A Patchwork Soul

By
Jeremy Varner

A Patchwork Soul
Book 2 of the Agent of Argyre Series

Second Edition

Copyright 2013, 2019 by Jeremy Varner
All rights reserved.

www.jeremyvarner.com

First Edition Published in 2013
Second Edition Published in 2019

To Christi and Dawn for being extraordinarily patient with me.

Table of Contents

Prologue

A golden line broke the horizon, streams of light stretching through the dust in the air from the space between the trees. I sat in the dirt, watching the shadows begin to crawl across the rolling ground around us and up the slope of the hillside. My arm was aching again and the rest of me was starting to feel about the same. The sun rose behind the rocks ahead of us, an imposing form rising with it. Throwing his head back, that ominous shadow, "Patch", screamed at the oncoming light like King Canute commanding the sea.

It was an unnerving sound - pained and enraged like a wounded animal with hints of a man on the verge of murder. But it was too strong a sound to be a man. I felt it roll through me, like the shockwave of a gunshot or a sound system's bass centered under my ass. It wasn't a man, a beast, an Alter or a human - it was beyond us all.

He was beyond us all.

I considered for a minute that it was a good time to just cut and run. Hell, on any other day, I probably would have. But as the light continued on I caught sight of a shade of brown that wasn't from the dirt or the trees. Glancing over, I found the familiar outline of a slender Elven woman face down in the dirt, her hair catching the light, leaf-like ear stained red with blood from somewhere beneath those dark chestnut locks. She wasn't going to be able to run with me and I knew I couldn't carry her.

Standing up, I fought gravity and every part of my body telling me to just stay down. My arm throbbed, urging me not to use it and reminding me I had to do it just the same. Rising to my feet, looking at his shadow looming ahead of me, I started to think of the last time I'd been in this forest.

"Hey, ugly," I choked out, trying to ignore the taste of dried blood. "I've had my nap, ready for round two?"

Startled, probably surprised I could stand, he turned to me. His fearsome form backlit by the sun, beastly eyes shining against his dark skin, reminded me again of the time I'd spent here. It was almost the same back then, though so much less likely to get me killed.

The pieces of the puzzle, colored by time and stained by fresh blood, certainly weren't the same. But both times I was here as a matter of survival. Both times I was being pushed by her.

At least this time she was blissfully peaceful as I was about to have my ass kicked. I wish I could have said the same before.

On a midsummer morning that feels like a lifetime ago, a group of raw cadets were brought to these woods, away from the harsh concrete and busy crowds of the Seattle streets. Freshly out of my short-lived career in MMA, I was arrogant and ready for a job where the cage would separate me from the people who wanted to punch me in the face.

My friend and mentor Lucian had convinced me that it was what I needed. My father had been a cop and his father before him. According to Lucian, that'd gone on since before our family line even had a last name. Unfortunately, that history was also why my grandmother and I weren't too sure about the idea of doing it. Though, given that I was fighting for a living at the time, we eventually agreed I was slightly less likely to get pummeled in law enforcement.

Of course, when it happened, it was going to be by bigger and badder people than I ever could have found in my weight class. That was beside the point.

As they brought us to this forest there was a quiet tension among the cadets. We stood in front of a man that we knew could have torn us apart. Standing over seven feet tall, he looked down at us with a cold expression framed by a snow-white mane. His uniform strained to contain him as he paced in front of us, powerful arms swinging in a more ape-like fashion, legs shuffling more than the natural human gait. There was something unusual about the way that uniform fit, beyond just his build, but I was trying my best not to look directly at him for too long. His eyes, snow-white and cold, stared into ours like he was searching for something behind them. We all felt uncomfortable. Why wouldn't we? It was our first time coming face-to-face with a Yeti.

The tension was broken by a small, gleeful voice saying, "Everyone say hello to Agent Zhang!"

Most of us couldn't take our eyes off of him or think enough to even try to react. I was the only one to turn my head just long enough to see the Elven woman walking our way. She practically bounced towards us, energy coming off every step she took while chestnut hair waved about her face in the light breeze. Emerald eyes were alight with a strange sense of amusement for no apparent reason at all. Her coat hung over a park bench not far away, her t-shirt taunting the rest of us as we sweated in the summer sun. She came to stop by Zhang's side, standing as a complete contrast with the hulking, furry thing we'd been facing.

She felt different, she felt... lively.

Reaching overhead she placed a hand on Zhang's shoulder and declared to the rest of us in a bright tone, "You guys are going to run into a lot of things bigger, stronger and angrier than you." Patting the large shoulder she continued with a grin. "Like a Yeti."

We gazed his way, his nostrils flaring and a low grunt rumbling from deep inside his chest.

When we could bring ourselves to look away from him she continued, eyes wide with excitement, voice practically giddy, "So you're going to need to learn how to deal with people like him. You're going to have to find a way to successfully capture people who could cause you severe physical harm."

She stopped, shot a quick smile at Zhang and patted his back. "And you're going to have to do it even in less than optimal environments like this."

The two of them shared a knowing glance, Zhang looking mildly uncomfortable as the Elf at his side grinned back to him.

The cadets murmured, some sizing-up the agent once again, and I asked the question everyone else was thinking: "What exactly is he going to be doing with us?"

She looked my way, ears perking like a cat's, eyes alight with curiosity. "Leone, right?"

"Damn right" I replied, rolling my shoulders with an undue confidence, "Nathaniel Leone – 'Nate the Quake' in the MMA circuits."

She should have decked me just for the attitude but her smile only grew. I later learned she knew my family from a long time back, recognizing my name. Even then, I still didn't know what exactly went through her mind at that moment as she smiled at me.

Laughing with a wicked delight she said, "He's going to hunt you."

We stared at the man standing before us. I thought she was kidding at first, expecting her to take it back in a minute. Instead, she slapped the big man's shoulder and cried out, "Get 'em!"

The Yeti roared with a voice that couldn't have come from a normal man, like the creature in these forests so many years later. And, while we stared in shock, he charged at us for all he was worth. The lumbering, hulking figure stormed our way while stripping his coat off – revealing a series of icepacks he'd lined it with. He threw it aside while finding his stride, moving with the grace of an animal over the uneven ground.

Zhang threw back his shoulders and stuck out his chest as he prepared for the final lunge at our group. I recognized the posture and the look in his eyes. He wasn't just running at us, he was challenging us to stand our ground. This was the time for us as a group to stand together. We had an opportunity to show that we could work against a superior force. He was daring us to do it.

I wasn't the first to run but I sure as hell wasn't the last. I felt the group thin out at my back and realized rather quickly that not all the breaking twigs were under his feet. No, the group fled like roaches, scattering into the woods. And, as much as I wanted to meet Zhang's challenge, I knew he would flatten me in that instant. I also realized I didn't need to outrun the Yeti exactly – just the slowest guy in the group.

I don't know what was colder: the wind in my face, the feeling of cowardice or the fact I saw another cadet trip in front of me and jumped him like a hurdle. I do know who was hit first though – seeing as we made eye contact as I cleared him like a seasoned athlete. The last we ever heard of Brenton were his pained, humiliated screams of "boot camp sucks!" under the sound of our boots pounding the ground. In my haste, I didn't even stop to feel sorry for the guy. All I really thought about it was, "I hope they don't deduct points for that."

The group spread thin enough to lose sight of each other along the way. I'd made my way downhill before long, into thick brush and downwind of what I figured was a powerful nose. There weren't any signs of the rest of my group as I hid in the brush, the forest falling silent as the wind went still. I tried to quiet my breathing, doing what I could not to add noise to the peaceful woods. Nothing moved around me at all while the dry leaves of the bushes jabbed into me from every direction and the scent of tree sap and pine needles started to overtake me.

I sat there for what seemed like an eternity before a scream shattered the silence. I wasn't sure which one it was out there. Of the dozen people there I hadn't had the time to memorize their voices. Soon it didn't seem to matter.

One by one, Zhang worked through them. I know this because each voice was different than the last and seemed a lot closer than the one before. Was it an echo? Were they running my direction while fleeing him? Or did he just set me up to be the last one out?

Could you be downwind anymore if there was no wind?

A twig cracked somewhere nearby, the leaves blocking my view of what it could be. I knew only two people could be out there still given the screams. I glanced around at the ground to see what it might have been, hoping to catch sight of a shadow. Either it was going to be short with noticeable ears or gigantic and without many noticeable features at all. Though, as the sun hid behind a pine tree, I realized even it was against me. All I knew was that there was a feeling of pressure in the air and a strong musk that I was sure wasn't mine.

A clawed hand burst through the brush around me and grabbed at my clothes. The Yeti roared overhead as it tore away my temporary shelter and I glanced up at his eyes shining against his dark face. He yanked back hard enough to make me believe he was a whole team on the other side of a rope and my feet left the ground before I could even respond with a girlish scream. Whipping me around like a doll in his hand, he took a moment to

9

turn towards a tree and prepared to chuck me against it in some show of bravado.

I was in luck though: my coat wasn't secured. It was the summer and our uniforms are black. I'd left it unbuttoned and my zipper half way down. It was just a simple matter of pulling down on the zipper. As he threw me against the tree I kicked against the trunk and did my best attempt at a sprint, flying back over his shoulder. A complete fluke made me look like the baddest man in the forest.

It lasted about three seconds.

He struck the tree, still clutching my coat, and his claws dug into the bark like tissue paper. For a moment, feeling smug, I smirked at him and rolled my shoulders again like a big man. However, in the moment it took me to do that, he ripped a fistful of bark from the tree to show I wasn't quite the big man of the woods. Roaring, he threw the bark aside, his face twisting until almost all signs of humanity fell from it. My bravado disappeared just as fast, the smell of peppers on his breath filling the air and warming my face. I'll admit it, my ass clenched. And in a flash I was running for my life again.

Instinct took over while running from the beast, my short career in the cages telling me not to let him pin me against the trees. Running from him, I knew that was exactly what was about to happen, the trees were in front of me once again and he was right at my back. As I turned to face him, I realized I couldn't just throw him against the cage like anyone else – even if he was starting to look a little winded. Overheating or not, he was still coming at me like a furry truck with a grill made of claws and teeth. All I could do was try a trick that never would have worked in the MMA.

Taking a knee and spinning around, I threw my weight behind a sweep and tripped the Yeti as he barreled towards me. With a confused grunt he stumbled by, nearly stepping on my leg as he did, and crashed face first into the tree beyond with a powerful crack. The tree shook from the hit, leaves falling over us. For a moment, I wondered if the tree was going to fall too, watching the shadows for the slightest sign of a tip.

Luckily for me, only the Yeti fell. With a deep, rumbling groan he fell backwards, eyes glazed over, stumbling past me with a dazed expression and a few chunks of bark stuck to his skin. After a few feet, the big man's eyes rolled back and he surrendered the eternal battle guys that size fight with gravity. Zhang hit the ground hard, dust and freshly fallen leaves pushed out as air rushed away from the giant furry bastard.

Everything was quiet again as he drifted off to what I'll call sleep. There, alone with my thoughts, I let it sink in just how much damage he could have caused me if I hadn't tripped him. In the time since boot camp I've dealt with men bigger than Zhang. But at the time, he was the biggest man I'd ever seen.

Somehow I managed to feel cockier than ever before.

Rising to my feet I felt this swell of emotion in my chest and turned to face the sound of the rest of the group coming. They were all there, most of them looking pretty miserable, moving along as a group behind the perky Elf like scolded dogs. They were limping, wheezing and making cracking noises as they moved. She was practically skipping as she came right up into my personal space.

"Good work, Leone!" She squealed, slapping my shoulder with more force than I expected from someone her size. I smirked at it and rolled the tender shoulder, trying to pretend it didn't hurt. Regardless, I felt pretty damn good at that moment, looking at the rest of the guys on the verge of traction.

But she frowned, ears lowering, and quietly said in a very serious tone, "There's a problem, though."

I glanced down at her again, her slender ears slowly rising as she lifted her eyes to meet mine. With a smirk gradually returning to her face she gestured over her shoulder and said slyly, "These guys are all dead and Zhang had a partner."

"Partner?" I asked, scanning the tree line, expecting another Yeti. Instead, I only found blinding pain as the wind blew out of me and a powerful knee was wedged into my groin. My chest was on fire, my head was pounding and my eyes felt like they were going to pop. Before I could gather what had happened, I toppled to the ground, looking up through tear-filled eyes as she raised her hands in victory.

11

"Never expect it to be over until they drag him away!" she cheered, bouncing from foot to foot, punching into the air.

I learned three important lessons that day. The first was that you never leave a man behind. The second was that you always stand with your hip to the target so you can't get nailed in the jimmies. And, most importantly, the third thing I learned as I watched her dance over me was that you never let your guard down around an Elf.

That was how I met Dulaf Nénharma, one of my best friends, here in the place where we might be seeing each other for the last time.

Chapter 1
Notable Brutality

The smell of roasted coffee and dried blood drifted around me on the night the case began. Anywhere else, anyone else, and that would have probably been a concern. For me it was another day drowsily staring across the Ahab's coffee shop and watching the diverse crowd drink their red brew specials.

The line seemed to take forever as I stood and stared at the counter in the distance. A couple of people glanced my way and I hardly noticed. Even the Goblin child jabbing me in the knee didn't quite register to what little of my brain was functioning. The man behind the counter, my friend Trey, looked at me and immediately held out my usual order. His eyes told me I was practically a Zombie and, considering how many Zombies were in the shop at the time, that was saying a lot.

"Still not sleeping?" he asked, looking me over with concern. "I thought they gave you some sort of pills."

I took the coffee from him and nodded absently. "They can't quite put me out, it seems."

"Well, you take care of yourself," he replied, shaking his head and giving me a weak smile, "I don't want to lose my best customer."

My eyebrows rose as I sipped from the cup. I was his best customer? Maybe I was in the shop more often than I should have been and might have a few troubles waking up. But I knew, I still know, I could quit at any time. And, really, I would have told him that if I'd had a cup before I came. As it was I just shrugged, paid the man and shuffled away.

I couldn't really talk to him about what was keeping me up anyway. My arm hurt, an old wound throbbing in the middle of the night, waking me from my sleep just long enough to make sure I never got any rest. The doctors said it was mostly in my head, likely related to some dreams I had, memories of how I hurt it in the first place. But I knew there was some sort of arthritis or something involved, aching when the weather changed or on really cold nights.

Who really needs sleep when you have coffee? I read once that statistically most people my age were woefully sleep deprived anyway. And, glancing at a nearby Zombie family listening to the Alter jazz, ferociously eating a pile of Ahab's famous cookies, I was tempted to look for a reflection. Given how Trey looked at me, knowing I couldn't be the only one not sleeping, I wondered how people like me didn't all look like them. Was there a secret? Did I need makeup? Maybe I should get more sun.

I sat in what I considered my corner of the shop, hoping to shake off the numb, hazy feeling drifting through my head before starting my shift. The nearby window was cold, draining the heat around it like a piece of ice while I looked out and felt the bite of the chilling air. To my surprise I wasn't the only one staring into the window, a pair of bright green eyes reflecting against the glass, a red haired figure sitting at the table with me. Somehow, I was tired enough not to notice I sat next to a Leprechaun.

I peered over as he turned his nose to a tablet and flipped a few pages with a finger across the screen. He sat in a surprisingly expensive suit with what looked to be 24 carat gold cufflinks and a gold tie-pin to match. His bright red beard was neatly trimmed but shaped for a little flare at his chin. I watched for a moment longer, a familiar feeling coming over me as he swiped at the tablet while financial news reflected across the lenses of small glasses with golden frames.

"Oh, I know that look," he chuckled without looking up, "I've been that look."

"Sorry," I murmured, getting ready to get up again, "didn't notice you sitting there."

"Don't worry about it any," he said, waving me back down, eyes practically smiling over his glasses. "Short as I am, most people don't."

Normally I would have continued on anyway, I just didn't have the energy for the effort. Besides, it was my corner. Technically, he was the guest. I sat back down and took a large drink from my cup, hoping the sudden heat would shock me awake. And he went about reading the news, stopping at the front page to read over what they considered the most important articles of the day.

I'd taken to paying more attention to the news in the last year. There was a time I didn't care much about what was happening, figuring I'd see things personally rather than through a cold screen. I'd grown out of that habit, realizing my limits and the dangers of not being alert. Looking at the screen in front of him, seeing a couple of headlines that scrolled by as he read one of the stories, I could still feel my apathy growing. I don't know if it was because I was tired, jaded or just couldn't bring myself to care which celebrity had a baby bump. Whatever it was, I felt myself start to drift away until a single picture caught my eye: a bat-shaped shadow against a moon that struck to my core.

He glanced up from the screen again, catching me peeking at his reader and smiled. "Terrible isn't it?" he asked, turning the screen so we could both look at it. "They did a number on us."

I was confused at first, not able to connect a bat to a Leprechaun, before realizing his finger was on another article altogether.

"They talk about it like we destroy economies all on our own," he said bitterly, shaking his head. "So we over-hyped gold, it's not like it ever loses value, and silver's been climbing for twenty years straight."

Gazing over the headline I realized what he meant: "Leprechaun traders sink precious metals." I wasn't sure how to respond to it. What little I understood of markets was enough to know that I was lucky to have a Brounie managing my retirement accounts. I struggled to find the words that someone who gave a shit would say.

"Yeah," I said hesitantly, "real shame about that."

He smirked and took off his glasses, tapping the frames against his reader screen. "You know we Leprechauns have been driving the value of gold for hundreds of years. But when we go public suddenly people start blaming us when the value levels off or drops. What about when that crazy fellow tried to sell it back in the noughties as a 'safe bet'? Swear to the lord he thought he was sent by God to sell people shiny metals."

I vaguely remembered these events from my childhood, feeling a bit sheepish that I was only a toddler during these "noughties" he was talking about. I smiled anyway, nodding and taking another drink from my cup. At the very least I was starting to feel livelier, even enough to finally collect a thought. "Well if you guys *have* been driving the value for all that time" I said, gathering the courage to have an opinion, "wouldn't you be a little at fault for what direction the market takes?"

He stopped for a second, his bright red eyebrow quirking while he stared into empty air. Then, with a laugh he reached over and slapped me on the arm, "Guess you'd be having a point there, boy!"

Truthfully, I was relieved to know he agreed. Leprechauns can get a little heated and I wasn't much up for an argument. His smile gave me an all-clear sign, so I nodded along and sat a little straighter in my seat – still hunching slightly over my cup so the steam of the coffee could counteract the freezing air drifting off the window.

"Desmond Kelly!" He announced proudly with an outreached hand, a little red hair from his arm sticking out of his sleeve, gold cuff-links twinkling from his wrist and drawing my eye to them again.

"Nathaniel Leone," I replied, taking his hand and feeling the remarkably firm grip the little man had.

"You know, it's probably about time to get out of metals anyway," he said while shutting off the reader and packing it away in his bag. "If you stay too long in one place you start to get stagnant. I've heard there are big things going for medical tech soon. Maybe I'll put all of my money behind that."

I continued to nod along, feigning interest, glancing at the time to check if my shift was to start.

"There've been some real big developments around universal donors," he said brightly. "I've been researching a company I heard actually has a way of growing anything you need without a copy of your DNA. Imagine that!"

Suddenly interested, I asked, "Wouldn't you run the risk of rejection?"

He shook his head, bright eyes practically sparkling. "That's the fun part! They said it's all universal. Could you picture how they pull something like that off? It's probably worth my money at the very least."

I ignored the urge to make a liver joke and considered how they'd do it myself. Artificial organs had come a long way in my lifetime, but they were never quite like the originals. Even if the concept baffled me, I had to admit it was a tempting prospect. The bumps and bruises I'd gotten in the last year alone made me sometimes wonder if I could get spare parts. The idea that they could actually provide them now was a bit surreal. Rubbing my arm idly, I just chuckled and brushed it off.

"Have we met?" he asked curiously, leaning closer as he did. "I swear you have a familiar face."

Looking back at him, studying his features, with his rounded nose and curiously wild eyebrows the same bright shade of red as his hair, I started to feel it again. Leaning back and taking him all in, I had a flash of seeing him in a holding cell once before – flirting with Dulaf through the bars and asking if she was interested in his lucky charms.

It was an awkward moment for me.

"I don't think so," I replied warily, quickly looking at the clock again while standing up. "I think I just have one of those faces."

He watched me get up and stroked his chin, running his fingers through the red hairs of his beard. "I suppose you're right," he laughed, "sometimes you all look alike to me anyway!"

I fought back a grimace from the comment and nodded to him, saying as politely as possible, "My shift's starting soon, but it was nice sitting with you."

He nodded, lifted a little hat from the side of his chair and flipped it end over end before resting it on his head. "Stay safe out there m'boy," he said, hopping down from his seat.

I walked out the door, stopping to look back at him following me out. He was definitely less wild while sober. At least, that's if he was the same Leprechaun. As much as I hated to echo his sentiment: they all looked alike to me too.

17

Walking out, I glanced up into the golden sky and took in the neon skyline starting to light up against the sunset. The people around me didn't seem to realize how much things had changed recently. Desmond, only a few feet away, hailed a taxi driven by a regular human without a problem. A few months ago, that would have been almost unheard of. For some reason, I kept expecting the other shoe to drop. Maybe I was just paranoid but I couldn't quite shake it.

The city had taken strange turns in the last couple of months. Fangtown, normally content with its corner, had spread its influence to just about every street of Seattle. The Alters' night murals now decorated places they never would have been welcome in before, even the City Hall sported a new piece of art that changed with the time of day. Ahab's coffee and blood bars were on almost as many corners as their normal competitors. And people walked the streets almost confidently at night, some sporting obvious signs of their lineage, mingling with mainstream humans like never before.

The Alter population doubled almost overnight as people from every corner of America heard Seattle was a new safe haven for their kind, flocking to the protection of the first Mayor from their ranks. Benjamin Hale, former City Attorney turned apparent savior figure, made national headlines when he became the first active Alter to win a major election. A lot of latent Alters had done it in the past and some actives had done it on a smaller scale in little town elections. Hale was just the first to take an election for a city with a building taller than two stories, in no small part due to a heavy sympathy vote.

I guess an assassination attempt makes people feel sorry for you.

He'd narrowly escaped death, surviving thanks to some swift action by the Alter Control Task Force – one Agent Leone in particular. The gun aimed at him was designed to kill people like him, meant to wipe him from the face of the Earth with one pull of a trigger. Luckily for Hale, he wasn't in the path of the bullet and probably only needed a new pair of pants. Not everyone was so lucky.

As clouds rolled in over the city and my left arm started to throb, I thought back on that night. Honestly, I probably think back on it a little too often. Sometimes, I still hear the sounds from when that gun went off and tore through those rooftop solar panels. Somehow everyone else had just seemed to forget it. I wasn't sure what bothered me most about that.

It was something to figure out on another day.

On this cold winter evening, getting my first call and driving into the sunset, I passed under those rolling clouds as they threatened to choke off the last remnants of light from the horizon. The Seattle PD sent out a request for one of our agents just as I got in my car and started my shift for the night. It was at least a mile north of my usual patrols, but it wasn't often the SPD called for a hand. So before I could finish my "morning" coffee I was driving through the center of downtown Seattle.

An Alter woman, a Vampire from what we'd heard on the call, had been found lying in an alley by tourists walking from Olympic Sculpture Park to the Seattle Center. She'd managed to go unseen for hours somehow, crumpled over in the shadow of a high-rise, obscured by a dumpster. It was an impressive trick in one of the busiest parts of town, the Space Needle looming in my rear view as I came to the scene. It lit up in the twilight hours, putting on a friendly face, hiding the fact someone was dead only about a quarter mile away.

The SPD and a couple ACTF investigators were on the scene, making sure it was taped off and keeping anyone from contaminating the place. Though, seeing the clouds above, I figured nature was going to take care of that for us soon enough. With night setting in, I put on my shades and let my visor's night-vision light the alley. The police's biometrics made their auras light up more than humans usually do with colors in their spectrum that told me they were way more agitated than they should have been even around a dead body. Unfortunately, I knew it probably wasn't something they'd be too open about.

I did what I could to ignore them for the time being and turned my attention to the investigators. A pair of Elves, wearing a uniform similar to mine but sporting patches for the science division, hovered over the woman's body in a hurried pace. Their slim figures and bladed ears told me who they were even from behind, recognizing Dulaf's "minions": Philip and Xander. They were younger than her, their ears short enough to almost pass as a pair of overzealous Trekkies. But their lean figures and the way they moved easily gave away their identities.

It was a bit strange they were here first – field agents usually call in the investigators after taking a quick look around. Either I was late or they were early on this one. It was still fortunate, given the weather. The longer she sat outside, the more time there was for us to lose everything that could be of use. With the weather rolling in, I was more than sure the important details were going to be washed away soon. Documenting things now was vital and we were running out of time. Even my first look at her revealed that nature had done some of that work already.

Her clothes were tattered and stained - office attire shredded and soaked in her own blood like something had pounced on her. Beyond the clothes she was covered in burns and open sores. Her face wasn't recognizable, a pained expression frozen in what was left past the burns, cracks and blisters. She'd turned towards the wall and dumpster before the end, possibly trying to hide in what little shade she found. Our victim had been caught out in the sun while she was still alive.

Before she died her body started to destroy itself, reacting to the UV radiation in a violent outburst of blisters and ulcers. The old myth that they burst into flame was more of a translation error - she'd sun-burned to death. The third degree burns might have been what did her in, but the condition of her clothes told me she wasn't left in the sun by accident.

Kneeling by her carefully and taking a few shots of the scene myself, I muttered quietly, "Hate crime?"

The Elves tensed at the words, their sharp ears being the only ones to pick up what I'd said but still worried about the other "normal" people in the alley. Philip shot me a look with bright blue eyes that shined slightly in the shadows and whispered back, leaning close to make up for my woefully un-pointed ears, "Someone definitely left her to die out here."

Xander's ears folded down and back as his partner spoke, green eyes shining through a lock of over-styled platinum blonde

20

hair as he looked our way. "If it was a person at all – she's covered in slash marks."

He was right, even if his hair was silly; she'd definitely been gashed in several places before the sun rose over her. The bloodstains were too large for ulcers and her position was awkward. It hurt to curl up the way she had, cradling an arm before she died. The question was: what could have possibly attacked her in this part of town? It's not like people were torn apart on the streets of Seattle often, not even around the Werewolf heavy areas northwest of Fangtown. You didn't just find people mauled and left to die. Maybe, I thought, that was what was causing the police to look so agitated through my visor. Then again, it was too soon to tell anything. In fact, I realized at that moment that I didn't even know who she was yet.

"Did you two manage to ID the victim?" I asked, glancing between Philip and Xander.

They both shook their heads with a solemn look on their faces and ears folded down. Her face was beyond what our hand-links would recognize. The Oracle system, height of technology and biology it was, wouldn't be able to identify someone through the horrible burns. Even dental records were going to be something of a stretch with Vampires being able to grow new teeth like a shark. We were going to have to get DNA identification if we couldn't find something on her.

The air started to feel moist, the smell of a strong sea breeze blowing in from the water front, a chilling wind squeezed through the alley and washing over us. I glanced up at the clouds now fully covering the sky above and took a deep breath of the moist air.

"Is she ready to move yet? We're running out of time here."

They exchanged looks and Xander gave the go-ahead nod. The two of them stood and quickly unrolled a body bag to get her out of this place. Even if the rain hadn't been on the way we owed her some dignity. Someone who'd suffered like this, frozen in her agony as she burned away in the sun, didn't deserve to be left in an alley overnight.

Figuring we needed to identify her at the very least, I reached for her arm and carefully started to turn her away from the wall.

21

Her body was stiff, her skin cracking as her limbs were moved. Her face scraped the wall for a moment before I could wedge my hand between them. Slowly, I pulled her out of the position she'd died in and laid her as gently as possible across the ground. Though, as her body leaned away from the wall, we all got a glimpse of something that couldn't be seen before. My Elf friends hesitated with the bag and the few police that could see for themselves were sickened by the sight.

With her arm cradled and turned to the wall we couldn't see it before, but exposed finally we realized the full extent of how much harm had been done to the poor woman. Her hand was missing, wrist and all, cut away from midway up her forearm as a ragged stump. The wall she covered was soaked in her blood. Her left side, the one she'd been concealing before, was stained almost entirely red.

The police murmured among themselves, reeling back, their auras showing confusion and even heavier agitation than before. Meanwhile, Philip and Xander grew pale while standing with the bag and looking on with disgust.

"An animal," Xander muttered.

Philip shook his head and swallowed, taking a deep breath and opening the bag for her. "Focus, we don't have time to get squeamish about it."

I nodded to Xander, starting to feel a little sick myself while examining the bloody arm, seeing shattered bone jutting from the end. Until I turned her away, it was a fairly standard scene for a hate crime or some other crime of passion. Now, I knew this was a lot more than the ordinary. It was one of those times you'd normally hesitate, but we had to push on and do what we were meant to do. I calmed the feeling of disgust, took a couple shots of her with my hand-link and started to carefully search her for ID.

I managed to find a small wallet tucked away inside what was left of her coat. The money was all there, the credit cards untouched and not a sign anyone even tried to open it. Though the outside was covered in blood, everything inside was clean. I found her photo ID, seeing what she looked like before. Her raven hair and alabaster skin were a stark contrast to each other that made her soft features stand out. She was a beautiful girl before this had been done to her, practically a child by Vampire terms. She was 22, only a Vampire for the last two years of her life. Bright hazel eyes with flecks of gold in them stared back at me from the ID.

Her name was Alice.

Philip walked over and took shots of her condition himself. I handed him the wallet and lifted the ID in the other hand. "Alice Winchester," I said solemnly, looking up at him.

"She looks young," he replied, putting the wallet away in a baggy and writing her name across it. "Do you think whoever or whatever did this to her knew who she was?"

I swiped my hand-link over the card, the information from it being transferred to my screen, a high definition photo of her replacing the small, blurry photo from her card. Seeing her gently smile, a rarity for a young Vampire in front of a camera, it seemed hard to believe.

"I'm not sure," I said with a growing edge to my voice, standing and offering the card to Philip. "But we'll figure it out."

Xander walked around me and kneeled by her feet, preparing to move her into the bag. "The police over there aren't too happy about this."

Philip nodded, kneeling by her head. "Yeah, I was hearing that too."

I peered over my shoulder at the police, starting to pack it up and leave the alley without a word said to me, likely getting the standard conversation out of the way with the Elves on the scene. As they left they were still whispering, shaking their heads and exchanging concerned glances. As one climbed into his car he stopped for a minute to look back at us in stunned silence.

"What were they saying?" I asked the investigators.

Xander looked back over his shoulder while Philip zipped Alice's bag closed. Frowning, he watched the last car leaving before looking back to me and saying in a hushed tone, "I don't know about Philip, but I kept hearing the same phrase over and over again."

I watched the bag close and Alice's face disappear from view. "What phrase was that?"

23

Xander's ears dipped while he helped Philip lift the bag, glancing across to his partner. Philip cleared his throat and nodded along. Finally, with a bit of a bass I didn't expect from someone who looked like part of a boy band, Philip replied in a steadier voice than his friend could manage, "Yeah, I heard it too. Over and over, they kept saying, 'it's another one'."

The phrase hit me hard as it left his mouth, almost tangible in the way it pressed on me. I couldn't say anything, only silently step out of the alley and watch the police cars roll away. The rain finally started to fall over us as Philip and Xander loaded Alice's body into their van. My old paranoia flared again, thinking back on that unnoticed change and realizing the local police weren't being entirely honest with us about something. Watching their lights disappear past the bend, I reached up and absently rubbed my arm.

It was hurting again.

Chapter 2
Old Neighbors

I parted ways with Philip and Xander, letting them take the poor girl back to the station while I went to get a better idea of what happened. Her ID said she lived close to where she was found, probably on her way home from work before she was attacked. I doubted, from the way she was left, that it was someone she knew. Though most murders are someone that knows the victim, the location's usually less random. Still, even if it was unlikely, I had to follow the lead. Alice deserved that much.

I walked to her building from where she was found, not seeing a point in bringing the car just down the street. The rain was slowly building, starting to fall steadily over me while I walked. If she'd still been out there we would have had nothing. It was bad enough that she was left in the sun long enough for her wounds to lose shape. If those wounds had time in the rain we may have lost the last shred of hope in finding who did it.

Her building was surprisingly welcoming, recently renovated with some Alter-friendly features. The front doors were changed with simple push plates, the universal sign for Vampires and their kind that the building was "open entry". Hanging over the door was a sensor similar to my visor, wired into a civilian part of the Oracle network. Everyone that walked by could be identified by their biometrics to determine what race they were. In our hands it was a sign of big brother; in the civilian hands it was to control the dimmer switch for anyone that was light sensitive. It was a strange change of pace, seeing the city make little adjustments like that for people they weren't comfortable with before.

The doorman, a rather hefty looking Troll, stood by as I passed while his large, bulbous nose flared in my direction. Once upon a time they said that a Troll could smell the blood of a Christian man. I've never exactly been a pious type - so I wasn't too concerned. I honestly wondered what exactly they smelled in the first place. Looking at the nose, they could probably pick up just about anything, especially in the woods or mountains they would have lived in before. Still, it raised a lot of questions, especially growing up in an era where priests were coming under scrutiny. Examining him, I did my best not to smile at my stray thoughts. Funny enough, my visor caught a momentary increase in blood pressure at that exact moment.

Maybe they were just psychic... through their nose.

But those were just stray thoughts distracting my sleep deprived mind from thinking about what really concerned me. When the doors closed, I was left with the real problem on my hands. Alice stared up at me from the hand-link, the question of what might have happened to her too troubling for me to think about after a day of dreams and the paranoia that something was about to go wrong. And nothing made that more of a bother than the thought of the police murmuring "another one" in the background.

The two thoughts compounded. Once upon a time there were stories of Trolls eating people. Were the "other ones" people that lived in this building, too? The thought was disturbing enough to make the brain in the nose less amusing.

It was a relief to step out of the elevator. Though evening just fell, the floor she lived on was strangely silent. No one was coming, no one was going. Every door had a knob and the lights were the old fashioned CFL types from a couple decades ago. Though the building had been friendly to Alters, the floor wasn't populated by many. In fact, looking around, I got the impression she was the only one there.

I walked down the hallway, glancing from door to door, not even looking up at the numbers after confirming I was walking the right direction. I just kept an eye out for the familiar push plate and biometric locks. Even if I didn't know this particular Vampire, I knew that's what you saw in places like this, especially for Vampires that young. After some time they could push past their fear of entering closed spaces, a form of reverse agoraphobia, but at her age and as long as she'd been active - I knew Alice wasn't there yet.

With their distaste of entering private property, even if it was their own, Vampires have a tendency to hate using keys too. People who made thumbprint readers quickly made a fortune off of this, but I guess that's to be expected. And the telltale sign sprang to my attention from down the hall, a light catching my visor from a dozen apartments away.

Walking up to it, I pulled my hand-link out again, turning it to face the door. Part of the treaty, something a few groups aren't too fond of, meant that we didn't need a warrant to enter the home of an Alter so long as we had due cause. It also meant, with electronic locks like these, that I didn't need to ask someone to let me in. With a swipe of the hand-link over the reader and a quick flash of colors the door unlocked with a click and slowly drifted open.

The interior was spotless and meticulously organized, like any good obsessive compulsive, and featured very few reflective surfaces. Though the older Vampires had a sense of vanity after enough time had corrupted their minds, a baby like Alice was looking pretty textbook. No reflections, no disorder, no keys - nothing at all out of the ordinary and no sign someone might have lived with her.

"Completely alone," I muttered.

A throat was cleared behind me, a raspy, wet sound of an older man with a few too many cigarettes in his lifetime. I looked over my shoulder at him, his aura reading a cold blue tone that told me he was definitely human, his hunched stature and leathery skin confirming he sure as hell wasn't ageless. Gripping his cane tightly, raising it towards me in an attempt to be threatening, he said hoarsely, "You stay the hell outta Alice's place, she ain't done nothing to no one!"

He had spunk.

I turned and lifted the hand-link, showing her photo to him and nodding down at my badge. "I'm Agent Leone with the ACTF. Is this the Alice you're referring to?"

"I know who the hell you're with!" He barked, shuffling back to his open door that he somehow managed to open without alerting me. "That little girl's done nothing to be hunted for!"

Watching him shuffle about, surprised someone his age was so accepting of an Alter, I felt a twinge of guilt and sympathy about the whole situation. Placing a hand on his arm, I helped him along back into his apartment, quietly saying, "Unfortunately, I don't think everyone agreed."

He looked back up into the reflective surface of my visor, his old eyes lighting up with a sudden sense of panic I didn't need the visor to see. Shocked, he asked, "What's that supposed to mean?"

I took the visor off for the first time since I saw her body, looking him in the eyes as I replied, "We found her body, sir, not far from this building."

"But," he stammered, falling into an old leather chair, staring through me as he sat. "That couldn't be. Our whole building agreed to let them stay here."

"The whole building?" I asked, starting to take in the room around me, noticing family photos lining the walls and feeling the need to look closer.

"It took some convincing," he said, lowering his head and staring at his shaking hands, clasping them together to make them stop.

I watched him for a moment, then peered back at the photos on the walls. A family stood there, looking back at me, wearing unusually bright colors, over-sized tops and Members Only jackets. I vaguely remembered my grandfather owning one of those and mentioning they came from the 80s, a time when apparently everyone was a "member". To the right of that family, in clothes that seemed a lot more familiar to me, stood the same people, slightly older and joined by others. The man sitting behind me was there now, standing where the father was in the previous photo, hand on the shoulder of a girl I quickly recognized as Alice.

I looked back at him and asked, "What's your name, sir?"

He raised his head from his hands, his eyes red, tears running down his weathered face. He shook his head and replied mournfully, "Henry, Henry Winchester."

The door past the hall was still open, letting me see into Alice's apartment from where I stood inside Henry's. Nodding and rubbing my arm a little above the elbow, I walked over and knelt by him - not exactly something in the manual. "I'm sorry about your granddaughter," I said, taking my plated glove off and offering my hand to him.

He stared at my hand, taking it with both of his and nodding. "Who did this to my little girl?" he asked quietly, his voice shaking.

I squeezed his hand and looked away from him across the hallway. "I'm not sure yet," I replied before standing again. "I need to know more about Alice before I can get a good start on this."

"She wasn't very outgoing," he said, "always staying in her apartment when she didn't go to work. She almost never went anywhere else... always worried about how people were going to treat her."

I nodded along, knowing the story too well by now. I've heard it a million times with the younger ones. Leaving your home was usually seen as taking a risk – usually an unfounded fear. Unfortunately, for Alice that wasn't true this time.

"I fought so hard with the association to start making it so people like her could move in," he continued, clasping his hands together again, shaking his head with a growing look of anger. "But once she was here, no one had anything left to say about it. Almost a year now, a year, without any problems at all. Then they start seeing that bat and think she was some sort of monster again. If one of them did something to her," he said, trailing off as his hands trembled again.

I stared in silence for a moment, a sense of dread falling over me while I listened to him talk. It wasn't the implication the building tenants might have done something that set me on edge. No, it was something much worse. A single word, out of everything he said, was jumping at me more than anything while images from Desmond's news flashed through my mind.

"Did you say 'bat'?"

Nodding, he raised a hand and gestured something flying overhead. "We've been seeing this thing just shooting by lately, skimming the top of buildings, like a giant-," he paused, cringing at the word he had to use, "a giant vampire bat."

A chill ran through my body as details started to come together for me. The photo on the tablet, the description Henry just gave me and the condition Alice was in all started to mesh in my head. And, worse of all, the things Philip and Xander overheard would fit too.

Henry hesitated, choking on the next sentence, tears starting to well in his eyes, "Did she suffer?"

I looked at the poor old man as he shook, his eyes bloodshot and his lip quivering. Absently, I started to put my glove back on, feeling it on my hand again, remembering Alice's arm in a flash. Moving my hand, feeling it push against the material of my glove, hearing the plates on my fingers brush against each other, I started to consider just how much force would be required to take it from me. Gashed, brutalized and left to die in the sun, I had an idea of what she went through. I knew the answer to his question all too well.

"No," I said, putting my visor back on, "I think she went quickly, sir."

He took a deep, cleansing breath through his nose and nodded to me, clenching his hands and giving them one firm shake. I watched the gesture and felt the weight of it, wondering if I'd just done the right thing. It felt right at the time, it still does now, but the question of whether I protected him or gave him false hope likely won't go away any time soon. Either way, I couldn't linger on it just then, something more important had to be done.

"Others are going to come by," I said, turning to the door. "I'm going to let them know that you live across the hall, they're going to want to know about Alice and the people she knew." I stopped for a moment, standing at Alice's door and looking back at him while I closed it. "I don't think anyone from the building did this, though."

He nodded, a little more weight lifting from his body as he did. "How can you be sure?"

I reached for his door and took the knob, stopping to consider how to word what was going through my mind in a way that wouldn't scare him or anyone else in the building. "Well, the way she was found," I said as calmly as I could, "wasn't quite the same as what you'd expect from someone trying to get rid of her."

With a defiant frown he stood and shuffled my way, reaching to the door as he did. "You catch the son of a bitch," he said with quiet restraint. "You bring him down."

I nodded back to him, releasing the knob and letting him close the door himself. "I hope so, Mr. Winchester."

The strength left his expression for a moment, his hand sinking against the door as he looked away from me into thin air. He looked back again and nodded a half-hearted approval before closing the door. The sound of his fist bounced off the frame as I started to walk away, the heavy thump and gradual slide of it running down as the old man let out whatever else was behind those pained eyes.

I couldn't look back, though. If everything added up to what I thought, there wasn't any time to waste. I hurried through the building back to the elevator and up to the top floor. My journey to the top was surreal, my mind picturing a horror movie while the elevator cheerfully bombarded me with easy listening love songs. At least I was happy it wasn't Halloween, when the places that still insisted on adding music to their elevators would have been playing something like "Monster Mash" on the way up. I didn't need to be reminded of what waited for me.

Thinking of Alters, any Alters, as a monster is frowned on by the ACTF. Sure, sometimes they could lose themselves to the blood-lust or go feral on a really bad month. Even then, none of those people would be someone we'd consider a monster. They were always just "troubled". The thing that I was looking for, however, was probably the only exception the Force, or myself, would allow to the rule.

Practically lunging out the door, I scanned the area for a second, turned left and bolted down the hall. I wasn't even sure if I was headed in the right direction at the time, just that I didn't want to delay confirming my theory any longer than I had to. Luckily, the stairwell to the roof was easy to find and I bounded up the steps two at a time to get up there, using the rail to keep from slipping and breaking my damned neck... or comically rolling several stories down the building while doing my best rag-doll impression.

The roar of the rain was semi-steady on the other side of that door, gusting winds sending waves of water against the metal and causing a rising and falling rumble, like the breath of a dragon rolling by. I pushed it open between the gusts, getting a face full of rain and watching a sheet of water form across my visor, pushing out towards my ears as another gust blew by.

For a moment, I considered that the evidence I was looking for, if it existed, wasn't even going to be there anymore. The rain was hard, the winds were high and most of what I could be looking for would have been gone before I even reached that roof. I pushed through the rain and let the door slam shut behind me, lifting my arm to shield my visor from the rain and looking for any physical proof of my theory. I knew in my gut it was futile – no chemical traces or residues would have survived this. Still, I had to try.

I pushed on to the edges of the roof, looking across them, watching my visor display go crazy with the activity around me, hoping something would stand out between the little explosions of heavy rain cascading across the skyline. And through the tiny liquid bombs I saw something finally, the faintest of impressions, narrowly revealed to me by what little ambient light the visor could pick up. I pulled out my flashlight and lit the eaves, seeing it just clearly enough to know I didn't like it.

Gouged into the concrete of the building, at least an inch deep, were a series of claw marks about the width of two very large hands. I fought with the rain and fished my hand-link out, taking the best photo I could manage while clutching it tightly to make sure the damn thing didn't fall off the side of the roof. The hand-link started to analyze it too, running through every possibility it could before reaching the one I was expecting, almost like the Oracle herself was hoping it was something else too.

While she desperately looked for a different answer, I put the link away and rested my hand over one of the claw impressions, spreading my fingers, trying to compare hands. It dwarfed mine, easily large enough to palm a human head. Whatever it was, I thought, it wasn't something you'd want to be on the wrong side of. And, with the worst timing possible, that's when the first sounds of thunder rolled from the storm overhead.

"Hilarious," I said sarcastically, peeking over my visor at the clouds, getting a raindrop in the eye for my trouble. Wincing, I decided to get inside before that bitch, Mother Nature, could try to take me out.

Everything squished and sloshed as I stomped into the stairwell again, water pooling in my boots as it trickled down my uniform. I muttered bitterly about leaving the Pacific Northwest until it stopped raining before realizing that would mean never coming back. And as I sat to remove the boots and drain them, I found myself pleasantly daydreaming of a tropical resort. I tried to imagine the rain at my back and the water falling out of my boot as the sounds of waves crashing to shore. Images drifted through my mind of a place too sunny and too dry for the things I encountered on a day-to-day basis.

Then the sharp, cheerful ping from the link reminded me I was soggy, cold and the furthest thing possible from relaxed. Pulling it from the pouch at my belt, its screen reminded me of the harsh truths of my existence. I was in Seattle, I was working a case, and, worst of all, the Oracle confirmed the sick feeling I'd had most of the night and the hunch I'd had since Henry told me of giant bats. It wasn't 100% positive, but it was close enough for me.

We had a Nosferatu in the city.

Chapter 3
Ominous Updates

Nosferatu was a word we used to keep some of the darker aspects of Alters under wraps. If you watch the old movies and you read the old books you'll find Nosferatu used to reference just your everyday Vampire. Maybe, from time to time, the ones referred to as Nosferatu would be particularly ugly compared to their sexier brethren. Hell, that's why we used the term in our reports. Aside from that, the Nosferatu in fiction were almost universally regular Vampires that managed to hit every branch on the ugly tree on the way down.

Unfortunately, that wasn't what we had running around town.

There were always old myths that Vampires could shape-shift into bats, but Shifters and Werewolves are both a type of reactive Alter - what we call metamorphs. It wasn't until we started to really catalogue all of the Alter types that we realized where the myths came from: some Alters are unlucky enough to have multiple types of A-Cell. What you get is a Vampire-like creature that's permanently stuck in an enraged, bestial form that gradually worsens over time. Instinct, more than anything, drives them to force their shape painfully into something akin to a giant bat-like form. And, as you'd imagine, it doesn't produce a pleasant end result.

As I walked out of the building the sloshing and splashing sounds barely muffled the repeated alarms coming from my link as the Oracle alerted everyone that there might have been one in the area. The system was practically in a panic as the girl at its core tried to get a grip on the situation. Chirping and vibrating like a large cricket trapped in my pocket, it wanted my attention to tell me what I already knew. Walking to the car solemnly under a less aggressive version of the rain that assaulted me on the roof, I ignored the alerts until I slid into my car and they appeared on my windshield.

The normally blue hues of the HUD were now taking red and purple tones that were reserved for emergencies. The code for Nosferatu, a symbol vaguely shaped like a bat's face with the numbers "119" centered on it, hovered near the ceiling and stared down at me. Even if I wasn't completely sure myself - the Oracle was. At the very least she was trying to be extra cautious in the face of what was the ACTF equivalent of a natural disaster.

The electric motors in my car's wheels powered up and sent a vibration through the frame while the HUD display faded into a translucent overlay instead of the brilliant display of lights across my windshield. As I rolled away from the scene I reached over and tapped my finger against the touchscreen panel on my console, opening up the communications network.

"Lancer Lucian Descartes," I said as clearly as I could.

It took a moment before my mentor's profile picture appeared on the console and I heard the ever-calm tone of his voice. "Never good news, is it?" he remarked when the channel opened.

"I might be bad luck," I replied, keeping my eyes on the road and watching the people scramble for shelter. "They're, what, one in a million actives?"

"Something like that," he said, a hint of hesitation in his voice. "I'd say less but the higher ups never agree with me on it. It's been," he trailed off for a moment, drawing my attention to the screen as he started again, "centuries since I've seen of those things personally."

"What happened back then?"

He paused again, something he rarely did. Lucian was ancient compared to anyone else in the Force, practically a force of nature. Though he was still only a lancer, one rank above me, I was well aware that was by choice. He'd seen almost everything in the time he'd been around and nothing really shook him in a visible way. Though I was sure there were times he kept things from me, the wait for him to speak was never a good sign about what was to come.

"You have to understand," he finally said, "we didn't have the equipment we do now. The thing was able to escape capture regularly and it could cover more ground than us in a heartbeat."

"How bad?" I asked, starting to feel uncomfortable in my seat.

"It took almost three months for us to find the thing finally, almost two countries away from where it'd been originally sighted, holed up in caves in Estonia where it was lurking with regular bats. When we went after it, it escaped again and went downhill to a village with a bell tower on their church. There were still people in there, gathering for an evening service after sunset. By the time we reached the village on foot we found everyone in the church dead or maimed."

I winced and turned to try to get off of the main streets. It wasn't exactly easy in the downtown area, finding people and vehicles everywhere I turned. But I was getting uneasy listening to him and driving at the same time. One question had to be asked even if I wasn't sure I wanted to know the answer.

"How did you stop it?"

"We burned the church down," he said distantly. "We lobbed small explosives packed with ground garlic and silver dust into the bell tower to stun it and then followed that with torches."

His voice grew colder as he spoke, a tone I hadn't heard from him before, taking an almost haunted sound as he continued, "We watched it for the rest of the night, scaring away any villagers that tried to come and save their church, only letting them take away the surviving wounded."

We both stayed silent for a minute after that, the GPS map on my windshield showing the steadily approaching station only a couple minutes away. I wasn't sure what to say about it. No one had really seen a Nosferatu active and in the wild in some time. There had been a few cataloged and kept in research labs around the country. Having one out in the wild, unchecked and possibly unregistered? That was like having a legend come to life and walk up to your doorstep.

"Things will be different this time," I said defiantly, tightening my grip around the steering wheel.

"Maybe," he replied, "I'd like to hope so. Honestly, capturing them is easier than killing them from what I've heard."

I nodded to myself, turning the corner and seeing the dark flower-like building of our headquarters, the black lights highlighting the spaces between the "petals" and shining off of the falling rain to create an ethereal haze over its spires. "Someone had to do it before," I said, trying to bolster my own spirits. "There's a couple held in the Argyre pens, right?"

"I think so," he said with the tap of fingers against keys in the background. "When the treaty was signed, I wasn't assigned to checking into the Nosferatu situation. They assigned me to head the Red Cure SOL team."

I nodded along, knowing it made sense. The Republic of Argyre, the people we answered to, were founded on the condition they cleaned up a few messes for the rest of the world and set up our organization to make sure no others like it would appear. Things like the Nosferatu were rounded up and put in storage beneath the city on the sea, kept away from anyone they could harm while living in relative comfort. Unfortunately, while that operation was being handled, Lucian had other fish to fry - leaving both of us in the same boat on knowing how to handle this situation.

"I'm pulling in," I said, reaching for the console, "meet you inside."

"Agreed," he replied, closing the channel before I even had the chance.

I wasn't the only car coming in at the time, at least a half dozen other agents were driving into the underground parking lot around the same time I was, likely responding to the same call. Though it wasn't as serious as an earthquake or a tsunami, the idea of letting one of these creatures run wild through a major city wasn't something we were comfortable with. So, of course, we were all hurrying back to get an idea of just what the next move was. Sadly, for a gendarmerie group set up to deal with creatures that could maul us on a regular basis, we were apparently lost about what to do with animal control.

Maybe we needed a bat whisperer on the payroll.

There were grim expressions in the corridor to the offices. The lot of us walked with an uneasy gate, the tension only breaking by my clothes sloshing and squishing every time I moved. Even with everything on their minds it was hard to ignore the fact it looked like I took a swim in the harbor.

"Nate," one of them whispered to me as we walked, "where the hell have you been?"

I turned to the voice and found the bewildered face of one of my friends, Devotee Ramirez. Ramirez, one of the rare crossovers from the traditional red-and-blues, had only been with the Force for a few months, placed with Lancer Nguyen who'd known what it was like to cross over. Before Mayor Hale was elected he was one of the few traditional cops I knew I could trust and watching him walk by me made me realize I didn't have a friendly face with them anymore. I thought about the murmurs that the Elves heard in the alley and wondered what the police might have known that I didn't. Apparently, the extra concern was easy for him to see.

"It couldn't have been that bad," he said, patting my damp shoulder.

"I was the one that found the claw marks," I said, grinning like an idiot.

Ramirez laughed and shook his head; he wasn't quite as tense as the rest of the people in the hall with us. Despite his rank, he'd been working law enforcement for years in another uniform. If we were regular police, I probably would be answering to him. Here in the ACTF he wore a lower rank and waited to take his lumps like everyone else. He wasn't quite ready to do this on his own, the suspects we dealt with weren't the usual street criminals he'd dealt with in the past, but he was a lot more comfortable in the role than most devotees.

"Well I guess it was that bad, then," he teased, nudging me with an elbow. "Always running into trouble, aren't you?"

"Yeah, I guess I am," I replied sheepishly, running a hand through my hair and thinking about the police again. I looked at him out of the corner of my eye and thought about asking him if he might know anything. It'd been months since he'd been there but...

"Something on your mind?" he asked.

"Well," I lowered my hand and hesitated, thinking of the right way to word it all before saying, "there were some red-and-blues on the scene when I got there. They were acting a little unusual and saying some things that our investigators overheard."

His smile faded a bit and he suppressed a small cringe, rolling his neck a bit as we walked. "And you were going to pick my brain about it, huh?"

"Was thinking about it."

He stopped short of the elevator, letting the others pass us by and tapping my arm to keep me with him, sharing a nod with his lancer who stepped onto the elevator with the others and signaled it was okay with her too.

"So what'd they say?" he asked, crossing his arms as the doors closed again.

I hesitated, knowing some of these people were his friends. There was an infamous blue line that was rarely crossed, one that I was almost surprised he wasn't afraid of himself. But, with a vision of Alice and her grandfather's face running through my mind, I suddenly had a hard time restraining myself.

"They've been keeping us out of the loop on something," I said. "The Elves overheard them saying this wasn't the first body they've found."

"You sure?" he asked. "Sometimes they don't realize it's an Alter case until they see the fangs or something like that."

"She was mauled to death," I replied coldly.

A more visible wince crossed his face this time. "I don't know then," he admitted, shaking his head. "When I was there, we wouldn't have kept anything away from you guys. In fact, even though they really don't like the ACTF being on their turf, they kind of preferred it if you guys had to deal with it."

"So why would they hide something now?"

He shrugged and rubbed the back of his head, looking at the elevator behind me. "It'd have to be something from higher up," he said, "or they would've called on us in a heartbeat."

We entered the elevator on our own after that, an uneasy silence falling between us as we both realized "higher up" was never good. For me, it meant that there was a chance someone was working against us. For Ramirez, probably worse than that, he knew he would have had to cooperate with whatever those orders were himself in a past life.

After what felt like an eternity in the elevator we arrived to the offices to find the agents there buzzing with activity. The hub of monitors hanging from the ceiling twenty feet overhead was alight like a Christmas tree with a flurry of colors flashing by. Scanning the room, there were more people in the offices this time than I'd ever seen there at once. Normally we were a scattered bunch, undermanned and forced to keep every car on patrol. But tonight we'd had a reason to gather and put our heads together in a way we'd never had before. Even the Commissioner, Omero Alston, had walked down from his offices above to talk to the agents and brief them on what he knew of the beast from the early days.

I quickly spotted the tall, lean figure of Lucian standing over most of the others, his long, dark hair framing a sharp face with a deep frown I hadn't seen often, a visor covering what was likely a tense gaze. He spotted Ramirez and I stepping out of the elevator and waved us over to a shared desk. Seeing the visor, I quickly pulled mine out and put them on too, tapping Ramirez's shoulder and gesturing for him to do the same while cutting my way through the bustling crowd of every tech, agent and consultant we had in the headquarters. The minute I put on the shades, the room's already chaotic lights mingled with a terrible array of auras. I did my best to navigate the crowd and tune out the sea of anxiety and conflicted emotions the system could barely organize.

As I cleared the thickest part of the crowd, I could finally see the petite figure sitting at the desk in front of Lucian. Dulaf Nénharma, out of uniform more than usual, had come back from her off hours to join the cause and was busily tapping away at the desk's keyboard while the desktop surface shimmered with a light and projected a display towards our visors. Even Dulaf was wearing a visor for a change, her ears folded back almost perfectly in line with the frames as she chewed on her lower lip. I couldn't see her eyes either, but both of their auras were not comforting to look at. Dulaf's normally calm, silver aura was replaced with agitated red hues I rarely saw on her, matching the color of the lights flashing all around us. Finally turning my head toward the desk, the display hovered in front of me like a hologram and showed me exactly why.

Floating in the air in front of us was a map of the city that had been highlighted by the system with dozens of markers scattered in an irregular shape. No rhyme, no reason, just peppered about like a shotgun spray through the heart of the city.

"That's not," I started to say, trailing off before I could complete the sentence.

"It sure is," Lucian replied grimly, crossing his arms and lowering his head.

Dulaf looked up at Ramirez and I standing by them and shook her head solemnly. "The boys told me what they heard out there and I had to see for myself."

Ramirez stepped closer to the desk and stared into it with visible tension, fist clenched he rested his hands against the desk, grinding his knuckles into the surface as he looked through the map. I could understand how he felt, looking at the marks and realizing what they meant: dozens had been murdered in the same fashion without a single report reaching us. There was a killing spree and the police had silenced the whole thing.

"I don't get how they could have done this," Ramirez muttered, removing his visor and stepping back, rubbing the bridge of his nose. "Is that even possible?"

"It gets worse," Lucian said with an eerie calm, lifting his chin but not quite looking at us. "The Oracle spotted the actions as they happened and then never reported them."

Numb is the best way to describe how I felt just then. I felt like I was shaking for an instant without moving a muscle. The sensation simply rolled through me like a shudder without actually moving my body, leaving behind nothing in its wake. It was a cold feeling without an actual substance, purely in my head as I tried to grasp what Lucian just said.

"Can that even happen?" I asked, stunned.

Dulaf removed her visor too and leaned back, looking up at the three of us standing over her, spinning slowly in her chair. "It can if she's ordered not to disclose information to us."

I shot a look across the room to Commissioner Alston briefing the other agents, a projection of a Nosferatu's skeleton rotating on the wall behind him. "By one of ours?"

"No," Lucian said curtly. "If one of ours tried to do this then she would have been legally required to report them for the attempt."

"Then who?" Ramirez asked.

Dulaf took a deep breath and looked over to Ramirez sympathetically before putting the visor back on, turning back to the keyboard. Clicking on a marker on the desktop, she opened the case file and showed us what little of it was open: a name, a face, a location and the condition she'd been found in. The rest of the file was redacted in a pale grey. I'd heard of them in the academy but had never seen the "silver lines" before.

"Oh shit," I muttered absently while studying the heavily redacted page.

"What's wrong?" Ramirez asked, putting his visor back on. He scanned the file for a moment before asking, frustrated, "What the hell is that?"

"It's a silver line redaction," Dulaf said matter-of-factly, resting her elbows on the desk and her chin on her hands. "The Tolerance Day Treaty to acknowledge the Republic of Argyre had a stipulation that the ACTF could only operate on foreign soil if the local government had the right to maintain secrets from the Oracle system."

I grabbed a chair from the next desk over and pulled it into place, sitting down roughly. Exasperated, I barked, "I thought that was just so she wouldn't report overhearing the President hiding a Succubus under his desk."

Lucian chuckled and shook his head at me, "When have politicians ever kept that hidden?"

"Besides," Dulaf mused, turning her head my way, "That's the Clinton Clause."

I almost laughed at that but just rolled my eyes instead. I was too tired, sore and wet to be amused. Ramirez, on the other hand, was nearly ready to jump out of his boots over it. He paced a bit by the desk, almost frantic in the way he was moving. I could understand it with all I knew about him. To Ramirez the police were his friends, his family. He'd come to the ACTF to try to bridge the gap between our organizations. I could only imagine this was like watching an old friend take a piss on your new friend's shoes.

"So you guys are saying that this isn't even the SPD doing this?" he asked. "This is the Federal government?!"

We all took a moment to look his way and nod our confirmations. None of us really had anything good to say at the time. After what he'd said below about how the others would have wanted to call us, it was probably a dirty grey area for the red-and-blues too by this point. No one was winning right now.

"We'll probably move the SOL team on this whenever someone actually spots the thing," Lucian said. "We just need people to know how to deal with it if they actually see it."

He removed his visor finally, icy blue eyes sweeping across the three of us while he stood straighter and took on his near perfectly calm expression again. "In the meantime, find out what Omero knows on these things and warm up." He reached down, patting my shoulder and hearing the squish, "and try to dry off."

Dulaf's ears perked like an excited cat at the sound of my soaked clothes under Lucian's hand. She grinned at me and sat a little straighter, asking, "wet yourself when you found the scratches?"

I was baffled by her ability to tease me at a time like this. Either she was extremely confident, carefree or just enjoyed screwing with me too much to let it stop. Still, it did make me feel a little better that things were still somewhat normal even with the situation we'd just uncovered. Status quo, even at the butt's end of Dulaf's jokes, was preferable to worrying about the bat. Thinking about that for a moment, feeling a little grateful to her for being a constant heckler… I felt the need to fire back.

Getting up, I nodded back to Ramirez and started to walk to Alston's presentation, quipping, "Maybe we should suggest using Dulaf as bait."

Chapter 4
Nightclub Incidents

Commissioner Alston is an impressive man. It made sense, being a Golem, that he'd be a solid enforcer. Standing head and shoulders over everyone in the room, including the lithe figure of Lucian once again leaning on the wall, he had a commanding figure. His harsh features were embellished by his grey, hardened, stone-like skin. And while all that was enough to make us listen to him, especially considering his rank, what he had to say was good enough to do it too.

He put on a clinic on how to take down a Nosferatu, relating to us stories of his time on the "heavy payload" division that was formed in the early days of the official ACTF. For a period of time, before there was a headquarters and when things like the Nosferatu were out and about, Omero Alston was one of the few people in the world who'd encountered multiple and lived to tell the tale. It didn't hurt that his skin could have easily brushed off a few claw swipes and he was built like a frequent steroid abuser. The feat itself was still impressive none-the-less.

"The thing you must always remember," he said in a deep, gravely tone, "is that everything has a weakness."

Waving to the projection behind him of a hunched over, furry, bat-faced bastard, he continued, "These things have better senses of hearing and smell than you could possibly hope of having. So overwhelming these senses is your best option if you're faced with of one of them. They're sensitive to loud, disruptive noises and strong odors. Obviously, there's ways to take advantage of this."

"Shit yourself?" I joked, draping a towel over my head.

A laugh rolled through the group while Alston's face somehow managed to top the scowl almost permanently etched on his face without cracking. I sank in my seat for a moment while the Commissioner glared my way, feeling the rank insignia on my shoulder slowly melting away from the heat of his gaze.

Then Lucian spoke up over the laughter of the agents, adding, "*Scream* and shit yourself!"

Suddenly, the pissed off Golem wasn't glaring at me anymore and my mentor ensured, once again, that he'd never be promoted.

Sighing, the big man looked back at the group and said, "You've dealt with similar senses before; you know what to do. Remember, whatever you do, you won't have to do it alone for very long. The SOL team will be called in the minute someone reports seeing one - even if it's a false alarm."

Laughs faded as the group started to solemnly nod to what he said. It was reassuring to know that a Special Operations Lancer team would be on the scene when we needed them. Without them, independent agents like myself were in for a world of hurt. Maybe, with us as the ones looking and SOL coming in to clean the mess, this wouldn't be such a clusterfuck after all.

Nodding back at us, Alston shut off the projection. "Dismissed," he commanded, surveying the group, "and safe hunting out there."

The others stood and started to clear the room, murmuring about the giant piece of guano that landed in our laps. However, with what I'd seen, I realized there was something going on that was bigger than the Nosferatu. Looking over my shoulder, I stared at the desk Dulaf had used and walked over there instead. She'd shut it down and left the room as we'd been listening to Alston's briefing, but I knew the system would have the same search on file. Even though I'd seen it already, there was still something about it that needed to be examined closer. In this case, the silver lining around the clouds was the only clue we had to work with.

Starting it up and putting my visor back on, I gazed over the map and looked for any sign of a pattern. There had to be a reason these cases were hidden from us, something possibly about the victims. I couldn't read the actual files, just who and where things had happened, but even with that I still had the option and ability to carry on my work by following the names and piecing this together on my own. Even if the Oracle couldn't tell us what was happening, I could investigate myself.

Examining the map, I found a cluster of victims not far from the center of Fangtown. The cases were almost a month old without a single report made to us and involved women who were unmistakably Alters. More than that, by looking at the names I could already recognize a few of them and knew exactly where that small cluster tied together. The Nosferatu, for whatever reason, had been hovering over the Moirae Club.

The club had a history: it was one of the few clubs owned and operated by an Alter from the minute it broke ground and everyone knew that as a fact without even having to step foot inside. It was near the center of Fangtown, the primarily Alter enclave, and was owned by reformed members of the Third Avenue Hunt – a gang consisting mostly of Werewolves out of Pioneer Square. I admit I had to resist the urge to call the Moirae staff a wolf pack from time to time. But experience with them told me that, while they were legit, they were sometimes forced to look the other way to stay safe and clean.

Seeing this, I went to the locker rooms, got a dry uniform, and went to see the wolves instead of the bat. At the very least, I figured they could give me some idea of how things went down a month ago. With luck, they might even have something to clue me in on just what exactly was going on with the Federal government crawling over a case that smacked of ACTF jurisdiction. Either way, while the rest of the group was out to find the bat before it could cause more harm, I didn't want to let this cover up hide from the light of day. Someone out there was okay with the idea of these girls dying in agony on the streets and just letting the pattern continue.

I wasn't.

The rain was thinning now, turning to sheets of mist that rolled across my windshield in small waves on the gusts of wind. The umbrellas were out en masse now, like a rainbow of floating islands drifting on a shadowy river of people, the multicolored neon mist floating overhead in a haze. The Moirae wasn't far off, the crowd ahead of me getting thicker the nearer I came. As I rolled by I saw the same umbrellas covering the line that stood outside the doorways. Well, most of the line was covered while the few normal humans, lacking the ability to read the weather and standing out there too long for their own good, managed to forget theirs while their Alter companions conveniently didn't warn them.

I climbed out of the car into the same mist and walked confidently past the masses, ignoring their pecking order and moving like a man prepared to kick in the doors. The bouncers, a pair of Werewolves who were already big and ugly in their regular human forms, saw my badge coming from halfway down the line and quietly moved the hell out of my way. I admit I may have been overzealous intimidating them in the past.

You might even say I was a bit of a dick.

Everything was a little more solemn than usual once I stepped inside. The Moirae's a three-story club with each floor acting as a different theme from the rest. The ground floor, where I was standing, was normally a lively bar scene with pleasant music and a mostly laid back atmosphere. However, this time, I could see the staff was on edge in a way you didn't normally want to see in a pack of wolves.

Toward the back I could see their boss, Anubis - his dark complexion against his light suit making him one of the most striking in the entire room and his towering stature making the pale woman at his side seem tiny by comparison. His back was turned to me but the tension in his shoulders told a story all their own. The grey suit he wore was tight around him, uncharacteristically ill-fitting, like he'd been on the verge of growing and bursting through his clothes in a fit of rage. The woman at his side glanced my way with a concerned look that quickly vanished as we made eye contact across the room.

Unassuming but always present like his shadow, I'd run into his assistant Marionette quite a few times over the last few months. For some reason she always felt vaguely familiar to me, a feeling that caused some awkward silences between us whenever I came to talk to her boss. She wasn't that unusual, her dark hair cut to shoulder length, her eyes a shade of blue that was a bit more subdued than most Alters. Her aura on the visor, an uneasy restrained purple from some unpleasant feeling she couldn't express near her boss, was easily the thing that stood out

47

about her most at the time. Though, even with the visor, I wasn't quite sure what kind of Alter she might have been.

Maybe I was never comfortable enough to look close enough to figure it out.

She reached over and patted Anubis' arm as I cut my way through the crowd. The tension in his shoulders rose again, practically jumping out of his skin. Then, somehow, as he glimpsed over his shoulder the look on his face was even less friendly than his posture. His dark features cutting a sleek shape, his eyes reflecting the dim bar lights like a pair of polished mirrors, he glared at me as though I'd wronged him. With the vague hints of his more canine-like bone structure starting to peek through and his normally clean-shaven face starting to show stubble - I knew he was on the verge of howling and going on a rampage.

"Where the hell have you been?" he roared, scaring customers standing nearby. "This shit started a month ago!"

The power in his voice slowed my pace as I continued to approach, the bright red aura shining through my shades confirming he was ready to take a chunk out of me. Lifting my hand, I stroked fingers across the wristband of my gloves and activated the silver coating across the protective plates. Even if I was only there to ask him about the case I wasn't ready to be chewed on for my efforts. Looking up at him, I watched him back down from the sudden increase of silver on my gear and scowl into the mirrored surface of my shades.

"I'm not here to start problems," I said calmly, "I'm here to help."

"Damn lot of good you've done for us," he snapped. "We call in about our missing girls a month ago and not a damn thing has been done about it. The red-and-blues came by our door to talk to us about it but not a single silver badge or violet light in sight except to pass on by and act like there was nothing to talk to us about."

I shook my head and regretfully replied, "We didn't know."

"Didn't know?" he yelled. "How the hell could you not know? Don't you have an Oracle to see shit like this and take your calls? Did she go on vacation? Can she go on vacation?

48

Can't someone else pick up the fucking phone when we make the call?"

"She saw it," I answered while doing my best to not react to his tone, "she just didn't tell us about it, recorded it and didn't mention it to us."

A motion rolled up through his body from the waist to his shoulders as he reared back before whipping his hands in my direction, snarling, "Oh great! Now your house-elves ain't even willing work with you."

The motion should have startled me, but he didn't make contact and I understood where it came from. On the other hand, the phrase "house-elf" caught me off guard and almost broke my calm. The old folklore spoke of fairies and spirits that would live in people's houses and do chores for them while they slept, acting as servants to ungrateful humans. Even if I wasn't an Alter myself, the implications heated my blood.

"Don't call her that," I scolded.

He scoffed, "Guess if you stuffed my ass in a bottle and kept me locked in a room I'd stop cooperating with your asses too."

"Look," I said, taking off my visor as a show of good faith, "I just want to know what happened."

He glared down at me, making eye contact and losing the scowl that had been on his face since I entered. "Man, all I know is that I lost two of my best girls over a month ago, little less than a week apart, and you guys don't show up once. The regular cops, who aren't exactly our best friends, showed up at our door and talked to us about it instead. Meanwhile, three other girls have quit over the last month saying they saw giant bats flying overhead and they didn't feel safe working here anymore."

"Bats?" I echoed.

"Damn straight," he grunted. "And it shows up in the news today and all of a sudden here you are!"

I thought back on Kelly's reader and the picture of the bat again, realizing it wasn't coincidence that was in the news on the same day we finally got the call. "Yeah, it was in the news, wasn't it?"

"Hard to ignore after that, isn't it?" he chided.

Ignoring the accusations was starting to wear a little thin. He couldn't be blamed for feeling the way he did but I wasn't exactly the one to blame for it. Shaking my head, I folded the visor and put it away in the pouch on my belt, then shut off the silver plated nanites on my gloves.

Looking up again, I said sincerely, in the calmest tone I could, "Normally I'd stand here and trade shots with you, Anubis, but there's big issues going on here. I need to know more about the girls and if there was anything important that connected them."

He shook his head, walking away from me to the bar counter, saying darkly, "They worked the bottom floor and they died only a week apart."

I looked at the staircase not far from us, hearing the pulsing music from below and seeing the strobing lights reflect off the walls. The fact they worked specifically in the lower levels suggested to me that they weren't exactly waitresses. Not that the information really helped me figure out the silver line. Maybe a politician did something with them before they died but I couldn't be sure.

Anubis saw me looking down the stairs apparently, striking my shoulder with the back of his hand and spinning me to face him again, snarling, "Look, just because they were Succubi doesn't mean a fucking thing about them! You got me? Those girls were family and once again you people haven't done a damn thing to protect me and mine from shit like this!"

The reasons I could have locked him up for what he just did were easily enough to turn the plates back on. If I didn't understand where he was coming from, they probably would have. And as he glared down at me, taking his overly aggressive posture, I was sorely tempted. But I knew he was right even if his tone wasn't.

"Someone wanted to make sure we didn't know about their deaths," I replied, frustrated. "I'm going to find out who and why."

He turned away from me and rested his hands on the bar counter again, shaking his head. "In the meantime, I'm casting my lot in with Locusta. They actually show up."

That one stung on multiple levels. Really, there was nothing that I could say in response to it. I just nodded, took out my visor and put it back on before turning to walk out without a word. Anubis' head lowered out of the corner of my eye, the normally imposing Werewolf sinking to a stool and resting against the bar counter. Looking over my shoulder at him, he looked a lot more defeated than he let on before. He couldn't help me now, I figured, as he was too justifiably angry. The best I could do was get a court order to grab the security tapes and hope there was something on them.

Marionette, silent to that moment and staying out of our way, suddenly stepped into my field of vision.

"Nate," she started to say, hesitating, "Agent Leone, you need to know something."

We hadn't spoken very often in the time since I first met her. She was always the silent figure standing at Anubis' side while he snarled and growled at me over our various encounters. So hearing her call me Nate, even for a moment, was a strange sensation that made my whole body tense. I didn't like it. I don't know why exactly but something in me bristled at the sound of it.

Taking a deep breath, washing that thought out of my head, I asked, "What exactly do I need to know?"

I think she knew what was going through my head at the moment, which wasn't at all surprising in a society full of mind-readers. She stepped back and lowered her head, averting her eyes from the reflection of my visor and actively starting to suppress her biometrics until her aura turned a midnight blue. Mentally, I noted that was a practiced response. For some reason, Marionette had trained herself to avoid ACTF attention.

"The Locusta," she said as her aura nearly flat-lined, "They've been working at this for most of the month and they've reported back some results."

"What kind of results?"

Looking up again, she made eye contact the best she could and replied, "Leads that might be useful to you."

"Did you actually catch any specifics?" I asked, finally turning to fully face her.

She shook her head and averted her eyes again, letting her dark hair hang over her face. "They didn't tell us the information itself, just that they had it."

I nodded and turned to leave the building, looking back over my shoulder one more time before exiting. She continued to shy away from eye contact and I had a twinge of familiarity again that I couldn't shake.

Pushing it aside, I asked, "Which members of the Locusta?"

She lifted her chin, took a strangely telling breath and replied with a false calm, "They're the members that spend their time down at the Façade, the one next to the Zomboner off the Forum."

I winced at the sound of those words; the Façade was a seemingly unassuming location that was actually the viper's pit of Alter mafia activity. It was like she'd told me the best way to find the Nosferatu was to go into a dragon's den. But, even if that was the case, I knew I had to go anyway.

"Want to help?" I asked, nodding and taking one last good survey of the area. "Get me the security tapes and send them to the headquarters."

She turned her gaze to one of the cameras hanging in the corners and I took the moment to consider just where that feeling kept coming from. For all my efforts I'd still had no idea why I felt strange around her. But I pushed it aside and walked out the door. I still wasn't comfortable with her using my name and I certainly couldn't place her face. Still, whatever that feeling was, she'd given me a lead I could use.

Chapter 5
Enemy Territory

I found myself traveling up the street and into the Crepusculum Forum at the heart of Fangtown. At the center of the Forum, surrounded by slightly taller buildings covered with glow in the dark murals and slightly European architecture, the waters of the Twilight fountain battled the falling rain for attention. The light show normally shot through the mist of the fountain waters now shined through the falling rain as well, creating a field of dazzling light at the center of the forum that lit everything around it. The shimmering pool and sunset colored mingled with the overlays of the Oracle's displays against my windows. The place was still bustling with activity despite the weather - the covered, half-buried walkways meant for daylight travel now providing them some degree of shelter.

Past the fountain another landmark danced in the rain. There was a Zomboner club not far from the Forum, a unique establishment that was hard to miss even among the unusual style of the Fangtown nightlife. Even from the Forum, through all the light, sound and motion, I could see the holographic Zombie in the white dress dancing on the winds. To this day, mostly because of that image, I still haven't been brave enough to enter the Zomboner as a customer. But for this one time, I needed to approach it.

Next to that gaudy building flagrantly waving its unorthodoxy in the face of the world was a much less conspicuous place. The Façade seemed almost alien in how plain it was next to a place like that. It was shorter than the rest of the buildings, less colorful and less well lit. It was almost like it was trying to hide, make itself look smaller than it actually was. And, really, that was exactly what it was trying to do. As if the name wasn't a giveaway.

Years ago, before the Third Avenue Hunt and Jiangshi Tong were chased out of this part of Fangtown, The Façade was a guarded secret. It was a front where the Locusta could hold meetings or relay communications while hiding in the shadow of stranger establishments. There were others like it scattered throughout the city, but in the last big conflict between the gangs it became an important location for the Locusta. I'd never been inside or had any idea what it pretended to be, but I had a few ideas of what I'd find.

Stepping out of the car, I started to run the mental checklist on things to do before entering a place like this. The riot control tools were on my hip, my gloves and greaves were turned to silver and my gun was fully charged and loaded with a spare clip at my back. Momentarily, I considered what power setting the gun should be on. I wasn't sure what exactly their reaction would be to me stepping inside, what with being a front business. Though I did know it wasn't going to be a happy get-together with my old buddies in the Locusta. Stopping in front of the door, I decided to leave it on the default, put in the earplugs we used to filter out some of the louder bangs and screams that I could expect and stared at my reflection in the glass for a moment.

At least I didn't look as nervous as I felt.

Noting my visor and remembering a lesson I learned the hard way once, I reached up and took it off for a second, pulling a strap out of my pocket to connect to the frames and keep the thing secured to my head. It made me look like a geek, but you never knew when a Giant could shoot you a dozen feet through a wall while your visor goes sliding into oblivion.

It's a long story.

Taking a calming breath, I pushed open the door and stepped into the Façade, ready to defend myself if they forced me to. The doors swung open and a cheerful little bell rang, the interior brighter than the outside in so many ways. Honestly, it wasn't quite what I was expecting the den of a mafia family to look like.

Bright pink and red inside with rose colored carpeting, there were clothing racks along each side of me carrying darker colored suits and frilly outfits with lace for both men and women. The owner, a frail looking man in a purple silk shirt and a black vest, had a dim violet aura around him as I entered, except for a Technicolor nightmare flying around his head. His pink eyes glanced up from the counter to me, his aura gradually shifting towards red as I weaved through the lingerie section that stretched from the entrance. I passed a teddy with a pink heart across the chest, a subtle bat shaped design in the lace catching the corner of my eye.

Glancing over the bat shape, I nearly missed the lanky figure behind the counter move over nearly a foot to his left. He raised a hand and ran it through his stiff, blonde hair. The way it resisted his fingers and bounced, I could suddenly figure out why the scan on my shades was discovering new colors in the spectrum. Then, before I could look back at him, still apparently unaware of me being able to see him, he tugged the bottom of his vest to smooth it out and rested his hands on the counter, hanging his fingers over the back edge.

"Can I help you with anything sir?" he asked in a high, nasally voice. "Maybe a little something for the little lady?"

I pushed my shades back, making sure he couldn't see my eyes through the mirrored surface, replying, "I'm here to talk to someone about a bat."

"A bat?" he asked, shifting his footing a bit while keeping those hands secured on the counter. "We're a clothing store, sir. We serve all the needs of the classy Alter, even in their not so classy times. Which I'm sure you can understand."

He smirked at me and winked when he said that, making me realize another reason his readings were so strange. Incubi were rare in the area, much more than their female counterparts, and until that night I'd only known of one in the city. Somehow, it made sense this man was working retail in a slutty clothing store. It also made sense why I felt like he was flirting with me.

"There's a Nosferatu in town," I replied assuredly, brushing aside the uncomfortable feeling. "I heard your guys have information on it."

His left hand started to slide along the counter edge, his aura starting to show signs of added anxiety, like he was starting to become afraid of me. A part of me was, admittedly, a little too amused by this. A man who worked for some of the scariest people in Seattle was afraid of me? I smiled broadly as I slammed my hands down on the counter.

"So do you know anyone who can tell me anything about a bat?" I asked cheerfully.

"I don't know what you're talking about," he said, hand continuing to slide.

I observed the hand from behind the shades. "So why are you reaching for the alarm button then?"

His face sank into a deep, ugly frown like it'd melted. He commented sadly, "You were cute too."

As he flexed his hand to press the button he quickly found my pistol in his face, lights along the gun shining dimly, a low hum building inside.

"Now why'd you go and do something like that?" I asked.

The effeminate clerk ducked behind the counter, a hidden door on an adjacent wall slid open. I turned to face it in time to see the pale face of a Vampire emerge from the shadows, his dark suit blending with the environment around him. Before I had a chance to line up a shot he pulled a trigger of his own, the bang of his gun filtered by the earplugs but the shot to my chest confirming it all too well.

The wind was knocked out of me and a flash of pain rolled through my torso as I fell back to the floor like I'd been punched in the chest. My visor bounced off of my face, held on only by the strap as I whipped my head back up and fired off two quick shots back into the Vampire's knees. With the visor hanging around my neck they were unassisted and I probably should have fired for his core, but dumb luck and muscle memory won the day.

Blue bolts of light cleared through his suit and the skin underneath as he screamed in agony and dropped with a loud thud. Lifting my hands up and jerking to the right I fired off another shot into his shoulder, forcing him to drop the gun. Clutching it, he cried out and fell to the floor, the face of one of his friends emerging from the shadows behind him.

I rolled along the ground, behind racks of clothes and out of the new guy's line of sight. My chest throbbed under the coat, a blunted round still wedged into the Vesperadin armor weave.

Ignoring it the best I could, feeling an awesome kick of adrenaline, I pushed to my feet and ran behind the racks with my head low. The new guy fired off a couple shots across my path, missing and blowing holes into the wall behind me. I didn't catch sight of the gun he had, but I knew his friend was sporting a 9mm with an ammo capacity of fifteen rounds in the clip.

He wasn't about to run out of bullets.

Turning, I dove across the aisles and past the rows of racks, hitting the floor on my shoulder and sliding a bit before getting sight of him from the side. Firing again, an ionized bolt of UV light and a chemical cocktail burned through one of his ankles, leaving behind the haunting blue glow in its wake. He dropped hard against the counter, turning to face me with his gun. But before he could get the gun lined with me I had a chance to fire again, passing a searing bolt through his forearm and forcing him to drop the gun.

"Anatole," he screamed to the clerk behind the counter, "hit it again!"

"Anatole" rose behind the counter, making a move for the button again. Scrambling to my feet and dashing over, I planted my hands on the counter and vaulted over, ramming a knee into "Anatole's" face. He squealed as his head whipped aside, dramatically throwing himself against the back wall. A contact rash formed across his face the instant it broke away from my silver-plated knee pad. As he slid to the floor, he looked up at me with sad pink eyes.

"Aquamarine," he said, dazed, "how lovely."

Staring down at the strange man for a moment, I wondered what exactly he was talking about. Seconds later, lifting my dangling visor again, I realized he'd been talking about the color of my eyes. I'd heard Incubi were strangely single minded, but I'd never seen it in Trey before. Finally experiencing it, I found myself a little unnerved, shaking my head as I approached the newly revealed door.

The one against the counter lifted his head and screamed towards the doorway, "Agent coming! Agent com-"

Choking on his words, he stared into the barrel of the Helios pistol centered at his face while I lifted a finger to my lips and nodded silently. We came to a quiet understanding in that moment: I wouldn't shoot him again if he promised to shut the fuck up.

Unfortunately, it was too late. The distant sound of steps charged up the stairs: two, maybe three, men the size of the ones that just traded gunfire with me were coming up from the basement. The burning welt on my chest convinced me not to try to take these ones fairly. So I reached to my belt, felt one of the rods hanging from it and yanked it from the clip. Feeling the pop, I lifted it ahead of me, twisted the end of it and flung it into the stairwell underhanded, letting it bounce down the steps.

The chirping sound, one of the only sounds the device would make that could get through these earplugs, drifted down the stairs before and meeting with the steps below. All of a sudden the steps were moving in the other direction, faster than they were coming up, and the chirps went silent. One voice broke through the sound to scream, "Banshee!"

And then it went silent, the chirps, the screams, everything gone in an instant, drowned and consumed by something stronger. I felt the floor rumble under my feet and felt my clothes vibrate with it. I knew the sound was blasting from the stairwell in my face, muffled by the earplugs designed specifically for this sound. Feeling it, I prepped my gun, ensured my visor was back where it belonged, and walked down into the darkness and the wailing of the Banshee.

Their voices, distorted and weakened before they could reach me at the top, started to separate from the sonic grenade's wail. I think I could hear about four of them, though that may just be hindsight since that's how many I found at the bottom. Taking a moment to grab a different rod from the belt, I clicked a button at the end of it several times until I felt a slightly different click than the last, mentally prepared for whatever pissed off creatures I could find down there, and charged down the last few steps, leaping past the bottom three into the small room below.

In the split second before I hit the floor I found four Vampires, each taking a corner and trying to get some distance from the screaming Banshee at the center. I lobbed the second rod for the door at the far side, the end popping open and clinging to the wood surface with a dull thud that I knew was there but couldn't hear past the noise and the filters. Hitting the floor finally, tucking and rolling, I turned and fired back into one of the corners, aiming low again – this time intentionally and with the visor's help.

The rod at the door, a Will-O-Wisp, went off just then, a blinding flash flooding the room as another of the guards rushed me from the corner. The light blinded him as I turned and swept his legs with a kick, firing into the back of his knee as he hit the floor to keep him from getting back up.

A second flash and the room went dark, a small EMP taking out any electronics that weren't shielded. The other two in the room screwed up the courage to rush me anyway, my gear still functioning and letting me see the whole thing in night-vision. I shot one in the shoulder on his way in, spinning him off center and letting him tumble to the floor, where his head unfortunately bumped the Banshee and gave him an earful of the thing before it rolled away.

A third flash, this time stronger than the last two, actually hurt the fourth guy as UV light burst through the room and gave him an impromptu tan. I stood to meet with him and whipped the pistol across his head.

By the fourth flash the room was clear.

I backed away from the door, having seen the fourth flash and knowing what was next. My heart was pounding or my welt was throbbing, I couldn't exactly tell which at the time. I pictured what was beyond that door. There were six out here already, Vampires, and a seventh if you included Anatole the Incubus: so how many more would be inside? Were they all hostiles? My arm started throbbing with my chest as I reached back and pulled the last rod from my belt, clicking the button quickly to switch between modes.

I had to assume they weren't all hostile.

With five flashes, the Will-O-Wisp exploded with a concussive force, blowing the door off the hinges and dropping it into the darkened room beyond. The visor highlighted dozens of red auras and a few blue or purple throughout the room as the door cracked open. I didn't take time to worry about the number; I just threw the last rod into the room ahead of me.

The Manticore pack-buster, a nasty little grenade, flew into the room and opened into a vicious little metal pine-tree branch. A light from inside the rod made the needles clear for all to see and, suddenly, all those red auras cooled off real fast. Everyone became very tense for a moment, including me. Usually I'd throw it closed, but in this one case I wanted everyone to know what was entering the room.

It hit wood and skid, scraping and tumbling along the surface, stopping after a few inches and bobbing on its weighted end until it stood upright on a previously unseen table. The light from the rod lit the face of a grim, younger looking man sitting behind it, shadows cast across his face making his features severe. I couldn't see much of him as he sat unmoved by the weapon, only the collar of a suit and a tie visible under the shadows of his chin, his hands raised, tented, fingers laced.

Despite my efforts, he wasn't impressed.

"Are you done?" he asked, lowering his hands.

"I think I'll be done when the rest of you get carted out," I said warily, edging slowly to the door.

I hesitated to enter, the smell of tobacco smoke and a few other herbs drifting out of the room beyond blended with the chemical odor of the spent Will-O-Wisp at my feet. It was hard to get a headcount from where I stood, the shadows and auras blending together as the people seemed to crawl over each other. I wasn't sure if they were just that close together or if the pounding in my chest was starting to blur my vision. From where I stood, however, it looked like cockroaches swarming in the dark.

"No one will fire on you again," he replied sternly, leaning back in his chair.

I laughed, "Your men already opened fire on me."

A low, quiet grunt came from the shadows where he sat, a hand waving into the light. Exasperated, he sighed and said, "They fired on the wrong uniform. We didn't expect to see ACTF at our door."

The fact he said all of that took me aback. The sheer gall of what they were doing in that building was staggering to me: gathering for criminal activities, ordering to shoot on sight for any agency as if it were no big deal, and still waiting calmly in the next room. It wasn't the first time I'd seen an Alter boss refuse to get up, but it was definitely the most intense. I had to admit I felt some respect for the man's brass balls if nothing else.

"Sorry to wander into the shooting gallery then," I quipped, finally crossing the threshold and taking an account of the figures cowering in the corners. "Don't suppose you'll tell me who you were expecting to be up there, or how you expected to get away with it, will you?"

"The FBI for the most part," he said matter-of-factly, not an ounce of hesitation behind it. "And we would have killed them, burned the building down and relocated."

My respect for the man's brass ones continued to grow as I strolled into the darkened room, feeling easier about it as I saw everyone continue to shy away. I had to admit, I was a bit frightened by how calm he was about the prospect. Something about the FBI showing up was enough for them to napalm the area and he wasn't wary about the concept at all.

"Why?"

He gestured to the chair in front of me, only faintly visible with the help of the visor, and replied, "If they come here, it will likely be for the same reason you do, but for far different motives I'm afraid."

I looked at the chair for a moment and hesitated. On the one hand, sitting down right now wasn't exactly the best idea with a room full of potential hostiles. On the other, I was exhausted, had a live Manticore right in front of me, and my emergency beacon was lit as soon as they shot me. To be honest, my odds were about the same on my feet or on my ass.

I assessed the room one more time before cautiously sitting, gun still in hand and left where all could see, asking, "The Nosferatu?"

"We were wondering how long it would take your group to find out about our troubled cousin in the city," he said with a nod. "In fact, you caught on earlier than we thought you would, considering the cover up."

"You know about that?" I asked, surprised.

"The silver-line redaction?" he chuckled smugly, "not at first but it wasn't long before we found out about it. It's tricky how that system of yours hands control over to the people most likely to abuse it."

"What are you talking about?" I demanded, "What do you know?"

The lights came back on as we sat together, the man across from me lit under visible light for the first time and the image from my visor slowly merging with the visible spectrum. His dark suit was expensive, leaps and bounds over the value of the clothes around him. His silk tie was royal purple, gold cufflinks at his wrists and a griffon shaped tie-pin made of what I assumed was platinum since no sane Vampire would have worn silver.

"More than you, I imagine," he said smugly. "Agent..?"

"Leone," I replied, "and you would be?"

"My name is Dante," he said, leaning on the table and smiling broadly without a care despite the weapon no more than a foot in front of his face. "You're in my territory."

"You took the first shot. Were you that willing to kill people on your own ground?" I asked, studying the room, people gradually relaxing from the realization they hadn't been bombarded with needles. "What's going on here, Dante?"

Dante examined the base of the Manticore, eyebrow raised. He unlaced his fingers and took his elbows off the table, grasping at his chin and stroking fingers along his jaw while he adjusted in his seat, leaning hard onto the arm of a chair and looking around the room with a knowing expression. Shrugging, he gestured with a light wave to one of the men in the room and smiled at me again.

"A while back we were called about a Nosferatu roaming the city," he said, "the ACTF hadn't responded for some reason and our friend Anubis was convinced that you'd written him off. Of course," he chuckled, "we know differently now, don't we?"

I watched Dante's man weave through the crowd with a deliberate pace to the far end of the room and into an office space in the back. That simple gesture, whatever it meant, seemed to be important to the minion. The question I had was whether or not it was to fetch the bigger guns. But, seeing Dante's expression, hearing the confidence in his voice, I knew he didn't need to shoot me right now. Somehow we were both on the outside on this case, at odds with the same force.

"What would happen if the FBI were the ones to show up?" I asked tightly.

Dante's face went cold and his voice deep as he answered, "I already told you, we would have destroyed the building and left. Not just them, anyone working for the federal government asking about that bat."

"Why?" I asked, stunned.

"Because if we didn't, they would have come down on us with everything they had," he said in the same cold tone. "They don't want anyone to know what we know."

"What do they have to do with the Nosferatu?" I asked, raising my voice.

The man Dante sent to the back came to the table again. He produced something about the size of a phone with a reinforced case, a noticeable antenna nub on the corner of it. With a flick of a wrist he whipped the device onto the table in front of me. I glanced to the device and back to Dante as he gestured to it with a wave of his hand. Picking it up, it became immediately apparent what he was being so smug about. There on a GPS layout was a distinctive, quickly moving dot crossing traffic and buildings like they weren't even there.

Dante, smiling broadly, looked like a predator perched across the table as he gleefully said, "It's tagged."

Chapter 6
Troubling Assessment

It didn't take very long for the Special Operations Lancer to swarm that building after getting the GPS. The minute a bullet hit me the badge's homing beacon alerted every agent in the city that there was a problem. But that smug look never left Dante's face. He wasn't concerned about the ACTF at all while he was dead set to eliminate anything federal. As they burst into the room and started to sweep through it, stirring up a swarm and killing any chance I had for more information, I got up and got out of the basement.

Outside the Façade I watched the lancer teams and ambulances cart away the guards, a few members with some possession charges and Dante himself - who looked like he couldn't care less. It was surreal to see someone so content with the fact he was being marched out in cuffs. He even looked my way, still smiling, and nodded to me like an old friend noticing me on the street. And that's when I realized the really creepy part - we weren't the only things he didn't care about.

The Locusta are a pretty anti-human organization and they always have been. They would let the whole city burn so long as none of it belonged to them or another Alter. So if this Nosferatu had been rampaging through human victims, I imagine they would have just let it go. The victims were Alters, though, yet the Locusta were apparently in no hurry to catch this Nosferatu.

Jogging over, I called into the back of the SOL van, "You know more than you're telling me, don't you?"

Dante laughed, "Of course I do! And if you let me go, I might be willing to tell you."

Every agent standing there was uneasy about that prospect: I could see it in their body language even without checking their individual auras. The problem was we really didn't have the time to interrogate him the old fashioned way. But seeing the way that room moved for him, knowing that he told them to shoot at federal agents and no one hesitated to do it, this man was high on their totem pole - too high to just let go.

"I don't think so," I muttered, turning away from him.

His voice lost that jovial tone as my back was turned and he said, "You've got nothing on me, I ordered the defense of private property."

I shrugged and acknowledged to myself he was probably right about that. It was certain he had his hands in something, but who knows what we could actually make stick. Still, we could hold him for a while to try to figure that out - hopefully long enough. And as I looked away from him, I saw a much better opportunity.

Anatole, face swelling and blood running down that silk shirt of his, was getting walked away dazed and confused, his nose clearly broken. A guy like that, standing as the front for all that time and getting the same orders as the guards, he had to know something. And, despite pressing the button to get me shot at, he probably wasn't that big of a threat.

Walking over, I nodded to the agent at his side, "I've got this one."

Anatole, through his black eye, past a slightly crooked nose, looked at me pretty confused. I took his arm and guided him back to my car, asking smugly, "How would you like to get out of jail-time?"

The bruised and battered Incubus glanced nervously at me and replied, quietly, "Planning revenge for pressing the button?"

"Nah, I need information," I said, opening the door to the car and guiding him in, "you just pushed the button."

Still, as the words left my lips, I did think about the fact he was figuratively the one who pulled the trigger. In hindsight, I admit that's probably why I shoved him a little quickly and accidentally bounced his head off the doorframe. I don't think it made his face any worse and I'm pretty sure it was an accident.

Though, the therapist might call that rationalization.

Driving back to the headquarters, the first minute was unnaturally quiet, maybe he was frightened or wasn't sure what to say. Maybe he had a concussion. Whatever was behind it, I

65

broke the silence with the question heaviest on my mind: "Why aren't they going after the Nosferatu?"

Anatole glanced up, hesitantly replying, "They don't think it's the problem."

"And the FBI is?" I asked, glimpsing at him, catching sight of the new bruise on his face and quickly looking away again.

"We were told about the silver line before the Nosferatu sightings started," he murmured, sinking slightly in his chair. "That's why we started looking for the tag frequencies."

I tensed at the mention of the silver line, realizing the implications of someone knowing about it before we did, hoping it was from the FBI side and not ours. Something told me I knew who'd told them everything, though, despite how impossible it might have seemed.

"Your information, it came from...?" I trailed off as we came to a stoplight, looking at him directly for the first time since we sat down.

He looked back at me, practically shaking in his seat now, like even mentioning it was a cardinal sin. Then he nodded lightly, sighed and said, "From the 9th."

The two of us stayed silent the rest of the way to the headquarters, the neon light outside the windows hazy behind sheets of rain that started to fall again after a short reprieve we had on the way out of the Façade. He was probably frightened about the possibilities of what was going to happen next. Despite his involvement, I didn't get a sense he had a killer instinct about him. At least, I hoped it was just that he was nervous.

I, on the other hand, wasn't feeling too great after the rough tumble through the lingerie section. My chest had stopped pounding, the throbbing sensation fading away, but the pain lingered. I wasn't sure if I should tell the medics at the headquarters at this point. I knew I should get it looked at, but I didn't want to be pulled off of this now that we had a way to track the creature.

We pulled into the garage under the headquarters and I pulled Anatole out of the car a bit more gently than I had put him in. The guy looked a bit tenderized now that he'd had a chance for all of the swelling to reach its peak and I did feel a bit bad for doing that to him, even if it was in self-defense... the first time.

"We'll get you checked out by the medics," I said, guiding him through the underground entrance. The secured doors below ground had been upgraded recently, trying to make up for a few security glitches in recent history. A sound rolled through the corridor, pulsating through us, leaving an unnerving vibration as it passed, irritating my wounds as everything settled back into place.

"What the hell was that?" Anatole asked, cautiously scanning the corridor for an origin.

I sighed lightly. "A Shapeshifter got through a while ago. It's trying to look at our bones."

And, I hoped, not close enough to spot anything I didn't want grounding me for the night. If it did, it didn't let us know as it only acknowledged I was the real deal and welcomed me in the cold, distant tone you get from computers, the polite feminine voice greeting us, "Welcome Agent Leone and... guest."

All things considered, I was actually kind of relieved it didn't refer to Anatole as victim. Though I suppose the handcuffs had to be noticeable as I escorted him through the back door of the corridor and into the monitored elevator.

"A Shapeshifter?" he asked, smirking lightly with a busted lip. "You didn't see that coming?"

I glared his way and tipped my shades down so he could see, staring him down and thinking very bad thoughts in the hopes he might pick them up. And, considering he was an Incubus, there was a fifty-fifty shot on that. He squirmed nervously next to me and averted his eyes, staring off at the now apparently interesting wall of the elevator.

I escorted him through the maze of corridors around the tulip-like building, passing the mercurial surface of the memorial wall and into the depths of the medical wing. The ever-smiling face in the medical wing greeted us as we entered, the eternally youthful doctor staring across the room at us like he knew we were coming and smiling with the look of the cat catching the canary. Considering our doctor was a Reaper, the fact he was so happy to see us made me nervous about which one of us was dying. But Anatole, standing firm for the first time since my knee met his face, somehow managed to turn a couple shades paler than he already was.

"Anatole," the doctor said, rising slowly from his desk, "long time no see."

Anatole, beginning to fidget where he stood, responded nervously, "Lucas, how good it is to see you."

"Lucas?" I echoed.

"An alias," the doctor replied cheerfully, "from long ago."

To be honest, it was the first time I'd ever heard anyone refer to him by a name that I could remember. I'd never really questioned it much. The doctor, a Reaper, was ancient and mostly met people on the verge of death. And, honestly, after years of watching old sci-fi I'd been comfortable with the idea of someone just being known as "The Doctor". As strange as my life is, he could have been a time traveler for all I knew.

"How do you two know each other?" I asked, surveying the doctor's bright smile and Anatole's nervous grin.

"A story for another time," the doctor replied cheerfully. "You should probably leave me to my work and let me take care of Anatole here."

The doctor was always smiling: that was part of what was so creepy about him. But the smile he had just now, the sensation that he had something sinister working through his mind, was a new experience for me. It wasn't quite as genuine or compassionate as the other fake smiles he'd shown over the years. Something in his eyes told me that, of all the smiles he didn't mean, this was the one he meant the least. A certain Incubus, it seemed, was in trouble.

"I'm sure there's plenty of time for him to stay and chat," Anatole burst out. "There's no reason to rush the boy!"

He was definitely in trouble.

I patted Anatole on the shoulder, turned around, and waved to the doctor on the way out. "Just go easy on the face."

I was sure, leaving the room, that it wasn't something to worry about. Whatever was going on between them, I'd never known the doctor to be anything but professional and, despite his race's name, he was pretty enthusiastic about keeping people

68

breathing. I was sure there was an interesting story behind those expressions, but I knew because of the doctor's that it was a bad time to ask.

Though, when I saw Lucian, standing under the monitors and watching for all the activity now that the tracer was being patched into the network, I figured it couldn't hurt to ask a third party while we waited.

"Hey Lucian," I called, "any idea why someone from the Locusta would know the doctor's name?"

He gazed at me and shrugged lightly, casually replying, "Well he did work for them for a while."

"What?" I sputtered.

"You didn't know?" Lucian asked, raising an eyebrow and smiling. "He'd been a mob doctor for years until he got tired of the futility of it."

"What does that mean?"

"Every time he pulled a bullet out of someone, someone else put one back in," Lucian chuckled. "So he became an informant for us until one of them ratted him out to the higher ups."

A minor chill ran through me at the mention of a "rat" and I asked, hesitantly, "Any idea who?"

Lucian watched the monitors and thought for a moment before replying with another shrug, "Someone who ran one of their fronts."

I glanced over my shoulder at the corridor back to the medical wing and, for a brief moment, considered if I could hear the screams from there.

"You don't think he'd do anything to that person if they met again," I asked, looking nervously at Lucian, "do you?"

Lucian laughed, "Oh no, he's not a violent man. Though, I imagine if they ended up as one of his patients there'd be a less friendly bedside manner."

Ramirez walked over, soaked and shrugging off a raincoat over the top of his normal jacket, clutching a cup of coffee, laughing. "The city's telling us to get inside."

"Sunny enough in the day to burn evidence," Lucian said grimly, "followed by a downpour to wash away the rest."

"And who knows how many we've missed completely," I said solemnly.

Ramirez looked to the monitors above and shook his head, "I can't believe the Feds would have anything to do with this though. Why would they even need to?"

"Yeah, it's hard to wrap your head around," I replied, sighing, "But the Locusta confirmed it."

Ramirez laughed again. "The Locusta? We're following what they say?"

He looked our way, smiling broadly at first, and let the smile fade from his face. Lucian and I had the most serious expression possible while he searched for some sign of it all being a joke.

"Oh come on guys," he moaned. "We're going to put faith in the mafia and not the government?"

Lucian nodded and smirked. "That mafia tells us the truth more often," he said, "especially when it comes to Alters."

"And they knew about the silver line before I kicked in their door," I added, "They didn't even blink about me being there once they realized I wasn't FBI."

Ramirez is a good guy, he's always been a moderate type, but I've always felt like his biggest problem was that he couldn't understand the friction between the Force and the local police. Honestly, I used to feel the same way: my father was with the SPD. Even so, as I looked at the exasperated expression on his face and read the frustration with us building in him, I think I had my fill. Pulling the tracking device from the pouch I'd put it in, I dropped it onto the desk in front of us and waved at it.

"Besides, they gave us that," I said, frowning.

He picked it up and looked it over, the frustration fading into disappointment. "This is a military grade tracking device, isn't it?" he asked in hushed tones.

I patted him on the back and shook my head. "I know how you feel man, but this thing here says it's only one of two things."

"Either they're covering their asses," Lucian chimed in, a light grunt behind his voice, "Or someone released it on purpose."

"On purpose?" Ramirez asked, stunned.

I looked to Lucian, thinking heavily on the same part that caught Ramirez's attention, and said, "Which is pretty much what the Locusta front man replied on the way here from the Façade."

"What do you mean by that?" Lucian asked, raising an eyebrow and turning completely to face me.

"Well he didn't say anything about them releasing it," I replied, "but he said the Nosferatu wasn't *the* problem."

The three of us went still in that moment, our gazes lowering and averting like we all felt the same thing just then. There weren't a whole lot of reasons why a government would release such a dangerous Alter into the wild, especially one lost to their more primal instincts like a Nosferatu. Of the few reasons I could think of, at least one of them was the worst case scenario. And, from the feel around me, I don't think I was the only one to come to that conclusion.

Ramirez lifted his head and asked, "Are you sure about the guy's info?"

I nodded along and took the tracking device back from him, looking over the screen and watching the dot fly around in a flurry, "I made a deal with him not to go to jail."

"You're going to let him go?" Ramirez balked. "Weren't you the emergency signal from the Façade?"

I nodded and shrugged.

"So he tried to kill you," he continued, a pensive look on his face.

"He pushed a button," I replied. "So I made us even and kicked him in the-"

A hand cracked across the back of my head just then, my entire head throbbing as the impact aggravated my already tender skull. I staggered, clutching at the tracker to make sure I didn't fumble it, and looked back to see who'd so effectively laid hands on me. Emerald eyes met my gaze, glaring at me like a predator in the brush.

"You broke the fun one!" Dulaf exclaimed.

"The fun what?" I cried out, struggling to even hear my own voice over the drums pounding in my ears.

"Incubus!" she snapped back. "Only two in the entire city and you break the fun one!"

"What do you mean fun one?" I asked, stumbling around Ramirez and trying to use him as a buffer between me and the angry Elf. "Trey's a fun guy!"

Dulaf sighed angrily and rolled her eyes, resting hands on her hips. She shook her head and replied, "Trey's too restrained all the time, Anatole at least embraces his inner predator."

The conversation, with Ramirez stuck in the center and Lucian holding back laughter, had turned all too surreal. A man called for a group of armed thugs to try to put holes in me, and one of my friends was now angry I kicked him in the face. And, more than that, I wasn't aware she was into that sort of thing in the first place. Neither of these thoughts were particularly comforting to me as I circled around the desk and turned the tracker her way.

"The guy tried to have me taken out, so I took him down and went down into the lion's den to fetch this thing," I said hurriedly.

"And what the hell is that?" she barked, slender ears folding back like an irritated cat.

Lucian put a hand on her shoulder and, doing his best not to chuckle, answered, "It's a tracking device attached to the Nosferatu."

Those leaf-like ears rose again, slowly at first, then snapping back into position as her eyebrows rose. She turned her gaze to the ceiling and saw the same signal bouncing around on the monitors above. All at once, her tension faded.

"Well then," she said, almost cheerfully, "I guess it was worth breaking Anatole's nose."

I looked between Lucian and Ramirez, hoping to see some support out of the others, or at least a witness to confirm the Elf was out of her mind. Instead, I saw Lucian smiling and Ramirez walking out, coffee in hand, eyes rolling into the back of his head.

Dulaf snatched the tracker from me and curiously examined every angle of it, running her fingers along every seam and edge like she was trying to figure how to dismantle it. She looked to

Lucian, apparently deciding the tracking device was more interesting than beating on me.

"We should send it to the SOL team, shouldn't we?" she asked, waving the device at him.

Lucian looked at it for a moment, then back at me. I don't know what he expected to see from me - I was still stunned stupid from the assault. But after making eye contact with me, likely looking like a deer caught in the headlights, he turned back to her and shook his head.

"I think we need to catch this thing alive," he said. "For the sake of the investigation I think we still need it."

"Alive?" she asked, sly grin crossing her face. "You realize the thing can't be interrogated."

"No, but the body has evidence on it that would be destroyed in a hail of plasma fire if the SOL team went after it head on," he replied. "I think you need to get your guys working on a way to stop this thing without killing it."

Dulaf looked at the screen for a moment and traced a finger along the seam in the case again, scraping across the padded corner with her nail and chewing lightly on her lip. She smirked and patted Lucian's shoulder with the device, nodding. "Okay, I think I know what to do. I've got a rifle that should do the trick." A tone of concern entered her voice, "You aren't going to be sending out an agent with that gun alone, are you?"

Lucian shook his head and turned, waving off-handedly as he walked away from us. "You get the solution together, I'll tell Omero to give me the SOL teams to form a perimeter and maybe flush the thing out."

He stopped and looked back to her, the two of them exchanging a strange, knowing glance as he continued, "In the meantime, you get our best sharpshooter out there with that rifle."

"I'm sure that won't be a problem," she said, nodding and turning back for the labs.

Lucian looked at me again and pointed my way. "Nate, when the rifle's ready, you're escorting it out to the site."

The drumming had stopped in my ears and I'd regained my senses by that point but I still felt like I'd missed part of the conversation. I would have asked for more if they hadn't both left the room in such a hurry to handle their ends of this vague, unspoken plan. As it was, all I could do was sit, wait, and fish around the desk drawers hoping to find some Aspirin.

Chapter 7
Oberon's Troublemaker

I waited over half an hour for the sharpshooter, watching the room bustle with activity. Word had gotten out that I'd found a way to keep track of the thing's movements and a lot of the passing agents stopped to look at the updated screens overhead. There was still a hushed respect for the thing. Though none of us had actually seen it face to face yet, we'd all heard the stories.

It was a bit like watching the weather reports for tornado warnings. It had been a long time since one of them had free reign in a large city and it had us all a bit more nervous than it should have. I had to remind myself the people in the past didn't have the equipment at their disposal we did. The rifle the techs were sending out was going to be unlike anything the hunters and knights of old could have even dreamed. Admittedly, I still wasn't really prepared for what I saw coming my way.

Out of the corner of my eye, a familiar silhouette rose and moved through the crowd. It was refinished, decorated with our colors and insignias, and given a new barrel designed for what seemed to be a different sort of ammunition. There was still no mistaking it: it was the same model of rifle that wrecked my arm. A Salma Fattore, a miniature rail-gun that I'd hoped to never see again, was being carried through the room. And holding it was the sharpshooter, in full uniform with protective gear and a visor on, chestnut hair falling over her face while she smirked at me and lowered her shades.

"Ready to go?" Dulaf asked while I stared vacantly.

I stammered, "You? You're going to be the shooter?"

She smiled and nodded, resting the rifle on her shoulder and patting it lovingly like a pet, "Yeah, I'm the most experienced with firing Sexy here."

"Is that what I think it is?" I asked, mostly rhetorically.

She smiled and nodded in confirmation. "We modified it and did what we could to remove any of the really lethal bits, now she just fires specialized non-lethal ordinance."

"She?" I groaned, "It's not a pet!"

Dulaf removed her shades and tucked them away in her pocket, taking the large rifle off of her shoulder and brandishing it with a sense of pride on her face.

"Locklin asked me for a hand on putting her back together after her study," she said, "and I couldn't resist the chance to work on something this powerful."

"Do we really have to use that?" I asked.

She stopped smiling for a moment and looked me over, examining the gun and letting her ears relax just a moment, lowering very slightly. Shaking her head, she smiled at me and replied, "I'm afraid so, Nate. It's the only thing we have that can shoot a tranquilizer through that thing's hide. It's big enough and strong enough to pull it off and, thanks to your little tracker, it's going to be able to see where the bat is moving."

I glanced at the electronic scope on the rifle and nodded lightly. "Satellite assist?"

She nodded back to me and started walking out, patting my shoulder on her way by. "Get moving, Leone."

Watching her pass by, it was hard to recognize her after the years of seeing her laid back. She hadn't really been in full uniform since I was in boot camp and I sometimes thought to myself that version of her might have been a delusional false memory from too many head-shots. Though, for the years I'd been in the Force, I honestly didn't remember her ever firing a gun of any sort. And the one she had, "Sexy" as she was calling it, wasn't exactly a starter pistol. I rubbed my arm absently and stood to follow her out.

"You do know how to shoot that thing, right?" I asked, slipping my visor on again.

She laughed and waved me off, "I've been shooting since before you were born."

She said it so casually, forgetting for a minute it showed her age – a well-guarded secret. Before I was born was at least two and a half decades, despite how young she looked. And for a moment I think she forgot that blink of an eye for her was my entire life. When it caught up with her again, she chewed her lip a moment and looked my way. "I'm just saying that I have some experience at it."

I nodded and thought about picking on her for it after that slap over Anatole. Regardless, I was more curious than petty when I asked, "How much experience would that be?"

She shrugged one shoulder, the rifle still resting on the other, and walked on through to the garage elevator, thoughtfully saying, "I was a field agent before there was even an agency, back in the days when we had to rough it."

Memories of her standing with a Yeti sprang to mind.

"I stepped over to the tech side after I realized there wasn't a gun that really suited me," she continued. "Sammy and I worked on the new toy for months before we got something we were both happy with."

"Sammy?" I couldn't quite place the name, at least not any mutual friends.

"Oh," she chirped, "Samuel Colt."

The name and the history instantly dated her gun-slinging experience back to a time when it was still called "gun-slinging". It was sometimes easy to forget the perky woman with the mean right hook was ancient and timeless. Something so mean-spirited didn't seem wise enough to be so old. Yet she stood there name dropping someone from a time I could only imagine.

"How old are you?" I asked, braving the chance she might crack me across the temple.

To my surprise, she kind of... smiled. Looking at me with those emerald eyes, she said quietly, "My father's name was Oberon and I was born before the name was famous."

The elevator doors opened and she strolled out with a swagger to her steps and the gun swinging along on her shoulder, a sing-song tone to her voice as she said, "You do the math!"

We got into the car and drove from the station across Fangtown. The signal was following the long scar of New Skids and steadily making its way east. The ride was strangely quiet as we went, Dulaf watching out the window as we passed the fringes of New Skids and the dilapidated buildings that stood where a real neighborhood once existed. It was actually making me uncomfortable to sit in the car in silence for the first time in ages.

"So," I asked, "you like Incubi?"

She turned from the window and replied, "Actually I haven't been around one in ages, tend to prefer Succubi."

I couldn't help it, my mind wandered a little about then. A dirty little part of me needed details, I guess. "Why's that?"

"Ah, they tend to know what's what and they're a lot more attentive generally," she answered, "They know how treat you right."

"They're trying to eat you, you know." I scoffed.

"If they know what they're doing," she joked, slyly smirking.

The heat in my face and her growing grin told me it was a good time to shut up. The blush growing in my cheeks was like blood in the water and her toothy grin made her the shark. I'd hoped, driving down the hazy streets, it was too dark for her to really see clearly. Her reaction let me know I was wrong.

"Oh come on, don't be so dirty," she said cheerfully, "I'm old enough to be your ancestor."

"That doesn't help!" I yelled.

"Hell, I might actually be your ancestor for all you know."

The cold chill that ran over me nearly caused shock to my system, the pressure of the blush now subsiding since all the blood had drained from my face. The very idea of it almost made me swerve on the street. I gripped the wheel for all it was worth and wrung the surface of it like I was trying to strangle it instead. And all the while, she just laughed softly on her side of the car.

"You know that's the seat with the box," I reminded her, gesturing my finger towards the button that would close the frame around her and slip her under the dash like so many people who'd pissed me off on patrol.

She was clearly unfazed as she snorted and rolled her eyes.

"Eyes on the road, dumbass," she scoffed. "And get your mind out of the gutter. The kinky stuff with the box isn't going to work."

I searched for anything to look at other than her, settling on the display across the windshield, suddenly seeing a figure highlighted in the distance. We watched the bat's movements on our horizon, now fixated on what we were seeing. The overlay gave us a vague sense of its size for the first time. Even as a faint figure moving over the skyline for only a moment, it was an imposing figure in the second before dipping below the skyline again. I stopped wringing the wheel, though my hands were still clenched around it for all they were worth.

"How are you still giving me shit at a time like this, anyway?" I asked.

She rested her head back and smiled. Her smile was soft and sincere, lacking the mischief normally behind it. "I already told you once," she said, "You have to let some things go. No point being terrified."

I looked up at the light flickering over the skyline once again. And I could see what she meant for a moment. Regardless of what people could feel about it, we were going to have to confront it regardless. At the very least we could do it with a smile on our face.

"I guess it'll chew on us whether we're afraid of it or not, huh?"

She laughed lightly, crossing arms behind her head. "Chew on you," she quipped, "I've got a sniper rifle."

The bat's signal stopped moving, both the satellite and line of sight markers stopping cold without warning. A silence fell over both of us as we approached it, knowing what it meant. The line of sight marker was leveled on an old run-down building, the GPS stopped on the same.

"Damn," Dulaf hissed, "nesting."

I slowed the car and glanced up at the remains of an old, nearly abandoned high-rise at the far end of the New Skids slums. The signal wasn't moving still, the overlays on the windshield practically frozen in time. In the rear-view I could see the SOL vans coming behind us and parking down the block, the team exiting quickly and practically vanishing into the night save for a few staying behind to coordinate. Dulaf lifted her rifle and started it up, the computer powering up and the coils inside starting to make a distinctive buzz.

"We should check in with them," she said quietly.

She got ready to step out, hesitating for a moment before looking my way, ears lowered, a look of concern on her face. I looked back her way, the odd silence between us making me uncomfortable while the sound of the falling rain started to become the only thing I could hear anymore. Without warning, she leaned over and kissed my cheek, patting the other with her hand and giving me a light pinch.

"Be careful, Nate," she said with a smile.

I could feel the heat in my face again and waved her off. "What happened to not being afraid?"

She put her shades on and stepped out, leaning back in the door for a moment and smiling gently again. "You're young and stupid," she said. "Someone has to worry."

I tried to think of a comeback, but after she'd been nice enough not to smack me for asking her age, I figured a crack about her being old was out of line for once. Instead, I just nodded and smiled back to her.

"I guess it couldn't hurt."

She nodded, closed the door and turned away. Resting the great rifle on her shoulder again, she strolled away from the car. It was still the most surreal thing I'd seen in some time. Then again, two things that scared me were walking away from the car to try to cover me while I went to go pick a fight with a third.

At least this time she didn't have a Yeti.

Chapter 8
Unwelcome Guests

The group standing outside the van was a strange sight for me; you rarely saw the team before shit had actually hit the fan. They stood like a wall of helmeted, faceless statues around Lucian in the center, the dim light of a map display shining across all of their faces as they went over a layout of the block. Confidently, without hesitation, Dulaf broke through the wall and peered over Lucian's shoulder curiously, chiming in, "So what's the plan?"

Lucian nodded and pressed a finger to the screen. "You're here on the tallest rooftop in this area, giving you a clear shot at it when we get it out into the open."

He lifted his gaze from the screen and looked across our group, saying in a commanding tone, "We're going to do a vertical pincher maneuver to get that thing out into the open and then into a contained space. One half of the team is going in on the ground floor while the rest take positions on the rooftops. The ground team will move up through the building, force the Nosferatu outside and then the rooftop gunners will use suppressive fire to keep it from flying clear while Dulaf takes her shot."

The team nodded almost in perfect, silent unison, like a well-oiled machine. Frankly, I felt incredibly out of place until a small, confident voice interjected, "And what happens if it passes your ground team to get down to a lower floor and goes out into the alley?"

Once again, that well-oiled machine moved at once, their heads turning in unison towards Dulaf. She shrugged them off casually and traced her fingers along three sides of the building. "If it gets out through any direction except the top and front, I have no shot. You can't take the chance it gets down the stairwell past these guys."

Lucian winced slightly, a hardly noticeable twitch that Dulaf seemed to notice immediately, leaning with an arm resting on his shoulder. He murmured for a moment, and then spoke up, "Then we keep most of the ground team on the bottom floor and send a squad up through the building to press it out."

He looked across the faces around him, or really the complete lack of faces around him, and said solemnly, "The team through the building is going to avoid any direct conflict if possible – just enough to scare it up or down to let the rest of the team do their job. I'll take point on the team but I'm going to need volunteers."

The group started to move slightly, each of them looking to each other and measuring who was thinking of stepping forward. As they measured and weighed their options, only one person actually stepped up without hesitation. Honestly, I have no idea what the hell I was thinking. I was just suddenly saying, "Give me a helmet so it doesn't crack my coconut."

Lucian studied me for a moment, probably looking to see if I was joking. Somehow, for reasons I couldn't understand, I wasn't. He nodded and reached into the van, producing a helmet from the back and offering it to me. I could have refused, maybe even laughed and pretended it really was a joke. But I took that helmet and put it on without another word.

With my uniform on, I was pretty well padded and guarded for most situations. Then again, I've always thought my skull wasn't really rated for monsters punching it or trying to crack it open while brandishing one of those little umbrellas and a straw. So I gladly took the shiny black dome and donned it like I'd been offered it by the gods.

"How's it fit?" Lucian's now muffled voice asked.

I looked around, the helmet starting to adjust to the shape of my skull, flexing the pads inside it and squeezing tightly to my head. The visor on the helmet started to light up, an actual display appearing across it rather than just being colors I had to interpret for myself. The rain sounds were soon drowned out and the voice of Lucian came through clearly as a radio moved snugly into position by my ear.

"Nice, right?" he asked.

For a moment, I had a touch of envy for the SOL teams and the nice toys they got. Sure, no one had ever seen their faces and some people thought they might have had them removed in some sort of ceremony, but their stuff was cool. At least I could take comfort in the fact the helmet wasn't trying to peel my face off like the urban legends said. And all of these thoughts came out in the most concise and eloquent fashion possible.

"Oh hell yeah."

He slapped me across the helmet, an act I barely felt as the pads inside acted like little airbags. I looked around and saw their faces clearly for the first time as they appeared on my display. One next to me in particular stood out as someone else nodded and stepped forward. It was strangely rugged despite his age, a light scar across his cheek looking like someone had lunged at him with claws in the past. His eyes were glowing behind the visor, at least a part of the display I was seeing apparently being projected across our eyes instead of the visor, explaining the strange clarity it had compared to the windshield of my car.

I barely recognized Timothy Richards despite having seen him only a year ago.

"Richards?" I exclaimed. "I thought you quit!"

"Nah," he chuckled, "just joined the meat-grinder."

Tension lifted from our shoulders for that moment, postures lightened and the crowd loosened up. But the motion that stuck out most to me was Dulaf's, her ears perked, her attention turned away from the rest of us as Lucian followed suit. The helmet displays picked it up shortly after, a lone car with government plates coasting to a stop not far from us. It was just as the Locusta had said, the Feds had arrived.

Just two men, buttoned down and looking like they'd walked out of a mortuary, stepped out of the car and approached our group with a strange confidence in their stride. The man out of the driver's seat was clearly older, seasoned and projecting a sense he felt he owned the space around us. His partner was almost the opposite, though he tried real hard to fake it. We could all see the aura as clear as day, the new guy was pretty intimidated by even being here.

That didn't faze his partner, who strode up and flashed a badge at us that I didn't recognize at all. The helmet caught it and froze it in a small window to the side, letting me study it and seeing the name in full: "Alter Affairs Division". Quite frankly, I think the whole lot of us had to choke back our disbelief.

"Special Agent Carlson," the older man announced. "This is Special Agent Lynch."

Lucian, without missing a beat, sniped back at them, "Wouldn't happen to have first names to go with those aliases, would you?"

Lynch tensed at the comment, apparently surprised someone could see through their genius cover names, while Carlson just seemed to chuckle it off. "No, I'm afraid that's not issued to us for a few more years."

"So what are you here for?" Lucian asked sternly. "Or do you realize we're here to clean up your mess?"

Carlson didn't miss a beat, he didn't even pause, he just shot back, "And who asked you to do that?" The attitude was unmistakable, even in the face of overwhelming numbers and firepower, this guy felt like he was in charge. "We put a silver line on this for a reason."

Lucian's aura did something I rarely saw, a touch of red bleeding into his normally calm reading, the helmet showing a rise in his vitals. Angrily, he said to the agents, "Yes, there was a silver line on this. But we've found this creature by way of a legitimate investigation, one you didn't manage to block from us. And along the way we discovered that you let dozens of people die without making so much as a call."

"Yes, there was a series of fatalities that may or may not be related to this incident," Carlson replied calmly. "You immediately assume it's your jurisdiction?"

"I do when the victims are all Alters and the prime suspect is an Alter," Lucian said. "The good news is we've managed to track it to this location by way of the government tracking device implanted on the beast. How do you think one of those got out and about in Seattle?"

The agents didn't reply, Lynch trying his best not to react, Carlson's brow furrowing in a tell-tale way. Raindrops filled my ears as the group fell oddly silent, the steady beat of it across my helmet drowning out whatever stray sounds might have come from us. The tension was palpable as we stood frozen in front of these men, like a bear-trap Carlson and Lynch were dangerously close to stepping on. We were a soggy, miserable bunch standing in the rain under the shadows of a nest. And these men were telling us to turn around and pretend none of it was happening.

I wondered if similar events happened in the places where the treaty broke.

"Here's what I think is going on," Lucian said finally, punching through the sound of the rain. "I think the fact you're hiding this means either your government is up to something or someone fucked up so badly that admitting this would be an embarrassment to someone very important." Stepping uncomfortably closer, he asked, "So which is it?"

Carlson didn't flinch, maintaining a steady tone while the rest of us felt a little uneasy. "I'm under no obligation to answer that."

Lucian scowled and demanded with a bit of bass to his voice, "Then get out of our way."

Carlson's attitude didn't change, his vitals didn't move, but it didn't matter. We all knew he couldn't say or do anything at that moment. We were in the right, unless they planned to break the treaty, and they weren't prepared to bring that thing in like we were. Lucian raised a hand and waved for the building to command that well-oiled machine to move again. We all did as he ordered, even Dulaf as she broke from the pack and hurried to her designated building.

Our procession passed the agents and each took a look their way. It was hard to resist wanting to size up the guys that had made this problem so much larger than it had to be. Looking at Carlson, seeing the defiant expression on his face, I only had one thought crossing my mind.

These people killed Alice Winchester.

Chapter 9
Chance Hazards

The team entered the old building carefully and quietly, guns ready and lights in hand to try to spook the bat. Old wood cracked under our feet, cobwebs along the ceiling falling under their own weight in the humid air, dew glistening across them as a cold chill blew through. Dust, caught in a breeze from an unseen window, drifted across my line of sight as the helmet highlighted every interesting particle in the air. Everything from human dandruff to marijuana pollen floated around us. The walls looked like they'd been sprayed with luminol, old bloodstains glowing all around us, surrounded by patterns that didn't quite match the usual arterial spray.

Remembering an old special on hotels quickly convinced me to not look any closer. But, as we entered further and the team started to spread out to all possible exit points, it was hard not to notice old rusted chains on the floor next to a rubber ball-gag. It quickly became obvious what we'd stumbled into.

"Abandoned Succubi nest," I murmured.

Richards stepped next to me and kicked one of the chains, commenting, "Think they've been gone long?"

A flash of a memory came across me, a look on Anubis' face and his defense of the Succubi that worked for him. A small feeling of dread crossed over me as I considered the Nosferatu had parked overhead. "I hope for a long while."

The lean figure of Lucian drifted by without stopping, commenting off-handedly, "Could be left there from years ago, a little after the businesses and residents started to clear out of this area but before Fangtown was all sorted, the Succubi and Incubi tried to turn this place into an unlicensed red-light district buffet."

"So I'm guessing we caught them and cleared them out years ago," I mused, following him up the stairs.

"Oh no," he laughed, "Seattle figured it out and forced us to break them up. It wasn't exactly something we wanted to do."

Richards and I stalled on the steps for half a beat, staring up at the back of Lucian's head together before glancing at each other in a silent challenge to see who would respond.

Taking the challenge, I called out, "So why didn't we want to do it?"

Lucian shrugged, turning the corner of the stairs, "It was the only real positive Alter-Human relations at the time. The humans got a thrill and the residents got what they needed until we could get it legalized."

Richards nodded and jogged up the stairs to catch up to Lucian above, asking as he reached the top, "So why would they chain someone out in the open like that?"

And from higher up the stairwell, I heard Lucian reply, "When you have a business, you leave candy in the lobby, right?"

I followed them at a distance, thinking of the women from the Moirae and taking in the sounds around us. The interior was eerily quiet, not a sign of life anywhere, even the rats you'd expect from the neighborhood nowhere to be seen. The sound of the rain against the windows and walls, along with the footsteps of our team, reverberated through the stairwell. Occasionally, a wailing of wind joined the mix, a distant sound of another window cracked open somewhere above, the temperature dipping every time it was heard.

The place hadn't been abandoned long, the rails rubbed clean of dust from hands dragging across it fairly recently. I suspected the stories of the Nosferatu got out from the people that escaped this place. The only thing that likely slowed the story when they got out of here was the process of bouncing through blogs before it could get to legitimate news sites and past the silver line. I just couldn't imagine the people in this neighborhood could be silenced for very long. It was actually unnerving how empty and quiet the place had become already.

Then the extra footsteps sounded above us. We all tensed and scanned the area ahead, the reading of the Nosferatu quite a distance from us. And once we calmed down that made sense.

The footsteps were too light, too lean. Still, it skittered through an otherwise abandoned building darting around in short bursts. Shadows moved overhead, giving us all something to focus on, our guns leveled at it before taking time to think. A monitoring program in the helmets started to try to identify the sounds using the information we had.

Lights flickered in the floor above, the only ones we'd seen active in the building since we'd entered. The shadows continued to shift around, slowly gaining shape. It was short with a hunched back and long pointed ears stretching behind its head. Thoughts raced through my mind about what kind of shit storm we could have walked into if this thing had young. Soon the shadow stopped, head shifting like it was trying to see something, ears making an exaggerated twitch across the wall. They perked and the shadow's posture changed. Suddenly, it was aware we were there.

It scrambled out towards us, darting so fast we barely had time to react. In the quickest blur of a moment, the helmet was practically screaming figures at me and everything was moving too fast for us to think. Training kicked in and we all did the first thing reflex told us to do. A shot went off, a flash of light bursting through the stairwell, a glass shattering and a scream ringing out.

Richards was relatively new and he did exactly what a rookie SOL would have done. They were meant to deal with packs, covens, and fortified locations. In the heat of the moment, in this environment, with these conditions, he was trained to react as fast as possible to anything that rushed him. He did exactly that. In that same moment, Lucian and I acted as experienced patrol agents and saw something he couldn't: pink.

His round burned a hole into the nearby wall, where I'd shoved his barrel in the fraction of a second it took for his trigger to discharge the capacitors in his very impressive Helios rifle. Lucian, in the same moment, lunged at the target and tackled it to the floor, putting himself in Richards' line of fire. And Richards, from the expression on his face, clearly didn't understand what we'd done until Lucian got up again.

A small Elven girl, ten at the most, with tiny bladed ears that looked so much larger in the unfortunately placed lights, shook like a leaf as the imposing Vampire stood up again. Her pink hooded sweatshirt was soaked with water, a shattered drinking glass lying on the floor around her, glistening in the dim light.

"Oh man," Richards said breathlessly, "I'm so sorry guys."

Her eyes were huge, shining against her shadowed face. They were filled with terror and shock, her ears folding as far as they could at their size. The three of us were as shocked and confused as she was. It was hard to fathom how a kid her size could be in a building this barren while an apparently dangerous creature roamed the halls. As I considered this, the girl bolted up to her feet and sprinted down the hall, darting around a corner as fast as she came. And following that we all saw a sudden flash of movement on our helmet displays and heard a rumbling over the ceiling above us. It wasn't a smooth movement, more like the sound of furniture sliding across the floor, and the helmets told us exactly what it was.

"I think," Richards said hesitantly, "it heard us."

"You two get the girl now," Lucian ordered, "I'll slow it down."

I hesitated for a second as Lucian dashed up the next flight of stairs and into the floor above. I looked back to Richards and we nodded to each other like either one of us had any confidence at all. Deciding to trust my mentor, I ran for the corner the girl disappeared around and started down the new hall, following the distant sound of footsteps as far as I could before hearing a door slam around the next bend. Peering around it, I found a short row of doors with only the faint footprints left behind by the girl running through the spilled water.

Knocking at the door, I called out, "Please open the door, this is the ACTF. We have an emergency in the building."

We waited for only a heartbeat before a high-pitched shriek pierced the halls and set off every red light and warning signal the helmet could muster. Richards kicked into gear again and lunged for the door, giving me only a second to move clear as he kicked it open, breaking the old wood frame as the door slammed open. We braced for a moment, listening for a response, only to hear the slam of another door to the back and nothing else beyond.

"Little high strung?" I asked sarcastically. "What'd they do? Train you with a bell like Pavlov?"

He looked at me with deadpan expression and without a hint of hesitation replied, "Woof."

Shaking my head, I stepped through to see a dilapidated but lived in apartment on the other side. It was run down like the rest of the building with a couple of windows boarded up and furniture held together with duct tape and a couple of blankets. It was clearly dragged in from a curb somewhere but somehow well cared for. Despite the fact everything was falling apart there was an apparent care taken for everything in the room like they were the only possessions in the world for someone.

Two doors at the far end of the room were left to be examined, the only things to possibly be slammed. I nodded to Richards and took a door, passing a couch with symmetrically lined duct tape carefully placed to cover and camouflage what had to be severe wear and tear. Reaching the door, I rapped the back of my hand against it as Richards used his elbow on the other.

"ACTF," we called in unison.

Neither of us got a reply and we opened the doors without waiting. I'm not entirely sure what Richards saw in the next room over, but what I saw wasn't entirely pleasant to me. A woman across the room, human from the looks of her vitals, was lying in a bed, the girl standing guard over her defiantly and glaring like a small animal ready to pounce. The woman's vitals, though human, weren't stable in the least. She was feverish, her breathing labored and every movement seemed to cause her pain by the look on her face. It wasn't hard to connect the dots for me.

I lifted the visor of the helmet and kneeled, trying as hard as I could to sound gentle and look friendly. "Hi there, I'm Nate; I'm here to help you. We need to get you and your mom out of here, okay?"

She glared at me with deep green eyes, reminding me of Dulaf on another rooftop, watching over us. To think we carried all this hardware into this area to deal with a monster while this little girl stood here unafraid was astounding. But as she stood her ground, I couldn't ignore the breaking window not far away and the sound of car windows shattering below followed by the blaring of an alarm. She jumped, the defiant look fading from her eyes, and I couldn't blame her – I jumped too.

"That was me," Lucian said over the radio with a groan, "but the good news is I landed on Carlson's car."

The rumbling inside the building told me that there was bad news to go with it. Bringing down the helmet's visor again showed me the lit marker streaking through the hallways like it knew exactly where to go. Richards didn't hesitate a moment, rushing to the hallway and turning to intercept the charging beast, firing warning shots to slow its progress. A scream filled the air again, piercing the building and shaking the windows, a deafening roar the girl recoiled from that the helmet only barely muffled.

Grabbing for her, I commanded, "You have to get out of here now! There's a monster in the building!"

She stood her ground the best she could, yelling at me for the first time since I'd heard her scream, "No I don't! You're scaring him!"

I was taken aback, hearing her defend the thing at a time like that. Not only did she know it was there but she assumed it was afraid of us and not the other way around. How long could it have possibly been nesting there? I almost questioned her, but the sudden crash in the hallway and the sound of Richards' gun going off broke the train of thought.

I lifted the visor and made eye contact with the girl again, her intense gaze not breaking away from mine for even a second. She looked like she'd take a swing at me herself at any moment. Still, I tried not to sound threatening to her even if she seemed to want to be threatening to me.

"Stay here, please," I pleaded, closing the visor and standing again.

Looking around the room, I knew I only had one option as it charged the last leg to the apartment. These two weren't getting out of here before it got to us. I pulled my gun and quickly surveyed the furniture in the room, an old heavy wood dresser immediately beside the door. It seemed to be full from what I could see, stray clothes hanging over the edges of the higher drawers, probably just enough to keep the door shut if it needed to.

Looking back once more, I ordered, "Just stay with your mother until it gets quiet again."

Her expression softened for some reason just then, climbing onto her mother's bed and cradling her head gently. A few more bolts went off behind me, flashes of light shining across the walls and another screech filling the room. Her whole body tensed, eyes wide with fear for the first time in this room. I watched briefly, nodded and ran from the room firing two shots into the dresser legs on the way out. The bolts chewed through the legs and scorched the wood enough to weaken what was left. Dashing out the door, I heard them snap behind me, the dresser toppling into the door and slamming it shut with its heavy frame.

She screamed behind the door, probably shocked by the sudden crash. I was shocked myself that the idea even worked at all. I pushed at the door to try to open it again, finding it was solidly blocked and that the knob apparently broke off on the other side. It was strange, the relief I felt that the door was blocked and I was locked outside of it with a killer Nosferatu.

Then again, most of my life is strange. I imagine few other people would expect to see what I saw as I turned around again. Standing there, large as life and shadowing out the doorway as if the apartment had suddenly gotten smaller, the Nosferatu stared at me with bloodshot eyes. Lucian had been hurled out a window, Richards' gun had fallen silent and I was alone as I laid eyes on it.

I was the last man standing.

Chapter 10
Horribly Angry

Even with all the information the helmet gave me, it wouldn't register the Nosferatu existed in front of me, just the tracking signal we'd gotten for it. The silver line was still firmly in place in some weird fashion. However, those eyes told me everything I needed to know about the creature on the other side. They were berserk: full of pain, rage, fear and bloodlust. If the girl behind the door was right, it was afraid of us behind all of that. And more importantly than that, it was clearly wounded, blood staining its singed fur.

Afraid and wounded: exactly what you want with a wild animal.

It charged through the door, its wide shoulders barely making it through the suddenly too narrow frame, before standing its full height. It was easily three feet taller than me, if not more. The tips of its long, bat-like ears grazed the ceiling. It stuck out its barreled chest and flexed its unnaturally long arms, the wings that grew from them extending almost like a cape as it reared back, the fur across its body bristling as it inhaled. Remembering the shrieks, I dove behind the couch, dropping clear as the beast unleashed another powerful scream, shaking the door and making me feel the rush of air pushing me aside.

I tried to ignore the tiny scream on the other side of the door as I hit the floor, assured by the fact the door was even still there after the force I felt. I fired from the floor under the couch into the two huge feet I could see across the gap, like the man in the Façade earlier in the night. It hit the ankle, just like before, the thick hide resisting the bolt while its fur slowly burned. It screeched and staggered away as I kicked the couch over and charged over it, using it as a step to launch myself across the room. It looked up at me, screamed and lashed out as I was in the air, easily slapping me aside with the tree limb it considered an arm. I bounced from the wall, my helmet image distorting for a moment as the heat signature dropped low and lunged at me.

Reflex kicked in and I fired into the general vicinity of its head, dropping to a knee. A blood curdling shriek and a fleshy crack sounded overhead, the blinded bat smashing into the wall hard enough to pass its head clear through where my torso would have been. Viewing it from below, I became immediately aware of being between the now flailing arms. Despite hitting it with a wall, I definitely hadn't slowed it down. It slammed its palms against the wall, cracking the drywall with ease, and pushed away as hard as it could while ripping a hole nearly large enough to be considered a window. Glaring down at me with those bloodshot eyes through the burnt, bloodstained fur across its face, it roared.

Luckily, Richards wasn't dead. Using the new window as an opening, he shot the bastard in the chest and sent it reeling back across the room. I took a moment to catch my breath, assess the situation, and make sure the water in my pants was entirely the rain. Turning, I darted out the door and into the hallway. There was a moment of hesitation on what I planned to do next but I knew what I had to do. Knowing I couldn't leave it in the apartment with the girl, I fired a shot into its crotch, hoping to piss it off.

I was pretty sure it worked after hearing the sound it made.

Down to all fours again, a mass of fur and teeth rushed the doorways head on, claws gouging through the floors as it stampeded our way. I kicked through the door of the apartment across the hall, running into a darkened room and doing my best to ignore the sound made by a half-ton mass of flesh separating a doorframe from its wall. Richards yelped and dived clear as the two of us went stampeding by, likely dodging wood shards on the way down.

The next apartment was almost completely bare, only an old table and some run down plastic chairs inside. I pulled a Manticore from my back on the way in and dropped to a baseball slide, finally looking back into the enraged eyes of the beast while I cried out, "Pack-buster!"

Hurling the rod at its face, I rose to my knees under the table and grabbed at the legs, toppling it over in front of me a split second before the explosion of needles sprayed the room, echoing the sound of the rain outside like the world had gone stereo. The wounded beast let out a new moaning sound, standing upright again, covered in glistening silver spikes across its face and shoulders, one of which sticking out of one of those bloodshot eyes and causing bloody tears to run down the side of its face.

Screaming in pain, it lurched back before lashing out my way and kicking into the table between us, snapping the tabletop in half and planting a foot square in my chest. The hit was intense, easily felt through my padded coat and the armored inserts and sending me into the wall hard. The visor on the helmet cracked and the displays distorted for a moment as whatever electronics in the thing rattled around my head.

At least, I hoped the rattling sound was the helmet and not something inside my skull.

It thrashed around the room screeching and throwing itself against the wall in a desperate attempt to knock loose the needles embedded in its flesh. The chemical cocktail in them were working quick, causing clumps of hair to fall out as it flew against the walls. Richards peered through what was left of the exit, readying his rifle as it continued to wail.

By the time I was able to start pushing myself back up, the thing turned and rushed the exit, plowing through Richards and throwing him against the opposite wall just as easily as it did to me. Bounding off that same wall, it leapt back the way it came and fled down the hall for all it was worth. Crashing and scrambling noises rolled up the stairway, giving us a minor reprieve from the beating we took.

Labored breathing was starting to fog my visor. An intense heat was building in my chest and sharp pain ran up my side whenever I inhaled. Somewhere along the line I'd injured a rib or two. That many shots to the chest in one night couldn't have been good for me. Luckily, somehow, we managed to wound it more than it wounded us.

Stumbling into the hallway, I examined the gouges in the floor before looking over at Richards propped against the wall. We groaned and nodded to each other as I offered a hand to help him stand upright. Taking it, we steadied each other before I started to follow the trail to the stairs.

"You can't be that eager for round two," he protested.

I shook my head and peered warily up the darkened stairwell. "The girl knew it was here, it's definitely nesting."

He groaned and we followed the trail upstairs, knowing we had no guarantee it was going to leave the building. The marks were unsteady and erratic, only three of its claws touching the ground at once, rarely the same three. It was scrambling and panicked: the worst-case scenario if we ended up in a closed space with it. Its haggard breathing echoed through the stairwell as we climbed, sounding like the beast had surrounded us under the cover of darkness.

Richards looked up the stairs and commented, "I don't know if it's hurt or just pissed off."

Scanning the shadows ahead of us, the helmet showing me nothing but the waveform of the ragged sound, I couldn't figure it out either. Worse, because I'd already seen the blood in its fur before it threw us around, I knew it was a moot question.

The harsh breathing grew louder two stories up, fairly close to the top floor. The howl of wind from outside confirmed that somewhere the windows were either open or, given the Nosferatu's inability to pass through doors, possibly gone. There'd been no blood on the floor on the way up despite all the wounds across it and the injury that Manticore caused. Clearly it was moving so fast that the streams didn't have time to fall in any steady pattern. It wasn't until we neared what I assumed to be the nest that a blood trail was clearly glowing under the scans of the helmets.

We approached a ruined door with all the caution of a bomb squad. There was clutter lying around, dropped items left behind in a panic as most of the people in the building evacuated. A hard gust of wind masked the breathing sound for a moment, a distant thunder rolling by keeping us from hearing the fact the breathing had changed. It was only as everything went perfectly still and quiet that we heard a deep growl rising from inside the next room.

"Aw crap," I muttered.

A brief flash of light shone through a hole in the wall, a thunderclap rolled, and then the figure bolted from inside the room and lunged for me. Checked into the wall like a hockey player, I thought back on what Alston said and produced the only loud noise I could manage without shitting myself loudly: I grabbed at my belt, yanked, and shoved a Banshee in its mouth.

I didn't have the time to adjust any settings or set a timer, only pull the trigger and pull my hand away. A sound blasted me in the face as it nearly shattered the helmet's visor and rattled the Nosferatu's skull from the inside. It thrashed wildly, hacking and coughing before spitting out the rod onto the ground and making a beeline for the hole in the wall at the far end. Up and out, it scrambled through the broken frame and scaled the side of the building long before the Banshee was spent.

"Mission accomplished," Richards said as the noise died down.

"That means we can take a nap, right?" I joked, waiting for the ringing and blurring to stop.

The bolts firing over the building were barely audible over the rain and the wind. The flashes of light blended with the natural lightning and thunder. But the screams of the Nosferatu as it scrambled to get clear of the onslaught were unmistakable. Richards listened for only a moment before he ran ahead and started back up the stairs. I, on the other hand, lingered a bit while waiting for my knees to stop feeling like Jell-O.

Unfortunately, the screaming and scurrying noises continued across the rooftop. It wasn't in the air and it wasn't down yet, letting me know it somehow found cover on the roof. I sighed heavily and exhaled, rolling my head lightly and hearing my neck crack. Turning to the stairs, I hesitated and started to follow Richards up.

The door to the roof had been torn from its hinges, rain falling into the stairwell and right into my face. I could tell the gunfire apart from the thunder now, the distinctive hiss of the Helios rifles surrounding the building. Richards appeared and ducked into the stairwell, using the corner as cover as the Nosferatu slammed into the building, rolled by and bolted away.

"It's pissed," he said dryly.

I nodded and grasped around my belt for what gear I still had available. The Manticore had been thrown into the thing's chest, the Banshee had been stuffed down the throat and all that I had left on me as far as heavy control was concerned was the Will-O-Wisp at my side. At best I could only blind it and make it angrier with that unless I forced it to swallow.

"It's using the registers as cover and looking for a way out," Richards said. "Not that it has any options, but it's refusing to fly right now."

He looked my way, the visor on my helmet long having shortened out and leaving me without a clue what the expression on his face was anymore. I had a good guess it was at the very least flustered.

"Damn thing is smarter than it looks," he said, nodding.

"Lucky us," I grunted, moving up and peering around the corner.

The Nosferatu was hunched over near one of the air conditioning units on the roof, down on all fours and pacing around it like a caged tiger. The rifles had stopped, leaving me with what little light could be seen with the busted helmet.

"I've used my Banshee," I whispered. "Do the SOL carry any?"

Richards nodded, patting his rifle. "We have miniatures in a grenade launcher."

Examining the rifle, I glanced from it back to the shadow of the agitated creature crawling along the rooftop. Sighing, I lifted the visor of the helmet to clear the field of vision and put my shades on instead. Under the night-vision I watched the hulking mass edge along the registers.

"Get ready to fire, then," I said, pulling the 'Wisp from my belt.

"What are you planning?" He asked.

"Scaring the hell out of it, I hope."

Exhaling, I ran across the roof and chucked the Will-O-Wisp forward, screaming at it like a moron to get its attention. It turned as I let the rod fly, the light flashing between us and blinding it. Screaming, it lashed out blindly into the air and slapped me aside with its leathery wing, hurling me against the nearby air conditioner and nearly knocking the helmet clear off my head. I bounced off the unit and shoulder rolled away from it, dropping onto my back at the creature's feet.

Richards fired his mini-Banshee and struck it square in the chest despite the bright light flaring only inches from us. The shock of the sonic blast took the wind out of me and forced the bat a step back. With it moving to where I could see again, I aimed up and started firing frantically into the air without much care where it went.

The plan almost worked. The Nosferatu was spooked when faced with blinding light, screaming sounds and a flurry of bolts flying at its face from out of seemingly nowhere. Running for it, the only path left was the entrance again, leaving Richards square in its path.

Everything ran fairly slow motion just then, realizing we were about to lose it again. I tried to catch up to it and help Richards hold the front, but it was moving way too fast for me. I was hoping for something, anything, to break in our favor just then. I never expected the black figure that burst onto the roof past Richards just then, tackling the bat as hard as it'd manhandled us.

Somehow, Lucian got back up.

The two of them collided into me, my helmet being hurled off with one last strike, and went tumbling past. All that could be seen in that instance was a flurry of fur, teeth and flashes of pale skin as Lucian's exposed face emerged from the tussle. Through sheer strength of will, the lean figure managed to drag the bat out to the center of the roof and pulled it upright to its feet. And with that motion, the loud pop sound went off and a dart found itself square into the beast's chest.

There were things I'd seen in my time with the ACTF that I never imagined I would see in my lifetime. One of them was a man built like a supermodel suplexing a nine foot tall monster after it'd been shot by a sniper rifle. And yet, there it went, the rooftop cracking and nearly buckling under the weight of a half-ton of muscle being slammed with relative ease.

Another thing checked off the bucket list.

I got up and leveled my gun to its face, approaching cautiously and watching its eyes slowly drift away. It was a mess, absorbing enough needles, poison and gunfire to have killed anything else, and yet it still breathed strong enough for me to hear. It had the most impressive endurance I'd ever seen aside from the man who'd just peeled himself off the hood of a car.

However, there was still a question on my mind, one that I couldn't shake. It was smart, almost too smart, and the girl knew it was there but wasn't afraid of it. It didn't try to feed on her or her mother and it didn't attack in a primal rage until I'd been close. Approaching it as the eyes were closed, I reached over and lifted its lips to look at its teeth. The fangs were impressive, like I expected, but the molars on the thing told me that it was definitely still an omnivore.

Just being an omnivore didn't make it impossible it attacked those people. But if it had, why wouldn't it have attacked what was close to it? I thought of the tracking device and looked for it on the Nosferatu's ears, figuring it would be tagged like an animal in the wild. I didn't find a tag, just a mark, one that I recognized fairly quickly.

Lucian saw it too, hissing with irritation, "Shit."

Staring at us clear as day in a UV dye that our visors could pick up was a set of tattoos. On one ear was the eagle emblem of the United States. On that second ear we found the mark of a griffon. And together the two only meant one thing that made this all a lot more complicated.

"It wasn't just theirs," I muttered, backing away, "this is one of ours."

Chapter 11
Elven Apartment

The SOL team moved in quickly and met with us on the roof as I sat just inside the stairwell trying to avoid being rained on any more than I'd already been. They were looking pretty spry, having been comfortably firing at the thing from a couple buildings away while Richards and I got a taste of angry furball. Bringing up the rear, grinning ear to ear, was Dulaf – "Sexy" on her shoulder.

"You look like shit," she said cheerfully.

"I think I was saved from having my chest caved in by a really cheap table," I replied. "Remind me to buy one for my apartment."

The team surrounded the Nosferatu, now rolled over face down so all could see the brands on the ears. They started to discuss how to get that thing off the roof and down into their van before it could wake up. And I watched them, wearily, hoping that its eyes wouldn't open before I was long gone and it was someone else's problem again.

Suddenly Dulaf was crouched by my side, leaning by my ear. "Are you okay?" she asked.

I turned my head as far as I could with the growing stiff feeling in my neck and shoulders. "It has an Argyre mark on its ear."

She frowned and peered at the group huddled on the roof. "This thing is a bigger mess than we thought, isn't it?"

"Yeah, I think so," I murmured, glancing down at my shredded jacket and the shiny black plate under it. "Right now I'm just glad I had a helmet and that this thing didn't fall apart."

She nodded and ruffled my hair with a smile on her face. "So where is it then?"

I searched the roof for it, realizing it'd long tumbled off into the ether and possibly over the edge. "I have no damn idea," I said with a chuckle.

"Over here," Richards yelled, presenting the helmet and holding it over his head, "Congratulations on breaking it!"

He tossed it to me from across the roof, laughing. "Enjoy your new motorcycle helmet."

I caught it with the one hand I could manage to lift without falling on my face. It was a mess: a combination of cracks, dents and busted latches that would have been my skull. Examining the damaged visor, I figured it could be patched up. So I shrugged and asked, "How much?"

Shaking their heads, one of the guys standing over the Nosferatu laughed. "You don't want to know, just don't plan any fancy vacations for a while."

I withheld the smile I was about to give them. The joke was on them: my typical vacation was my recliner, ramen noodles and a blender I used to make fruit smoothies while pretending I was in the tropics. All this had done was enable my fictional bike trip through Malaysia.

Looking at the helmet in my hands, I soon lost that smug feeling, realizing my head had been behind the cracked shell and completely smashed visor. In a different situation, possibly with a different Nosferatu, I wouldn't have been well off enough to think about ramen and that chair.

Luckily, if the girl was telling the truth, I think we were dealing with a less violent creature than we'd been led to believe. Though I didn't have proof yet, I had a feeling that the Locusta were right. She seemed to share the opinion that the Nosferatu wasn't the problem. Us being here was the problem in her eyes. And I was starting to believe that the guys who were really a problem were now trying to hammer out the dents on their government issued car.

The thought brought on the realization that my work in the building wasn't done yet. I stood the best I could and started down the stairs, leaning heavily on the rail to keep myself stable.

Dulaf stood up and watched me, asking curtly, "Where the hell do you think you're going?"

I stopped and tightened my grip on the rail, gesturing with a nod downstairs, "There's a girl and her mother down there, looked like a BDA. I'm going to check into it."

102

"BDA," Dulaf echoed breathlessly before hurrying down after me. "There was a BDA and a Nosferatu in the same building?"

"It's just a guess," I replied. "But that's what it looked like to me."

They were haunting letters in the community, the rarest of the rare. Alters often go active because of physical threat to their life, a severe situation harsh enough to force the body to defend itself. So there were a rather unhealthy number of recovering, and not so recovering, drug addicts in their ranks.

Every once in a while there was a quirk, a rare abnormality as rare as the beast we had to take down on the roof: children who go active in the womb while their parents remain unaltered. Usually you'd just get a Cambion in that already rare case, but every once in a while you'd get a kid that defied all odds and was born fully transformed. If my hunch was right, the girl I met in the room below was one of those cases and her mother was still fighting those old demons years later. Worse, it looked like her mother was losing that fight.

Dulaf and I stepped into the wreckage of that apartment. The door was still secured shut on the far side, the faint sound of struggling and grunting seeping through the gap. Nodding, I walked over and knocked on it lightly.

"This is Agent Leone," I said. "It's all clear now. Can you step back?"

The defiant little voice on the other side yelled out, "How about *you* step back?!"

The smirk on my face was hard to hold back, the one on Dulaf's face was practically glowing. Rolling my eyes and shaking my head, I pressed my shoulder to the door and started to push at it for all I was worth, hoping to move that heavy wood dresser I'd dropped in front of it. It wasn't moving as easily as I'd hoped. More accurately, it was exactly what it needed to be when I put it down in the first place – a door stop. My eyes felt like they wanted to shoot from my skull as I strained against the thing, grunting and feeling my face turn a bright shade of red.

I stopped, exhaled and looked at Dulaf sheepishly. Stepping out of her way, I waved her to the door, rubbing my shoulder and

103

down my arm. She stepped up, put a hand against the door and another on the knob, and gave one quick push that slid everything back almost effortlessly.

It wasn't that I was weak, I was just beat up and she was an ancient Elf. On any other day I would have been able to move it, I assure you. Not that it stopped her from ruffling my hair and pinching my cheek like I was the most adorable thing she'd ever seen. Satisfied with tormenting me, she pushed it the rest of the way and stepped into the room.

The girl on the other side was now brandishing a broomstick and glaring at us, ears flexed like a cornered cat. "You're not touching my mom!" she cried out, swinging the stick as a warning.

Dulaf held up her hands and shook her head. "It's okay; I'm Dulaf Nénharma. We're here to help you."

The girl clicked her tongue and stamped her foot, pointing the stick at us like a sword. "That's not what my mom said!"

Her mother was still sweating and shivering under the blankets in the corner of the room. She looked frail and malnourished, hardly having the strength to move the blankets over her as she shook there. My hunch was that she hadn't said anything to her daughter in quite a while.

"Well we're here to help her," Dulaf insisted, kneeling and holding a hand out to the girl. "We're going to try to get her to a doctor that could help her and see what might be wrong."

"You will?" the girl asked, lowering the broomstick and looking between us, maintaining her white knuckled grip on it even if she wasn't ready to swing.

I nodded confirmation and gestured to Dulaf. "I brought my friend here to help out."

Dulaf's hand was still outstretched, a gentle smile on her face. She nodded and asked, "What's your name?"

The girl's shoulders relaxed some, the tension in her posture starting to break as she loosened the grip on the stick. Quietly, hesitantly, she answered, "Amelia."

Dulaf reached out and placed her hands on Amelia's, rubbing them gently and trying to loosen the death grip she maintained on the stick. Cheerfully Dulaf said, "That's a pretty name, Amelia."

104

Dulaf gave me a look and nodded, gesturing over to the bed as she did. I took the hint and moved over, sitting by Amelia's mother and checking her pulse when I had the chance. It was as erratic as I thought – not a good sign. I frowned and shook my head to Dulaf, gesturing a pair of fingers to my badge to let her know I wanted to call in help. She nodded, smiled, and stood with Amelia's hands firmly in hers.

"Can you help me clear out the stuff in the next room so we can try to get your mom out of here?"

Amelia looked back at me and I gave her the best smile I could. She didn't look too convinced, her brow furrowing slightly, tiny worry lines in her forehead that someone her age shouldn't have had. I tried a little harder to smile sincerely, saying, "I'm going to get her ready and we can all get her out of here together, okay?"

She frowned and nodded again, being towed out of the room gently but firmly by Dulaf's carefully adjusted grip. We both knew what I had to say over the communications wasn't something Amelia needed to hear.

I pressed the badge and opened the communications channel, quietly speaking down to the badge, "This is Leone, I need an ambulance on the scene. We have a civilian that seems to be crashing. Her vitals are rough and I think she's getting worse."

There wasn't a verbal response, just a brief flash of the center insignia on the badge to let me know the signal was received. Amelia's mother was showing symptoms that told me she was in a world of trouble that Amelia wasn't likely old enough to understand. I'd seen the same in my family before, withdrawals at the very least, possibly even shock.

I stood up and went to the next room. Amelia was shuffling debris out of the way the best she could as the broomstick she had was lacking a broom on the end. I gestured to Dulaf while she was busy, hoping to wave her over while Amelia wasn't looking. Dulaf caught sight and quietly edged around the room to me.

"She's bad, her heart's racing and she's sweating like crazy but seems to be pretty cold," I whispered. "I think she might be going into shock."

Dulaf looked at Amelia sweeping away the debris and nodded, backing up into the room with me and whispering back, "If she's going through withdrawals she might be dehydrating from all the sweating, it could cause some issues if she's dehydrated enough."

My shoulders tensed and I fought back the urge to clench while hearing it. My tightened jaw hurt a bit more than it should have, still tender from getting smacked around only minutes before. I took a deep, cleansing breath and tried to let it go, looking back her way.

"Yeah, I know," she said, rubbing my upper back lightly and giving me a sharp pat. "Let me keep an eye on her and you keep an eye on Amelia, you've got some experience here."

I sighed, rubbing the bridge of my nose lightly as I muttered, "Yeah, I guess I do."

Another quick slap on my back and Dulaf bounded back to the mother's side, leaving me with Amelia and a pit in my stomach.

"How's this?" Amelia asked, looking up at me.

I examined the floor and found she'd done fairly well getting all the drywall and wood out of the way. It was clear now the kind of weight and power the Nosferatu's movements had even when it wasn't on the attack. The deep gouges from the claws were random, chaotic scratches that looked like it'd been dancing frantically through the room and tearing chunks out of the floor with every step. As for the hole in the wall, it was clean and clear like it'd been punched through with a sledgehammer instead of a living, breathing creature's skull.

"Is it that bad?" Amelia asked, studying my expression.

"Uh," I stammered, "No, it's good, just thinking you guys might need to move after all of this."

She looked around, hands at her hips and trying to stand taller like she was attempting to appear more grown up for my sake. Sternly, she said in a matter-of-fact tone, "We can fix it."

I looked at her posture and felt a little bit of respect for the kid. She was small and kind of reminded me of Dulaf but with a touch of something else. In a way she also reminded me of another kid who had a rough hand dealt to them so many years ago. I remembered how it felt when things started falling apart, how much I wished I could control something. So I quickly examined the room again, a gesture to humor her a little, and shrugged lightly.

"Well, it could be fixed," I said, "but I think we could manage a better neighborhood at least."

Her stance shifted, that posture sinking as she sulked and said mournfully, "You're going to try to put me in a foster home aren't you?"

The flinch was hard to hold back, my arm shaking a bit as it tensed. I recognized the tone and the emotion behind it pretty well. Hesitating, I said to her, "Well, we wouldn't go to that right away. Sometimes there can be alternatives."

"Like what?" She demanded.

I rubbed the back of my head and squatted to get down to eye level, a position I wasn't too sure I could get back up from right at that moment. Meeting her gaze, seeing the tears she was trying to hold back, I answered sincerely, "I lived with my grandmother after my dad got really bad."

Her lip quivered as she replied, "I don't think I have a grandma."

The pain of the night and her tone started to get to me. I rubbed my arm idly and chewed my lip a little while I thought it over. She looked at me and started to sniff slightly, tears beginning to roll down her cheeks.

"Hey," I said quietly, resting a hand on her shoulder and squeezing it lightly, "we won't let anything happen to you if we can help it."

"You're going to put me in a foster home," she said, sniffling.

I thought and looked back at the room, thinking about her mother in there and wondering how long it was going to take for that ambulance to arrive. What I didn't mention to her, what I couldn't say to her at a time like this, was that my dad died before I moved in with my grandmother. And, as much as I hated to think it, I was pretty sure the same was about to happen with her mother. Even then, I could understand why she didn't want to go into the system.

I felt the same way, once.

I really didn't know what to do with Amelia and her situation. I lucked out when it happened to me; my grandmother was there for me when things went bad. Amelia didn't really seem to have that kind of safety net to fall back on. The Argyre social services were rumored to be a lot more reliable than elsewhere, with so few kids going through it and more than enough volunteers in a community of outcasts. But I couldn't help thinking about what exactly would become of the kid if I just walked away from it after that night.

We watched her mother getting taken out to the ambulance together, the Nosferatu being carted away by the SOL at the same time. Amelia stood between Dulaf and I on the curb, taking it all in with big wide eyes and alert ears. She stared intently at the Nosferatu, showing more fear of it than I'd thought she would after her defiance, but soon lost interest in that as she heard the familiar clank of the stretcher being guided into the back of the ambulance.

"It's not so bad in an ambulance," I said, smiling down at her, "I've been in plenty."

Dulaf laughed and said, "Understatement if I ever heard one."

Cutting me off at the knees was usually a bad thing, but the kid giggled and it wasn't quite so bad anymore. Dulaf, at the very least, was in tune with immature people. To be fair to Amelia, I wouldn't have called her immature for her age, so it might have been easier to step down to her level. Not that being down to that level helped much in knowing what to do for her next.

But with everything being cleared away and my legs feeling like they were about to give out, I knew it was time to leave. We stuffed ourselves into my car, me sitting in the bucket seat behind the driver, "Sexy" in the little half seat behind the passenger and the Elves taking the front for themselves. I saw my life flash before my eyes as Dulaf sped through the neighborhood like a bat out of hell, completely ignoring the rain. Amelia, on the other hand, thought it was the best thing she'd ever seen and laughed the whole way.

Cheerfully, the Elf, the big one, yelled out, "Hit the siren!"

Amelia laughed, clapped and hit the button, the blast of sound shocking the people on the sidewalks. The crowds scattered and the two of them reveled in the show, breaking into hysterical laughter like a pair of hyenas.

"You know," I said scornfully, "we're not supposed to be doing that."

Dulaf huffed and rolled her eyes, waving at me over her shoulder and remarking, "There's a lot of things people aren't supposed to do."

"And that's the fun part!" Amelia laughed.

I shook my head and stared out the windows while we cruised through Fangtown back to the station. I didn't really have the strength to fight them over a siren. The adrenaline was fading now and I'd given into the bumps and bruises of the night. This many encounters in a row usually meant someone needed to take the rest of the night off. I wasn't fond of the concept most of the time since it'd usually meant you'd fucked up. But on a night like this I was ready to call it a day and just sink into a really old recliner in front of a TV.

Unfortunately, seeing Amelia out of the corner of my eye, I realized there were questions to be asked and mysteries to be solved. It had already been a long night and it was still going to get longer. I just wasn't sure how to strike up the conversation with a little girl.

Thankfully, Dulaf did it for me. "So Amelia," she said, "you were in that building with the Nosferatu for a while, right?"

Amelia nodded quickly and kicked her feet. Brightly she answered, "For a whole month at least."

A month? Something like that had been in that building for a month and she wasn't worried about getting out? It was like hearing someone tell you they didn't mind the lion in their living room. It was surprising how she said it without the slightest hint of deception or hesitation.

"Why weren't you scared?" Dulaf asked, bringing the car to a stop in the ACTF's garage.

Amelia looked at Dulaf and back at me, thoughtfully saying, "Well, it looks mean but it shared its fruit with me."

"Fruit?" I asked, "What do you mean it shared its fruit?"

She smiled, "It had so much that it let me take some."

Dulaf and I exchanged a look: the comment was way outside of what we both expected. But Amelia seemed perfectly unaware of how strange it must have sounded to us, smiling on and ignoring the awkward silence like it wasn't there.

"Is that all it ate?" I asked, shocked.

Amelia nodded quickly again and tilted her head slightly while her ears folded down. "I really don't know where it got all of it, though."

Dulaf laughed and turned in her seat, cheerfully gloating, "You got your ass kicked by a fruit bat!"

"Is that even possible?" I asked, trying not to yell.

"Apparently!" She exclaimed, laughing. "It's not like it could have been living off of the stuff if it wasn't!"

And it was then I realized the horrible truth: I'd gotten my ass kicked by a fruit bat.

Amelia looked extremely confused by the way we were acting. For all the things she probably expected from people in our position, laughing hysterically and dying of embarrassment over a "fruit bat" was probably not one of them. She raised her hand calmly, waiting like a kid in class for her turn to speak while Dulaf was practically rolling in her seat.

I nodded to her and waved in acknowledgement.

"What did you think it was?" she asked, looking between us quickly.

Dulaf cleared her throat and sat straighter, replying earnestly, "A vampire bat."

Amelia gasped and leaned over to Dulaf, asking excitedly, "You mean those really exist?!"

We both nodded, Dulaf smiling broadly, me trying to hide my face behind my hands. Dulaf ruffled Amelia's hair and laughed heartily, "We totally thought it was going to eat you."

Amelia laughed too, clapping her hands, "Not unless I was a melon!"

The girls continued to laugh away while I wished it was a four door car so I could escape. Unfortunately, it was a two door and both of them were in the front. So I got to sit there and listen to them celebrate the misunderstanding at my expense. And it didn't really stop once we'd gotten into the building either.

Though the beast was large and fierce, it was apparently mostly harmless if we'd just approached it differently. Nosferatu weren't usually herbivores but, strangely enough, it was apparently possible. I'd known Vampires who were vegetarian, requiring only a liquid diet rather than the actual blood. Hell, I'd known a few of them to live off of protein shakes and even a couple that had a concoction akin to the world's nastiest tomato juice. It just never occurred to me that trait could have crossed over to their primal, berserk cousins. I guess most people don't expect bears to live off berries either after hearing stories of them mauling people.

It did raise a terrifying question, though: What exactly happened with the victims?

We entered the shared office space with Amelia, the energy of the room calming some now that the creature had been captured safely. Lucian was standing with a SOL member and Commissioner Alston as we came in, all of them taking notice of us and acknowledging our arrival. For a moment, the agents still in the room applauded us for our safe return and I felt a little pride about taking down a legendary beast.

And then, as if to ruin it all, Dulaf announced, "It was a fruit bat!"

After a long night of being beat on, shot at and thrown into walls I had come to a point where my investigation only turned up more questions and bruises than answers. It didn't stop the Elves from tormenting me. No, instead of letting me have my moment, Dulaf found the one thing to poke at to deflate our small victory. I knew she didn't mean to make me that miserable and, given her ways, it was probably just to avoid the thought that was haunting me at that moment.

If it was a fruit bat then we still hadn't found the actual culprit.

Chapter 12
Shared Enemy

The snickers lasted for a lot longer than I would have liked, but they didn't much matter once I went to get my "fruit bat" trauma looked at in the medical bay. The doctor was giving the most sincere smile I'd ever seen on his face when I walked in. Anatole, for his part, was unconscious on a bed in the corner, his wounds treated and his face taped up. Unfortunately, his head was also shaved.

All things considered, he got away pretty lightly.

"Ah, Leone!" the doctor cheerfully greeted me, "Welcome back from the hunt, we've had a bed ready for you since you left."

"Thanks for the faith doc," I replied, sitting on the bed and taking off the torn jacket. "How was your reunion with the snitch?"

He chuckled, picking up a couple syringes and an icepack as he waltzed to my side and gave me a jab in the arm without a word of warning. Grinning ear to ear, he told me, "It was splendid, I haven't felt better."

"And him?" I asked.

"He may disagree."

I looked back at Anatole, face bandaged like a mummy, head shined like it'd been polished during his involuntary nap. It would grow back eventually, but my limited experience with Incubi said they were at least a little vain. He would definitely be disagreeing later.

I idly rubbed my arm after getting a few quick jabs to it, looking up at the ceiling and waiting while he checked over a few of the nastier bruises I got under the coat. My eyes were burning and my head was starting to ache. My whole body wanted to just collapse onto the bed and take a nap for the next few days in the hope that it would all blow over while I slept.

"You're looking surprisingly well," he commented.

I looked back at him and raised an eyebrow, surprised to hear that from anyone after so many people said the exact opposite before. "What exactly did you expect me to look like?" I asked.

He shrugged with his ever-present toothy grin and waved a finger my way, replying in an overly cheerful yet matter-of-fact tone, "Hamburger."

The vote of confidence screamed again through his shark-like grin. He really expected me to walk away from the encounter looking like I'd fallen through a meat grinder. Though, I couldn't be sure if that was a judgment of me or the Nosferatu. To tell the truth, with my history of getting clobbered by larger Alters, it might have been a valid prediction.

The doctor danced away to another room, leaving me behind with my thoughts. It was a good moment, fruit bat or not, we'd taken down one hell of a large beast. So why wasn't it the threat? Those tattoos on the ears and Amelia's account were troubling. Because, if the Nosferatu didn't attack those people, who or what did? Maybe I just needed to clear my head for a bit to figure it out.

I laid down, figuring it was as good a time as any to try to sneak in that nap I'd been desperately wanting since the rooftop. My mind drifted as my eyes closed, flashing the griffon in my memory and hearing the voice of Dante talking so smugly about how they knew more than we did. I knew where to find out what they knew, it just wasn't pleasant. That led to images of the deepest, darkest pit the ACTF had at their disposal. It led to the visions of a creepy little garden under serene music that shouldn't have existed in such a terrible place.

Lost in my thoughts and drifting to sleep, I didn't notice the hand hovering over my face and edging ever closer to my unsuspecting nose. With a pinch, my air was cut off and I snapped awake, flailing to slap it away.

Dulaf and Amelia laughed as Dulaf's hand swiftly snapped out of my reach, the two of them hopping back almost in perfect unison like they'd reached some state of synchronicity through the magic of being Elves. I grunted and sat up, wearily staring at them and hoping they could read my deepest inner thoughts so I wouldn't have to curse out a kid.

It was the first time I'd actually seen Amelia without a visor and under full lighting, her sandy blonde hair in a short bob cut, face covered in smudges of dirt and grease that I couldn't see before. Her clothes were old: the edges frayed, looking like hand-me-downs from only god knows where. The only thing she really owned that seemed to be relatively new was the pink hooded sweatshirt she was wearing over the top of her t-shirt with a white cartoon cat I vaguely remembered from my childhood.

She smiled at me and waved lightly with her free hand, the other clutched around Dulaf's tightly. Giggling, she said cheerfully, "Good morning sleepy-head!"

"It's not morning," I sadly muttered, "if it were morning I'd be allowed to sleep."

Dulaf swept Amelia off of the floor quickly and sat her on a bed with a gentle poetry to her motion. Amelia glided into the air and onto the bed in one fluid arc and sat cheerfully on the edge as if nothing had happened.

"So," Dulaf said, turning to me, "what're we going to do about the tats?"

I sighed heavily and rubbed my arm, saying, "There's really only one thing we can do about it."

She rubbed her forehead, ears tensing a bit as she replied knowingly, "You're really going that way? Couldn't you just ask one of the people they brought in tonight?"

She was right to suggest it but I really didn't have many other choices. Dante could know something, but I wasn't about to give him the satisfaction of having something to negotiate with. Anatole already seemed to tell me everything he actually knew and that made sense for a guy acting as the front man. I didn't imagine anyone else having something I could use, especially with the rest of them in hospitals or down in the prison levels we called Limbo.

"He's the only one who couldn't use it for a power play," I said, frowning.

Dulaf's deadpan expression said just about all it could. We both knew that what I said was pretty silly. The man I was speaking of used everything as a power play, even if it looked to be something he couldn't benefit from. I just regretted it was the only real option I had that wouldn't let someone walk free. Despite all common sense I had to go to the Devil of the Ninth, Rufus Plagas.

Concerned, she said, "You know he's going to try to play you."

I nodded and stood up, starting to feel a bit warm and fuzzy from whatever the doctor had given me. I wasn't thrilled about the sensation, old ghosts haunting me from time to time, but a year of chronic pains had convinced me to let up on my fears so long as the doctor gave it to me. Bending my knees and testing their strength, I figured I was at least good enough to walk and picked up my jacket from the bed.

"I don't really have much of a choice," I said, putting the coat on.

Dulaf studied the jacket and looked at me with the faint sight of a frown at the corners of her lips. For a moment she watched me silently, finally breaking out into a smile and slapping my shoulders harder than I would have liked. "I'll come with," she said cheerfully.

Amelia frowned at us, verging on tears again. "You aren't leaving me are you?"

Brilliant green eyes alight, Dulaf announced brightly, "We'll take you with us and I'll show you the garden!"

"Uh, wait a minute," I interrupted, "I haven't agreed to you coming with me and I'm sure as hell not taking her down there."

The look I got, the coldest look I've ever seen, was a bone chilling, soul piercing gaze of discontent and judgment. It was the infamous "look" so many men had feared before, perfected over centuries since time immemorial to make guys like me know it was time to shut the hell up.

"Not that one you idiot," she said darkly. "And as for the other, after a night like this, you're trying to keep me away from a man in a box?"

"It wasn't like that," I said, trying to avert my eyes. "I just don't really need help talking to him."

With a quick shove she tapped my shoulder and nearly sent me tumbling back across the bed. It wasn't a very hard shove, especially not for her, but it was still more than I could stand against right then. Whatever the cause, my knees weren't exactly as stable as I thought they were at the moment.

"Okay, okay," I admitted, "maybe I'm not in the best shape right now."

Her eyes rolled practically into the back of her head as she turned on her heel and walked for the doors. "Get a move on it then," she ordered, "so we can get this done with before you collapse."

I looked at Amelia, who seemed delighted by my torment. "I was just trying to make sure she wouldn't leave you," I assured, trying to cover my ass for the peanut gallery.

She giggled, hopped down from the bed and skipped along after Dulaf, chiding with a sing-song tone, "Sure you were."

I buttoned up my coat as I followed them out. Tracing my fingers along the tear in the chest and running them across the protective plate beneath, I considered whether I was really okay to leave the clinic at all. The doctor hadn't given me permission, not that it mattered usually. But with Dulaf demanding I go with her right at that moment, I was extra motivated to disobey the Reaper.

The halls were a lot calmer now, the sense of order settling in over the compound and everyone moving at a much more leisurely pace. We'd been a beehive only a couple hours ago, in that brief moment of panic when we thought something dangerous was on the loose. No one could have guessed it'd be a fruit bat of all things. Then again, the person or thing that really did it was still out there, a fact I imagined escaped everyone else at the moment. For now, I just considered it might be a good idea to let them go on thinking that everything was cool until someone higher up decided to break their Zen. After all, those halls wouldn't be peaceful much longer.

The journey down through the building led us into the basement levels, the silver lined walls and UV lights creating a bright, shimmering corridor for us to pass through. Amelia jogged ahead to take Dulaf's hand again, curiously peering at the end. The sound of laughing children and an artificial breeze greeted us, the smell of flowers on the air like a perfume,

116

possibly artificial itself. We exited the corridor into the underground garden, the small waterfall and babbling brook almost overwhelming the sound of Amelia's awed gasp.

The shelter space we had in the area below the headquarters was lively and active at this time of night, refugees from the surface having a leisurely time while watching their children run and play among the flowers and trees. I glanced up as we entered and saw the sky through the monitor laden ceiling, clouds still rolling high overhead, raining down through the scenic landscape of Kobe Terrace Park as it seemed to float magically above.

Amelia ran down the stairs, bounding over steps and taking them two at a time, grabbing the rail and using it to glide down. For a moment I was worried about her going down the stairs like that, but I figured anyone who lived where she did had to be used to running like hell down a flight of stairs. A little gravity wasn't about to get her down.

At the bottom a Dryad woman, with a faint green tint to her skin and the light leafy texture to her hair, waved up to Dulaf and called out, "Welcome home! How'd the hunt go?"

Boastfully Dulaf replied, "Oh quite well, I bagged me a bat and brought back an Elf girl as a trophy."

Amelia squeaked, "Trophy?!"

Laughing maniacally, Dulaf swept Amelia up into the air and spun around with her across her shoulders, declaring, "And you'll be mounted over the mantle!"

I hung back and watched them from the steps; it was actually kind of unusual for me to see Dulaf like this. She swayed from taunting and manipulative to supportive often, a mercurial personality most of the time. I'd never really seen her be completely supportive of someone before. Amelia wasn't just under her watch; Dulaf seemed genuinely wanting to see the little girl happy. I guess, for once, I was admiring my tormentor.

The Dryad smiled and looked over at me, waving and smiling my way. "And Nate, how are you holding up today?"

I was confused for a second, guilty that I didn't know the woman's name even though she apparently knew mine.

"I'm sorry," I said, rubbing the back of my head, "have we met?"

She laughed and waved her hand quickly. "No, we haven't," she said, "I've just heard the stories."

It was confusing still, but at least I didn't have to worry about disrespecting her now. I glanced to where Dulaf and Amelia had been, Amelia now darting across the grass to meet with a pair of little girls, a Satyr and a Siren, making flower crowns. Dulaf reached over and tapped the Dryad woman's shoulder, smiling and shaking her head while she commented, "He's had a bit of a rough night, but it wasn't my doing. Mind taking care of the girl for us? We're headed down into Acheron."

The Dryad nodded, her hair rustling like a bush and a faint, sweet scent of flowers floating from her head. She got up and walked over to Amelia, who'd now joined the other kids, leaving us to continue on into the prison gates at the far end of their scenic little world. Briefly, I watched to make sure Amelia didn't notice us walking on before hurrying to keep up with Dulaf.

"There's stories of me?" I asked as we made our way through the gates.

"Oh sure," she replied with a wicked grin, "None of them are really good though."

I let the comment slide as we entered the section we called "Limbo". It was always a little uncomfortable there, trying to ignore the faint wails and howls of disturbed Alters lingering just out of sight. It always felt like a place to stay quiet and remain unnoticed. And it stayed quiet between us as we continued on before meeting with the smiling face of Joe the Curate, elevator man to the depths of Acheron.

Joe's a friendly man, nearing retirement and really only there to throw the switch and call for help. But even then his job wasn't one I envied. The man had taken the same stretch of tunnel up and down every day for as long as the building had existed. And, while you'd consider it boring, the fact of the matter was the man got to see the worst of Alter society from a bird's eye view everyday

It was all you could see down the long, coiling tunnel, looking down through the common areas of the cellblocks. Orange jumpsuits spread out as far as the eye could see: worn by Giants, Golems, Ogres and everything in between as they stewed under watch of the heavily armed guards. The platform we stood on went down the slope, the common areas and prisoner population progressively becoming more hardened and compact as we passed. It was like watching the darkness becoming concentrated as we descended to the ninth circle.

He looked over at us with bushy grey eyebrows furrowed and asked us in a friendly tone, "Never a fun ride to see the devil, is it?"

Dulaf laughed lightly, "You should have seen what we're dealing with above."

He chuckled and opened the door to the guard station at the lowest level. A mass of guards greeted us in the tiny lounge-like space they had available, too many people for a single prisoner and smelling like a locker room of all things. There were as many guards here as any other level, despite a prisoner population of just one, and each of them seemed as uncomfortable to be there as we were. They patted us down and put us through scans to make sure we weren't smuggling anything in. The scans were more thorough than they'd once been - a precaution after past mistakes. In fact, given those mistakes, I almost welcomed it.

As they waved us through to the next room we were greeted by the equally strong smell of garlic on the air. The fine mist on the air was highlighted by UV light-strips running the edge of every floor-plate. They weren't enough to harm any Alters walking through, not like this, but the emergency switch on the wall could have changed that quickly. Residue on the walls hinted at test fires over the years.

Approaching the core of the basement we could see the shine of glass walls surrounding the small hotel suite the ninth level considered a prison cell. The garlic essence mist I'd smelled since the entrance was thickest around those walls, forming the ghostly image of a second wall of mist surrounding the perimeter.

Once, it seemed extreme to build all of this for a single prisoner. It was only through experience that I realized it may be inadequate from time to time. The current walls of the suite were replacements for a set he'd nearly destroyed with a pair of gardening shears nearly a year before.

His lean figure loomed in the back as he thumbed through a relatively new looking book. He'd once had a tablet for all of his reading materials before he'd found a way to shut off the lights with it. The bookshelf he'd been given to replace it was now filled to the brim with an otherwise archaic form, all of them leather-bound and treated with the best of care. The wooden shelf was polished and cleaned meticulously like he'd spent great deals of time focused on maintaining perfect order in that corner.

The rest of the rooms were similarly spotless, every surface cleared and cleaned of any stain or smudge there might have been, the glass shining and polished both inside and out. I understood the outside, the guards not wanting him to be able to hide behind any hazy surface. But the inside? That was all Rufus.

The commanding yet airy voice broke the silence as he lifted his head from his book and said, "I suppose you've come to talk to me about a bat."

He put the book away carefully and strolled from one room to the next with a willowy grace, his long platinum hair bouncing and waving lightly in the perfectly controlled atmosphere. His jumpsuit, the one thing that tied him to everyone else in the compound, was still defined from the others with slightly better materials and a sense that they'd been hand tailored for him. They were new, better than what he'd been wearing the last time I'd seen him, and telling me that he was somehow still getting his way.

"I heard you cast Dante into your little inferno," he said, turning the corner into the visitor's alcove. He lifted his chin, the corner of his lips upturned just slightly enough to make me question whether or not he was smirking.

"I have no idea what you're talking about," I replied, trying to deny him the satisfaction.

He stepped up to the glass, our reflections overlapping on the double-paned wall. Smugly he said, "Still trying to pretend you have control?"

I gestured with a nod at him, sweeping an arm at his surroundings, "And yet we're still the ones out here, despite whatever you think you know."

He looked us over and gestured our way, Dulaf moving at my back, her ears perking on the reflection I could see out of the corner of my eye. Dryly he said, "I see you're still watching Lucian's pet."

I stepped over to get directly between the two of them, staring him in the eye and doing my best to seem intimidating to him. "She's with me," I declared.

He laughed and waved dismissively at me, shaking his head. "I'm not talking to you, boy. I'm talking to her."

I looked back at Dulaf, her intense gaze unwavering as she kept her eyes fixed on Rufus over my shoulder. I'd heard there was history between them at some point, but with people who'd lived that long it wasn't all that surprising.

"Why are you so sure she's here to watch out for me?" I asked, crossing my arms. "You're in the bad position right now."

His eyebrow perked lightly, the twist at the corners of his mouth becoming more severe as he broke into a full smile. "Oh, she's here to watch over you," he assured. "She's been doing it for centuries, keeping an eye on you and yours. Who do you think named your family?"

Dulaf's ears flexed and the glare grew darker, her normally soft features hardening as her brow furrowed and she stepped in closer, slamming her palm against the wall with a swift jab. The material shook under the force of it, stirring me and spooking the guard at the end of the small bridge leading into the alcove. All he did in response to it was smile at her, unmoved, unfazed.

"Stay on the subject!" Dulaf demanded.

I moved around behind her to avoid being in range of the next swing, looking over her shoulder while I said, "We need to know about the Nosferatu and your men implied you knew something about it."

He lifted a hand to his chin and turned his back on us. "I do know something about it, actually."

"Specifics," Dulaf said darkly, "now."

It wasn't the most elegant approach to the interrogation but I wasn't about to question her when she was in that kind of mood. All of the training told us to never lose our cool. The aggression was considered bad form, especially out of a former instructor. Yet, strangely, it worked.

"There's a facility you should look into," he said calmly, continuing to face away from us, "It has aspects to it that would connect quite a few dots for you."

"How would you know about some facility outside of these walls?" I asked.

He turned his head enough to let us see his face in profile, smirking as he replied, "I know many things you don't, like why they activated the silver line and what exactly caused the release of that bat."

Dulaf's shoulders tensed, her posture stiffening as she squeezed her outstretched palm into a fist against the wall. I watched her, seeing a rage in her body language that I wasn't aware she was capable of. No one was easy down in the ninth but Dulaf was practically enraged being face-to-face with this man.

I looked up from her shoulders and asked him, "So you're saying the Nosferatu was released on purpose?"

He nodded, lowering his chin to his chest, showing us the back of his head again. "It's a cover-up; they did it to keep you from looking into the facility I mentioned."

I'd been using Rufus as an informant for some time, at least a year by the time we were standing there, and I'd never quite figured out how he got the information he did. He once had a person who could slip inside undetected. They died an unceremonious death on a cold rooftop. And yet, somehow, he was talking to us like he knew for a fact that everything he was saying was accurate.

"In fact, the facility in question is public, but their operations are classified," he continued, walking around a corner and into an adjacent room. "It was classified by both nations funding the project."

Dulaf and I turned to watch him move around us and towards a desk in the corner, a tidy stack of papers laid next to an old fashioned inkwell and a set of notebooks. He lifted the first couple of sheets from the pile and pulled one from the middle of the stack, approaching the wall with it in hand.

"It had markings on its ears, correct?" he asked, lifting the paper. "One was for the United States and one was for Argyre."

I watched the sheet, light passing through it showing the outlines of a detailed drawing: a pair of claws in the air and an unmistakable beak opened wide. He turned the sheet and put the drawing of the griffon against the glass, identical to the one on the Nosferatu's ear.

"It looked like this, didn't it?"

I nodded silently. It was identical down to the last detail like he'd plucked it from my memories. It wasn't the same griffon on everything else I'd seen from Argyre, though I'd known the animal was the symbol of our country. Something about it, the way it was positioned, was different from the standard.

Dulaf stared at it and looked at me with shock and surprise in her eyes. The tips of her ears sank slowly and her eyes grew wide as I nodded. Her jaw slowly opened and she was left agape for some reason. I realized then that she hadn't looked at the ears before we met Amelia and I was suddenly very uncomfortable as these two people stared at me.

"It's just a griffon," I said, pointing at it off-handedly, "I know it's from Argyre already, it's not news to me."

Rufus crumpled the paper abruptly and frowned at me. "Nations which use heraldry in their symbols sometimes use special positions or elements to denote messages," he said. "This one here means that the marking was placed by the military of the Republic of Argyre."

"Military?" I asked, looking between them. "Why would the military be involved in this?"

Dulaf shook her head and gestured to the badge she rarely wore. "We are the military, Nate. He's saying someone in the ACTF released it into the public."

Rufus nodded and threw the crumpled paper over his shoulder, sending it into a wastebasket next to his desk. He crossed his arms and turned up his chin to us, scowling. "It wasn't your branch specifically, it was one closer to the seat of power," he said scornfully. "But yes, it was one of yours."

I rubbed my arm lightly, clenched my fist and crossed my arms to mirror him, asking, "So where's the facility then?"

He studied my position and smirked, shaking his head as he walked back to his desk, "It's a public facility on international waters, positioned out near the border of the United States and Canada. It shouldn't be a long drive and there's transport onto their platform available from the shore."

I watched him sit at the desk and lean back in his chair. He was so direct about the information, I felt uneasy about just taking it straight out of his hands. "How do we know you're telling us the truth?" I asked, "Who's your informant?"

He chuckled and shook his head. "I'm not ready to give up that sort of information to you just yet, but I assure you everything I'm saying is true."

"And if it is," I asked, "why are you giving it to us so easily?"

He stopped leaning back and shifted forward to the edge of his seat, looking up at us, face cast in shadows as he tried to hide a strange twitch. "When you see the facility," he said, practically growling, "you'll understand what I mean when I say I don't approve of what they're doing."

It was an unnerving tone, almost born out of pure hatred and loathing instead of his usual cocky bravado. I stared at him and saw the shine of his eyes in the shadows around his face; they were piercing, practically staring through the visor into my eyes. And the visor itself, it gave me the calmest, most serene blue colors I'd ever seen on an Alter: it was one of the coldest stares I'd ever seen.

Chapter 13
Old Nemesis

I reported what Rufus said and tried to press for an investigation. But in my condition it wasn't easy to argue the validity of sending me back out. The doctor at least confirmed that my ribs weren't shattered, just bruised, and gave me a heavy dose of omega to try to speed along my recovery. It hurt like hell, nonetheless, and we all agreed it was probably for the best to take the rest of the night off. In the meantime, none of us could say a damned thing to anyone else.

Alston himself agreed that we should keep a lid on the situation until we could figure out what we were really looking for. The case stunk too many ways for us to treat it normally. If the people who released the thing knew we were onto them they'd likely find a new way to hide their tracks from us, and that could mean something worse than a fruit bat.

So Dulaf went back to the garden to meet with Amelia while I dragged myself home. When I got there I collapsed into the old beat up recliner and dozed off while watching shitty television, embraced in the familiar smells of ramen and my father's cologne. After all these years sitting in my living room and a year of me trying to clean the thing, I couldn't get that smell out. It must have become part of the chair at some point. Though, I suppose it wasn't a deal-breaker.

I could have stayed there for the rest of the day had I not gotten a sharp slap in the face. I woke with a start and reflexively jabbed into the air, hitting what felt like a wall that shouldn't have been so close to the recliner. Squinting and covering my eyes from the sunlight shining through the window, I could only see the faint outline of the thing I'd hit. Long locks of brown hair and slender, bladed ears caught the light and moved ever so slightly as a breeze came through my now open window. Dulaf grinned as her grip tightened on the fist she so effortlessly caught.

"You need to work on your follow through," she teased, shoving my fist aside.

Rubbing my eyes, I shifted to the end of the recliner, trying to clear the waking haze and understand what was going on. The sun hadn't set yet, the city outside lit like mid-day, the clouds from the night before gone while I was in my drug induced mini-coma. So why the hell was Dulaf there?

"Aren't you on duty?" I asked, looking at her blearily.

"Yep!" she chirped, bouncing around my living room, sweeping up the clutter around me. You could call her a morning person if it weren't somewhere around three in the afternoon. "I'm working," she announced, "And you're coming with me!"

I strained to see the nearest clock-face and found the horrible truth of it only being a little after two. With a stubborn grunt I reclined the chair and covered my eyes again.

"Wait a couple hours," I muttered, "I'm not on duty until seven."

The shadow of the Elf darted across the room, looming at the foot of the recliner as she stomped heavily on the end of it. Nearly breaking my ancient chair, she launched me to my feet.

"Tough," she chirped, "I'm investigating and they told me to bring a field agent!"

I grunted, "What about Lucian? He'd go!"

Shaking her head, she snapped, "It's two in the afternoon, I need someone who won't burst into flames!"

I groaned and grumbled, "There's nobody else? Nguyen, Ramirez, anybody?"

Grinning mischievously, she ruffled my hair and laughed off my protests. "I don't want to disrupt their beauty sleep."

"What about mine?" I whined.

She shut off the TV left on across the room, looking back over her shoulder and smiling brightly as she said, "You're not that pretty."

Reluctantly, I put on my spare jacket and followed her out as she fluttered around like a hummingbird. The sun was unwelcome when we stepped outside, my eyes burned and my head pounded before I hid behind my shades. I had to be the only sober person in Seattle cursing the lack of rain.

126

"Where are you dragging me, anyway?" I asked her, awkwardly stretching to ease stiff joints and trying to look anywhere but at the light.

She slung a bag over her shoulder and spun to show off her brightly colored sun-dress, announcing with a grin, "Makah Bay."

"And where the hell is Makah Bay?" I asked, regretting my uniform. With a dark black suit of the thick material and metal plates everywhere it was like I was going to the beach in a fucking heat sink.

She was unfazed by my misery, however, walking with a bounce to her step. "It's out past Olympic National Park. I looked into Rufus' tip and found the only place that matched out on international waters is at the mouth of the Salish Sea."

Old family trips to the National Forest and boot camp made me realize just what she expected us to do. From Seattle that trip meant driving past a handful of cities wrapped around the Puget Sound and then past all the little ports between us and the Pacific Ocean.

I grumbled, "That's a four hour drive."

Swinging the bag around again, she shrugged. "Yeah, I packed for an overnight stay."

I sighed, "You couldn't warn me before we left my apartment?"

Rolling her eyes, she replied, "Oh stop being a baby. I packed something for you too. Why do you think I went through your stuff before slapping you around?"

It took a second for that to sink in: Dulaf had gone through my things while I was unconscious. The thought of her rummaging through my apartment was kind of embarrassing, but at least there wasn't anything worth being embarrassed about in my dresser.

"Though," she said in a sing-song tone, "I'm curious about the magazines."

"Magazines?" I echoed, feeling a faint blush rise.

An awkward silence grew along with the heat in my face. Being so rare, there weren't a whole lot of printed materials in the apartment. But that wasn't to say I didn't have some in a few places.

"Oh god," she exclaimed, "I was just kidding!"

And then my face was on fire. Rubbing the bridge of my nose, I just walked around to the passenger side of the car and tossed my keys to her. "Just shut up and drive," I muttered. "I'm going to take a nap on the way."

She had a wicked grin as I slipped into the car. I knew, even if I slept for a while, it wasn't going to go away before Makah. There was really only one thing left to do. Reaching over to the console, I hit a switch and braced myself. The framework around the chair whirred as it fell back, laid down, and snapped a metal box closed around me. My nice metal cocoon formed, a personal air conditioner making it comfy inside, and everything went dark as the "casket" slid partially under the dash.

Closing my eyes, I drifted off in the comfort of my new personal safety zone, hoping I wouldn't get another slap in the face.

Luckily, instead of slapping me she decided to pinch my nose instead. Joints popped and an old man grunted as I sat up and saw the waterfront from along the seaside roads. The radio and the Oracle were off, leaving us alone with the sounds of the ocean, my world-weary joints and the obnoxious pop music she'd chosen for the trip.

Dulaf glanced my way behind a pair of shades and smiled gently. She patted my shoulder and asked cheerfully, "Nice nap?"

Surprisingly, gazing out over the ocean, I was more rested than I should have been. "You know," I said, "These things might be too comfortable for prisoners."

She nodded with a light shrug and said, "We had to design them to avoid any human rights violations."

"You helped design the car?" I asked, resting my arm on the door. "Do we use anything you didn't have a hand in?"

She chuckled and shook her head. "Honestly," she said, "I lost track years ago. My parents were Magi with the original order and the family business just dropped into my lap."

Magi, a word usually not heard in a contemporary context. Old stories of intellectuals in the Bronze Age, like the three wise men of the bible, referred to "Magi". Once upon a time, the order of knights that eventually became the ACTF used Magi to do real science under terms like "Alchemy" and "Astrology".

"So you weren't kidding about the Oberon comment," I mused. "I guess the thing about naming my family was accurate too, wasn't it?"

I could hear her hands wringing the wheel from where I sat. Peering across the seat, I could see her knuckles turning white.

"That a bad memory?" I asked.

For a moment she looked conflicted, taking her eyes off the road for a second to look me over. Blowing a strand of hair out of her face, she shook her head and replied, "I just have a bad history with Rufus."

Chuckling, I replied a little smugly, "Welcome to the club."

"Lucian and I founded the club," she said coldly. "We've been hating that man forever."

Tension continued to build in her hands and her arms strained like she was ready to rip the steering wheel out. I didn't know what to do. Despite being hours away from the man she was still incensed. She bounced a knee, tapping a heel on the floor like a nervous twitch. And all I could think of was doing what she would do.

I socked her in the shoulder.

Swerving lightly, her grip relaxed, a look of shock appearing in her wide green eyes. Jokingly, she threatened, "I'm so going to shove you out, jerk."

Ignoring idle threats, moving past the specter of Rufus, I asked, "Why Leone?"

Starting to relax, she answered matter-of-factly, "It was the name of a great man."

Gazing over the ocean, it stung a little to hear that for some reason. It was a ghost that always left me feeling uncomfortable. I couldn't resist asking, "Why was Leo such a big deal?"

"For me, personally," she replied, trailing off and restarting with a bit of a stammer. "When I was young, my parents were these great minds in the order. They worked on a whole load of

129

things no one had at the time. A lot of what they made eventually became things used today. We even had gunpowder centuries before anyone else."

With a nostalgic look in her eyes and a fondness in her voice she laughed and said, "I nearly burned down the house with it."

"Not surprising," I remarked, "I know how often your lab's caught on fire."

She shoved my shoulder lightly. "I was a kid, totally different."

I chuckled, commenting sarcastically, "Because you're so mature today."

"Hah, no way," she said, gesturing at the radio as some twelve-year-old sang about girls.

I glanced over and reached to turn it off, getting a sharp slap to the hand for trying. She glared my way for a moment, smirked and continued, "Really, I guess that was always the problem. My parents were so good at everything they did and I was just some immature kid. They were untouchable."

She squirmed slightly in her seat, adjusting her position while trying to keep the car straight. "I was an easier target than they were: young, inexperienced, kind of stupid. I was taken captive by Rufus' forces so they could try to get me to work for them or get my parents to."

"Did it work?" I asked.

"Nah," she replied, "the first hunter I ever met face-to-face rescued me and we ran like hell to Rome."

"Lucian?"

She smiled and glanced my way, "No, a rough, backwater human named Leo from Tuscany."

I nodded along and felt a little understanding why she was so loyal to his memory. I'd seen his name on the memorial wall for years but never knew anything he'd done to get there. Though, it was bittersweet, considering the one thing I knew everyone on the wall had done was die in the line of duty.

My expression must have been obvious as she said wistfully, "He didn't die for several more years."

I nodded silently, trying not to think about it too hard. I'd researched my family history when I first joined the ACTF, finding secrets that were never known to me or my grandmother from ages past. Of the dozens of Leones to follow Leo's footsteps, more than half of them shared his fate. It wasn't something I liked to linger on.

"I was the godmother of his children," she said sadly, "so I was the one to actually tell them what happened."

We exchanged a look, a faint frown on her lips. Without her sunglasses, I imagined she would have been getting teary as her voice cracked when she said, "I told them to carry on his name. But they didn't have a family name. He was an orphan and even Leo wasn't really his name, it was just given to him by Lucian."

"So what was his real name?" I asked, trying to avoid her saddened face.

Shakily she laughed. "The hell if I can remember anymore."

She wiped a thumb across her cheek just under the edge of the shades. "He was my best friend for years but it never really came up. He liked being Leo, he said it was blessing."

"What," I asked, "being a hunter?"

She shook her head, replying, "Being anybody. He was a street urchin before Lucian found him, a survivor of the Justinian Plague."

The word "plague" was shocking by the ancient implications. I didn't recognize "Justinian", but I had a feeling it wouldn't have been anytime in the last millennia.

Pushing the thought aside, I tried to focus on something more positive. "So, I guess we're family."

She went strangely calm with a serious expression that rarely crossed her face. The corners of her lips turned up very slightly and she quietly hummed before the subtle smirk grew and she said mischievously, "You have no idea."

Flinching, I asked hesitantly, "What's that supposed to mean?"

"Let's just say," she mused, "If things had worked out better I would have been more than just the godmother."

A wave of emotions flashed through me just then. It was easy to see how it could be true, but for some reason a lot of other thoughts crossed my mind. In the end, all I could say was "Ew."

Throwing her head back, she laughed as I searched for something to change the subject. To my surprise, on the shoreline stood a building that seemed to be cut from a block of silver sparkling against the setting sun. A strange, archaic rune re-imagined with a modern style graced the signs and seemed important enough to acknowledge. It couldn't have come a moment too soon.

"Is that the place?" I asked, gesturing ahead.

Dulaf looked and nodded. "Sindri Industries," she said, parking the car. "There's another facility out over the ocean like Rufus said."

"And what do they do there?" I asked.

She nodded to the horizon, resting her arms on the steering wheel. "They're an Alter owned pharmaceutical company specializing in surgical equipment and medical supplies."

The words raised red flags for me and I gave her an uneasy look.

She met my gaze and said knowingly, "Yeah, it's an orchard."

I shuddered, flashing back to the first and last time I'd been to a so-called "orchard". They weren't the friendly, lively places with trees you'd picture with such a benign name. They were where the legendary "blood apples" were grown.

I probably turned a few shades that humans normally couldn't reach. At least, Dulaf seemed to think so as she reached over and pinched my cheek. Happily, she assured, "It won't be so bad, just don't look at the tanks."

We stepped out of the car, Dulaf tossing the keys over the roof to me and walking to the building casually like it wasn't an issue. The area around us was strangely quiet, even the office seeming practically abandoned despite every light being on as the sun dipped below the horizon. We were in a quiet, uninteresting part of Washington, featuring only one notable tourist trap to the southeast that some cultists claimed long ago. But even in a place like this I expected more activity around a major corporation.

Calmly, she said, "Just act natural and keep an eye out for anything unusual."

Picturing the orchards again, I knew that was easier said than done.

Chapter 14
Unpleasant Experience

The office looked like the lobby for a building much larger than it was. The girl behind the desk was lively and energetic as she greeted us, despite the late hour. Of course, considering I recognized the technology, I knew that was because she was a projection like the receptionist in the ACTF headquarters. In fact, looking around the entrance and seeing how few chairs were there, I realized that there was likely no one alive in that building.

"Welcome to Sindri," she said mechanically, "How may we help you today?"

Dulaf approached, removing her shades and examining the room herself before asking, "Does anyone actually work in this building or is this just the entrance to the actual facility?"

The artificial girl waited for a moment, silently staring at us with a broad smile for a few seconds while she processed the request. After what seemed like way too long of a pause, she spoke up with the same bright, oblivious tone, "We are currently standing in the debarkation building for those who wish to be transported to the offshore platform where we do the majority of our business. For various legal reasons we keep our operations offshore where they will not fall under any specific jurisdiction. How may we help you today?"

"Ugh, bots," I muttered, moving to examine the pane of glass the girl was being projected on. "Not even one of the high-end models."

Dulaf giggled and nodded, leaning against the counter and staring into what would have been the girl's "eyes". "We'd like to go to the offshore facility and take a look around if you don't mind," she said.

The girl stood there blankly again, processing it for a moment before replying, "I'm sorry, while our company is open to the public we do not allow individuals to tour the grounds without being escorted by an officially approved tour group."

I studied the room again and looked for some sign of a camera or microphone that let her know we were there. I was sure it had to be somewhere, but the people who built these things always went out of their way to hide the methods to their smoke and mirrors. Catching sight of a camera lens sticking out of the wall behind her, I stepped around the counter and removed my badge, holding it up where the camera could clearly see.

The girl started to protest as I walked around, beginning to say "please do not go behind the counter" before coming to an abrupt stop and freezing at the sight of the badge in front of her camera. The freeze lasted for longer than the other times, the girl's jaw left wide open as she stared into space.

Holograms, especially the interactive ones, have always been a little unnerving. When they work perfectly it's hard not to be disturbed by how lifelike ghosts on a pane of glass could be. When they didn't work perfectly, like this poor girl, they were blank and emotionless figures with uncannily human-like faces that froze into awkward positions.

It took seemingly forever for the girl to close her mouth and return to her default smile. After that long stretch of deep "thinking" she announced with the friendliest tone a computer could muster, "We welcome ACTF to our facility and will have you transported to the offshore platform immediately."

Gesturing to a wall, the surface shifted and opened like an elevator door, showing us a corridor that hadn't been visible before. Dulaf rested her shades on top of her head and walked that way, hanging her bag over her shoulder again and entering the newly opened door casually without any sense of hesitation.

I, on the other hand, took my time, wary of hidden doors after my experience the night before. The bruises under my coat were more than enough of a reminder to watch where I step. To her credit, at least, the hologram girl was slightly less unnerving than an Incubus. So I gave her a bit of a salute before entering the doors.

Turning the corner, Dulaf was half way down the long corridor. It was filled with artificial plants lining the walls and glass doors showing us a small pier and the ocean beyond. There were a dozen boats docked by it, standing out with their white polished surface against the darkening seas and the violet sky. The sea breeze blew in through the far door as Dulaf passed through, everything strangely peaceful after the previous night of noise and fury.

She walked along the dock, a string of lights along the edges showing us a path to one of the boats. The boat itself was small, just large enough for a couple of people but seeming to lack any sort of steering mechanism, just a monitor and a set of seats lining the edges. A canopy over the deck was held on hinges and seemed to be large enough and shaped in a way that it could close completely over the top of the boat like a capsule. As we approached, the girl's voice spoke from the ship and greeted us again, "Welcome aboard agents, the trip to the Sindri plant will take approximately 10 minutes."

I wondered just why their entire staff would be located offshore in what could be considered international waters. The hologram mentioned "legal concerns" and that, in turn, had me concerned. What sort of legal concerns could they possibly have at a pharmaceutical plant? Especially concerning was that it was one that Rufus himself didn't "approve" of.

And, honestly, there's never been much that Rufus hasn't approved of.

Dulaf stepped onto the small boat, once again without hesitation, and sat down as I followed her on. She dropped the bag to the deck, making a noticeable heavy thump like she'd been carrying a pile of bricks in it. It didn't look that heavy the way she whipped it around so carelessly, but it shook the deck-plates under my feet. I gave her a curious look and glanced down at it, watching the bag settle into place and yet not actually lose much of its shape.

"What the hell are you carrying in there?" I whispered, sitting next to her.

She rested her feet on top of the bag, which still kept its shape like it'd been solid. Leaning back, she winked and whispered, "Sexy."

136

I looked at the bag with its flower print and canvas surface, thinking about how insane it was that she'd disassembled a gauss rifle and stuffed it into something a tourist would have been carrying.

"Urban camouflage," she joked. "Don't leave home without it."

I took a breath and tried not to make a big deal out of it, not knowing how well these boats might have been watched by their owners. The canopy closed over the top of us and the craft steered away from the dock, turning out to the open ocean and speeding along. The low rumble of the ocean water against the hull was smooth, no sense of chopping as it cut through the water like a knife.

I started to recognize the design while we rode, realizing the craft was something the government used in the actual city of Argyre. Being an artificial island, Argyre had more than enough reason to build a fleet of small watercraft like this and they'd gotten good at it over the years. If I recalled correctly, it was even designed to be submersible if someone could get at the controls. Though this had been the first one I'd seen automated.

"These guys have a lot of connections," I said to Dulaf.

She was frowning, chewing her lip, the tips of her ears dipping slightly. She took a deep breath through the nose and exhaled from the mouth, looking at me and nodding.

"Yeah, there's no other way they could have gotten these," she confirmed.

The boat coasted to a stop, the canopy sliding open to expose us to the much brighter compound on the other end. It stood as a towering structure of glass and steel, every surface reflecting the scenery and the lights from the campus grounds. It was arched in a way that made it look like a blade piercing the sky, the backbone glistening like a sharpened edge, shimmering under the starlight and the rising moon.

Dulaf stood and looked at it, the grounds at the base of the tower resting atop an artificial island clearly designed like the hull of several very large ships tied together into a star formation. The decks of these ships were covered in trees and patches of grass, looking like a small park set adrift. Despite all of this, from the way it was designed and the sleek, curved edges of the base platform, I had a good feeling this thing was designed to move.

Dulaf gasped sharply, like she was reminding herself to breathe after seeing the structure ahead of us. Lifting the bag from the deck with ease, she flung it over her shoulder again and shot me a harsh look behind her, asking, "Do you recognize it?"

I shook my head, looking again at the design and trying to place what she might have been referring to.

"It's one of Argyre's satellite ships," she muttered, stepping off the boat.

"You mean they don't just have the boats," I said, gazing at the tip of the tower again, "they have part of the city?"

With a stiff gait she began to walk down the dock, looking ready for something to charge from the brush, like a cat aware of something crawling in the shadows. It was the first time she'd shown tension since the afternoon about something in the here and now, making me more aware of the surroundings myself.

"Something wrong here?" I asked quietly.

She nodded, eyes darting around as we crossed the courtyard on the ship deck. The walkways were stone covered, grass growing in boxed off patches across the yard, each with a tree that rustled in the sea breeze. The sloshing of the ocean could be heard against the far off walls but wasn't felt at all in the center, the ground like a solid island under our feet. Everything was perfectly organized and maintained, yet hid the artificial nature of what we stood on.

"It's like walking through Argyre," she said through a tense jaw.

I'd never been to Argyre, knowing only roughly where it was and what the culture was like. What little I knew was the pictures I'd seen in the guides easily matched the scenery around us.

The tower we could see from the boat was just the central building, one of several arranged in a tight group at the center, coming together almost at random, blending into each other like waves crashing together in a crest. They weaved into each other much like our headquarters, the sense of many structures into one.

A man stepped out of the building, wearing an old, worn down lab-coat covered with the faint stains of projects past. His hair was thinning and peppered with grey near the temples. He seemed haggard, weary and not entirely there as he walked up to us, coke bottle glasses catching the light as he walked our way.

His aura wasn't making the situation any better. He was a deep, dark shade of blue, telling me he was either a human on an Argyre platform or hiding something. Considering everyone who could be hiding something at this place and this time was likely to kill me, it made uneasy. Either way he wasn't someone I was going to read with the visor, so I took it off and looked at him with my own eyes.

He was a nervous, fidgety little man, toying with his glasses as he approached and looking like he wasn't sure which one of us he was supposed to talk to. His head darted back and forth between us, getting quicker the closer he got, beady eyes getting a bit wider as he reached out with a hand into open air, hesitating for a moment before turning it Dulaf's direction.

She stepped up and took his hand. "Hello, I'm Sage Dulaf Nénharma from the ACTF; we're here to ask you a few questions about your products."

Staring semi-blankly into her eyes, the odd man stammered, "Our products?"

She smiled reassuringly and said, "We've been following some recent activity involving blood packs and we noticed you were the closest production facility for omega."

A bold-faced lie told without an ounce of hesitation, like she'd been practicing it on the way in. The anxious man holding her hand looked between us one last time, released his grip and wiped it off on his coat.

"I'm Archibald, Archie," he stammered, still nervously looking between us. "I'm the head of the bio-synthetics development team. Usually one of the executives would have come out here to see you miss...Nénharma, wasn't it?"

"Sage Nénharma," Dulaf corrected, her smile straining. "I came in casual clothes because it's quite a drive from Seattle but I assure you I'm the highest ranking agent here."

Archie paled at her tone, running a hand through his thinning hair and adjusting his stained tie on the way down. I was getting the distinct impression the man hadn't been out of the lab in some time and speaking to a woman was a new experience for him, especially one that was so quick to put him in his place.

Stepping over, I offered my hand and tried to reassure, "We're just here to check into your production, make sure no one's sneaking anything out."

If he was unsettled by touching Dulaf's hand, mine was made of plutonium. Glancing down at it and back up at me, he stepped back quickly and turned around, waving for us to follow. "Then let's get to it," he said quickly, "I'm sure you'll see everything's in order."

Looking down at my hand, I questioned why he wouldn't touch it with the glove on. Maybe he was an Alter after all, avoiding the nano-particle silver plates running along my fingers. Then again, maybe he was just a dick.

He led the way at a hurried pace, practically scrambling back into the building like a roach being exposed to the light. He opened the door, stepped through and just let it close before we could even catch up.

"Either he's done something," Dulaf commented, "Or this man's terrified of human contact."

I nodded and opened the door for her, looking around the grounds one last time, pulling my visor from my pocket. Putting the shades back on now that I'd had a good look at Archie, I stepped in after Dulaf and kept an eye out for any strange sights from the rear of the group.

The interior was sterile, every surface polished to a shine with glass, metal and ceramic all reflecting back at us like mirrors. The reception desk ahead of us was a shade of teal mirroring the color of an ocean, curved in a semi-circle with a single chair positioned behind it, monitors on either side of it like it was meant to be used for security purposes as well.

The receptionist, a living, breathing woman as far as the visor was concerned, was the spitting image of the hologram on the shore, smiling in the same way and practically unmoving as Archie marched by with us in tow. For us, however, she turned and raised a hand to wave, showing she was actually aware we were there. One of the two monitors at her desk showed the interior of the beachfront office, a console and a microphone below it showing she was actually involved in that strangely stilted conversation.

"So where do you want to start?" Archie asked, continuing to walk at a steady clip and not looking back at all. "There's a lot of space to cover in here, the facility stretches over and under the sea level."

Dulaf lowered her shades and peered at a series of doors we passed on the way to the elevator before settling on the back of Archie's head and replying, "I'd like to see the bio-synthetics department first."

Archie stopped and finally turned to face us again, pushing his glasses back up his hooked nose. "I suppose that'd be a good place to start if you're looking for omega," he said, stepping into the elevator as it opened. "We'll stop by the orchard first and work down from there."

It took some effort not to react to that as Dulaf shot me a look and followed him in. Climbing into the elevator, the three of us descended beneath the ocean into the bowels of the giant ship. The doors opened several floors below to a place lit slightly darker then the offices above and keeping long strips of the compartment in relative darkness, visible from where we stood only by the reflection of ambient light.

"This is our orchard," Archie said, stepping off the elevator onto a catwalk. "We keep it a bit darker here since some of the imperfect batches of omega can become light sensitive before processing."

I tensed lightly while entering that room, the air chilled and smelling like disinfectant, the sound of gurgling fluids and mechanical pumps all around us. Archie led along the lit catwalk and past a series of large translucent tubes. Shadows cast through them while a faint red light escaped giant pools of blood thinned with a chemical cocktail. Inside were shadowy masses of flesh seen dangling from a series of tubes, pulsating in the center with a rhythmic beat. Every flutter could be heard, the pressure of the

141

fluid being pushed against the glass causing them to amplify the sound.

"How many production tubes do you have active at one time?" Dulaf asked, looking around at crimson towers surrounding us.

Archie stopped, looked up at one and rubbed a finger under his nose, shrugging. "It depends on the day and how fast they go since you can't get perfect timing out of organics," he said, nodding to us with a look of pride, "but on a good day we've had five to six hundred running at once."

Feeling something churn, I sputtered, "Did it *have* to be organic then?"

"Artificial blood existed before omega," he said, nodding to the tubes, "but it was a more involved process. It was still useful because it meant you didn't need to rely on donors. But the apples, strange as they seem, are a perfect donor. They could practically bleed forever."

As he answered me, my eyes drifted in the direction he gestured. My visor was picking up more detail from within the tubes, enhancing every edge and surface on these blobs of flesh floating in their own juices. I caught sight of one towards the back, nearly empty of its fluids, the exposed organ flexing and oozing blood out of every crevasse, a stream of the thicker blood slowly trickling down into the chemical pool below, the IV lines straining to remain anchored in as it struggled against them, a series of tendrils weaved around the cap of its tube shuddering with every hard jolt.

I was going to hurl.

A hand landed gently on my shoulder and Dulaf gave me a light squeeze, gesturing me to a doorway not far away where the catwalk left the room. She looked to Archie and asked, "So is this the only thing you produce here?"

Archie shook his head and looked to the same door Dulaf was nudging me towards as I began walking that direction. "We have two floors and multiple wings," he said idly, "That door over there goes to the organ transplant development wing."

Freezing in front of the door, I hesitated to move any further or look at anything but the floor. Dulaf walked behind me, her casual sandals making a distinctive noise as she crossed the metal grate of the catwalk.

Shoving me lightly, she cheerfully said, "Well then let's take the tour then!"

Archie hung back for a moment before following. He stammered, "I suppose so, but we should really hurry, I have work to finish before the morning."

"Are you the only one working right now?" she asked, putting her arm around my shoulders casually.

"Oh no," he said, "But the others would be down in this direction over here. Most of the orchard operations are automated."

Dulaf started walking me along to the door, arm around my shoulders keeping me on a straight path while I tried to hide my embarrassing nausea. I'd seen people torn apart, horrible bite wounds in human flesh and the corpses of victims burned alive by fire or sunlight. Yet I was a mess in the room with the pulsating mutant hearts. They continued to beat, drip and gurgle behind us as we left, reminding me they were still very much alive without any form of body to speak of.

I was pleasantly surprised by the next room. We crossed the threshold while I braced for another gore-fest and listened for any more throbbing out of sight. Soft lights and earth-tone tiles greeted us instead, feeling less like the sterile environment above and more like a home.

I lifted my head to see what looked like the entrance of a doctor's office: a rug on the floor with the company logo, simple paintings of quaint landscapes on the walls. The room was a hexagon shape with the wall in the back divided into three angled surfaces, two with doors and one with a wood reception desk. Unlike the last two we'd seen this one wasn't manned, likely expecting no visitors down into these floors at this time of night.

It was shocking that the room was there at all. Stepping out of the elevator, you would have expected them to hide away the horror show from the sight of the public. Yet here we were standing in what was clearly a better room only after walking through the nightmare fuel of the orchard.

143

"Why would you have a reception desk here in the back?" I asked, marveling at the concept.

Archie faltered slightly, "Well, you see, the tour passes through the orchard room to show people where omega comes from but this room here actually accepts patients."

We both turned to look at Archie, the word "patients" instantly grabbing me. "What do you mean by patients?" I asked, dumbfounded.

He responded to the question with a simple wave, gesturing us towards the right-hand door at the back of the room. We followed his direction, walking into a carpeted hallway with more of their artificial plants placed evenly along the walls. It curved through the building, the end of the hall vanishing after a distance and showing us only the large glass wall following the edge ahead of us. On the other side of the glass we saw what appeared to be an outdoor patio.

Like the Purgatory shelter under headquarters, the Sindri platform had an artificial landscape in it, decorated like a tropical resort, featuring, strangely, a wave pool to mimic the ocean that was already crashing against their hull.

"Who is this for?" I asked, nearing the glass, listening to the crashing waves and what sounded like a seagull.

Archie stepped over and pointed into the water, saying proudly, "Our master project."

A figure rose from the "ocean", wading back towards the sandy beach. It was a man, tall and lean with bronzed skin and jet-black hair. He was cut like a statue, moving fluidly through the water with ease as it rolled past him. As he looked our way, he raised a single hand into the air and smiled broadly.

Dulaf squeaked a little, apparently enjoying their work and completely forgetting what we were there for. I rolled my eyes behind the visor and looked over at Archie. "What do you mean by 'master project'?"

For the first time since we got there, Archie seemed perfectly calm, smiling and waving his finger out at the beach as he said, "This was the next logical conclusion. Omega was the answer to blood donations, a truly universal donor compatible with all blood types. But this here is the *true* universal donor."

"You mean this guy's compatible with everyone?" I asked, looking out at the Adonis walking onto the beach again.

"He's more than just compatible," Archie said excitedly, "the donors are factories in the same sense the omega organs are."

When I looked out at the man on the beach and started to realize what exactly the excitable researcher meant. My skin crawled at the implication. The "donor" went on with his activities like he was oblivious, grabbing a towel off of a beach chair and drying himself off, gazing at Dulaf the whole time with a sly, confident smile.

I wasn't sure if he knew he was cattle.

"Our friend Marcus here is going to be donating one of his hearts tomorrow," Archie commented casually.

Anxiously, I asked, "What do you mean by one of his hearts?"

Dulaf looked over, ears folded back, snapping at Archie, "You're going to be cutting into his chest?!"

Archie jumped, stepping back from us and holding up his hands, trying to wave us down. "It's not like it isn't something we've done hundreds of times now!" he exclaimed.

"Marcus" looked at us curiously, apparently unable to hear our conversation through the glass but seeing the sudden shift in Dulaf's mood. He shook his head and sat on his beach chair, looking back out over his artificial ocean, living his artificial life, apparently working with more than one heart.

Watching him, realizing this meant he had to know, I wasn't exactly feeling assured. "I want details."

Archie nodded and stepped around Dulaf, keeping just out of arm's length from her and passing us. He walked down the curved corridor backwards for a bit, keeping his eye on the high strung Elf at my side.

"The others should be processing some of our recent orders as we speak," he said nervously, "so let me show you how it all works."

Returning the favor, I put an arm around Dulaf's shoulders and gave her a quick squeeze, waving her on to follow the neurotic scientist through whatever strange lab he was leading us to. She looked out the window again at Marcus on the beach with a furrowed brow, clenching her fist and her jaw as she started to walk again.

Archie led us down the curved corridor, the doors on the wall adjacent to us marked like hotel rooms, a stretch of these rooms bridging the gap between the serene artificial environment and the once again sterile labs beyond. There were windows on the other side of what was apparently a circle, mirroring the ones facing out into the ocean landscape. Unfortunately, what lie beyond those windows wasn't the tropical paradise seen at the other end.

The earth tones faded into a set of pure white rooms with highly polished surfaces and airlocks bridging them together. To the right-hand side was a room bustling with activity, people working carefully in self-contained suits. They placed a series of organs into tubes of clear fluid I assumed were there to preserve them for transport.

On the left I could see what looked to be a hospital room considerably less active, a nurse standing watch over a man in a bed, monitors checking his vitals while my visor confirmed he was still, at the very least, alive. The aura was a set of violet shades and his bone structure was harder and sharper than the typical human. His nose and chin were more defined and his eyes slightly sunken. It was probably a good hunch he was a metamorph of some sort and probably one of their donors.

And in the center room, separated from us by yet another airlock, was a room with medical equipment, surgical tools on a tray, and monitors of every kind surrounding a table under harsh lights. Though it was a clean-room in the sense nothing got through without being sterilized, I could see from where I stood the faint traces of a recent pool of blood.

"We just harvested a series of organs from one of our universal donors," Archie said proudly.

Dulaf growled, "I take it the man on the monitors was your 'volunteer'."

"Yes, he made a couple of donations that will be shipped within the week," Archie replied. Taking a quick look at Dulaf, he hastily assured, "But he's going to be compensated for his time, we take good care of our subjects."

146

"Is your 'subject' a metamorph?" I asked, stepping around Archie and Dulaf to get a better look at him through the window.

"Ah, yes," Archie replied, on the verge of a chuckle as a grin crossed his face. "We keep different body types ready for any needs. You couldn't very well put a human heart in a Werewolf; the adrenaline spikes would cause severe damage."

"So you keep one handy for every race?" I asked, taking off the shades to take a look at the patient unfiltered, seeing his slightly gaunt, paled features that told the tale of how much of an ordeal it actually was.

"No, not quite," Archie said, gesturing into the room, "he's more for any that would have a standard metamorph physiology - the ones who suffer from dramatic chemical and physical changes during times of stress."

Watching the man's vitals on the monitors, I commented idly, "So you transplant from these guys only to people with similar bodies."

Archie went silent for a moment, then protractedly said, "Well, not quite, you could place organs into different breeds provided the one you placed in was a step up from what their body required. We've placed Werewolf specific hearts in humans a few times, athletes especially."

A chill ran down my spine, considering what Rufus had said about the marking on the Nosferatu's ears. "So you could optimize someone," I said distantly, "like a custom car."

He smiled and nodded along. "We've researched just about every breed we could find to see where the superior materials lie."

Dulaf backed away from the window, her ears twitching lightly out of the corner of my eye.

"We even had a Nosferatu for a while before we had to give it up," Archie continued, "it was a shame too, they have some interesting features."

Dulaf spoke up behind us, saying tightly, "I suppose there's a lot of use for this, fixing problems, improving performance, practically making Alter abilities available for everyone."

Archie nodded excitedly and looked back at her. "Exactly! It's something to bring us all together – an equalizer!"

147

I stared at the man on the table, commenting, "Probably even military applications for this."

Archie's enthusiasm faded for a moment, a new, calm restraint taking its place as he replied, "We've considered it."

Dulaf stepped up and looked up at Archie, smiling to him while she asked in a friendly manner, "Could we see your files? You know, inventory, shipping records, stuff like that?"

Archie thought on it or a moment, eyebrows rising lightly before he shrugged and started walking down the hall. "We'll put in the request," he said. "It's not my department but I'm sure they won't mind releasing that information to your organization."

We followed him and I put my visor back on, scanning the room with the patient one last time as I walked by. Dulaf was hanging back and gripped at my sleeve before I could get out of earshot, whispering, "I heard something else in here, something angry."

It obviously wasn't something I could hear, human ears not quite hitting the range of an Elf's, but I knew not to question it. Glancing her way, seeing her aura again, she was a shade of orange verging on the traditionally aggressive red. She was bordering on fight or flight like she felt threatened.

"We have to find it," she said quietly, "whatever it was."

Feeling her grip tighten on my sleeve, I realized two things while following Archie out of the transplant wing into the orchard that put me on edge earlier. The first was that I was wrong about which wing was more disturbing. The second, more frightening to me, was that I actually agreed with Rufus: I did not approve of this.

Chapter 15
Repulsive Knowledge

Quiet would be the best way to describe the ride back to the shore. Dulaf was nearly completely silent as she sat on her side of the little craft. The hum of the engine and the continuous rush of the water across the hull were easily louder than any noise she made. Not once did she even move or look my way. Frankly, it was unnerving.

And as we reached the shore she fled from the boat like it was on fire. By the time I stood, she was already a good seven feet ahead, moving down the dock like she was on a mission. Following her, I had to pick up the pace more than usual to keep up. Each step was falling sharp and fast, like she was ready to sprint but not quite throwing her all into it just yet. Though, the sound of it would have had me fooled if I just closed my eyes.

She rushed through the office building and out to the car, the artificial girl behind the desk hardly getting the chance to repeat "How can we help you today?" before she was already out the door. It swung closed again just as I reached it, whipping back from the hard bang Dulaf made as she threw it open.

I pushed through and yelled for her, "Dulaf, wait!"

She snapped back at me, yelling "What?!" at the top of her lungs. Hearing the tone in her voice, a near shriek, made me stop cold and step back. Elves weren't exactly known as short-tempered people, they've always been the long fuse, big explosion types. She was boiling before my eyes, pacing back and forth in front of the car before suddenly driving her fist into the hood.

"We need to take this situation calmly," I said quietly, inching closer.

She shot me a glare and pointed at me, ears flexed, face turning red at the cheeks, yelling, "You don't get it!"

"I probably don't," I answered, trying my best to keep a calm tone and hoping she wasn't going to take a swing at me next.

"But I know we need to handle this right or it's going to get nasty."

A shuddering sigh left her as she crumpled back against the car and sat on the hood. Her hands were shaking as she clutched them together as tightly as she could to hold them still. Quietly she started crying.

"We waited centuries to do this," she said tearfully. "We were trying so hard to wait for the right time. We just couldn't wait anymore."

I moved in closer and sat on the hood next to her, not sure if I should risk putting a hand on her at the moment, seeing the faint twitches as she tried to control herself.

Looking up at me, tears running down her face, she said, "Guys like Rufus said if we ever revealed ourselves without declaring war, they were going to find ways to torture us."

I looked out at the ocean, trying to think of what I could even try to say about a situation like this. Gathering up the courage to put myself in reach, I put an arm around her shoulders. She flinched at first, clenching her hands into fists. Squeezing her shoulder, I hoped she would relax instead of punching me into orbit.

It wasn't the first time I'd seen this kind of situation. My parents worried about stuff like this in the short time they were still together. Mom was always sure that there'd be experiments like this, that it would go unchecked and we'd essentially "eat each other". But dad...

"My dad used to say that the job of people like us was to force people to accept other's right to live," I said. "Didn't matter if it was human, Alter or anything else – everyone had the right to live so long as they didn't hurt someone else."

She shoved my arm away and bolted up to her feet, turning and screaming at me, "They're using us for parts, Nate! Parts! Like we were just things to be taken apart and put back together for their god damn curiosity!"

She turned and kicked the dirt, losing one of her sandals as it flew off. In a fury she pulled off the other and reached back to pitch it through the window of the office. Past her long hair I could see the shoulders and back flex, the hidden tone of the

Elves' slender but dense muscles starting to show. I was pretty sure she could have broken the window with that flimsy shoe. Instead, with a heavy grunt, she flung it past the office building, clearing it well enough to easily hit the ocean.

Slumping, hanging her head low, she muttered, "We're calling a fucking SOL team."

I hesitated for a moment to reply to her, finally saying, "That'd be a bad move."

"Bad move?" she snapped, glaring back at me. "What the hell would be a good move right now, Nate?!"

I looked up at the clear night sky, pointing up to it while I said, "Sun's down, Lucian could be here in a couple hours the way he sometimes drives."

"You think you, me and Lucian could take that place down?" she asked scornfully. "Are you stupid?"

Assuredly, and without getting reeled into matching her tone, I replied, "We need evidence they've done something wrong before we can take them down. The place is Makah territory, thus the name, right?"

She nodded lightly, turning to face me again, tears finally starting to dry up behind the mess of hair that'd fallen over her face.

"So then if we rolled a couple black vans through tribal lands, someone's going to notice and close up fast, right?" I continued.

Chewing her lip, she looked off to the north, a thoughtful look in her eyes. She swept the chestnut hair from her face and sighed heavily, saying, "I saw a place in the reservation we passed through where we could wait for him to meet with us."

I got up, walked around the car and opened the passenger door for her. "Were you serious about bringing a change of clothes before or is there only enough room for Sexy in that bag?"

Running fingers through her hair, she walked over and climbed into the car. "Actually I stuffed your trunk full of crap we might need," she said, tone getting a little lighter. "You know you really need to get a better lock for your apartment."

We went north to another bay in the Makah reservation, finding a small, quiet town up there that I apparently missed during my nap. On the way Dulaf thought to connect the car to the Argyre database, bypassing the Oracle to prevent the system from actually knowing what we were looking for, and started to dig up the schematics of the platform we were just on.

"Think we can find a way in that they wouldn't see?" I asked her, coming to a stop in front of a small place marked like a restaurant but looking more like an old two story house.

She nodded, bringing up a 3D model on the windshield and tracing her finger along the edges of it. "I'm going to have to look at it carefully, but I've known some maintenance workers from the city-state that talked about hatches they use to get in and out of these things."

She wasn't shaking anymore, her voice regaining that steady confidence she usually had. Having something to occupy her time seemed to be calming her as she focused her anguish on the concept of making these guys pay for what they were doing. It made me feel a little better about going in with just her and Lucian at my side. So I produced a pamphlet from my coat, opening it to show the tour route's map of the facility. Exchanging a quick smile, she took it, removed a small projector from the dash and we both climbed out of the car.

Having skipped breakfast, dinner and everything in between, we decided to pass our time eating while she studied the two maps. The food wasn't as bad as I figured it'd be for a location that didn't really even have an actual sign in front of it. We were there for about an hour, me eating and trying to set a record for amount of coffee consumed in one sitting, Dulaf going over a holographic map and looking for weak points in the structure. And before long we heard the hum of another of our vehicles outside, the buzz of the wheel-mounted electric motors standard to our cars coasting to a stop outside.

To my surprise, Lucian got off of a motorcycle in the black and silver colors of our vehicles, lacking his badge and wearing a helmet that completely covered his head and face from view. At first I wasn't even sure it was actually him, wondering if he'd sent some traffic agent in his place. But as he stepped off and pulled a

152

case of tactical gear from a hidden storage compartment, I caught on to what he'd done.

"I guess he took the stealth thing seriously," I commented to Dulaf, nudging her shoulder lightly.

Lucian strolled in and dropped the case onto the table by us, sitting next to Dulaf and looking over the map she'd been studying, his arm rested across the back of her chair. At first I couldn't help noticing how casual he was being, but then I decided to judge how well he was prepared for our trip. Peeking at the toys he brought with him, I pulled the case over, cracking it open and taking inventory of what looked like a portable set of the SOL gear. Looking at the helmet he had while driving the bike, I wondered if he might have broken one himself at some point.

"How bad was it in there?" he asked.

Dulaf lowered the map and answered solemnly, "They grew Alters to be harvested endlessly."

Lucian was reserved in his response, a light grimace on his face quickly pushed aside, a fist clenching subtly behind Dulaf's shoulder. He rested his other hand on the helmet and idly rapped his fingers along the top of it.

Finally, he asked tightly, "What exactly are we looking for in there?"

"Dulaf heard something while we were in there," I replied, closing the case again. "Which isn't too surprising. I seriously doubt the guys we saw walking around that area were capable of dismembering Alice Winchester."

Lucian nodded, taking the cool tone I knew him for and smirking lightly as he remarked, "Guess that means we storm the castle through the culverts."

"If we can find the entrances," Dulaf said, returning to the map. It was a more complex structure than I imagined, the weaving corridors and pockets of space maximized to work every inch of the body. The walkways seemed to move mostly where traditional ceilings and walls would have been, nothing cleanly boxed away or having a clean right angle. I hadn't noticed it as we moved through but there was a very organic nature to how it all weaved together, like the organs of a great monster we'd escaped.

"These satellites always were like ant-hills," Lucian said, running his finger across the display methodically. "But if you know where they have to get in, you can find the places where they would do it."

He traced his finger across the map for quite a distance, moving across what appeared to be a power plant and stopping his fingertip hovering just outside a space where two of the wings met near the glowing object I assumed to be a reactor.

"There's internal access to some of these lines, but since space is so tight, they'd have to climb in to reach some of the power conduits," he said confidently. "We can climb through there and take out their lights at the same time."

"Just one problem with that, guys," I said, crossing my arms and resting over the toy-chest Lucian brought. "How do we get out there to the platform over the open ocean when we've only got a car and a motorcycle? Vampires can't swim and I'm not sure we'd be too fresh after swimming twelve miles."

Lucian nodded and gave a light, bemused shrug at his unfortunate lack of buoyancy. "We're probably going to need to rent a boat then, something small enough not to make a lot of noise but fast enough to get us there before dawn."

Outside was a sleepy little town that didn't exactly scream "speedboat" to me. There were docks out there, fishing boats and some personal boats I'm sure could make the trip. But none of it was exactly designed to be fast and stealthy at the same time. Honestly, I think half of them would have been heard from a mile away.

"It won't be a problem," Dulaf assured. "We'll just take one of theirs."

Looking back at her, ears starting to perk, amused and slightly devilish, I hesitated to reply, "I don't think we want to take the boat they can track."

Grinning, she replied in a darkly amused tone, "I didn't mean 'take' as in 'use', I meant 'take' as in 'steal'."

"Borrow," Lucian interjected, "we're still law-enforcement here, even if we're going out to international waters."

Honestly, I was kind of hyped to play pirate for a bit. It was one of those strange little childhood fantasies you always want to try out just once but knew would never happen: going to space, fighting ninjas, stealing a boat or slaying a Vampire. Though, that last one might have been a bad example as one was grinning at me from across the table.

"To borrowing," I toasted, lifting my glass of water into the air.

Dulaf grinned, lifted hers and cheered, "To borrowing!"

Chapter 16
Terrible Realization

Under the cover of darkness, somewhere around midnight, the three of us approached the Sindri building and made our way around its perimeter towards the shore. Dulaf and I dove in as we reached the water, swimming for the docks as quietly as possible, Lucian deciding not to risk drowning and staying on the shore for the time being.

The water was chilled in the late night air on the dark shore. There was very little light to make out what might have been ahead of us without the visors and a good deal of guess work was required every time a wave splashed across our faces. The distant lights of a resort on the north end of the bay were visible from where we were, but the office building's back-end was a solid wall without a sign of light or windows to speak of - only the small, covered dock jutting out and cutting across the horizon.

Swimming for the shadow, we soon heard the familiar splash of waves against the hulls of small boats and saw the glimmer of light from the covered dock. Entering through an alcove, slipping in past one of the boats, Dulaf lifted herself from the water and peered over the edge of the dock, searching the ceilings for cameras or motion detectors. There was a faint trace of infrared shining from somewhere close to the building, likely positioned over the doorway. We knew that had a good chance of being a motion detector, likely connected to a camera.

Luckily, we had Will-O-Wisps.

Treading water behind her, I set the Wisp and passed it to her. With a quick toss, angling it to bounce off a support so she wouldn't have to reach her arm into the line of sight, Dulaf chucked the device up the docks. In a moment, the lights around us suffered an unceremonious death, the motion detector's sweeps coming to an abrupt end.

Dulaf held her breath and continued to dangle from the dock for a second, ears stretched to take everything in, likely listening for anything resembling an alarm. With a quick nod she waved me over, gracefully pulled herself over the edge and up onto the dock.

Following her with a little less grace, I asked, "So you're sure about being able to hijack one of these?"

Getting onto the boat we just squeezed past, Dulaf produced a knife from the back of her uniform and jabbed it into the console. She didn't respond or take time to explain herself, she just started to rip the thing apart and get to the wires underneath. Swiftly she gathered the wires together and started to connect them to her hand-link. Her fingers were nimble and moved fast, naturally and without hesitation. She hardly had to look to see where they were going and by the time I was on the deck with her she was already cracking into the boat's computer.

I looked around us, searching for any sign that someone else might have been there but only saw the dead of the night beyond the dock. Even with the visor enhancing every shred of light it could find, there was nothing out there to see. Deciding we were the only things alive out there, I returned to Dulaf.

Peering over her shoulder, I asked, "Where'd you learn to crack into computers anyway?"

"Programming languages were an Alter creation," she commented, "based in old signals we used to communicate under the noses of the humans."

"Are you serious?"

She looked up and smiled, dozens of red indicators quickly starting to flash to green as a control display appeared on her link. "Completely," she said, "espionage and information transfer techniques always go hand in hand."

Sitting next to her, I asked, "Are you saying you were a spy?"

She punched in her first command to the boat and started us south along the beach to where we'd left Lucian. Sitting back in a seat across from me she waved and laughed, "Oh no, that would require more self-control than I have."

Excitedly she continued, "This is my first time stealing my way *into* a castle."

"So why'd you learn the language for sneaking messages?" I asked, leaning back and wondering if I should try to drain the water from my boots while I had the chance.

"Oh," she laughed, "I wasn't a spy, but I was the one they reported to."

The thought of Dulaf being the head of an organization of covert Alters was slightly intimidating. I'd seen how she was with her lab boys; the idea that she might have had something akin to ninjas at one point was like finding out your neighbor was raising attack dogs. I was sure she wouldn't have used something like that on me so the fear was moot. But it did leave me with a thought.

"Do we still have a covert division?" I asked curiously.

She looked out to the ocean and thoughtfully answered, "You know, I wasn't really sure before. But it would definitely explain a whole operation supplied by Argyre, especially one that could silver-line the Force."

We coasted to a stop by the shore, the canopy over our heads lifting away. She looked at me, then at the shore, then leaned over and whispered, "Though if anyone did know about something like that, it'd probably be the guy who formed the original."

Looking over my shoulder, Lucian waded out a bit and climbed into the boat, sitting next to me and waving. "Let's make this quick, I don't like being soggy," he quipped.

Dulaf nodded and shut the canopy, turned the boat around and took it out to the platform. She steered us on a slightly more scenic route in case they watched the waters a little more carefully than they watched their dock. After taking around twice as long, circling in towards the shining blades piercing the night sky, we reached the platform and Dulaf cut the engines, drifting us in the rest of the way so we'd approach silently.

Using the hand-link to monitor their system, she nodded to us. "We're good; they didn't seem to notice us. Their security is still on standby."

Lucian nodded and opened the tactical case, producing a pair of large flat pads with handgrips on the back and straps. He handed them to me and nodded, saying, "Put these on, they're setae surfaced grips with magnet supports, they'll help you climb the hull."

I took them, putting one on and strapping it to my arm, examining it carefully. I could see a texture on the bottom of the shiny metal plate, like a piece of steel had grown hair. Running my finger across it, I could feel the surface grip at the tip of my glove for a moment before I pulled it away. "So these will help us climb that thing?" I asked, looking between them.

Lucian patted my shoulder and smirked. "They'll help you, Leone."

And with that, he stood from his chair, moved to the nose of our boat and leapt off of it like a god-damned leopard. He hit the wall of the ship near a corner where two wings met and bounced off of it, throwing himself to the other wall. With quick, springing motions he ricocheted from one wall to the other, swiftly scaling the structure with an incredible ease.

Leaning over the nose and watching him from below, I commented sarcastically, "He can't swim, but apparently he can fly."

"Of course," Dulaf said, pulling her rifle out of her bag, "All muscle, no buoyancy but a hell of a lot of strength."

She stood after him and slung "Sexy" over her shoulder, the gun having a new look now with a shorter barrel and a new ammo clip I hadn't seen before.

"Did you change that?" I asked, standing and backing up to take it all in.

"I swapped it for the automatic configuration," she said, ecstatic, "I've been wanting to try this in the field for months."

Flatly, I remarked, "You put an automatic configuration on a gauss rifle."

"Of course," she said. "If one shot was always enough then Sammy and I wouldn't have worked so hard on those revolvers."

I nearly palmed my face before realizing the thing strapped to my hand might have peeled the skin off. Surprising myself with it, I flinched and quickly lowered my arms to my side, hoping she didn't notice. Luckily, she followed Lucian, springing up the side of the facility with an effortless grace.

Watching her follow him up, I murmured to myself, "Elven Ninjas."

My climb was considerably less graceful or easy. Though the pads were great, gripping at the metal with an incredible efficiency yet releasing when needed, it still took a good minute or two to get up as high as they had. Several times I had to take a moment to adjust my footing so I wouldn't be lifting myself entirely with my upper body strength. Every moment I was on the wall I was reminded of the height by the sound of waves crashing far below. All the while I thought to myself, "the dock was at sea level guys, we could have just kicked in their door."

When I arrived to the top of the climb I found the two of them in a small alcove with an electronically locked hatch, a ladder built into the wall giving people access to the area from above. I hoisted myself into the alcove, collapsed to the floor and rested against the wall, staring at the bars of that ladder and wondering just how far we would have had to sneak into the compound before we could have just used that thing.

Dulaf giggled at my expense. "Maybe I should have carried him."

"No," Lucian replied calmly, amused, "we needed you up here to work on this lock. The boy just needs to work out more."

I would have shot him a glare if I could spare the time to focus on it over trying to catch my breath. Not that I would have had a long time to worry about it since Dulaf cracked the door open seconds later, cutting my brief reprieve short. With that, I just removed the grips and dropped them onto the deck, figuring we'd be running back out this way if anything went wrong since Lucian wasn't about to swim. Pulling my Helios, I walked over to join them at the newly opened door.

The air from the other side of it had a strange medicated smell, like the interior of a hospital but more so than the lab we'd been to earlier. It wasn't just sterile in the sense of absence: it was practically anti-biotic. The space beyond was well lit but narrow, allowing only one person at most and even then only just. It was built for people with a slim profile: Dulaf getting through easier than Lucian who still managed to make it through easier than me.

160

We slipped through the narrow passage, keeping an eye out for anything looking like a security sensor or camera. It was clear along that stretch since only maintenance workers came anywhere close to it on a day-to-day basis. But as we reached the end it was a whole different matter, standing at the edge of a room looking like a more advanced version of the omega plant above. The lights were set as bright as they could, creating an incredible glare off of the control consoles lining the edges of the polished steel walkways. And over the top of it all, there was enough infrared to think the place might have been on fire.

The fluid in the tubes was opaque while reflecting the light, preventing us from seeing what was inside. Though, I couldn't help but notice that they were deathly quiet without the single hint of a heartbeat or a throbbing mass. The fluid itself was a different color as well, verging on a dark blue rather than the crimson blend of the twisted cocktail only another level over our heads. The light reflecting off of them gave the room itself an eerie blue glow. These were clearly not meant for the same thing as the ones above.

Dulaf perched at the end of the passage like the edge of a precipice, whispering, "I've never seen so much security over an orchard."

Lucian and I silently agreed, edging towards the room ourselves as much as the passage would allow. There were motion sensors all around and cameras mounted in every possible corner. Really, the only thing preventing this room from being the most secured place I'd ever seen was the lack of a mile of tunnel and a troop of armed stormtroopers. For now, that record was held by Rufus, whose disapproval was starting to echo in my head.

Leaning back towards us, Dulaf whispered, "the cameras are going to be a problem but I think we can break the motion sensors by scattering the infrared."

Frankly, I was stumped by the suggestion and wasn't sure what to say. But Lucian pulled his gun out like it was the most logical thing he'd ever heard and aimed over her shoulder with it. After a second of leveling it and adjusting it to a higher setting, he quietly ordered, "Eyes up."

I secured my visor and backed out of the way, Dulaf looking to the floor and covering her face. He fired a shot across the room, the ball of ionized gas and scattered particles not triggering the motion sensors: too fast and not nearly dense enough. It flashed across the room, casting new shadows inside the tubes and striking a fire extinguisher on the far end of the room, venting its contents into the air.

Dulaf nodded and leaned out, poking her head out just a bit as my visor saw the infrared scramble through the cloud spewing out of the canister. Waving, she pointed in another direction and leaned against the wall to get out of Lucian's way. He leaned out, turned and fired again around the corner. There was another loud bang and a hiss going off through the room while more of the sweeping light started to scramble and go dark.

Looking at my perplexed face, Dulaf grinned and waved, saying off-handedly, "Carbon dioxide reflects infrared."

I'd known this once before, I was sure, but it hadn't occurred to me as we were perched there at the edge of the room. Watching it in action, I could see why it would be something to remember in the future. What was once a crossing maelstrom of heat now started to look like a pitch black void in the center of a growing cloud of gas.

Lucian turned and fired yet again, hitting another in the distance, this time shattering glass as the bolt caused an explosive decompression. He nudged Dulaf and she darted off into the gas, hurrying out himself and waving for me to follow. Unsure what exactly was going on, I just nodded and figured the best option was to keep my eyes on his back and watch for any entrances. Running into the cloud, just about everything started to vanish into the fog.

Through ambient ultraviolet light, the shades turned the room into a silhouette around us, a room of living shadows. Lacking any sense of heat, only the movement showed a difference between what was alive and what was just a tube. We weaved through the room as quickly as possible, the air fairly thin and my lungs starting to burn from the vapor surrounding us. The others didn't seem as bothered by it, quickly moving through like they'd memorized the layout of the floor from the passage.

162

Suddenly darting aside, Dulaf waved us over and the three of us stepped out of the gas, my lungs aching at the sudden reintroduction to air. While I leaned on the wall in coughing fits she produced her knife again and jabbed it into a locked panel in the wall. Prying at it caused the panel to groan against the knife but hardly budge, provoking an angry sigh from Dulaf as she pulled out a small kit from her belt and started to pick the lock.

"We really need to cook up something to just burn through locks," Lucian commented, leaning on the wall across from me and watching the cloud dissipate. "It took me a week to get Nate picking locks effectively."

To be fair to me, I learned to do it on the job, often in a place where I could be shot at. It's hard to focus on the idea of hitting tumbler pins when you look over your shoulder every thirty seconds. And when it wasn't on the job it was somewhere that could have just gotten me fired. I still wonder from time to time why he wanted me to crack into Commissioner Alston's locker in the headquarters' gym.

The panel cracked open and Dulaf found herself looking at a mess of switches with no clear labels. Muttering to herself she ran her fingers along the space between them. "Of course they wouldn't be labeled," she complained, "that would make it easy."

With a sigh and crossed fingers on the other hand she flipped one of the switches and braced for it. The lights stayed on, the consoles remained powered, but the infrared sweeps that had been scattering through the air now vanished all together. With a silent cheer and a fist pump in the air she hit another switch, hopefully taking out the cameras.

The vapor in the air thinned enough for us to see again and Lucian stepped cautiously into the open space, looking at the entrances to make sure they were still closed. The majority of the facility seemed to be closed down for the night but there were still clearly lab rats wandering the floors above. Any one of those people could have come down without much warning.

"Well, we're in," he said, walking over to one of the tubes, trying to peer through the opaque fluid inside. "Now to find out what's inside these things."

Dulaf and I nodded and the three of us split up, taking different rows of tubes and hoping one of us would find one that didn't seem to be flooded with blue miso soup. At least, that was my goal while Dulaf went the more practical route of cracking into their system and Lucian checked the doorways to see what was connected to the room we were in.

"There should be a monitoring station of some sort around here," Lucian said from across the room. "They'd have to keep records of their experiments somewhere."

Dulaf, face lit with the colors of the new screens appearing on her display, replied distantly, "Hopefully on this floor."

When she hit pay dirt it wasn't with a cheer or even a signal to us to come see it. She just made a simple, pained gasp. I couldn't see the screen from where I was, but between those slimy tubes I could see her face over the console, uncomfortable and frustrated.

"What is it?" I asked, jogging over.

Fixated on at the screen, Dulaf lowered her hands and let me see the display for myself. There were readings and measurements on the screen for a man, but like none I'd seen before. He was at least the height of the Nosferatu, densely muscled, yet lean enough to still move effectively. The monitors for his vitals showed two heartbeats steadily running harder than I'd ever seen and yet his brainwaves were minimal, like someone in a deep coma.

"The military project," Dulaf muttered, turning away from it.

And that's when I saw the last thing on the screen to really unnerve me: a griffon emblem in the corner, plainly visible and positioned like it was ready to pounce. The Argyre military had been behind it. I looked back at her and searched for Lucian, only to find him standing by us again now that I'd taken the moment to look his way.

"It's not a real surprise," he said calmly, walking over to view the console with me. "There have been people in the Argyre government, Rufus supporters, looking to create a military force capable of going to war."

"War with whom?" I asked, studying his face and his visor readings, wondering why he was so damn calm.

Coldly, with a calm aura and a subtly disappointed look in his eyes, he replied, "Everyone."

Examining the screen, I wondered if every part were plucked from the body of a donor like Marcus. Maybe they'd been grown intact, like a mix and match of parts brewed in these strange soups like the primordial ooze. Or maybe these things were weaved together like patchwork quilts, stitched from pieces and parts. If they were, were they alive? Did they have a mind to go with the body? Did they have a "soul"?

I looked between Lucian and Dulaf, feeling uncomfortable just standing there, and walked away from them to give them some space. At the very least I could try to get a head count of the tubes and see how many of these things, or people, we would have to deal with. There were at least a dozen in the first row I counted, none of them visible behind their brew. But when I turned to look at the next row, I found something wholly more disturbing.

One of them was empty.

"Uh, guys," I said, backing away from the tube and glancing around to make sure the thing wasn't hiding out of my peripheral vision, "We have a problem here."

Lucian joined me first, staring into the glass tube and examining it much more closely than I was secure in doing myself. Stepping within inches of the surface he gazed down into the bottom of the tube, searching for something along the floor. Quietly he said, "I think it's been empty for a while."

Dulaf grazed past me, nearly pushing me aside. Looking in with Lucian she muttered, "No chemical traces down there at all."

He shook his head while I tried to catch up to what they were saying. Honestly, I was feeling amazingly out of my environment here. The facility already made me uncomfortable and the concept of what was happening here was over my head. The thing that really chilled me was the idea that either humans were doing this to control Alters, or Alters were doing this to control humans. Either way, for the first time in a while, I felt that line between myself and the others in the room.

We might have all agreed that this was horrible, but it was impossible to ignore the fact that one of our groups was conspiring against the other. I just hoped, while Lucian turned to stare at me, that he wasn't seeing me as a proxy.

"Nate," he said calmly, "I need you to go find the office and get any documents you can find while Dulaf and I see what we can do about burning all the data here."

Tensions relieved for me as he said it, even if the chill in my bones wouldn't pass. I nodded and jogged out of the room as quickly as I could, looking for any doors Lucian hadn't already pried open during the first round of searches.

The one I found led into a small, claustrophobic space with wall-to-wall counters and desks. Monitors wired into terminals were so heavily packed that they had to be arranged into the corners of the rooms and up onto rigs overhead. The electrical hum in the room was enough to hear it before the door was fully open, felt through me like an underlying vibration to the air. When I stepped in and saw all of the information across the screens I just hoped these guys had a way of getting the information out that I actually understood.

The terminal was, blissfully, something I'd seen before. It wasn't that I was particularly behind on modern technology. I just knew my limits and the field of bio-synthetics was definitely beyond my ken. Everything else in that level was beyond my range of expertise, so it was nice to see something I could call familiar. Fetching my hand-link, I was happy to see a compatible port and connected them, beginning the transfer and watching the steady progress bar.

The subtle sound of whispers drifted to me over the electric hum and the quiet droning of the cooling fans in the terminals. I looked out the door to see my friends gathered around the same console, Dulaf hunched over it, squeezing the sides of the display hard enough that I could hear the sound of twisting plastic and straining metal. Something was clearly about to break.

It was hard to put myself in their shoes. On a surface level we all knew it was wrong and that these things in the tubes were the end result of a whole race being experimented on. But I couldn't really say I'd fought for someone's rights before, not like they had. I couldn't say that I'd devoted my life to preventing something like this from happening. To me, it was a lab of monsters. What was it to them?

The link chimed at me, reminding me I should be worrying more about what I was supposed to be doing than what they were. Still, gathering it up, I thought back on the things I'd learned in history class about operations like this. I wondered what happened to guys like Marcus if they were unsuccessful. Worse, I wondered what that empty tube meant.

If the Nosferatu didn't attack the women like Alice, what did?

A flash of movement caught the corner of my eye just then, the monitors showing a team of security guards running down a corridor towards us. Apparently, there were security measures we missed. Running out of the room, tucking the link away, I yelled to them, "We've got company!"

Dulaf's already tense muscles flexed one more time, their slender form moving ever so slightly as she effortlessly ripped the monitor from the console and threw it aside. Shooting me a look over her shoulder, her eyes narrowed like daggers, she responded grimly, "Let's fry the place and get the hell out."

A little chill ran up my spine, looking around the room and realizing we might not be allowed to do something like that. Even if this felt morally wrong, we were the police for these people, not random vandals. Then again, we *had* already broken in.

Cutting off my train of thought, Lucian lifted a Will-O-Wisp in front of my face and clicked the button. "We have a moral obligation to do anything we can to defend the rights of Alters," he said with a similarly cold tone, "including turning this place inside out."

I took the Wisp from him and nodded, pulling another from my belt and running off to the far corner of the room. Planting the Wisps around the room, setting them to be trigger activated, I repeatedly told myself they were right, we had to do this. If it was really our government, I realized, this was probably going to be the last "moral obligation" I was going to be filling as an agent. Hell, it might have been the last I was going to fill as a free man.

Pushing the thought aside, I stepped back from one before hearing the growing whine of another activating behind me and seeing Dulaf dash for the corridor we entered through. The sound of her feet falling against the floor nearly blended with the sound of a lot more footsteps coming towards one of those doors.

Lucian stepped ahead of me and ran back for that door. The footsteps beyond were getting close enough to practically count them. But he didn't slow, he didn't hesitate, he just leapt at the door and kicked it off its hinges right into the face of the group on the other side. Tumbling, crashing and grunts were muffled by a face full of door, a lean figure somehow plowing through what seemed to be a half dozen men.

He nodded back to me and ran for our exit, chucking a Banshee over his shoulder to add salt to the wound. The shriek shook the tubes, the blue fluid bubbling and the bodies rattling inside. As I started to follow, a stray hand struck the glass near my face.

Startled, I fired a shot through the tube, burning a hole into the glass and causing a leak. A figure started to take shape at the faded end of the arm. For a moment, the guards under the door stopped existing to me, Dulaf and Lucian with them, and all I could see was the looming body ahead of me. Easily eight feet tall, a striking silhouette like the outline of a statue, it blocked any light behind it as the fluids continued to drain from my accidental hole. Finally getting a good look at the hand against the glass, limply hanging in the quickly thinning pool, I realized it could have palmed my head and easily held on.

"Come on!" Lucian called out, waving to the tunnel.

I stepped back from the tube while the sound of guns cocking echoed through the room. Instinctively I dropped my head just in time for bullets to rip through the glass. My legs took over and I scrambled away from that thing as fast as I could, firing a few blind shots back in their direction.

Lucian stepped over confidently and took a few, clearly more controlled, shots over my head. A loud crack rung out, the wiring behind the wall frying in an instant as the heated gas burst through the cover of a light switch. The lights went dark and the guards in the room scrambled to get a better view of us. Unfortunately for them, we were gone.

That narrow tunnel we came through seemed a lot less narrow during an adrenaline-fueled rush. Lucian was ahead of me, his lithe frame moving like he had all the room in the world. He scrambled like a feral animal, his hands lashing out to grab onto surfaces and pull himself along faster, using the narrow space to his advantage. Reaching Dulaf, who stood her ground half way through the corridor, he deftly stepped around her, disproving the idea that only one person could walk that path at a time.

Pressing against the wall and trying to slide by as easily as Lucian, I couldn't help but push her back up against the opposite wall. She backed up as hard as she could, keeping one arm down at her side, staring down the hall with an intense look in her eyes. Grabbing my coat by the shoulder, she shoved me ahead and pulled her other arm up, lifting "Sexy" into the air and leveling it at the guards behind me.

The pulsing hum of the shots sweeping across the tunnel mouth echoed off the metal walls. The light off the ionized shots lit the corridor, backlighting her as I watched from the other side. Hearing the men panic and scatter from the shots, I realized it was my turn.

"Wisps!" I yelled, getting the trigger ready. Lucian ducked at the opposite end of the tunnel and covered his head while I hit the button.

The confused, overwhelmed grunting and yelling from the men hiding from Dulaf's wrath only got more tormented as the whole room lit up around them and every electronic in the area started to fry. The shrill hissing and crackling sounds of the consoles breaking down filled the air and blended with their screams to form an unnatural wailing. Dulaf stood there, staring defiantly into the blinding light, her rifle continuing to ring out, nearly drowned out by the sounds beyond.

As the light started to clear and the room at the end fell into shadows, she turned to me and we made our escape under the dim glow of phosphorescent markings on the walls. The shadow of Lucian stood ahead of us, hands pressed to each wall with a strong stance. As we neared, a loud twisting metal crunch sound rang out ahead of us, his hands pulling away from two rods firmly pressed into the walls like they were thumbtacks.

Stepping out to the alcove, Lucian waved us through. Shots rang out behind us, the guards apparently deciding a blind shot was better than none. Whizzing past us, I felt the small wind break from the bullet, my hair moving slightly like it'd been a gentle breeze, but my heart practically jumped out of my chest.

It was damned close to my head.

Dropping to a knee and throwing my weight forward, I got as low as I could by shoulder rolling into the alcove. Anything was worth getting my head clear of whatever was blindly firing past us. Dulaf ran out with her head low, spinning on a heel as she exited and leaping backwards from the door, soaring into the open air and falling over the edge. She fired back at the hallway as long as she could, as if the gesture was as simple as giving them the finger on her way out the door.

Lucian chuckled, ducking the shots zipping by, nodding to me to get out too. Returning to my feet as Dulaf vanished past the edge, I darted after her, forgetting the grips I'd had wedged into the corner, and leapt off the platform, diving for the water and hoping I wouldn't hit the boat instead. As I cleared the edge and was starting down I could see the brief flash of Lucian stepping back into the entry way and firing two shots into the room, winging the rods he'd anchored into the wall and turning them ever so slightly.

As I dropped out of sight, I could hear the tell-tale bang of Manticores detonating, the whistling zip and rain-like sound of the ricochets ringing through the hall. The stunned cries of the guards became distant and easily forgotten as I looked down and realized just how fast the ocean waves were approaching. I hit the water hard despite what I hoped was a perfect dive. It rushed past me hard and fast, pulling the visor up over my head and stinging my eyes. When I could look up again, blurry and hazy, I saw the boat practically overhead, the slight foam where I entered no more than a couple feet from its hull.

I nearly went through the damn thing.

Surfacing, I grabbed onto the edge of the deck, gasping to recover the air the impact had squeezed out of me. Dulaf's hand reached out and grabbed me by the wrist, quickly and effortlessly lifting me from the water and rolling me out across the deck. Looking up at her, a crimson streak was running down the lobe of her slender ear, a gash out near the point.

"You're hit," I said breathlessly.

She just nodded and dragged me off the center of the deck, running a command off her link with the other hand and moving the boat away from the facility. "Yeah," she said coolly, "no time for that right now."

Sitting up, I watched the widening gap between us and the platform, hearing the banging sounds and watching the lights flash up on the high wall. Looking to her, I asked tensely, "Are we just leaving him there?"

She shook her head, steering the ship with her link and keeping her eyes on the status updates flashing across her screen, the blood from her ear starting to run down her jaw to her neck. "We're the only ones that can swim," she said. "He'd never be able to jump down to the ship the regular way."

I looked back to the platform, listening to the ringing of the shots fired through the metal frame. It was hard to make out anything in that corner of the facility, with or without the visor. The sound of the Helios was too distant to hear anymore, so I couldn't be sure if Lucian was giving as good as he got. Suddenly there was a faint shadow darting out of that alcove and up across the hull like a flea jumping across a dog.

He made it up the side of the facility the way he had before and headed towards the deck. Sirens blared as he reached the top and vanished over the edge. Dulaf nodded out of the corner of my eye and turned the ship to circle around the platform, headed to the docks we'd entered before. Speeding along, she pushed the ship to its limits, tilting hard enough that one side of the boat was nearly submerged while the other side sprayed a wall of water high into the air.

Bracing myself, all I could do was watch as she flew towards the docks and grazed past them with reckless abandonment. Lucian sprinted up the length of it after apparently leapfrogging across the facility. With one last jump, he leapt off the end of the dock and out towards the ship as Dulaf made a sharp, hard turn. I was thrown across the small deck while she exposed the side to Lucian and he came bursting through the canopy, tumbling over me.

Looking up, dazed, I saw into his grinning face as he sat comfortably where I'd been sitting before I was flung like a ragdoll. Sarcastically, he said, "Thanks for coming to pick me up, I always hated walking on water."

Dulaf cranked the controls up and fled for land, somehow finding room for the craft to accelerate as we left the horror show behind in a fine mist, the distant sirens fading into the sound of the ocean and the roar of the engine.

Chapter 17
Obscuring Sindri

The ride back to Seattle was probably fairly quiet in my car. I imagine it was a solemn moment for my Alter friends. But I wouldn't know because I ended up on the motorcycle instead. We were taking the long way to avoid being followed and that meant we had to put Lucian in the car with the tinted windows.

I didn't mind a bit.

The thing cooked like a bat out of hell with its ass on fire. I broke the speed limit at least a couple times on the way home, not looking at the gauge past the flies randomly splattering across the helmet visor. I think I heard them telling me to slow the hell down over the radio. Unfortunately, it was hard to make out their words over the sounds of my giddy laughter.

I wasn't very concerned about traffic. The route was considerably longer than the one we took across the north side of Olympic National Park, passing the west-end and going around the south-side to circle back into Seattle. It was a strangely quiet stretch of road so long as everyone ignored the maniac trying to break the sound barrier on an electric bike. In fact, nothing much was out there besides a few odd sights scattered across the landscape.

Quite a few Alter shrines dotted the roadside, a common sight in certain parts of the world. Anywhere that could be connected to an Alter race in pop culture would be littered with the things, usually actors who weren't even Alters and generally not even from the same franchises. In this place, it was easiest to find people from Vampire and Werewolf movies and TV shows – and rarely the good ones. Their soggy cardboard cutouts were covered in offerings of what I hoped to just be animal blood. At least one actor with a popular shrine faced down a crazed fan with a pair of scissors once. You could never really be sure what lengths these people would go to.

At one point I thought it was just a joke when someone said she was trying to get a sample to clone him. However, after the night I had, I wasn't so sure anymore. People could apparently go to great lengths without anyone noticing. Who's to know what dark, twisted things could be done by someone with enough money and the right connections? At the very least her creation wouldn't have been a homicidal monster.

Maybe a bad actor, but that's not a crime the last I checked.

Our route brought us towards the city just as the silver line started to break the horizon over the skyline. It was starting to creep into that time of morning when Seattle finally went quiet, the changing of the guard between the mostly nocturnal Alters and their daylight cousins. The faint light of the sun past the horizon caused the phosphorescent murals of the city to slowly fade from sight. We coasted down the street, heading into Fangtown and on the way back to the headquarters, passing through the city as it gradually returned to normal.

The quiet little village started to look like any other part of the city besides the covered walkways bridging the few businesses open after dawn. Peering over my shoulder, I admired myself on the back of the bike as I was reflected on those walkways. Looking in that direction, a sign soon caught my eye and I realized I'd missed one of the most important parts of the day. So I stopped at Ahab's.

Climbing off the bike, I watched the others pass me in the car and stop another couple spaces down the sidewalk where the shadows could cover Lucian. They stepped out and nodded to me, obviously understanding my intentions to chug coffee and possibly snort the grounds to keep myself functioning for another couple hours. Looking at them, I figured it was probably about the same, especially for Dulaf and her usual day shift hours. Of course, their growing grins told me another reason they stopped.

Bemused, I asked, "You're going to pull rank on me, aren't you?"

Dulaf laughed and practically skipped over, slapping my shoulder and answering, "Yep!"

Shaking my head, I walked in with the greedy Alters looming at my back with their sinister expressions. The room

174

inside was strangely quiet, the faint sound of Alter Jazz playing in the background, only half of it audible to me and all of it strangely low volume compared to usual. The tables were mostly empty, a couple Alters still in the seats, notably daytime Fae who weren't afraid of the coming dawn. And behind the counter, despite the fact I was sure sunlight didn't agree with his kind, stood Trey, waving at us and going to get our order before I'd even had a chance to make it.

"Sit," he said, gesturing over his shoulder. "I figure if you guys are showing up this late then you've had an interesting night."

Dulaf and Lucian sat at the table closest to the counter, just under the partially concealed speakers playing the music, the two of them moving their heads to what I assumed were notes I couldn't hear. I hesitated and peered across the room to my table out by the window, thinking for a moment I could ditch them and sit where I always did. My better judgment was that it'd be best to keep an eye on them since I was covering their tabs.

Sitting by them, I took off my gloves and put them down on the table, feeling just how wet they'd become over the course of the night. I'd been in the ocean twice after midnight and somehow didn't notice the cold the entire time. Though the clothes were well insulated, I think a good deal of it was because it'd been the first time my hands had touched reasonably warm air since sunset. Flexing my fingers, I also realized several hours on the bike had made them a little stiff. I was definitely going to sleep well through the day, provided I made it that long.

"I think I'm just going to take the day off," Dulaf said listlessly, staring at the table. "I'm sure I could push through the shift but I'm not even happy with the idea of going home right now."

Lucian nodded and looked out the window, the tinted glass slowly darkening against the rising sun. "Purgatory doesn't quite seem so safe," he remarked, "when you consider what Argyre is apparently willing to do."

Watching him, I thought about what Dulaf had said about the people who could have been involved and the implication Lucian would know them. I knew already that he wasn't, but I wouldn't

175

have been honest with myself if I didn't admit that was just wishful thinking and a blind guess. Tapping my knuckles against the table, I felt the notion sinking in along with the weight of a long night. My arm started to throb lightly from a night of dragging myself up a steel wall and paddling through ocean currents. And as the sound of my pulse echoed in my ears, I just shot it out without warning.

"Do you know who did this?" I asked point-blank.

If the room wasn't quiet before, it sure as hell was right then. The two of them fell eerily silent and their eyes turned my way. Dulaf seemed almost understanding of it with a softer, warmer look in her eyes bordering on concern. Lucian, meanwhile, was incredibly unnerving by how unfazed he looked by it. A chill ran down my spine as he looked at me unwavering with a cold, steely gaze. Confidently he said, "I haven't been with that part of the government in a very long time."

I nodded and averted my eyes back to the counter. Trey's friendly face greeted me as he stood next to the table with a tray and a set of drinks.

"You guys look rough," he said to us, carefully lowering the tray to the table, steam rising off of the cups. The familiar scents of Ahab's all flowed around the three cups on the table, the savory scent of warm roasted coffee after a cold, soggy night mingling with the sweet, slightly metallic scents of things that really didn't belong there.

"But I got just what you all could use," he cheered, putting out a cup with a red lid in front of Lucian. "For Lucian, the red brew special, fresh pack of omega just opened up right now, nice and sweet."

For Dulaf, her usual cup of jet fuel. "The double mocha triple filtered omega red with ten shots of espresso."

"And Mr. Boring," he sang, "gets the coffee with cream and two sugars."

I didn't care, I was proud of the fact I was the only one not sucking the blood of an undead pulsating heart. Waving the coffee under my nose, I only hoped it would overwhelm the slightly sweet smell coming off of their cups as they drank the horrors within.

"You should really cut the caffeine though," he said. I looked to him thinking he was directing his comments towards Dulaf, only to see his eyes squarely on me.

"What, you're talking about me?" I asked, shocked. "You realize the girl across the table should be lifting off like a hummingbird, right?"

Trey laughed and put a hand on Dulaf's shoulder, smirking at me. "She wasn't the one that knocked Anatole on his ass."

"You know about that already?" I asked, frustrated. "How come everyone knew this guy except me?"

Trey replied sarcastically, "You mean you *don't* get the Incubus newsletter?"

I was not amused. Sipping my coffee, I just scanned the room and watched the others around me. The few that were in there weren't hard to identify. They were clearly Faelish, a lot of them visibly so, like the Dwarves in the corner making a small building of sugar packets, standing on their chairs to reach the center. To their right sat a Brounie couple, husband eyeing the Dwarves' project curiously and wife pouring enough honey into her cup to give Dulaf diabetic shock. And as I looked past them my eyes met with a beautiful face across the room.

A Nereid sat in the corner with an olive complexion, sea-foam green eyes and dark wavy hair. She gazed back at me from across the room. After a second she smiled warmly and I smiled back. For a moment, I forgot all of the problems of the night, until she lifted a finger and poked the top of her head.

I spent a confused moment wondering if she might be crazy as she continued to smile, starting to giggle at my new expression. Finally, I realized she was gesturing for me. Reaching up, I found a bit of kelp there that I'd somehow missed and no one had pointed out. Though, it did explain the strange aquarium smell I had in the helmet for the whole ride in.

Dulaf laughed and shook her head. "Oh man, you should have seen the look on your face for the couple seconds you thought you had a chance."

"Hey," I protested, "she smiled at me too!"

Slyly, Lucian remarked, "Maybe she was hungry."

I sighed and rested the cup on the table, looking between the two of them. "So," I started hesitantly, "How do we track down a creature we only just discovered tonight?"

Dulaf's smile faded and she swirled her cup idly, watching the contents mix. Lucian rested his cup in his palm and watched the steam rise from it. Looking up, he nodded lightly and said, "We figure out where it's been, where it's going, and how it thinks."

Drinking, Dulaf murmured, "There's always a pattern of behavior."

"Not that we know how it's supposed to act," Lucian said grimly. "No one knows what this thing was programmed to do in that tube. Who even knows what they're telling it to do right now?"

The thought wasn't comforting. We were dealing with something born and bred to serve a function. It was made from the best parts of whatever those guys at Sindri could patch together. Though, the fact they needed to release that Nosferatu didn't quite make sense.

Idly thinking aloud, I said, "Unless it's not acting like it's supposed to."

The two of them looked at me, Lucian's eyebrow quirked while Dulaf's ears slowly rose. It was uncomfortable watching them watch me. Squirming, I continued with a slight stammer, "Well, if it was acting the way it was supposed to be, then they wouldn't have gone so long without catching it."

Sounding slightly awed by the fact I figured it out, Dulaf commented, "That's why they worked so hard to make a cover-up instead of just silver-lining it and leaving it there."

Nodding, I continued, "Exactly, this thing was supposed to be controlled but it's gone way off the grid. It's gone so badly that they released that Nosferatu to try to cover their tracks in case it went on too long for the silver-line to work."

Dulaf's mood was rising considerably, sounding almost excited when she said, "And you can't have soldiers just go berserk in the middle of a metropolis. So we track it by what it's been doing and don't worry about what it was supposed to be doing."

I nodded, glancing between them. "We just have to figure out when it got out, what's happened since it got out and see if there's anything else it does besides attack women in the middle of the night."

Lucian tensed as the words left my mouth, lowering his cup to the table and frowning. "It really has only been women, hasn't it?"

Dulaf stared at him for a moment before asking no one in particular, "Why would an out of control monster have a pattern?"

"Maybe if we discover a pattern we'll figure out the motive," I said hopefully. "But we're going to need to find out more about this company and the people that work there, I think."

Lucian nodded and remarked, "There's always a crack in the cover-up. We just have to find one we can use. One of the researchers might be willing to talk if we can isolate them."

"You're assuming they don't just live on that platform," Dulaf chided. "Even if there were boats there, we don't know they were the ones to use that building. For all we know that was just the visitors' center."

"Then we find out for sure," I said to her. "Go in today, take a look through the Oracle System's satellite feed and see how much activity has been around that building. If there's a lot of traffic in and out of it every day..."

Annoyed, Dulaf interjected, "Then they live on the mainland, right."

Nodding, I glanced past her, seeing a familiar bolt of red hair as Desmond Kelly wandered in, his tablet under his arm. "Meanwhile," I said, getting up, "I think I can try to get more information about the company from someone I met earlier."

Dulaf glanced over and smiled broadly with a mischievous glint in her eyes. She'd met Desmond once before in the prison, commenting he was "adorable" during an alcohol fueled rage that got him stuck in a holding cell. "Oh, not Desmond," she said, giggling, "You think he could help?"

I nodded. "We were talking about medical companies a couple days ago. He works the stock market and said some medical technologies were on the rise. I imagine he knows more than we do right now, at least."

Glancing to the darkening windows, Lucian stood with me and patted my shoulder. "Take it easy for now," he said. "I'll meet with you two after the sun sets to see what you've gathered. It's getting a little too bright for my tastes."

I gave him a simple nod and a light wave before walking over to strike up a conversation with Desmond. He sat in the same place he had before, scrolling through the news idly, scanning the headlines for anything of interest and apparently finding none. Getting closer, I suddenly wasn't sure how you would ask someone what they knew about something like this.

Rushing past me, Dulaf squealed, "Dessy!"

Looking up, the diminutive Irishman smiled broadly and winked at her. "Dulaf, my sweet, how's my favorite officer?"

"Could be better," she said earnestly. "But you're looking good! Sticking with the rehab program?"

He laughed heartily and shook his head, waving at her. "Oh not a bit," he said, "I just make sure not to get caught anymore."

The two shared a laugh over it, Dulaf leaning over and kissing his cheek. "You stay out of trouble, okay?"

The little man blushed, his face almost as red as his hair, smiling to her as he winked again and wiggled his eyebrows. Whimsically, he said, "The trouble is usually the fun part."

She smirked and shook her head, standing and backing out of the way. Gesturing to me, she nodded and said, "My friend Nate has some questions he thinks you might know the answers to. Do you think you can give him what he needs?"

I stood there and watched the two of them, feeling strangely uneasy about watching her talk to the guy. It wasn't the first time I'd seen her halfway flirting with someone, but it was more uncomfortable than usual this time. Trying to shake it off, I stepped in and nodded to him.

"Mr. Kelly, you mentioned investments into medical technology earlier."

"Please," he said, waving, "Desmond for a friend."

"Right, okay," I replied, sitting across from him, "Desmond it is."

180

Dulaf rolled her eyes and patted my shoulder, gesturing with her free hand for me to give her something. "Give me your link," she said, waving her finger, "So I can go through those files."

I felt a little sheepish; I thought she might have been asking for money at first. Handing it over to her, she quickly turned to walk away, waving over her shoulder with the link in one hand and cup in the other. I glanced her way and watched her exit, feeling a touch of concern that I couldn't quite understand.

"What's on your mind, m'boy?" Desmond asked, looking through the news again.

Shaking off the feeling, I turned back to Desmond and answered, "You were talking about a company a couple days ago that could make compatible body parts without DNA. That company wouldn't happen to be Sindri, would it?"

He lowered the tablet, fiery eyebrow rising lightly as he did. "Sure would be, m'boy. But why would you be asking about them right now?"

"Well," I started to reply, trailing off as I second-guessed my approach. "What do you know about their operations? Is their headquarters local? What kind of people do they employ?"

He put the tablet down entirely and laced his fingers together, leaning towards me to look across the table. "You wouldn't happen to be looking to start a portfolio yourself, would you?"

It wasn't exactly the response I expected, but it worked.

"Well," I said, grinning sheepishly, "ACTF pension is still up in the air."

He chuckled and nodded along. "Never know when the hammer might drop and the organization turns tail and runs, eh?"

Smiling, I shrugged and nodded, playing along. He probably wouldn't have responded badly to the truth, but I didn't want to give out the information I had in exchange of information he *might* have had.

"They have an offshore platform," he said. "The employees have to go back and forth in little boats to make it to work, passing through a checkpoint and having their route controlled. It's surprisingly secured for a pharmaceutical company."

"Why would they be so worried about security?" I asked quietly, leaning in like we were discussing national secrets.

He looked around at the rest of the patrons in the shop with the same sort of suspicion. Quietly, secretively, he whispered, "I heard they were suspecting sabotage about a year ago, one of their researchers died and their setup for their employees changed."

"Someone died?" I asked. "Was it really sabotage?"

The little man shrugged his shoulders and shook his head. He leaned back a bit and said in a bit more confident tone, "No one knows for sure, in fact the incident was mostly swept under the rug."

Another cover-up was the last thing I needed at a time like this. But it was something I should have been expecting none-the-less. Frustrated, I asked, "So besides covering it up, what did they do to deal with it?"

Rubbing the back of his neck and starting to look slightly uncomfortable in his seat, he replied, "The word I've got is that no one enters or leaves that place without someone knowing for sure they're coming and going. They don't really much care about visitors, for instance, being in their labs because the visitors are always being watched."

Leaning forward again, he whispered with a curious, almost amused tone, "I heard they have a lab so wired with motion detectors that some of the researchers are worried the room could cook them."

The vision of a room filled with red beams crossed my mind, a thought I quickly suppressed so I could continue to fake ignorance. "Why not use sonar based detectors then?"

He shrugged. "I guess something in that room is sensitive to sound."

I can't accurately describe the feeling I had in that moment. It was like feeling my chest getting ready to leap out of my body and dance around the room. That "something" could have only been a couple objects in the entire lab, if it was the lab I was thinking of, and I've yet to see one of the simple sound-based motion detectors damage a modern console. The tubes and the fluid inside might have been sensitive to sound in some small part. Still, something deep down told me I was just given a clue on how to take the thing down if we found it. After all of the tinkering, they left the things with a pretty clear flaw if my luck was holding out.

"Where'd you find this out, Desmond?" I asked, curious if I could follow the source.

He laughed and waved at me off-handedly. "You think I'd give up my sources so easily?" he mused, chuckling. "I'm not a new player on the field, m'boy."

"Come on, what threat am I to you?" I asked, doing my best to smile back at him. "I'm just trying to figure out how accurate your information is."

He looked around the room again, lowered his voice and raised his eyebrow. "Not all of the researchers appreciate being watched all the time, you know."

I wasn't sure if I could press it further, there was a chance he might not want to give up more information about these precious contacts. But part of me knew I had to take my shot.

"So," I started, trying to act casually about it, "Would you have a list of some of these researchers?"

Looking me over warily, he raised that eyebrow again. A little motion in his face suggested to me he was probably chewing his lip. Normally the visor would have filled in the rest, but wearing it while having a "casual chat" would have made it not so "casual" anymore.

Feeling the energy of the conversation starting to shift, I chuckled and said, "Can you blame a guy for trying to double check his information?"

The fiery eyebrows lifted a bit more and a sly smirk crossed the little man's face. "You know something too, don't you?"

He laced his fingers together again and rested them on the table. Slyly, he said, "I want in."

Chapter 18
Yearning Facts

I couldn't give him everything he wanted to know with an ongoing investigation and a pretty high-level conspiracy at hand. I was a little irked that my casual act failed so miserably. But Leprechauns are infamous for the ability to see past bullshit – either for the fact they're fairy-folk or because they've talked to so many drunks.

The luck was on my side for this instance. He really only wanted to know if there was an investigation going on. Somehow, according to him, that was enough to make him a lot of money. I was sure there was more to discuss about that, but I didn't figure it would be legal for either one of us so I left it at that.

For my efforts, though, I walked out of Ahab's triumphantly with a list of names written on a napkin. I was a little annoyed to not have the link at the time, seeing as Dulaf swiped it and walked away to analyze it. Though that didn't quite match how pissed I was when I walked out and realized that she'd also taken my car. Annoyed, I really didn't have a lot of recourse to take against her, so I did the only thing I could in that situation... I walked home.

There was still another hour or so I could have worked, maybe walk into the headquarters and stand around for a while before clocking out. But after a day way out on the fringe of our jurisdiction there really wasn't anyone who was going to question where I was today. Really, at that point I just had to leave the badge on to be considered "on duty".

I would have called her to give her the list on the way home if she hadn't swiped all my things and forced me to pick up the tab at Ahab's. Unfortunately the hand-link was also my private line during duty and the badge radio wasn't exactly "secured" as far as I knew. The people who I knew in the station were probably okay, but I couldn't be entirely sure about everyone else that could follow the radio traffic at the time. All I could do was drag myself into my apartment and go to my personal phone which I'd left sitting by my bed. At first I was a bit annoyed with myself for that, but swimming in the ocean has a way of ruining most electronics.

Flopping down on the bed was like having my entire body instantly thank me for the opportunity to give in. I wasn't aching as bad as I would have figured, the arm really being the only thing that hurt, but I was pretty tired from hours of driving and the late night swims. It was a long night and I wasn't sure if I actually wanted to extend it by calling her.

I grunted and lifted the phone, staring at it for a moment before deciding to snap a shot with the camera and just send the list that way. Watching the message send, I gave in and closed my eyes hoping for the world to melt away.

There was just one problem: I couldn't sleep. I'm not sure if it was the early morning coffee or just my conscience, but my mind was racing when it should have been shutting down. The partially crumpled list in my hand was drawing my eye, thoughts of Alice lying in the alley haunting me. If that thing was ordered, it was ordered to do that to her. If it was wild, someone lost control of it.

Someone on the list might have even been the one to pull the proverbial trigger. There were roughly a dozen scribbled down hastily in a Leprechaun's tricky handwriting. Some letters were easily interchangeable, possibly being one or the other, hardly any clue except context. I'd heard there was some deep need for them to hide things in plain sight but I hadn't seen it for myself before. Browsing the list, one suddenly leapt out at me: Archibald Faber.

"Well, well Archie," I murmured, "someone's proud of their work."

Debating with myself, I rose from the bed and glanced at my closet, considering getting my fresh uniform and possibly taking a shower. Images passed through my mind as I thought of whether it would be worth staying up all day or not. I could see Alice's arm, the feverish woman living in the same building as a Nosferatu, the haunted faces around the Moirae Club while I was

185

there. But the last I saw run through my mind was the one that made it up: the tears running down Dulaf's face after finding out what these people had been doing.

I couldn't sleep: I had to set things right.

Putting the paper down, I went to the closet and grabbed my spare uniform and some dry gear. I threw them out across the bed and closed the door, getting ready to change before I caught sight of myself in the mirror unmistakably smeared in the dry remains of sludge from the shore.

"Shower first."

Roughly twenty minutes later, second-guessing my decisions, I stepped out into the hallway. I stood outside my door a lot longer than I should have and debated with myself once again before gazing up and catching a strange sight. The ceiling had an odd stain on it I hadn't noticed before, sitting over the top of my landlady's door. It looked like smoke damage but in a color I hadn't seen on a ceiling before. It was a faintly bruise-like image I should have noticed at least out of the corner of my eye.

"I did it a few days ago," a small, frail voice called out to me from across the hall. "You've been too distracted lately to see it."

Looking down, I saw the little old lady in the tie-dye shirt standing across the hall from me, gingerly holding a travel mug in both hands and lifting it to my face. "You should take this," she said warmly, "to put a little pep in your step."

Taking the mug from her, smelling the faint scent of roasted coffee drifting out of it, I replied, "Peeking through minds again, Babs?"

She smiled sweetly and patted my good arm, resting her other hand on the bad arm gently and just running it down to my elbow. "You've been a little louder than usual," she said quietly, brow furrowing, "something's had you in something of a tizzy."

"Yeah," I said, hesitantly, "I guess I've had a rough couple of days."

She nodded, squeezing at my elbow tightly and moving it just a touch. "This thing has been bothering you again."

I glanced at my arm. It had been throbbing more in the last couple days since I found Alice. Looking back into her warm

186

eyes, meeting the compassionate smile crossing her weathered face, I chuckled.

"Ah, I'm getting old," I said jokingly. "You need to tell me your secret to staying so fresh. The weather's been taking it out of me."

She nodded, the smile fading slightly, saying in a hushed tone, "And that poor girl, so sad."

I looked at the mug and took a sip from it, finding a livelier flavor than I was used to, an unusual nutty taste I couldn't quite place. Lifting my eyes from it, I asked, "What's in it, Babs?"

Lightly laughing, she turned away and waved me down the hallway, "Never you mind that, Nate. You just drink up and try to have a nice day, dear."

Closing the door, Babs left me with a haunting question to consider. Barbara Zdunk, a Witch, wouldn't tell me what was in the coffee. I briefly considered throwing it out, picturing the things that could be in her pantry. Unfortunately, she would know, she always knew. Grimacing, I took another swig and walked out.

The sun was blindingly bright at that time of the morning, breaking down the street and shining right into my eyes. Even the visor couldn't quite remove the glare, like a spotlight pointed directly in my face as I made my way up the block to go fetch my car from the short Elven thief. Looking away from it helped, but I kept making eye contact with confused people looking at me like they hadn't seen an agent in the daylight before. Though, knowing our practices, it was a little surreal for both of us. I couldn't help having some fun with it.

"I'm on a special assignment," I said to one staring harder than the rest, "doing a spot check for day-walkers."

Lowering my head and looking at his feet, I slowly looked up and scanned over him with a very measured pace, taking a sip from my mug and raising an eyebrow at him like I'd seen something. His colors on the visor were a solid blue, standard human through and through, but I swear I saw a flash of orange leap in him. It was like I saw his heart skip a beat as he took a ninety-degree turn and crossed the street like a power-walker in training.

And there I was, with my flower decal travel mug, trying my best not laugh.

Sadly I didn't get to do the same to anyone else for the rest of the walk, getting slightly more Fae-type Alters and agents the closer I got to the headquarters. There were quite a few there that had the faint agitated state, standing in line up at the surface reception desk, obviously there to bail out a friend or something equally unpleasant. I tried not to smile at them as I strutted by unimpeded. It was especially annoying of me since the holographic girl at the reception desk stopped dealing with a visitor to turn her head and greet me on the way through.

I found Dulaf in her lab, the minions darting around busily while she sat at a computer. Amelia sat by her side wearing a lab-coat too large for her and a little badge drawn in crayon. The screen was linked to the Oracle system in front of her, some of the data flashing across on my visor as if it were dancing around her. Archie's name floated into the air, a slightly outdated photo sitting almost on top of Dulaf's head.

Walking over quietly, Amelia looked up and smiled while Dulaf seemed to be too engrossed in the screen to notice. Her ears didn't even twitch while I stood behind her, so I made a shushing motion to Amelia and smirked. Amelia nodded quickly and sat back while I set down my coffee cup on another table and pulled off my glove.

There are a lot of things you don't do to an Elf: You don't talk about how feminine their men look, you don't bring attention to the fact they remind you of cat people and you don't flick their ears. But no one ever said anything about a wet-willy. Licking my fingertip, I didn't hesitate a second to jab my finger into her pointy ear.

The scream was a mix of rage and panic and I thoroughly enjoyed it for the split second before her fist jabbed me in the breadbasket. I think I saw colors that didn't exist in the visible spectrum as the wind was knocked out of me. Nearly collapsing, I braced myself on Amelia's chair and wheezed hard while the little girl laughed hysterically.

She was a tiny traitor.

A faint voice of disapproval came from Philip chiming in behind me, "We don't interrupt her while she's working."

I looked back to him, his striking blue eyes looking exhausted, dark circles forming under them. He was haggard for an Elf, not at all like their usual selves and entirely too stressed to be compared to the other two by my side. He looked worse than I felt.

"When'd you last sleep?" I asked.

He looked me in the eye, expression unfazed but ears drooping slightly. "I've slept," he said wearily, putting a folder on the desk in front of Dulaf, "just not well."

I watched him skulk away, shoulders hanging at the same angle as his nimble ears. He was hardly there with the rest of us. Even Xander, who I'd understood to have the same schedule as Philip, darted about the lab space with his usual rigor and energy.

"What's wrong with him?" I asked Dulaf quietly, lightly nodding to Philip.

She studied the back of his head, the tips of her ears starting to ever so slightly drift down like his. "It's nothing," she refuted, "just some rough nights since finding the Winchester case."

It was almost comforting, hearing that I wasn't the only one with a sleepless night from thinking of Alice and the case around her. My stomach was still tight though, reminding me the day wasn't going nearly as well as it would have been if I'd stayed in bed. The nausea was slowly rising, boiling up from my gut and pushing the burning sensation of coffee towards my throat.

"However," Dulaf chided, "you look like the one that's about to be sick."

Trying to smile through the pain, I sarcastically replied, "I can't imagine why I suddenly have stomach pains."

Amelia giggled, spinning in her chair by my side and rending the support from my hand like she hoped to throw me to the floor. I took a deep breath through my nose to try to clear the pain and steady myself. It smelled unusually cheerful for once; the normally sterile and polished smell of the lab was now covered by the scent of wildflowers and cinnamon disks. It was the strongest around Amelia, but a flash of color caught my eye as one of those wildflowers sat in Dulaf's hair by her temple.

189

She returned my gaze and frowned. "What the hell are you doing here?"

I grabbed one of the free chairs in the room and rolled it over, sitting across from her. The wind didn't return to me as I did, the pain only shifting as a warm sensation spreading across my midsection like a slowly dying fire moving across a dry forest. I shrugged and crossed my arms, trying not to hint at my discomfort. "I need my link, my car and anything you've fetched off the link so far."

A deadpan look crossed her face. She turned her chair to face me and looked me over with a skeptical expression. "You're really going to work right now?" she asked. "After all of that?"

Peeking over my shoulder and watching Philip wander around the lab at half mast, I nodded back to her, held out my hand and said, "I think what Philip has is going around."

Amelia stopped spinning her chair and stared at the two us. Her bright eyes narrowed slightly and she wrinkled her nose like the conversation was either boring or frustrating her.

"We're all kind of busy," I said to the little girl, "it's keeping us up all night."

Her expression softened and the little ears lowered slightly. They couldn't quite move like the ones on her elders but they were still able to do just enough to echo the saddened look in her eyes. Solemnly she said, "Like when I had to take care of mom."

It halted me, hearing her say that, reminding me I didn't know her mother's status. After fishing her out of that building and clearing the Nosferatu away, I'd been too caught up with getting to that platform and finding out what was really going on to consider the poor woman in the slum. Eyeing Dulaf, I hoped she could read my intention and answer me about the woman's fate.

She shook her head once, slowly and silently. It was a soft gesture, something I hoped Amelia wouldn't notice while she was looking at me, but it told me everything I needed to know. Just the weight of her expression, the sadness in her eyes, told me that simple shake of the head was the worst possible news.

I just didn't know if Amelia knew.

Reaching over, I patted her head and ruffled her hair lightly. "I used to have to do the same thing," I said to her, lowering my hand and tapping it under her chin. "But you're doing a lot better than I ever did."

She smiled faintly and nodded to me, saying happily, "When she gets better I'll keep an eye on her too."

My heart sank a little. My chair was awkward to sit in now, the feeling coursing through my body telling me to try to get away from it before I could say or do anything to make it worse. I knew what it was like, finding out about something like this, realizing what had happened. I knew what it was like to be left behind like that. I didn't want to have to be there when she found out.

Luckily, Dulaf handed me the link and my keys, giving me a pat on the shoulder.

"Get out of here," she said softly, "before I kick your ass again."

I looked down at the link like it was a life preserver thrown to me in the ocean. Clutching it, I stood up and tucked it away quickly, picking up the flower decal mug and lifting it to them like a toast, nodding my thanks to her. "Just try to take it easy on Philip and Xander," I said, turning to walk out. "And don't you go learning any bad habits from Dulaf, Amelia."

The little voice giggled as I crossed the threshold, calling out to me, "But Dulaf's so cool!"

I looked back before turning the corner and smiled at the round little face. "Yeah, sometimes, even if she swiped my car."

"No," Dulaf corrected, "*Lucian* took your car and went down to the nocturnal wing of the sanctuary so he wouldn't burn."

I felt a little bad just then, realizing I'd jumped to blaming Dulaf for that one a bit too soon. I should have realized my mentor, while certifiably badass, had a long standing problem with sunshine, rainbows and morning dew. Wincing, I smiled sheepishly and said, "Well then, thanks for holding onto my keys for me. Maybe Amelia's right about you."

Turning away and walking out, I swear I could almost see Dulaf blush off to the side. Someone with that sort of ego probably couldn't do something like that, though. So I quickly decided it was just a hallucination from the mix of sleep deprivation, caffeine and whatever else Babs slipped in my coffee. Strangely, the stuff was otherwise making me feel pretty damn good. Whatever was in that peculiar little travel mug, it was like a shot of adrenaline.

So, obviously, it was mind altering at the very least.

I hurried out of the headquarters and through the underground garage, lifting the keys into the air and pressing the button. My car's motors revved with a distinct electric hum from the corner, greeting me like a wild animal in a cage. The lights turned on and guided me over, the doors unlocking as I approached. For a moment, standing at the door, I reconsidered the idea of going out there in the shape I was in. Even if it was helping me now, I feared the crash of Babs' brew.

A thought of Philip wandering the halls back there, haunted by what had happened and not knowing the truth, pushed me into the car. I put the keys in, leaned back slightly in the chair and exhaled, wedging the odd mug into the cup-holder at my side. It didn't fit in any way possible: not by shape, not by color and sure as hell not by pattern. The woman needed to update her decor out of the 1960s. I hated to admit it brought a touch of warmth to the dark interior of the car, almost encouraging me in my altered state to drive out and confront the world.

So I took the wheel and left the garage, loading the address for Archie into the console and getting all the information we had on him, just like the display Dulaf had hovering over her head. Strangely, seeing it all laid out before me, I realized his profile, like so much about this case, had been redacted with the same silver strips that marred every report and piece of evidence gathered before we caught on. Frankly, by this point I was surprised to see his face.

Despite the fact he worked out over the ocean, he lived in a city at least a couple hours inland. Port Angeles is a small town marked as an evacuation point for a Code 88 and only two hours out from Seattle. In all honesty, it wasn't really that small, being the largest city west of Seattle before hitting the ocean that I could think of. It just wasn't a place that really caught the attention of the Alter community outside a small enclave of sea faring breeds. The ACTF, on the other hand, saw it as a safe harbor for a couple reasons.

Just across a small straight from a peninsula on Vancouver Island, we'd marked Port Angeles years ago as a good place to jump the Alters across the border into Victoria, British Columbia. Even before the Seattle headquarters was finished the Force set up a secondary headquarters out that way. Though we trained in the Olympic Mountains, Port Angeles was basically the Cascadia boot camp.

Considering we just trashed that platform, I fully expected someone at that sub-station to be dealing with Sindri security about now. With any luck, I hoped, it wouldn't be the Yeti. I was sure if it got to him, it would have probably been something I would regret.

The drive didn't quite last two hours, a Witch's brew fueled maniac behind the wheel and tunes from the 1970s rocking out from my radio made quick work of what was a pretty scenic trip. The Olympic Mountains out the window were nostalgic to look at from this angle. They painted the horizon, cutting through the sky with slate and green colors contrasted against a vibrant blue sky. I remembered this place, this road, from the time I was first brought to those mountains at the start of my career. I'm sure this was the road we took on the way to the coast as well. At least this time I was awake to see it.

When I arrived to Port Angeles I could see all the places I'd passed through during the time we had leave from the camp, or the times when we just snuck out in hopes the sneaky ninja Elf didn't come cracking down on us. It hadn't been that long, only a couple years at most, but it felt like an eternity. I was a different person in Port Angeles and those years had been practically a lifetime.

Climbing out of the car in front of the station, I saw the black vans parked around it, the Sindri logos printed across the sides in a sparkling metallic paint that caught the sun just right. It was the only real dazzle around an otherwise simple building. The place was constructed in only a couple months as a stopgap measure that was never really meant to last. The headquarters in Seattle is a piece of modern art, a black shard shaped into the form of a flower glowing against the night skyline. The Port Angeles station was a grey brick against a blue backdrop. It was wide and only two stories tall, practically looking like a wall with doors instead of the usual Dwarven craftsmanship you'd expect.

I walked up to the door and hesitated, surveying the number of black vans out front and considering just how much they knew about the team that hit them. We knew when we did it that it was sketchy at best. Though the entire operation was out in the international waters, a place we still had jurisdiction, the idea that Argyre might be backing them lingered while I rested my hand against the frame. Pushing the thought aside, I stepped inside.

The plain look outside was mirrored by the stark interior, looking more like a post office than the familiar environment I was used to. The smell of the sea breeze and the scent of what seemed to be a wet animal were apparent as I stepped on the muddy doormat with the Cascadia branch's logo centered on it. The receptionist, an older man with leathery skin and a silver mustache, sat where I normally would have expected our artificial girl back in Seattle.

"Hello there," he said cheerfully in his raspy voice. Adjusting his thick glasses, he studied me from across the room. "You're not one of ours," he remarked, "come from the big city?"

I nodded and walked closer so he could see the emblems on my sleeves. Trying to use my impressive voice, which I'm sure isn't as impressive as I'd hoped, I introduced myself, "Agent Leone from the Seattle Headquarters, here to investigate a possible witness in the Port Angeles area. Just letting you know the extra signal wandering the city was me."

The old man nodded and pushed his glasses back, turning to a keyboard on his desk and idly commenting, "I'll just put the note in the system here then, wait here for a minute."

He hunted and pecked his way across the thing. I was surprised someone in this age couldn't use a keyboard but assumed the man was just old enough to be forgetting where the keys were. Even as a child my grandparents knew how to type. So, trying not to show my impatience I turned away and rested against the counter, looking out the glass door of the entrance.

The shadow to step through was almost instantly recognizable by its posture. It was stiff, rigid and moving like someone on the verge of road rage. With the cold, harsh voice, the figure called out to me, "Leone, funny seeing you here."

My body tensed just from the sound. It wasn't a pleasant voice and I was surprised to know he bothered to look up my name. It took a moment to control my disdain. Pushing up my shades, I let it filter out the backlight so I could see his uncomfortable scowl clearly. Resisting the urge to sigh, I just stood straight and crossed my arms, replying just as coldly, "Hello, Carlson."

Chapter 19
Sacred Flowers

There was a palpable tension on the air as we stood on opposite ends of the plain white tile floor under the glow and faint buzz of rather old and shoddy fluorescent lights. I couldn't say I was surprised to see the man there, given what had happened and the general vibe I'd gotten that he was connected to the silver line. I was just more annoyed *he'd* found me than I would have been if it were Sindri security. At least those guys could claim to have a legitimate beef.

Lynch drove away in a remarkably un-dented car while Carlson remarked smugly, "You're a little far outside of your jurisdiction, aren't you?"

"International gendarmerie," I replied a little snottily, "My jurisdiction is where ever the hell I'm standing."

The raspy chuckle behind me let me know the receptionist approved as the typing stopped and I heard the chime from the system update.

"You're good to go, Leone," he said, upbeat. "We'll keep watch over you if there's any trouble."

I nodded back to the old man and started for the door, Carlson turning to watch me pass. Lowering his sunglasses he chimed in, "Of course there wouldn't be any trouble if you weren't putting your nose where it didn't belong."

My better judgment told me to keep on moving and ignore he existed. It wasn't easy, some cheap cologne leaving an overwhelming impression of the man floating by the door. I turned my head to look into his eyes and watched his aura, a faint orange bleeding through the normal human blue. He was agitated about something more than just the stick up his ass.

Looking at him and seeing the aura, I almost didn't notice what he'd just said. At least, I didn't fully register it at the time. He'd told me I was putting my nose somewhere it didn't belong and that meant that there was still something to put my nose in.

Suddenly smirking, I replied warmly to him, "Well that's okay, I'm just here to find a witness, there's nothing to stick my nose into anymore, right? We caught that Nosferatu a couple nights ago so it shouldn't really be a problem."

Carlson's tense expression faded as his tightened jaw suddenly slacked while he realized what he'd just said. So convinced I was there to get involved in his case, he'd overlooked the fact the official story said the case was over. Sure, he might have been right about me and my motives, but I wasn't about to let him know that.

"It was nice talking to you," I said, patting his shoulder. "Keep out of trouble."

Walking out, I smiled the whole way back to the car, a little spring in my step. I got back in, took the final swig out of Babs' old mug and drove away. Something about the encounter was actually uplifting for me, I found myself whistling one of Lucian's old show-tunes about a block away. Maybe I'm just an ass, but it felt good.

Archie's house was out towards the mountains on the horizon and just on the fringe between the city of Port Angeles and the edge of the wilderness beyond. The neighborhood out that way was actually vaguely familiar to me. I could recall passing by parts of it in the back of one of the ACTF vans on the way up to getting hunted down by a furry Chinese man. I wondered if the things at Sindri were already at work when I crossed this pleasant neighborhood the first time through.

Unfortunately, the present day was a lot less pleasant, or at least a lot more obvious about its bad vibes. Lynch and Carlson's car was parked on the corner, Lynch's shadow sitting in the driver's seat unmoving as I passed. When I approached Archie's house, I could see the car driving off in my rear-view, turning back towards the station and speeding away. I briefly considered pulling him over for speeding just for more shits and giggles but decided I preferred to just let them go – so long as it was somewhere else.

Archie's house caught my eye as I decided to ignore the Feds again. It was small home, one story with a white picket fence and a well-groomed but strangely unnatural garden of roses surrounding it. They seemed too bright, like they'd never been sick or dry. It was the garden of someone who could spend all day, every day working on maintaining them and, as far as I knew, that wasn't Archie's schedule.

When I came to a stop in front of it, looking at the cream walls and the tan roof, I could see the colorful decorations of lawn gnomes peeking out from between the bushes like they were watching for me. For most people this wouldn't have been all that unnerving, lawn gnomes being tacky but harmless. For someone like me? I considered he might have had a Gnome security detail I didn't know about.

The Gnome people are the smallest of all the shorter Fae I've known but they're scrappy as all hell and brave in numbers. The Red Caps alone were infamous for their ferocity and quick as all hell. Of course, my paranoia probably wasn't helped by whatever I'd been drinking all morning. But the visor didn't read any biometrics out of the bushes so I felt safe enough to at least climb out of the car.

As I approached the fence I saw the small house-shaped mailbox to my left, "Faber" written across it in an old English text. I didn't exactly see any of this fitting the nervous, mawkish man that I met on that platform. It all seemed too cute and over-involved in the landscaping. And the closer I got, the nearer to those strangely bright roses, the more that feeling grew. They were absolutely perfect, even for a flower laymen like me. The petals just opened in such an orderly, ornate way, unfurled for all they were worth and displaying a shade of red you'd rarely see in nature. I had to lower my shades to confirm it wasn't just the visor screwing with my perception.

Standing there, looking for a sign they might have been plastic, I could smell them all around me and see the last remains of morning dew drip off one of the lower buds that still sat partially in the shade. It was curled up, unlike the rest, just starting to open now that the sun was beginning to reach it. These flowers were real and being taken care of very well. Someone cared deeply about this garden.

I pushed the visor back, ignored those thoughts and rang the doorbell, a faint chiming sound like an old grandfather clock sounding at the back of the house. It fell quiet around me aside from a faint rustling as a breeze flowed over the bushes and filled my lungs with rose scented air. It was cool, refreshing and I turned slightly to face it, the sun shining on my face. I hadn't actually been awake at this time of day in a really long time. It was nice to take it in for that one moment.

And I stood like that until the door opened, the half-awake Archie standing in a robe and peering through the crack. His schedule was a lot like mine, apparently. His hair, what was left of it, was a rat nest fringing the top of his head. His glasses were on slightly crooked and his robe was hastily tied closed. The robe itself, an old, stained red one with a small Sindri logo on it, was looking unlike the landscape outside, hardly washed in who knows how long. And his aura, shining through the visor, was barely there, much like the man himself.

"Doctor Faber, good morning," I said, surprisingly chipper. "I need to ask you a couple of questions about what we talked about last night and the operations around Sindri."

He warily pushed back his glasses and took a long, hard look at me. His brow was furrowed, his nose wrinkled and his mouth partially open. In his half-awake state, I was pretty sure he didn't remember being visited by a couple of agents the night before. Tapping my badge, I gave him a brief reminder. "Agent Leone, from the ACTF, we met last night."

His face lit up, an expression of understanding crossing it as he nodded and opened the door wider. Exhausted but somehow pleased to see me, he waved me inside and said abruptly, "Yes, yes, come on in!"

The interior was strangely dusty, the air slightly stale as I entered. The furniture in the living room to my right was faded under the thick dust covering the room, the colors a shadow of themselves like the grey and brown had saturated into the very fiber. The furniture that wasn't covered in dust was just covered in plastic like an old woman's house and seemingly left that way for ages.

Hardly any lights were on inside, though given how he looked I figured he was sleeping before I rang the bell. The interior was still strangely vacant of any sign of life despite the man standing right next to me.

Jittery, Archie hurried past me and towards a kitchen down the hall, waving for me to follow. "Come, come," he beckoned, "do you like coffee?"

I started to follow him, looking into the living room again as we left it behind, seeing old photos hanging on the wall and sitting on the tables. One with a small wooden frame sat on a corner table at the end of a loveseat showed a younger Archie from the days of his profile. He stood in a mountain landscape, a young woman with golden hair standing at his side, smiling broadly under a straw hat in a blue sundress. The man in the photo seemed so much calmer, serene, like he had no concerns in the world.

Looking at the back of his head in the modern day, I could hardly believe they were the same man.

"I apologize for the mess," he said, walking through to the kitchen and turning on the light. "I don't really have much time to clean these days, you understand."

I nodded and followed him into the kitchen, glancing around and responding almost absently, "not enough hours in the day."

The kitchen was much better maintained than the living room, the floors mopped and the counters wiped down, though there wasn't much there to maintain. The appliances were modern, but only covered the bare essentials: a toaster oven, coffee pot, microwave and a refrigerator. A small table sat in the corner with only two simple wooden chairs. A photo of the woman with the golden hair hung over that space, the only real decoration in the otherwise spartan room. She stood against the backdrop of yet another mountain, hair catching the light of the setting sun as she smiled broadly under the warm light of a rose colored sky.

The realization of what I was looking at settled over me like a thick, chilling fog. I was standing in front of a shrine. The house was in disrepair, left to collect dust and haunted by memories of times long past. Furniture showed when things were used and it was clear this was the only room he actually touched. He'd placed one photo in the entire kitchen, in the room that seemed to be where he did everything while home. I'd seen it before, rooms left the way they had been the last time someone was there, old pieces of furniture left untouched because it had belonged to them. I'd seen an old chair, a recliner, sitting in a corner and left as little more than a memento while wounds could heal.

Almost to myself, not really even sure if I was loud enough for him to hear, I murmured, "The garden was hers."

Breathlessly, he said behind me, "She couldn't take care of it anymore, so I bred it to take care of itself."

Placing a cup of coffee on the table under the photo, he gestured to one of the two simple chairs in the room and nodded. Sitting, I peered at the photo again and then across to him, considering whether or not I should have my visor on. Was it necessary to read the man's emotions? Would it be disrespectful? Could I see anything from it?

Folding them quietly and slipping them into a pouch on my belt, I took the cup and lifted it, wondering if I should tell him about the great amounts of caffeine I'd already had in the last couple hours. Suppressing a chuckle, trying not to smile at such a bad time, I just started to drink and hope my bladder and heart would hold.

"How long has she been gone?" I asked, gesturing to the photo with my eyes.

Hesitantly, he raised his eyes to the photo above with a haunted reverence and replied, "Sometimes it feels like forever."

I nodded along, feeling a twinge of a spasm running along my arm, wondering if it was the first of many signs of "the shakes" coming over me. Glancing down at the cup I pushed the thought aside and took another sip, letting him have his moment of silence and keeping my mouth busy.

"Heart defect," he said quietly, making eye contact as I lowered the mug. "Fought it off for years but just couldn't survive without a transplant anymore. She died of a broken heart and left me to deal with mine."

Taken aback would be putting it lightly. I'd just watched this man's coworkers harvesting organs in a lab no more than 24 hours prior. Yet here he was, a man that literally created hearts

201

telling me that his wife died from lack of a transplant. Tellingly, I asked, "How?"

He chuckled softly, apparently knowing my train of thought, pointing at me across the table with a waving finger. "I did start working for them for the sake of getting her on the list," he said. "I just wasn't able to convince them that she should be at the front of it."

"So how long is that list?" I asked, resting the cup on the table and letting this concept seep through my mind.

"Back then?" He replied, voice catching and eyes starting to well up, "Too long, it seems."

I didn't know what to say, frozen there as I realized the thing he was working on, the thing that hurt Dulaf, was also something that could have saved his wife.

"Do you know what that's like?" He asked, probably rhetorically, though I couldn't be sure in my daze. "You have the ability to just save someone, it's right there in your hands, and you can't make it happen."

Gazing down at my hand, watching it idly flex as I tried to work through another spasm in my arm, I answered, "Yes, I actually do."

"It's worse than just losing someone, isn't it?" He asked. "Because you wonder and you ask the same question over and over whenever you think about it."

Nodding, I murmured softly, "Was it my fault?"

"Never as easy an answer as people make it out to be, is it?" He asked knowingly. "You know, logically, it wasn't something you had any control over, especially if the decisions or the work of other people is involved."

Looking away from my own hand, I saw his, noticing him rolling his wedding ring lightly around his finger, the tan marks so crisp that I couldn't help noting he somehow could have been paler than he already was. It was his tick, the thing he did when thinking about that unpleasant little part of his life and everything around it, like a few things of mine had been for me. I felt guilty thinking about how I could use that to gauge how honest he was being with me. I felt guilty just thinking about the fact I had to ask him questions after this.

"That's why I work so hard at what I do now," he said with conviction, "so that list will always get shorter."

That didn't help me at all.

I considered right then and there that I should just get up and leave before I could bully the poor widow. But, glancing up at her, I thought about the people I'd known and lost.

"It'd be a sin to let noble work be used for sinister deeds," I remarked, feeling a tad poetic. "It'd be a dishonor to her memory."

Gazing into his eyes, I saw that knowing expression. His eyes locked with mine, relaxed and unsurprised. The corners of his mouth sank lightly into a barely visible frown. His nostrils flared just a bit to let in one cleansing breath as he resigned himself to the elephant in the room. Clearly, we both knew what else had been worked on in the floor below his.

"I had a feeling it was you that broke in last night," he said. "The way it happened exactly after a couple of agents walked through like that. They're thinking it too."

I nodded. "They have a security detail hovering around the local station here, probably trying to figure out who exactly we are."

"So why are you here?" he asked. "I'm sure it's not to talk about my growth controlled rose bushes or my dead wife."

He was suddenly more confident than he had been before, like he wasn't afraid of what I was going to say next. No, not quite confident, reserved. His shoulders were relaxed, his expression was nearly blank. It was like this man had been waiting for this conversation for some time. Glancing down at the cup in my hands, I momentarily considered how likely it was someone would try to poison an agent to cover something like that up.

Irritated, I snapped, "I don't see how anything I saw down there could improve the chances of someone getting a transplant."

The nervous little man I'd known the night before emerged again for a split-second, a slight shake to his hands as I scolded him. Then he lowered his head, closed his eyes and seemed to swallow that part of himself, forcing it back down and regaining control. Calmly, he looked back up, sighed heavily and said with a troubled tone, "Sometimes you have to make deals with the devil to get what you want, Agent Leone."

Shaking my head in disgust, I nearly threw the mug in my hands. I'd heard that phrase so many times in Fangtown, always an excuse for every awful thing people had just allowed to happen. Like every soldier saying they were just "following orders" the "deal with the devil" was a natural part of crimes where I came from. Naturally, I would have suspected Archie's devil to be the same as my own if that devil hadn't pointed me this way in the first place.

Calming myself as much as I could, I said, "The devil usually finds a way to get what he wants while making you think you got yours."

The mousey man's face hardened, his features sharpening as he strained to hold something back: a quivering lip, an angry snarl, maybe even a breakdown. Once again he managed to swallow it, managed to push it down somewhere deep and regain his composure. Something about that was incredibly unnerving to me.

"I do the work I do," he said quietly, voice steadily growing stronger, "because I promised I would never let it happen again."

"But that doesn't mean you build them weapons," I sniped. "There's no reason to create these monsters for them."

His shoulders slumped hard, his body nearly crumpling over the table, and silently he nodded along.

"One of them is on a mission, isn't it?" I asked directly.

He shook his head and sipped his coffee, eyes still moist and starting to well up again ever so slightly. "Not officially," he answered quietly. "No one in the lab was informed of any mission, at least."

Lowering the cup, a deep, troubled frown crossed his face and his brow furrowed, hand shaking as he held onto the handle as tight as he could. "I can tell you this much, it didn't leave during my shift and I'm sure you saw that capsule while you were there."

I thought back on the empty glass tube surrounded by shadows in a milky ooze. I knew exactly what he was talking about as I thought back on it: it was entirely intact when I saw it.

"So even the people at Sindri don't know how to find it?" I asked sternly, frustrated.

"It stopped responding to the lab signals the day it left," he replied, finally relaxing his grip around that mug. "Not a sign of it or what it's objective is since it left that room."

Sighing, I asked in a softer tone, "Is there any reason why this thing would be sent to kill seemingly random Alters in the middle of Seattle?"

He shook his head, eyes locked on the table between us.

Pensively, I asked, "Is it possible this thing got away from them after they sent it out?"

He lifted his eyes from the tabletop and shrugged his shoulders. "They're operated by a unit at the base of their skull, a remote that translates the electronic signals into something the brain can understand."

"Wait, wait," I stammered. "They have communication between biological and artificial signals?"

Nodding, he rubbed the bridge of his nose between his finger and thumb, mumbling slightly as he replied, "Like your Oracle."

"Like your Oracle" were dangerous words. They completely confirmed the suspicions we'd had before. It was the second time these people had used the same materials against us that I knew of. First they had complete control of our system, and then they had control of the technology behind it. The people supporting this whole thing, the weaponized Alters and the harvested organs: they were ACTF.

He looked at me after a moment of silence, studying my expression with a raised eyebrow and a curious glint in his reddening eyes. Leaning closer he said quietly, "Our version of the technology is based in the fact these creatures are mentally wired in a similar fashion, but it's a crude comparison to the Oracle, much smaller and much less versatile."

"Why would you even need that?!" I asked harshly.

205

He flinched, sitting stiffly upright again and watching me carefully as he replied nervously, "S-so we could network the soldiers."

"Okay," I said, leaning back in the chair, running my hand through my hair and trying to ignore the sudden tension running from my elbow up to the shoulder. "So, say, in theory, that we happen to find this thing: how do we stop it?"

He shook his head rapidly, waving his hands in a frantic sweeping motion. "You can't!" he declared in a panic, "You shouldn't even try to think of it like that!"

"Why?" I asked, glaring. "What the hell do you expect us to do, just bring the damn thing in alive like nothing has happened?"

He shook his head and ran both hands through his thinning hair, sweat starting to bead across his brow. "It's not like that," he said, strained. "These things, they're practically perfect. We designed them to take all of the strengths and none of the weaknesses."

I stood up and pulled my visor from my belt, snapping the shades open with a flick of my wrist and putting them on as I started to walk out the door, taking a quick look at the cup while I had a chance. My momentary paranoia was averted, the cup reading clean, but I couldn't say I felt any better after what he'd just said.

"We're just going to have to cook up a new way of killing your monster," I said.

His chair scraped across the floor and rattled as he stood behind me, the sound of his slippers hitting the linoleum floor a couple times before stopping. "I'm not boasting about this," he insisted, starting to lose that edge to his voice, the nervous little man seeping through again. "They're bio-weapons, super soldiers, meant to withstand warzones and come out of it alive."

Peering over my shoulder at him, I looked at his aura and saw the faint traces of legitimate concern painted across it. It was harder to see, being human, but the chemical traces of sincere fear were similar in any race. "Everything has a flaw," I told him, "we just have to find it."

"Not this time, they're perfect," he said quietly, raising his voice to repeat, "Perfect."

I nodded and continued walking on, wondering just what about this situation was making him nervous. Was he concerned that we would somehow destroy his creation? Or did he really mean everything he'd just said?

That last thought echoed in my head a bit as a growing need to go to the restroom came over me. Was it the coffee or the fear of something a mad scientist built in a tube? As I exited the door in a slightly greater hurry than I would have normally, I realized the answer was probably both.

Chapter 20
Eager Enemies

Outside his house, arriving a lot later than I expected them to, I could see Carlson and Lynch exiting their black car and approaching with determination. Normally, I'm all for the idea of mouthing off to guys like Carlson, but the multiple cups of coffee and a several hour drive left me with only one instinct: find a rest room that wasn't owned by a widow with a creepy everlasting garden.

Jogging away from the door and out the gate before they could reach it, I darted by them and opened the car door remotely, letting the car start itself while I slipped in and slammed the door behind me. My belt hadn't even been buckled by the time I was half way down the street. I wasn't in that much of an emergency, but I didn't want to risk wasting time with them and the sticks they'd sat on during their traumatic childhood. Honestly, if they were that eager to have a really awkward conversation with me where no one said what they were thinking out loud then they could have it with me in the same place everyone else did: the men's room.

I felt a little silly, speeding away from the place like it was a crime scene, but even if I didn't have to go I wouldn't have wanted to talk to them any more than absolutely necessary. I just hoped they couldn't figure out where I was going in all my haste as I weaved through town looking for a convenience store or a public restroom.

Parking and practically sprinting out the car, I power walked the last leg of the trip. Pushing the door open, I became immediately aware of what was creepier than some poor man's potential restroom shrine to a long lost wife: the men's room. I realized at that moment that I had never actually looked at one while wearing the visor.

I never want to do it again.

The colors radiating from every surface were like a rainbow of woe. I could see four shades of yellow and none of them were particularly screaming "urine" to me. In fact, sad as it was, I had immediately stopped breathing the moment I saw it. I didn't realize it at first, too busy watching the colors like an acid trip, but it was just a reflex that left me literally breathless.

Taking off my shades for peace of mind, I put them on the counter by the mirror. I decided to ignore my better judgment and told myself I'd probably been exposed to everything in there at some point anyway. I'd survived drug labs, I could survive this. Whatever she'd brewed, Babs' concoction was coming back with a vengeance and I couldn't sweat the small details no matter how bright, vibrant and terrifying they were. And, for one moment, as I reached my goal, I had experienced a true sense of contentment. I'd even say it was the best part of my day right up to the moment a gun was being cocked behind my back.

"Bad form, Carlson," I groaned.

A second click rang out from the entrance of the restroom, Carlson standing there at a reasonably secure distance with his gun leveled on me. Lynch, on the other hand, was the guy who decided to sneak up on me at a urinal. The two of them were tense, shoulders tight and grips on their guns a little too secure. Lynch was particularly unusual, his knuckles practically white and his hand subtly shaking in my peripheral vision.

"What the hell are you doing here, Leone?" Carlson demanded from the door.

I seriously thought that question over for a moment. Was I supposed to just tell him the truth? And, if I was to tell him the truth, how much of it was I to say? My inner smart-ass told me there was something more pressing on my response: it was kind of a stupid question.

Tongue-in-cheek, I replied, "Taking a piss."

Carlson grunted and rolled his eyes, snapping at me, demanding "What do you know?"

"For one," I said, glancing over my shoulder at Lynch, barrel fully pressed into my back still, "I know Lynch is new."

"W what?" Lynch stammered, sweat streaming down his face. "What's that supposed to mean?"

Carlson glanced at us, looked down at Lynch's hands and sighed. "It means his jacket is bullet proof, jackass."

"Also," I interjected, "I could turn around and, while your shot goes off and grazes across my back, I could use your arm to throw you face first into this urinal."

Turning to face the wall again, I was satisfied to hear the validating sound of two footsteps and feel the gun retreat from my back. I taught him something at the very least.

Again, Carlson barked, "What do you know?"

I still wasn't exactly sure how I was supposed to respond to the question. He was assuming too much and had tipped his hand ages ago when he told me to leave the case alone. Was I supposed to tip my hand too? His scowl told me that I wouldn't exactly win him over by arguing my case and the two of them pulled guns on me the minute they got the chance. At best, they were incredibly intimidated by the ACTF's reputation. At worst, they were waiting for me to start a fight so they could be justified in trying to take me out.

"I don't think there's any reason to explain my current investigation," I finally said, deciding to be honest and dismissive at the same time. "It's in my jurisdiction."

Lynch piped up behind me, his shaky voice steadier now that he was a good foot back from me, "You went straight to Dr. Faber's house."

"And there's no jurisdiction for ACTF over a human researcher," Carlson added. "So you're going to need a better explanation than that."

I shook my head and glared at him. "I don't see how talking to a researcher for an Alter owned and operated business is somehow outside of my jurisdiction. If anything, I'd think it'd be outside of yours since this isn't a national security issue."

His posture shifted, his gun lowered and his expression became distant. I was fairly sure the man had realized he couldn't correct me without telling me too much. In fact, I was pretty sure he'd just had the thought that he could be fired, or worse, for what he'd already divulged.

Frustrated, he asked the only question he could actually ask in his position: "What the hell are you doing here, Leone?"

I looked him over, seeing the slight tremor in his hands and the way his shoulders were practically locked. There was something seriously upsetting about the situation to the man, something that I'd been missing from the fact he'd seemed to have no personality beyond whatever the job required of him. The situation was physically affecting him now that he stood there, more so than the nervous Lynch at my back.

Zipping up and turning to face them, I decided to push my luck. "We figured out where that Nosferatu came from," I said, staring down the gun now. "And we've been trying to figure out how it got out and reached the city."

Carlson frowned and holstered his gun, waving for Lynch to do the same and pointing a finger at my face with determination. "You were supposed to stay away from the case all together!" He scolded, nearly cracking his facade to yell at me. "The entire thing is silver-lined and the whole bunch of you are supposed to stay the hell away from it."

I sighed and walked around Lynch, going to the sink by my visor. Lynch was still fairly nervous about the whole thing as I crossed, half-circling with a slight crab walk as he shuffled his feet along and turned to face me the entire way. Carlson, on the other hand, was growing considerably more at ease as I walked by.

"Silver line doesn't hold," I commented, washing my hands, "Unless your national security problem is from the fact that bat made it into the country from international waters."

He glared and searched my face with quick, darting glances. I imagine he was trying to figure how much I actually knew again. So I did my damned best to pull off a poker face without reaching for the visor.

"You'd think you'd want us to be able to figure out where that leak in security happened," I remarked, peeking at the visor by my side. "Unless there's something else you'd like to tell me about the case that I'm missing."

Even without the visor, I could see the disbelief in his eyes as he strolled over and leaned against the counter, crossing his arms. "We want the ACTF off of this," he replied, "and as far away from any part of the case as you can get."

I shut off the water, watching it drip into the sink and thinking of the rainy night I first stumbled onto their damned crime-scene. Quietly, tightly, I asked, "Do you even know who Alice Winchester is?"

He studied me, eyebrow raised, lips pursed slightly like he wasn't sure if he should respond or not. After a moment he asked obliviously, "Who?"

Rage nearly overtook me in the moment he said that. They'd been covering everything and keeping us at bay this entire time and it had almost nothing to do with the victims. I wanted to scream at him, I wanted to take the first swing and I sure as hell wanted to put these guys in their place. But even if I did, it would have only made things worse. Closing my eyes, lowering my head, I breathed deeply through my nose and exhaled slowly from my mouth, trying to wash away the fury and disgust welling up in my chest.

"She was one of the victims," I said with a light hiss, "The one we first caught sight of."

Lifting my eyes, I saw the look on Lynch's face, a sorrowful, downward gaze like he'd been ashamed of the fact he didn't know. Carlson, looking smug and indifferent to my side, just scoffed at the notion.

"You can't memorize every damn victim in a case like this," he remarked, "we have more important things to worry about."

"More important?" I snapped, turning with a clenched fist but not actually swinging at him. "Who the hell are you to decide they weren't important?!"

Cold eyes stared back into mine, unfazed by my motion, unafraid of the fist and seemingly looking through me like I didn't matter. He didn't move, his shoulders tense but only as much as they'd been when he held the gun. The only motion I caught in him as I faced him head on was a twitch of the hand tucked into his elbow.

It was almost like he was just waiting for me to finish throwing my tantrum and walk away in a huff. I was as much of an inconvenience to him as they were to me. I was just someone who was in the way of whatever his actual objective was. I don't

212

know if that's how he actually felt, but it felt that way to me. It felt like I was better off walking away.

Seeing my fist unclench, he answered calmly, "I have only one job in this: to tie up all the loose ends and make sure that people like you stay the hell away from it. If you'd do that, then my job would be easier and we could all move on with our lives."

Lynch stepped up, eyes darting between us, head hanging low, looking like he was going to be sick. "This whole case," he commented, voice wavering, "It's got everyone on edge. It's not perfect, but it's what we've got to deal with."

I looked at Lynch and considered what he said. Sighing, I realized he was right and turned back to Carlson, saying, "Move, I need my visor."

Carlson's posture eased and he glanced back at the counter he'd been leaning on, seeing the shades sitting behind him and reaching to them. I watched him warily, almost defensive for the simple sunglasses as he lifted them from the counter and examined them.

"They almost got these for us," he said, lifting them towards his eyes, "How do you turn them on?"

The flash of colors shone through the lenses and Carlson saw what I'd seen when I first walked in, a Technicolor haze with a sickening feeling of chemical waste.

"You don't," I replied, reaching over and snatching them away from him. "They're always on so the system can keep analyzing one state to the next. Keeps the readings current."

"Current?" he echoed, quizzically. "Isn't it just some sort of chemical reaction in the glass?"

For an agent meant to monitor our activities, I was almost amused by the fact he didn't know how they worked. Smugly, I replied, "Well we use magical little devices to transmit the data from the visor back to the system, have that analyzed and shot back to the glass where little Gnomes reassemble it all into pretty colors."

His tongue rolled behind his lip and his eyebrows rose as he nodded along. Shrugging off my attitude, he responded casually,

"I guess if you need help to investigate a crime scene it might as well be the equivalent of a whole lab strapped to your face."

Avoiding eye contact, I waited to put them on before facing him again. "Funny," I said sarcastically, "I don't remember you guys finding that bat before us." Shooting a look at both of them, I shrugged. "Of course, I'm assuming you were looking for him."

Lynch looked away, his aura registering slightly off like the comment made him nervous. Carlson, on the other hand, read cold as ice yet again. Shaking his head and walking away from the counter, he mused, "At least our investigations don't fall apart if we can't get a connection."

Like a bolt of lightning the comment struck me and turned on that little light-bulb I'd hoped would flick on the whole damn morning. We'd never had a broken connection as long as I'd been there, but the visor hadn't always worked. I couldn't see the Nosferatu's signature on my visor the night we found it, blocked by the silver line as the Oracle was told it couldn't show us. Suddenly, thanks to Carlson, I realized how to find Archie's beast: The Oracle knew where it was.

Chuckling, I followed Carlson out of the restroom and slapped Lynch on the shoulder on the way. "Don't worry, it gets easier," I assured, "Sometimes the answer just falls into your lap."

He flinched and watched me pass, standing his ground and not moving to follow us. It was strange to see an agent, someone trained to be in situations like these, frozen in place at a time like this. I thought back to when I first started, fraught with uncertainty and doubt in my actions. I knew the feeling of what Lynch was going through.

It didn't make him any less of a wuss, though.

"Your boy's cracking," I said to Carlson, gesturing a thumb over my shoulder. "He's only been at it for a couple months, hasn't he?"

Carlson nodded, putting his own sunglasses on as he stepped out into the light. "First confrontation with ACTF," he mused. "It usually isn't the smoothest event for the FNGs."

I nodded along, squinting into the sunlight and letting the visor adjust to it. For a small moment, standing in the warm sunshine, listening to him call the new guy an FNG, I almost felt a sense of camaraderie with Carlson outside that restroom.

If only he actually gave a shit about the murders he covered up, I probably wouldn't have hated him.

Chapter 21
Xenolithic Objects

Carlson and Lynch followed me out of Port Angeles, coasting on the road at a relatively safe distance and doing their best not to make it obvious they were making sure I left town. I could understand why, they didn't want me snooping around anymore. Unfortunately for them, I didn't need to. They'd given me the kind of information I needed without intending to, accidentally pointing out something I'd overlooked the whole time without being any the wiser.

Settling back into my seat, the fairly quiet roads outside of the cities let me relax again and let go for a minute. Babs' brew and the couple cups of coffee I'd had for the day were starting to wear off and I was starting to feel the weight of the day again. Though, strangely, I didn't feel as dead as I should have at a time like that. The faint headache growing behind my eyes and wrapping around to the base of my skull was expected but strangely weaker than it could have been. I imagine I had Babs to thank for that.

Realizing I was pretty much the only car on the road except for the one purposefully following my lead, I set it to network with the system and start driving itself. The Oracle's icon appeared on the windshield, hovering over my steering wheel. The holographic eye, a simple, colorful depiction to represent the all-seeing eye we relied on, now literally kept an eye on the road for me. And while it drove, I called back to the headquarters, patching through to Dulaf.

She answered the call, her face appearing on the communications console. Her ears were hanging slightly, her eyelids sagging and her posture drooping as she blearily looked into the screen. She looked surprisingly more tired than I felt.

"Find anything useful?" She asked, stifling back a yawn.

Chuckling, I questioned her back. "Are you going to be okay there?" I asked. "You look pretty dead."

An exasperated sigh left her and she sat up straighter, trying to fake being alert while I watched on. "I sent the kid out for coffee," she said bluntly, "I just hope she manages to keep the minions in line."

"Well at least they have supervision," I quipped, nodding along to her, "I think I'd prefer it if you got some sleep though, I'm going to need you tonight."

"Tonight?" she asked with an eyebrow and an ear-tip raised. "What do you need me to do tonight?"

"Well," I replied, leaning my chair back and getting comfortable while the wheel ahead of me steered itself, "I think I figured out how to find that creature out of Sindri."

"Did Archie give you the information?" she asked, adjusting her position and resting her elbows against her desk.

"Not exactly," I replied. "He told me something important, but I wasn't sure how to use it until Carlson snuck up on me at the urinal."

A little spark of life came to her eyes again as she grinned and asked, "So you're saying he snuck a peek, huh?"

I laughed. "Well he did have his gun out the whole time. I think he might have had some envy." Nodding to the monitor, I took a more serious tone. "But I think I figured something out that we should have realized ages ago."

"What's that?" she asked, letting a yawn escape finally. She was trying so hard to stay up and fight back the urge to collapse on me. She was normally a day-shift worker but she hadn't been to bed in probably longer than me by now. With helping the Nosferatu hunt, going out to Sindri and breaking in the night before: I was fairly sure she hadn't been to bed in a couple of days. I actually felt a twinge of sympathy for her and knew I had to make it quick.

"The creature uses a biomechanical transmitter to allow remote control," I said. "The Oracle should be able to track it down through that."

"But it hasn't given us anything," she protested, face pinching as she fought back what I figured was the desire to roll her eyes at me. "Your brilliant idea failed to work days ago."

I shook my head and ignored the protest. "This thing was meant to be operated through some sort of remote system, something like our Oracle system but, according to Archie, way less involved."

Her eyes shifted to the side and she chewed on her lip, nodding and huffing. "Yeah, it would make sense they'd want to network their super-soldiers to keep them in line, like drones."

Nodding, I continued, "and if they're going to be networked then it has to be a two way connection, like our visors. It can't just be commands being sent to them, the controller has to see what's happening around the soldiers while they move."

She flung her hands up and slapped them down on the desk, frustrated. "But that doesn't change the fact the Oracle hasn't seen a damn thing from it, Nate."

"Because it was silver lined," I corrected, "Just like the Nosferatu."

Her eyes shifted down and started to dart around while she thought about that, her ears slowly rising and her brow gradually furrowing. The growing glare started to put some life back into her while she stared at the desk between her and her console.

"Right?" I asked, looking for some sort of response out of her. "The Nosferatu wouldn't appear on the readings despite being tagged. Its aura wouldn't even show up when I was face-to-face with it."

"So their other creature wouldn't show up either," she responded, nodding along with it. "It might be reading it right now and not showing us anything," she continued, starting to get some pep in her voice, "because it couldn't."

Feeling better about the theory now that I heard her say it and confident she'd give me an answer I could work with, I asked, "So how do we get that damn line off?"

She looked back into the monitor again, making "eye contact" as far as the consoles were concerned, eyes wide and a little lost when she said, "I have no clue yet."

Of course, that wasn't exactly what I wanted to hear.

Confused, even a little annoyed, I asked, disbelieving, "So you're telling me someone working with those systems for all these years has no idea how to take out a command like that?"

She snapped back at me with a matter-of-fact, patronizing tone, "Well we weren't supposed to take out a command like that, stupid! That was the fucking point!"

My head bounced off the headrest as I watched the ceiling of the car and tried to control my frustration. I balked, "Well I guess that idea's gone down the shitter."

After a moment of silence she chimed in with a touch of mischief in her voice, "Not necessarily."

Curiosity piqued, I studied her expression on the monitor, trying to figure what was going through her mind. A subtle smirk grew across her face, the beginnings of a cat-like grin.

Impatiently, I asked, "What're you thinking?"

Energetically, she replied, "Get home and you'll see."

Before I could ask what that meant, she shot up from her chair and cut our connection, hanging up on me and leaving me to think about what was cooking in her devious mind for the next couple hours I'd be on the road.

Resting back in the chair, I mumbled to myself like I needed to keep it quiet, "I just hope she's not planning to shove me into the ocean two nights in a row."

They were prophetic words.

You could probably imagine the look on my face when I stood on the edge of the harbor, looking out over the Puget Sound while Dulaf eagerly headed for the waterside with a determined stride. At the very least I knew we wouldn't be out on international waters this time around, the next shoreline was visible on the horizon and the only artificial island was Harbor Island to the south. They were less hostile waters, to be sure, but I'd had my fill of soggy clothes for the week.

"Get a move on," she demanded with a hard swipe of her hand, "We don't have time to be standing around right now, Nate."

"Why are we going into the harbor?" I asked warily, slowly starting to follow her.

She didn't answer as her stride broke into a jog and she skipped down a small set of stairs to a pier standing slightly lower than the rest. It was quiet, empty, not even trash or the usual evidence of seagulls around it. There were no boats, no people and no sign of the years of wear and tear you'd see on any of the others. In fact, it looked almost brand new, completely pristine in a way that shouldn't have been possible on the edge of the sea.

Finally, she stopped at a small structure at the end of the pier the size of a tool shed. The structure was anchored into the surface of the pier and, studying our surroundings, I realized that it was the only thing out there. She opened the door, stepped inside and started to climb down a ladder through the deck. Peeking back at me from the ladder, she waved for me to follow before disappearing into a long, dark shaft. I approached cautiously and looked over the edge to a surprisingly long drop.

Moments later, echoing from the shadows far below, she called to me brightly, "This is where we fix the silver-line problem!"

After a moment of hesitation I sighed, climbed onto the ladder, and started my way down grumbling, "We better not be getting into a submarine."

It wasn't as bad as it seemed from above, the shaft wider than it should have been and accommodating to someone much larger than me. I figured, as roomy as it felt, it could have likely fit someone as large as Alston, maybe even an Ettin or average Giant. I couldn't figure why they would create a shaft that large, maybe those kinds of people were in mind as they were constructing this odd pier wedged between the rest. Odd as it was, the thought was soon washed from my mind by a feeling I couldn't quite pin.

It was disorienting, almost like vertigo, but not enough to have pulled me from the ladder. My head was light, fuzzy, but still firmly aware of the area around me. Everything suddenly felt clearer, crisp, like the world had gone into high definition. Every rung of the ladder suddenly felt more tangible to me, like they'd instantly become the most important thing in the world. I felt my hand wrap around it, I noticed how ungiving the metal bars were, something you'd never stop to notice on an average day. Even the sound of the ocean sloshing around us filled the passage with a buzz. There was a movement in the air I could feel throughout my body with the same clarity as the ladder.

Once, I'd gotten a contact high from a room full of chemicals – a place where you could practically stew in the air around you to achieve hallucinations. This passage, whatever it was, was starting to give me the same vibe. It wasn't quite the same; I didn't feel altered in the way I was there. Instead, this was giving me a feeling of being beyond myself, existing above my standard existence. It was more like a feeling I had in another place once before.

It was like being in a room with an Oracle.

The room at the bottom was an incredibly controlled environment, the air chilled like the inside of a refrigerator and the faint hum of electronics working behind the walls. It wasn't a very large room, enough for a group of four to five people to walk around, but it made use of its space as effectively as it could. Three of the four walls were covered in computer equipment and switchboards like we'd stepped into the control room of a much bigger operation. The fourth wall, however, was another matter altogether.

Floating in a strange, gel-like liquid, bathed in an eerie green light, was a strange, alien organism suspended in the center of the jar. Leathery but translucent, the creature's internal organs were visible as they pulsed and flashed with faint sparks of electricity from electrodes piercing its skin. The fleshy surface branched out like tendrils, bundles of nerves weaved through them and bound to what seemed to be fiber-optic cables.

There was a heart beating steadily inside the fluid filled mass, but that wasn't the core of it, not like the blood apples of the factory. No, for all the parts moving and flexing inside that creature, it all existed to support one thing: a huge brain. I stood there and stared at it, slightly ill from the sight of this thing as it seemed to float there and stare back at me without eyes. It'd been the first time I'd actually seen a brain in a jar and certainly the first time I'd seen whatever the hell was wrapped around it.

"There's a brain in a jar," I said warily. "We're in a room with a brain in a jar."

She giggled and glanced over her shoulder as she sat by a terminal at the far end of the room, opening a control panel that bore the distinct iconography of the Oracle system. Calmly, she said, "This is one of the buffering stations."

"This," I stammered, waving at the brain in the jar staring at me, "this is what the relay stations for the Oracle look like?"

"We didn't exactly stop at the blood apples in the realm of bio-engineering," she said, slightly annoyed, "though I was never too fond of the idea of creating a brain."

I turned away from the jar and quipped, "Well yeah, a bleeding, pulsating lump of flesh is *way* less disturbing than a brain in a jar."

"Hearts don't think," she said distantly, almost under her breath but just loud enough to be heard past the buzz and rapid tapping of keys.

Suddenly I felt a little sorry for the disgusting thing behind me. Hesitantly, I asked with concern, "Does it know it's in a jar?"

Pointed ears flexed as the tendons in her neck tightened and shoulders stiffened. Tightly, she replied, "*She* does, I don't know why they would be any different."

A flash of a girl suspended in a similar tank crossed my mind, floating in a room no one else could stand in. We'd created a barrier around her, one that this room was apparently a part of. Remembering the faint smile she had when I actually stood in the room, I remarked, "I try not to think about the fact we keep a girl in a jar, either."

"That part isn't quite as bad," she noted, "at least the Oracles volunteered for that job. At least they get something out of our arrangement. The modern world isn't friendly to people overwhelmed by too much information."

Peeking over my shoulder at the tank in the room, I commented, "But that meant having to put brains in jars."

Quietly, angrily, she made a frustrated grunt, nimble fingers falling on the keys just a touch harder than they had before. "Yeah, well," she muttered, "we had to out-do the enemy."

"Ah, the great organ race," I replied sarcastically. "And just who else was shoving body parts in jars?"

"Rufus!" she snapped, slamming a palm next to the keyboard, rattling the keys. "He started the biological warfare, eugenics, race wars, and all that other crap and we had to figure out how to stop it!"

I stepped back, studying her posture, frowning as I asked, "He was into biological weapons?"

"You have no idea," she replied mournfully. "Before we really understood what we were, before we even knew what bacteria were, he figured it out. He saw all these people he was recruiting had gotten sick in the Plague of Justinian and then he tried to restart the plague. He started experimenting on people."

Thinking about the blood apples, the donors, and the Oracle – I felt ill, a chill running over me, my arm starting to ache. "So you started to experiment on people."

She glared back at me fiercely, correcting, "On ourselves."

Spinning her chair around, she turned to face me, gesturing at her arm as she hurriedly continued, "We were trying to figure out how to take what we had and then give it to everyone else. The blood transfusions, the organ transplants, the gene therapies – it was supposed to prevent wars!"

I turned away to take in the room, asking quietly, "So how does that lead to this?"

"This," she replied, pausing to look around the room, turning away to face the terminal again, "wasn't exactly something we all agreed on. I just made sure that it was as humane as possible. I try not to think about the rest."

"I thought you had sway with these people," I said, coming closer again now that she'd calmed down, "the Elf ninjas and all."

"Rangers," she corrected. "And, actually, I kind of stepped down from that position when the order went separate ways."

"Went separate ways?" I asked, "When'd that happen?"

Matter-of-factly she replied, "The colonial period. Rufus and his men wanted to start their own country somewhere else. The order followed him."

"Followed?" I asked. "As in hunted, or joined?"

Hesitantly, she answered, "A little of both."

I dwelled on the implications for a moment before I realized how ancient she must have felt at times. Without hesitation she'd told me she'd been around for colonialism with the same nonchalant attitude she had name-dropping Samuel Colt. To me it seemed like a great big period of time that couldn't be easily overlooked, but the sound of her voice was like someone talking about events from only a year ago.

Shaking it off, I asked, "And where did you end up?"

"I stayed behind, had things to keep an eye on," she responded, continuing to work on a long string of code in a strange, seemingly archaic language.

I studied the codes, the old symbols so out of place on the digital display, an anachronism right in front of my eyes. "But you were around to help build all of this and meet 'Sammy' back in the day. You couldn't have been gone that long."

"Several generations," she replied, the hint of a soft smile crossing her face under the glow of the screens. "Until my charge moved to America."

"Why would you stay behind for so long?" I asked, leaning over, hoping I wasn't moving into swinging range.

She looked up, pinched my cheek and replied nostalgically, "Old saying in the order: 'You need a lion to fight a griffon'."

The grip of her pinch grew tighter, my face burning as she squeezed, tears starting to well in my eyes.

"Now stop asking stupid questions and help me," she scolded, releasing my face and turning me towards the terminal.

Staring at the console ahead of me, I asked, "What exactly are we doing here?"

Presenting her badge, Dulaf answered, "You need two officers to activate the command."

I pulled mine from my jacket and nodded to her. She reached for a hand scanner and nodded to me, gesturing me for me to remove the glove. Though I wasn't sure what she was doing, I followed her command and pulled my glove off, reaching for the other scanner. Together, we placed our badges into grooves in the consoles and put our palms against the scanners. With a hum and a buzz we looked on as one of the status symbols turned red and an icon of a lock changed.

Puzzled, I asked, "What exactly did we just do?"

She nodded sagely and said, "Untied her hands."

"What do you mean by untying her hands?" I asked.

With a sly smile she leaned back in her chair and replied, "The silver-line is software, it's part of the buffering system preventing her from sending out the information she has."

The dots started to connect for me and I stared back at the brain in the jar, "So what you're saying is that we turn off this buffer's part of the silver-line and she can start getting information out to us again."

Happily, she nodded and said, "So that's precisely what I did. And I opened the door just a crack so no one will notice except for the people tuned directly to this section of the network."

I examined the room again and thought about how much of what was happening now wouldn't have happened without these overlapping technologies. Though, if they hadn't used those same technologies we might not have even been able to track it either. The room was bathed in green light but all I could see were the shades of grey.

Slender hands wrapped around my forearm and wrist. She pulled me to face her again as she said thoughtfully, "Someday, when we have the chance, maybe I'll tell you the rest of how we got here, okay?"

I nodded and reached into a pouch on my belt, fishing out the hand-link and showing it to her. Placing it in her hands, I asked, "How hard is it to make it so this can see through that hole you just made?"

"It won't be too hard to do," she said. "We just have to remember to close the hole after we're done."

As she said it, I wondered for a moment if we should actually "tie her hands" again. I guess the system was arranged like this for some reason, so we had to remember to return it to the way it was. It just felt wrong to build things like this and wall off a girl behind firewalls. I'd never fully understood the arrangement with them. Maybe when it was time to put things back to normal I could raise an objection or get an explanation. In the meantime, I looked at her and nodded my consent.

"Let's find us a monster."

Chapter 22
Crazed Monster

We weren't sure who could be trusted with the new leak in the security, so we kept it to ourselves as much as possible over what was left of the day. Dulaf, weary and ready to collapse, finally seemed at peace enough to drag herself to Purgatory and sleep. Luckily, with as much time as I'd spent active for the last couple of days, I was able to take the rest of the night off myself. It was long overdue as I went home to my apartment and once again collapsed to the old, comfy chair that I'd been daydreaming about on and off since leaving Port Angeles.

It didn't take long for me to drift off once there, watching old reruns of sci-fi shows in between the blinks that occasionally lasted minutes. When one of those slightly involuntary naps took hold I found myself drift away for a decent couple of hours where I became dead to the world. It was a dreamless sleep, even a slightly restless one. I simply sank into the chair and let the darkness take hold. And when I woke up, hearing the sounds of bad actors discussing techno-babble, I momentarily felt worse than I did when I first drifted off.

The sun had long since set and I could hear the sounds of the people of Fangtown going about their busy lives. The neon glow outside and the sound of cars passing by made me rise from the chair and wander to the window, feeling every ache and pain that I imagine I'd ignored for the last couple of days. I'd almost forgotten the bruised ribs and the slightly battered torso thanks to omega packs and whatever it was Babs slipped in that decal thermos.

"Ah, damn," I groaned, "the thermos."

Fetching my keys, I walked out of the apartment in only half my uniform, leaving the coat, badge and belt behind, hurrying downstairs to get find the flower-power mug that Babs had given me that morning. Strolling past a few people, I waved and smiled and no one seemed to think it was odd. The lack of the coat and the badge always made people friendlier. At least, they were friendlier until I reached the car and they realized the gloves weren't a fashion statement. I opened the passenger side door, reached into the half-seat in the back and took out the oddly decorated container.

Standing with the thermos by the car, I closed my eyes and took a deep breath, enjoying the cool night air while people continued to walk by. It was strangely invigorating being out of my building that late without having somewhere to go. The air was crisp and clean from a couple days of rain and I felt the bite of a chilling breeze. It was refreshing and helped stir me from the hangover I'd had from the short nap in the old recliner.

Waking from my haze, I suddenly realized something strange was in the air, something I felt but wasn't immediately aware of. People had been walking and talking along the sidewalk, quite a few given how close I lived to the center of Fangtown. But then I realized I couldn't hear them anymore. In fact, I realized that everything had gone strangely still all together and that the people had started to scatter.

And then, opening my eyes, I could see a shadow casted from somewhere above stretching out over me and the car. Looking back, I saw a huge figure standing against the full moon, like the old images of Werewolves I'd learned long ago were nothing more than fairytales. When it clicked, my heart nearly jumped from my chest as I realized why it would be there of all places.

The damn thing had come for me.

Without warning, the creature leapt from the rooftop above and plummeted towards me. I don't remember thinking anything just then, or feeling anything, just reacting in an instant and ducking into the car as fast as I could. The creature landed just outside the door with a heavy, fleshy crack and rushed the car. I managed to slam the door shut and lock it, pushing myself across the passenger seat just as its massive hand burst through the window and reached for me, catching my ankle.

Visions of Alice flashed through my mind as it started to pull. In a panic I lashed out for the only thing I could find, the button to turn on the siren, blaring it in the creature's face. The hunch about the lack of sonar in that room proved right as the beast got an ear-full and instantly reacted like I'd stabbed it. It reared back from the car for just a second, giving me the window of opportunity to sit up and put the key in the ignition. Turning it over, I saw the system come online just long enough for the voice recognition to kick in. Seeing that, I screamed, "Oracle, activate riot control!"

I'd never used the feature before, never even thought of doing it, but there couldn't have been a better time to try. With a sudden shriek, the car's siren mirrored the power of a Banshee. The creature on the sidewalk roared in agony and clasped its hands over its ears.

It was the first time I'd seen one of these things clearly. The monstrous figure towered by the car, its near jet black skin making it look like a moving shadow against the side of my building. As it moved, every muscle flexing and rippling, I realized that it stood naked, as if there was no need for it to shield itself from the elements. Watching it in awe, I wasn't sure what to do next. It growled heavily and glared at me with piercing eyes, lunging towards the car with a ferocious speed and ramming into it hard enough to rock it onto one set of wheels before rocking back to its waiting arms. The arm reached for me again, a clawed hand coming towards my face.

Lacking any weapons or gear to speak of except my gloves, I have to admit I panicked a little. Flooring it seemed like the best option at the time. We sped down the street, luckily cleared by the people panicked from the creature dropping out of the sky and my siren blasting at full power. And without missing a beat the creature at my side slammed its claws in through the windshield to hold on as I broke about half a dozen traffic laws.

Steering onto a blissfully abandoned sidewalk corner, I jumped the curb and clipped the corner of a building, hoping to scrape the monster off like gum off my boot. The crunch from that mountain of flesh hitting a solid wall sent a chill through my bones. Sparks flew from the side of the car, what was left of the windows shattering on that side. When I finally pulled away and hit the brakes I found myself taking a moment to stop shaking, my heart pounding in my ears.

And then, as I glanced into the rear view, it got back up.

At that moment I could have probably driven away, left it alone and gone for help. In fact, looking at the console, I wondered if help wasn't already on the way. But with the way it got back up I knew I hadn't hurt it enough to make sure it couldn't hurt someone else that night. So I buckled up and threw the car into reverse, looking back over my shoulder so I could make eye contact with it… and flip it off as I ran it over.

It fell under the back of the car fairly easily, but the sound it made as it went down was more rage than pain. You'd think a heavily modified armored supercar with four-wheel drive would have done the trick. But as the back lifted over it like a beefy speed-bump, I heard that roar muffled through the undercarriage and felt a sudden lift in the car. Time slowed down as the car rolled over. It flipped, skidding along its roof out onto the blacktop as the siren went dead and the airbags deployed.

On what was left of my windshield I saw the flickering status display of an emergency beacon starting to broadcast. Nearly instantaneously that beacon shut down and silver text flickered into view letting me know the network had disconnected. Dazed and confused, I was still alert enough to laugh at the absurdity of that god-damned system.

The patchwork monstrosity wasn't about to just lie down even after being run over by a car. I saw it lurch back to its feet, staggered but still somehow breathing. It began to shuffle towards the car again, undeterred by my attempts at vehicular manslaughter, and locked eyes on me as it did.

Almost admiring it, I screamed in frustration, "You've got to be fucking kidding me!"

And that frustrated admiration grew pretty quickly when the thing seemed to walk off its injuries. The hitch in its step gradually faded and by the time it was walking up to the front end of the car it was looking ready for round two with my fender. Unfortunately, for the time being, my car had had it and was left to the mercy of the beast as it grabbed onto the bumper and started to shake the car violently.

My mind raced for options at the time. The car's siren had gone silent, the lights were probably no good and I had no

229

weapons on hand thanks to feeling like I could walk out of my apartment unarmed. With the Oracle blocking my way, I couldn't even call for help at the time and my hand-link was back in the apartment. Screwed would have been the best word to describe my situation.

The car's frame groaned and creaked as the creature started to slowly spin it on its roof like a top, likely either too pissed off or lazy to realize it could walk around the car to reach into the driver's side window. The sparks striking off of the pavement and the ear-piercing shriek of metal against asphalt filled my ears. The retractable part of the roof started to buckle, the lights shattering, and glass scattered across the street. I knew I had to leave the car but my only options out of it weren't looking too pleasant as all I could do was put the car's width between me and a creature that just jumped off a building.

When I could see the thing's feet out the driver's side window I remembered the one place I still had weapons on hand. Unlocking the trunk, I removed my seatbelt and fell hard against the car's ceiling, scrambling for the shattered windows of the passenger side. The trunk fell open hard, cracking against the street, the tumbling sounds of cases and weapons falling out of it and bouncing along the blacktop. Thankfully "Patch" out there didn't seem to think any of it was worth noting as he continued to turn the car like a big, unwieldy merry-go-round.

Crawling out the opposite side, staying as low as I could, I scrambled for the cache of weapons that'd scattered from the back of the car. In a moment of adrenaline fueled stupid, I just grabbed the nearest Banshee and set it off in my hands. Lobbing it over the car, I grabbed another and took a moment to actually set it before rolling it around the side of the car. Ten, twenty, I couldn't be sure how many I set off. Each of them rattled my bones while Patch roared in agony. I felt the area around me practically wobble from the sound waves, glass in the nearest windows beginning to crack and dogs howling for blocks around us. At the very least, if no one had called the cops yet, I was hoping someone would do it now for disturbing the peace.

Exhausting my supply of Banshees, I fetched a Manticore from the ground and sprinted back for my building as fast as I possibly could. I didn't bother looking back while I ran down the street and ducked through the door. If it was following me then I was lucky it hadn't caught up, and if it wasn't then there wasn't any reason for me to want it to. I just needed to get up the stairs and get to my link so I could call for help since the Oracle wasn't going to do it for me.

Running through the entrance and up the stairs, I considered yelling for others not to come outside. Realizing that would draw attention, I figured it was best to keep my mouth shut and hoped that thing would focus strictly on me. Those stairs have never been so tall or flown by so fast as that moment I was leaping up them. Taking them two at a time, using the rail to pull myself up, I got to my floor and dashed for the door as fast as I could. Throwing the door open, I bolted for my gear next to the recliner and gathered it up, doing my best to throw it on before that thing could recover.

Buttoning the coat, I froze as the sound of the Banshees faded outside the window. Their charges had run their course and either that thing was about to be on the way or it'd already come for the building. I couldn't be sure which without poking my head out again and that didn't sound like a great idea at all. But then the strangest thing happened: I saw red and blue lights outside and felt an immense feeling of relief. Their sirens blared, somewhat quieter than the one I'd been blasting the neighborhood with, and I realized there were at least two outside.

Finishing with my coat and walking to the window, I looked outside to get an idea of just what the new situation was. Patrol cars were parked by the overturned wreck outside and the police surrounded it to examine the scene. Patch, it seemed, was nowhere to be found out there. I considered he may have run from the onslaught of Banshees, which I realized had left a prolonged whistling noise in my ears. I took the opportunity to get out the hand-link and make my call to Dulaf.

"Hey, this is Dulaf," her voice rang out, "I'm not able to take your call right now, but…"

My head hit the wall a little hard about then as I groaned and bounced it off the nearest surface, listening to the rest of her message. Hanging up, I started trying to dial for the next person I

231

knew I could trust: Lucian. The sun had thankfully set and I knew he could suplex something the size of a Nosferatu if he had to. But before I sent the call my personal cell rang across the room. Hurrying over, I snatched it off a corner table and started my way for the door, seeing Babs' name on the Caller ID.

"Hey, Babs," I answered with short breath, "Not really the best time to talk right now, something's up."

"I know sweetie," she said gently with concern, "that's why I'm calling you. You really don't want to go outside right now."

I shook my head furiously, as if she could have seen me, and replied, "No, you don't understand, the noise outside is something I have to deal with right now. The cops around my car are here to help me."

Her protests started to bleed into the background noise of me fumbling with the doorknob and the ringing in my ears. And as I cleared the door and heard a new breathing sound rumbling behind me, her voice melted away almost entirely. Looking up the hallway, I found the massive figure standing roughly a dozen feet from me. My hearing cleared up just enough for me to hear one last thing before I dropped the phone.

"You should probably run now, sweetie."

Babs didn't need to say a word, my phone was already dropping from my hands as she finished the sentence and I was sprinting for the stairs for all I was worth. Patch roared behind me and charged the corridor like a fucking rhinoceros on my heels. Vaulting over the banister, I found myself thankful for boot camp and put my parkour training to the best use I'd ever had to make my way to the bottom floor without breaking my neck.

The front door had to be open if that thing was in there. I couldn't picture it opening a door without smashing through it. I couldn't picture it having the ability to think that through. So it was only a matter of sprinting down that last stretch of hallway and out into the open where I could be joined by the boys in blue.

There was just one problem: the door was closed. I slowed to reach for the knob and immediately felt the pressure at my back. The lights dimmed and the temperature rose. The hairs on the back of my neck stood on end. Suddenly a pair of massive hands slammed into my back hard enough to lift me from my feet, through the door and out across the sidewalk. The door came with me.

Frantic screaming and gunfire followed. Patch and the police laid eyes on each other for the first time and the whizzing of bullets forced me to scramble clear of it. I never got completely upright, still winded from getting literally shoved through a door. When I tumbled over and rolled onto my back I was well out onto the black top. He was walking through their bullets like they were hardly there, the sound of ricochets and chipped brick echoing around us. I squeezed off a few shots into his chest myself, watching the Helios bolts hit almost harmlessly as his skin hissed and smoldered. And for all of our efforts, he only seemed to get angrier and glared intensely my way.

So I increased my settings and shot him in the face.

It was probably the first time he'd been wounded, the anguish in the sound he made being new and different from what he'd done before. Giant hands clasped over his eyes and he turned his back to me. A glint of steel appeared at the nape of his neck, a strange electronic port embedded at the base of his skull. I tried to get a closer look, but in an instant a small light flashed on that metal plate and Patch turned yet again. That light was only a momentary change, but he moved like it mattered.

He crouched, legs rippling as he brought down his weight on them, and then leapt like a leopard from the street into the side of the building. Driving his claws deep into the wall, he made a few quick motions and scaled the side like it was a ladder before disappearing over the eaves.

The dust started to settle around us in that awkwardly silent moment. The police probably didn't know what to do except wait for me to give them a sign. I couldn't have told them anything at that moment myself. It was the first time anything had actually come to my doorstep like that and it was certainly the first time it had been done by something like Patch. I holstered the gun and started to slowly get up from the pavement, keeping my eyes fixed to the skyline above.

Buzzing at my hip, the hand-link finally came to life when I stood upright. Taking it out, I answered without looking, "Leone."

Dulaf's voice pushed past the buzzing in my ears just narrowly, asking groggily, "Do you have any idea how little sleep I've had?"

"Yes," I replied, still stunned, "I guess I shouldn't have expected you to be awake yet."

Her voice rose as she snapped, "You're damned right you shouldn't have. What the hell were you thinking calling at this hour?"

My mind raced to try to find a way to turn the raw emotion of what had just happened into coherent thoughts I could communicate to her. I was coming down off a pretty heavy adrenaline kick and everything was still a bit hazy. Two thoughts emerged from the haze and came together for me after what seemed like an eternity.

"Well," I said quietly, "I think I have proof that someone's firmly in control of our escaped monster."

"How do you know that?" she asked, trying to suppress a yawn.

I hesitated, making my way back to the building very slowly and waving for the police to follow. Stepping inside, I started to feel some ease, even with the signs of broken wood from the creature smashing the handrail along the stairs. I hadn't noticed it when running from it – the sound of wood shattering at my back. I think I fell silent just then, staring at the fragments along the floor.

Angrily, she demanded, "Well out with it already!"

Quietly, I finally answered, "They just tried to kill me."

Chapter 23
Emergency Report

The ACTF arrived once Dulaf got the word out to the rest. With the help of a dozen guys we flipped the car over and got a good look at the kind of damage done to it by running into that wall of flesh. Most of it was cosmetic, but it was more than enough to take it off the streets so the Dwarves could get to work on the body. I'd lost all of the windows, which was a fact I didn't fully appreciate until I had the time to cool down and realize Patch had just punched through reinforced bullet proof glass with his bare hand. The full weight of what happened finally sank in.

That creature, Sindri's Frankenstein, was strong enough and indestructible enough to shrug off everything we threw at it and punch through tempered, reinforced glass. The fact that I was alive at all was a miracle of dumb luck and me being stubborn. Though, if I'd driven away when I had the chance there would have been a lot less damage all around. Being stubborn was a double-edged sword.

Trying to shake it off, I walked back to what was left of the door and tried to examine it. Feeling pretty sure that he wouldn't have been able to think through closing the door behind himself after he entered the building, I wondered if there might have been another way inside. With a shadow of an agent passing by, I felt the urge to look to the sky again and peer at the eaves of the building.

"The roof," I muttered to myself.

Every agent and police officer for blocks seemed to be stuffed into that building, scouring every crevasse for some clue as to what the hell Patch might have been or where he could have come from. We had just gotten past another large, scary beast rampaging through the city and I don't think anyone was prepared for the new one that jumped onto the scene. Worse, they weren't finding anything of value besides confusing claw marks and old wood shattered into fresh kindling. When I arrived to the top of the building and looked at the rooftop entrance, I saw the one shred of evidence to the mystery of Patch.

It swayed lightly on its hinges, the lock broken away from the frame and the evening breeze pushing through the crack. Clearly it was locked, the deadbolt still jutting out of the side of the door, wrapped in concrete ripped from the exterior wall. The outer knob, still locked itself, was surrounded in vague claw markings arcing around it in a half circle. Before busting the door down Patch had tried to open it like any other person. Apparently, he was capable of thought.

Lucian strolled up behind me as I stared over the mysterious doorknob like one of the ape men staring at a black obelisk. He reached over and squeezed my shoulder lightly while I was entranced with the scratches and said calmly, "The first cold blooded attempt on your life, it's always a little jarring."

I jerked lightly from the sudden contact, shooting a look up to him and saying, "You say it like it's a regular occurrence."

Slyly he smirked, shrugged and replied, "It's happened more than once to me. You get used to it after enough times."

Studying the scratches again, I replied distantly, "I think it has a transceiver in the back of its neck."

"Because of a doorknob?" he asked.

"It tried to open the door with its hand, but when it had its sights on me it just slammed me through the frame," I commented, standing and facing him, "so it's capable of thinking at the very least. But when I shot it in the face, I noticed a light flash on this metal plate on his neck and that's when he decided to jump away."

Eyebrow raised, Lucian dragged a gloved hand down the edge of the door and asked, "So you think it was receiving an order when that light activated?"

I nodded and started down the stairs. "I think it gets orders that it has to follow, and then it thinks for itself as far as the orders will allow."

The silence behind me was deafening when he didn't respond or follow me down. I stopped and looked up at him, seeing a concerned look on his face as he looked down at me with a deep frown. Nodding lightly and finally walking down to meet with me, he patted my arm and asked in a strangely gentle tone, "Are you okay, Nate?"

A chill ran through me at the very sound of the question. I wasn't really hurt and, at the moment, I wasn't much scared. The adrenaline was wearing off and I was feeling a pretty numb feeling starting to take its place. When he asked me if I was okay, I suddenly wasn't.

"I could really use a ride back to the headquarters," I answered hesitantly. "And probably a room down in Purgatory for the next couple nights."

He nodded lightly and walked next to me, putting an arm around my shoulders and patting it lightly. I kind of lost my train of thought just then, maybe deciding it really was time to just let go and go lick my wounds down in a safe space where I knew I wouldn't have anything kick in my door.

Babs waited for us down at the bottom floor, handing out brownies to officer and agent alike. She smiled up at us as we made our way down, pushed her glasses up lightly and held up a bag with a blue ribbon tied around it. When I took it from her the smell of fudge coming from it was hard to mistake and I couldn't help but chuckle at the strange little woman giving out sweets to people at a crime scene.

Softly, she said, "To cheer you up while you're staying in Purgatory, sweetie."

Lucian sniffed at it, an eyebrow rising once again and a slight smirk on his face like he had a mind to take my little bag of sweets. But as he did, she reached over with a similar bag with a bright red ribbon and smiled just as sincerely his way.

"And for you I have these," she said brightly. "They're special ones that will be easy enough for you to digest."

A toothy, fanged grin crossed his face as he asked cheerfully, "A special recipe for Vampires?"

She pushed her glasses back lightly, reached up and patted his cheek. "No honey," she said warmly, "it's for old people."

The grin faded from his face briefly before returning with a hearty laugh. The two of them exchanged a knowing nod and Lucian walked me out of the building as Babs waved us off. He happily opened the bag of "old people" fudge and snacked on it as we passed my car being towed away and crossed the street to his familiar old unit.

I stopped by the door and stared at it for a moment as a small wave of nostalgia ran over me. I hadn't sat in that car, in that seat, for over a year after having been in it so many times before. It was almost comforting to be back there, like going home again. Sitting down, getting adjusted to the old seat, it even felt like it did the last time I was there.

"You know," he commented when sitting back down, "It used to be that you'd be the one who handed me snacks when you got into the car instead of the landlady."

I chuckled softly, nodded and played with the blue ribbon around the baggy. Looking over to him, I smirked and said, "Well Babs thinks these wouldn't be good for you old man."

A sharp jab landed on my shoulder. I winced, realizing it was a little tenderer than I'd imagined it was. It wasn't that hard to understand either with the fact I'd gone through a door and had been flipped in a car. It would have been more surprising to find out that I wasn't bruised and battered under the coat.

"Dulaf let us know what the two of you did," he said after turning the first corner towards the headquarters. "She said she had good reasons for it, but Alston wasn't exactly thrilled to hear it."

I shrugged lightly and tried to relax for the couple blocks we were going to travel. My eyes drifted up towards the skyline, watching the rooftops as we passed through the heart of Fangtown. Flashes of that thing coming down at me crossed my mind, then memories of the brain in the jar.

"I didn't know what she was thinking until we got there," I replied hesitantly. "But I think if she'd told me what I was going to find down there I would have done it anyway."

Out of the corner of my eye I could see a subtle nod. He said in a strong, confident tone, "I think you guys did the right thing too, and I'm pretty sure I can convince Alston of the same when we get there."

I broke my gaze from the rooftops and looked at my old mentor. "So it's time to face the Commissioner with our misdeeds," I mused.

"No," Lucian replied, "it's time to bring him into the fold."

We coasted into the garage before long and exited the car almost at once like the old days. I wasn't too thrilled about facing Alston after a few of the shady things we'd done in the last few days. Knowing Lucian was going to stand at my side made it easier to accept the fact. At best, we would have a man with a lot more authority on our side. At worst, Alston would probably take it out on the higher ranking agents long before he took it out on me. And, for all the rumors and the speculation about why Lucian wasn't the man in charge, I knew at the very least that he was well respected by everyone there.

We entered the building and were almost instantly greeted with the broad shouldered, stone-faced man in the corridor. He stared at us with his piercing eyes and nodded sternly before turning and waving for us to follow to another elevator beyond the usual entrance for the headquarters. Hesitating, I looked to Lucian for reassurance and watched him walk ahead of me towards the elevator doors. Following him in was surreal, knowing where this new shaft was taking us. It wasn't every day you stepped into the elevator that linked directly to the Commissioner's office.

Standing shoulder to shoulder with them, the silence was making me uncomfortable.

Relief came over me when Alston started to talk, which was pretty surreal considering he was the most intimidating person in that little metal box. "So I've heard from Dulaf," he said in his deep, gravelly voice, "that you two broke down part of the relay network's defenses so you can try to track this thing with the system."

I nodded and glanced over to him as subtly as I could. "Whoever's in control of it doesn't care about the safety of Alters," I said as confidently as I could. "I don't think we should let protocol stand in the way of us protecting the people we were put here to protect."

He turned his head just enough for us to make eye contact. The stony brow over his eyes furrowed enough that I swore I could hear a crack from his skin. The longer we maintained that eye contact, in fact, the more I started to feel like I stared into the face of a statue to some ancient god. And while he kept his eyes locked on me that feeling grew ever deeper until he finally closed his eyes and dipped his chin in one of the faintest nods I'd ever seen.

Firmly, he commented, "Whoever's doing this isn't a friend of ours to be sure. We can't afford to let them control the tools at our disposal."

Lucian, standing between us unfazed, interjected matter-of-factly. "Besides," he said, "It seems appropriate we fight one human rights violation by lifting another."

The words felt heavy when he said it but I couldn't object to their use. Even if you could argue that the brain in the jar wasn't a human with rights to speak of, there was still something troubling about it to me. I couldn't understand it and I certainly wasn't in on the full story. However, Dulaf and Lucian were certainly sounding against it and that in itself confirmed some of the squeamish feelings deep in my gut.

We stepped out of the elevator to be greeted by Dulaf on the top floor. I'd rarely seen that part of the headquarters before and almost never without being in trouble. It was a strange room with angled glass walls meeting at a point over our head. The windows forming the far wall were curved and marked with the seals of the Force. The black light that shone from the gaps between the different "petals" of our strange tulip-like building was shining off the darkened glass and creating a distant, faint glow that couldn't quite be placed. And as Dulaf stood from her chair, backlit by it all, I saw a relief on her face that took me off guard.

"You look okay," she said quietly. "It didn't break anything off of you did it?"

I shook my head and rubbed it lightly, answering brashly, "I think hitting it with the car made it think twice about removing my limbs."

Alston passed us, the movement of the air brushing by like a great ship passing in the sea. Circling his desk, he said in a commanding voice, "So now it's time for us to figure out what to hit it with that could cause more harm than a simple car."

Lucian sat by the desk and nodded along, crossing his arms. "We don't exactly have tanks handy," he sniped.

Dulaf patted my arm and returned to her seat, tugging on my sleeve lightly as she stepped away and nodding over at another chair in front of the desk. That seat looked fairly comfortable to me from where I stood, but the idea of sitting down with these people so casually just didn't feel nearly as easy. Everyone in the room outranked me by at least one stage and one of them was the commander of everyone in the city. How was I supposed to sit and talk with a man like that? It felt like being called to the principal's office.

"Sit, Leone," he ordered from behind his desk.

And just like that, I did as I was told by the scary rock man.

Dulaf giggled at me as I parked it next to her and the Golem across the desk glared intensely at me. It wasn't making me any more comfortable that he kept glaring, but I could at least adjust to it with the knowledge his face was in a near permanent scowl.

When she stopped being amused at my situation, Dulaf remarked, "It's obvious that we can't try to take it down by brute force without a whole team. The reports from the scene said the same thing from multiple accounts: nothing injured that thing until Nate shot it in the face."

I winced. "Even then it really didn't seem to do much except hurt it really bad and piss it off even worse."

"Scream and shit yourself loudly," Lucian joked.

Alston nodded along as he listened and sat back in his chair. "So we're looking at mobilizing an entire SOL team like with the Nosferatu. Do we have any alternatives?"

Dulaf shook her head idly, but a thought crossed my mind as I watched her. That little light at the back of his neck was flashing in my memory and I couldn't push it aside.

"Someone was controlling it," I said, looking back at the Commissioner, "they were sending signals to it, I'm almost sure of it."

He brought a hand down on the glossy surface of the desk, over a space that had been worn and scratched repeatedly like the old weathered face of a watch. Idly, he started to rap his fingertip against the surface with a dull, thick crack noise that reverberated

241

through the surface. There was a definite groove in the desk where his finger fell, a long-standing habit of his that had crept to view. After a few taps, he nodded and asked Dulaf, "Do you think we can try to control it ourselves with the Oracle?"

Dulaf fidgeted in her seat and shrugged. "I couldn't be absolutely sure. I think we'd need to drop the entire buffering system to give her direct access to the thing like that. At least without finding a way to force his transceiver, if that's what he actually has, to tie into our system."

"Then get to work on finding a way," Alston said, running his finger idly along the groove in the desk and scraping away at its surface. "The only thing left is to try to find the ones at the wheel and we can't be sure that isn't someone we don't want to tangle with."

Indignantly, I remarked, "Lord knows the Feds tried to crawl up my ass in Port Angeles."

"Which really leads one to wonder," Lucian commented. "It's one thing to want to silence Nate. I think we can all acknowledge he can be a pain in the ass from time to time. But can we be sure that they're the ones who wanted to do it? Sindri and the Port Angeles ACTF were in contact when he was entered into that system."

Dulaf uneasily remarked, "And no one knows why any of them would want to kill some random women around Seattle."

"Two of them were Succubi," I added. "Maybe one of the Senators was experiencing the local night-life."

"Regardless," Alston rumbled, "That means there's three potential organizations behind this thing. All three of them have some potential sway with our government. We can't just randomly take a swing at one of them."

The three of them silently came to a consensus around the desk. The idea behind it was true, but it nagged me that we couldn't identify the one at the wheel. Even the Locusta had known more than us from the start of the case.

"We could try to finally squeeze Rufus," I muttered bitterly.

I wasn't looking up at the time, but I could feel that steely glare aimed my way again. I knew Lucian and Dulaf weren't above asking Rufus for information, all personal feelings towards him aside. But the Commissioner was a staunch supporter of keeping that genie in the bottle as much as possible. It was rare anyone even so much as mentioned his name in the man's presence.

I guess I got over that intimidated feeling from the elevator... or the concussion had caught up to me.

"It's true," I continued defiantly, looking up to meet his gaze. "He knew about everything before we did, even from down where he's been locked up. He knew about the Nosferatu, he knew about Sindri, he knew about these creatures."

"Janice Gray has been dead for some time," Alston said. "There's no way that Rufus Plagas could still be getting current information down there, at all."

Forgetting the rank on my sleeve, the mention of that name crawled under my skin and I snapped at him, "The hell he doesn't! He's given us everything since this started! Right down to searching for that damned lab!"

He fell silent, lacing his thick fingers together and resting his hands against the desk as he studied me. And that courage I had suddenly faded away while I began to shrink back in my seat, quickly following with a forced, "Sir."

"We can't be sure of anything coming out of the man," Alston replied, surprisingly calm. "He may have information but he's also a professional liar."

"We could use the Oracle to try to crack him," I answered, trying to take a more respectful tone. "She can gather all the information around the city, I'm sure she could squeeze the information out of a guy like that."

Dulaf shook her head, frowning and saying with a dripping disdain, "Getting to the deep, dark secrets of someone like Rufus would require him being actually in the same room with her, it would be like removing all of her buffers."

Lucian stood up again, saying, "And that would be like willingly subjecting her to torture."

Dulaf watched Lucian and rose next to him as Alston nodded their way and said, "You two get to work on finding a way to get our system in control of that thing."

They turned and walked out casually, leaving me behind with no clue what to do next. Uncomfortable in the seat again, I started to get up before the graveled voice grunted and the Commissioner cleared his throat at me.

"As for you, agent," he said while beginning to stand himself, towering over me, "You have a sharp tongue, but you may be right about the information. I want you to see what else that man might have."

I nodded and started for the door myself, looking back his way. "Are we sure that we can't let her crack him?"

He shook his head almost as subtly as he nodded and rested his hands behind his back as he circled around the desk once again. "We wouldn't do that except in the most dire of emergencies," he said, looking me over, "and I don't think any of us would approve of something like that."

I wasn't quite sure what would happen to her without the buffer. Everything about the Oracle at the moment was sounding like a complicated issue that I didn't know nearly enough about. So once again I went with the reactions everyone around me had and nodded in agreement with what he said. He returned the nod, lifted a great big hand, and patted me squarely across the back with a sharp thud.

Watching my wince, he guided me back to the elevator and nudged me through a bit more gently. "You might want to take the rest of the night off," he said. "You're starting to look a little tenderized."

Chapter 24
Plagas' Guy

I sat in Purgatory for the rest of the night, watching the kids run around the field outside the apartments and watching the sky drifting by on the ceiling. A cool breeze crossed my face and the smell of flowers filled the air. The stream running by occasionally lulled me to sleep long enough for the kids to skip over and drop bugs or dirt on me for shits and giggles. When I startled awake and they ran away giggling, I couldn't draw up the motivation or the energy to chase them. And, really, it was my own fault for dozing off in their playground so many times.

When the sun rose in the morning I was stirred awake by the feeling of warmth across my face. Those projectors, though they filtered the UV out, still generated enough light to make me feel the rays touching down on me. I raised my hand to it and squinted through my fingers, never having actually lingered in this place during the daytime before. After a moment, a shadow stood over me and shielded me from the brilliant light above.

"Hey there," Dulaf said warmly. "Finally get some rest?"

Sitting up, I looked around at the deceptive grassy field around me and said sleepily, "I guess the stuff the doctor gave me did the trick."

"Good," she said with a giggle.

Glancing up at her, I caught her smile and noticed the sound of rustling grass as another figure darted nearby. With a swift, surprising motion a little shadow came around behind me and a bucket of water was dumped across my head, Amelia and Dulaf cackling as they fled the scene, Dulaf sweeping Amelia into the air and running for all she was worth. With the swift, cat-like movements of Dulaf it wasn't long before they disappeared around a bend and vanished away to another part of the sanctuary.

"Damned Elves," I muttered, getting up and shaking the water out of my hair.

My surprise at the fact I could stand was hard to contain. Realizing that I somehow wasn't cracking and popping when I stood there, I bounced and hopped from foot to foot and marveled at the cocktail the doctor had used on me before I dragged myself to this place. A few of the adults down below grinned at my energetic skipping and a couple of giggles were heard before I remembered myself and stopped celebrating my miraculous recovery.

As if to bring me back down to Earth, a grinding metal sound came from the far end, the gates to the prison space opening and closing as the guards rotated for a new shift. I watched them walk through like the living dead rising from the depths and remembered where I needed to go. Picking my jacket up from the grass, I started to put it back on, pausing for a moment to examine an amazingly dark bruise on my arm that I hadn't felt during my cheerful bouncing.

I chuckled and shrugged it off. "I'll probably feel it tomorrow."

Still buttoning the coat as I walked up, I got some strange looks from the guards standing at the gates to Limbo. One gestured at me and commented, "Apartment burn down or something?"

Trying to stay casual, I replied with a grin, "Giant busted down the door to my building."

They laughed it off and waved me through the gates, the howling normally found in the asylum quieted in these morning hours. Joe the curate was missing, his shift having ended, and a new man I didn't recognize was sitting at his desk. Silly as it was, I assumed Joe was always there like the hologram standing at the entrance above.

The usual protocol escaped me as I walked closer, trying my hardest to remember what I'd said to Joe in the times before Joe and I came to know each other. After a momentary pause, I stood where he could see my badge and announced in an awkwardly stilted way, "Agent Leone, requesting entrance to Acheron and transport to the ninth level."

The curate, far younger than Joe, smirked and replied smugly, "New guy, huh?"

He stood and walked with me to the lift. His cocky attitude even came out in the way he walked, a strut in his stride as he stuck his chest out and twirled a set of keys playfully. I brushed off the feeling and followed him to the lift, deciding to play along and figuring there was no harm in the fact he didn't recognize me. I was well liked, but it wasn't like I was famous for anything except getting shot once with one of the worst guns ever built. So I gave him a pass, figuring there was no reason to hold it against the guy.

"Don't worry kid," he said reassuringly, "You're going to be just fine so long as you don't make eye contact with anyone down there. I'll take care of you."

Maybe there was some reason to hold it against him.

We went through the prison complex on the lift and I did my best to look presentable on the way down. There was grass everywhere and my hair was a bit of a mess. And as silly as it might have been, I didn't want Rufus to have any ammo to use against me that he didn't already have. So I groomed myself in the reflection off of the glass of the lift and played with my hair like some teenager getting ready for a date. The curate, who didn't speak a word for the entire mile trip down the coiling shaft, could easily be seen smirking in the reflection of the glass. Despite the attitude, I couldn't bring myself to give a shit what that man thought of me. For once I was in a good mood first thing in the day.

It was strangely the best sleep I'd had in some time, lying there in the dirt and the grass, surrounded by giggling children and occasionally being tormented. Maybe it was the first time in a while that I was too exhausted to keep myself awake. Maybe it even had something to do with the doctor's cocktail or the lingering effects of Babs' potion from the day before. But, whatever it was, I was well rested. Even without coffee, when that door opened at the bottom, I was ready and willing to face the people beyond.

The curate chuckled and nodded to me as the doors opened, slapping my shoulder and nudging me along saying, "Don't worry, there's going to be glass between you and him, and you look fine."

Humoring him, I smiled, waved and walked out as quickly as possible. The guards checked me and escorted me through, and for the first time ever I walked into Rufus' vault and saw the lights in his glass house turned off.

A guard by my side whispered, "He turned in about two hours ago. I don't know if you can wake him up but, if you can, he's all yours."

Grinning a little too much, I marched over to the bridge and quickly crossed into the alcove. I pounded my fist on the door-frame to try to get his attention, the banging echoing off the cavernous walls of the chamber. Peering through the glass showed me faint outlines, the glow of dim running lights making it possible to still see many of the shapes, including Rufus in a bedroom at the far end, stiff as possible, looking like a corpse as his rigid form laid flat. Nothing moved, not a hint of a reaction anywhere, the sound of my banging reaching deaf ears as he seemed to be dead to the world.

Glimpsing back at the guard, I asked, "Can I do anything I want to try to wake him up?"

The guard contemplated for a second, shrugged and replied, "I don't see why not so long as you don't hurt him any."

Reaching down, I fished out my earplugs and grabbed a Banshee I'd borrowed from another agent after the clusterfuck in my building. I'd intended to keep it handy in case I ran into Patch again. Though it may have been a waste of resources, before I knew it I was opening a slot in the door, turning it on, and jabbing the end through the slot.

The scream from the back of the box was almost as loud as the one from the rod. His shadow bolted up from the bed and practically into the air before hitting the floor running and dashing through the apartment towards me. The lights flashed on and in an instant he was grabbing for the rod in an enraged, disheveled state, eyes blood red and fangs bared. Jerking the rod back from the slot, I removed it from the box and shut it off before he slammed against the wall and glared menacingly at me.

"So I take it you're not a morning person," I joked, brandishing the rod and tapping it against the glass.

Hissing, he demanded, "What do you want, Leone?!"

My smile faded and my humor passed as I asked sternly, "Who's behind the creature that escaped from Sindri?"

Practically growling, he snapped back at me, "How the hell would I know?"

"Because you knew everything else," I said. "Someone's giving you information still and the people who are giving it to you know things no one else does."

He turned away and ran bone-like fingers through his hair to straighten it. Keeping his back to me, he tried to compose himself in a corner while I watched on, beginning to wander back towards a chair with a clumsy gait. He sat with a heavy groan and stared to the floor for a few moments before lifting his eyes to me again. The red color was already beginning to pass and the calm facade once again took hold of the slender man.

Finally composed, he replied to me in his usual tone, "So because you can't find these things on your own you're going to try to strong arm them out of me?"

"I'm not here to strong arm anything," I answered. "But I know you know more than you're letting on. These things were created by people who support your philosophy, you knew they existed and the Locusta have been acting like the murders weren't a problem. Why is it that they knew there was a tracking device on that Nosferatu but they didn't act on it? Why didn't any of you act on what you know so far?"

He smiled broadly at me with a fanged, toothy grin. "Ah, yes, it would seem that my men haven't been very proactive about the situation with those creatures," he said. "I suppose it would seem a bit strange to you."

Studying him, I considered reaching for the visor, but held off and asked, "Do you know who's doing it?"

For all the bluster, the old creature sitting in the chair sat back and looked almost defeated as he crossed his arms and said, "Even I don't know that much."

Frowning, I tapped the Banshee against the slot. "But you knew about those creatures didn't you?"

His eyes drifted down to the slot, then back up at me, an eyebrow rising subtly. "I think what you found when I sent you speaks for itself, doesn't it?"

My hand tightened around the rod. "You're involved in that, aren't you? You had someone on the inside with that operation."

A corner of his mouth lifted slightly while he suppressed a smirk, exhaling sharply as he shook his head. "Now why would I possibly send you to go break up an operation I had a stake in? It seems to me that sending you there makes no sense at all if I have any control of it."

The word "control" echoed in my head for a moment, almost overwhelming me as I started to physically feel a realization come over me. "You lost control somehow, didn't you? That's why you want us to put it back in the bottle for you."

Smugly, he remarked, "Well I wouldn't exactly want anyone playing with my toys, would I?"

Hiding my disgust wasn't easy while I asked, "When did you lose control of your 'toys'? Who took it from you?"

He shrugged and waved to me, "My contacts with that organization were higher up, people in the executive levels. I had someone who was attached to the project itself for some time. Somewhere along the line he was eliminated."

Desmond's talk of a man dying on the job came to mind. There was a chance the two incidents weren't isolated after all. "How do you know it wasn't an accident?" I asked. "A lot of people get hurt or killed on the job, especially in a place where they deal with biological hazards like that."

"You've heard about that one, haven't you?" He asked, sitting at attention.

"I was informed about someone dying on the job there, causing the increase in security," I said. "You're telling me that was your man?"

Hesitating, he eventually shrugged and nodded. "It doesn't help to hide it anymore; you've already figured that my supporters are behind the project. You may as well know he was involved. His name was Oliver Smith. He wasn't a member of the Locusta but he wasn't against taking their money."

Putting the rod away at my belt, I turned towards the bridge and asked, "You wouldn't happen to know who killed Oliver, would you?"

"If I did," Rufus said, rising from the seat, "they wouldn't be alive anymore."

We were both thinking the same thing at that moment; I didn't even have to ask him as I started walking out. When I passed the bridge and turned for the exit he called out to me, "When you find the man at the switch, be sure to let him know who sent you."

It halted me to hear it, wondering if I was being Rufus' enforcer for a fleeting moment. Rubbing my head, I averted my eyes from him and hurried down the hallway. The rested feeling I'd had from the field quickly faded and the minor aches were starting to flare by the time I reached the far end. The dirty, uneasy feeling grew all the way back to the surface as I fidgeted and squirmed. My skin crawled at the idea of busting someone Rufus wanted taken down.

The curate patted my back and grinned. "Take it easy kid, new guys usually don't go down this far. Did he give you what you wanted to know?"

"I got enough," I replied, crossing my arms, fingers starting to massage into my arthritic arm idly. "I think he's using us to carry out a hit."

The curate examined me suspiciously and reached to slap my shoulder again before hesitating and lowering his hand. "Well luckily we don't take orders from Rufus Plagas then."

My lip curled a bit and I tried to hold back the comment floating at the back of my throat. I bit it back, swallowed my pride and tried my best to fake a smile. "Yeah," I said through my teeth with a strained grin, "He's toothless."

Ignorant to the end, he smiled and waved me out as we reached the top again. I stormed out the door and cut through Purgatory as fast as I could, passing the giggling children and trying not to look their way. Amelia waved as I passed, but I couldn't bring myself to look her way and tried to act like I just hadn't noticed.

It wasn't that I felt bad stopping whoever was behind this. It was just knowing that this entire thing may have stayed under our radar if Rufus hadn't started to clue us in, if the Locusta hadn't given us the tracking device instead of resolving it themselves. Whatever was happening, it was something he wanted us to take care of so his people could keep their hands clean. And they weren't even afraid of killing the FBI so that spoke volumes about what kind of shit I was stepping into now.

An eerie silence filled the room ahead of me. Every agent on the scene was entranced, left frozen in their places as they watched something playing out on the status monitors above. I scanned the ceiling myself and tried to make out what they saw, the indicators showing dozens of emergency beacons triggered at once in a tight cluster. A team had been hit hard. My heart started to sink and I slowed to a stop as I realized which team it would have been.

As we watched those flashing points of light, seeing another team on the move to assist, I knew everyone had just been introduced to Patch. Alston sent a team to try to stop it as I slept and now I was awake in time to see it fail. And as I watched on, Dulaf approached me and rested a hand on my arm.

"SOL made contact," she said quietly in my ear. "And it's looking like he wiped them out."

Chapter 25
The Survivor

We stood among the debris of what was once a small business office. The pieces of broken gear were scattered among shattered furniture and destroyed computers. There were holes in the walls roughly the size of full grown men going clear through to other rooms. And, as I entered, several of those men were carted out on stretchers as the medical teams scrambled to find them all.

Watching one of them roll by, I walked deeper into the office and carefully made my way around anything that could have been evidence: broken furniture, claw marks, bloodstains and the like. The investigators were already busy at work cataloguing everything the best they could with their cameras. In a room like this one, there was really very little they could do to sort it all on the scene. Moving to join them, Dulaf brushed past me with a large case hanging over her shoulder, longer than even the one she used for "Sexy".

Though, it disturbed me that I was starting to mentally refer to the gun by that name.

I followed her in, tracing her steps as she weaved through the scene, making sure to only put my foot down in roughly the same places she did. She didn't seem to have to think about it at all, never even looking down at the floor as she seemed to instinctively float past the rubble around her. When I glanced up for a moment to try to see how she was doing it, I felt my foot hit something with a metallic clink. A distorted, weakened little beep like an alarm clock on the verge of dying came out from under whitewall dust in front of my foot. A faint red light flickered on for just a flash, like the last flare of a candle before dying out.

Kneeling, I took a shot of the scene with the hand-link to preserve it for their information, reached down and brushed away just enough dust to see what was there. A badge laid on the floor under the dust, dented and bent, the beacon light cracked and the electronics partially hanging out of it. The hand-link didn't even recognize it as a badge, the beacon not showing on the Oracle's feed. But the lion's face was still unmistakable, scarred and contorted it may have been, and the name on the plate was one I recognized.

Lifting it from the floor, taking shots of it as I did, I murmured to myself, "Richards."

Dulaf glanced back at me, saying, "I think I saw him in one of the ambulances outside."

Running my thumb across the plate, feeling the raised letters, I stared at the bent surface and wondered how you'd manage something like that. Did the creature bend it on purpose? Was it the force of an impact or some random act in the middle of the fray? As I looked up from it and scanned around me, my eyes became fixed on one of their helmets, caved in with a dent about the size of Patch's fist. It was answering my questions, harkening back to shattered windows and overturned cars.

"How was he?" I asked sadly.

She turned her back to me again and opened the case, Xander and Philip joining her side as she replied hesitantly, "It wasn't looking good."

The three of them pulled equipment from the case, long mechanical devices with tripod legs and spheres on the ends like crystal balls. Each of them took to a corner of a room and set up these machines, standing them upright and extending the necks until the spherical objects were extended to eye level. I'd never actually seen these devices before, whatever they'd been, and curiously wandered over to peer into the case over Dulaf's shoulder.

"New toy?" I asked quietly, seeing her pull smaller devices from inside.

She shook her head and grinned at me. "If you'd gone into the smart people's division," she chided, "you'd have seen these before."

I shook my head back at her before catching a glimpse of her aura. There was a faint nervousness she was trying to suppress.

And, for a moment, I knew what she needed was a taste of the status quo.

Grinning, I asked, "Is it really 'smart' when you've been studying for over two millennia?"

She shot me a glare and walked away from the case, backing up with the devices in hand. "I'm not *that* old," she scolded, turning away on a heel and tossing her hair with a snap.

Other investigators I hadn't known strolled into the room for a moment, catching sight of the three with their crystal balls and quickly retreating back to where they came. Though I didn't know why they'd left, I started to feel uncomfortable about standing there. Fidgeting in my place, I looked around for some sign of what the devices might do. And as I studied them, Xander threw a switch and a deep electrical hum rolled from the base of the machine and towards that sphere. Suddenly, I was half way across the room and letting my feet do the thinking as I hurried out for the hallway.

The three of them followed me out shortly after, Dulaf taking up the rear as she threw one of the smaller devices to the ceiling, closed up the case and lugged it back out of the room with her. Lights and sounds went off in the room behind her as the rest of us watched on. The spheres lit up like stars as things outside of the visible spectrum swept across every surface of the room.

"Imaging equipment?" I asked.

Xander nodded along and replied cheerfully, "They really take a lot of the grunt work out of places like this, leaves us to just photograph stains and residue patterns instead of every damn surface."

Chuckling, I marveled at the lightshow at play and watched as lasers crawled along the floors, ceiling and every scrap of furniture still left standing. None of what was intact looked all that impressive, most of it just your standard fare. Strangely, not long into the scan I started to notice the odd lack of any electronics not scattered across the floor. It wasn't some advanced lab or an important location. In fact, looking at the room made me wonder why it would come into a building like this at all, especially in broad daylight.

"Why was it here?" I asked, looking around at the Elves.

The minions looked as puzzled as me and shrugged their shoulders while Dulaf replied, "The Oracle got into its head, but it wasn't very useful. She couldn't get into any of his thoughts; just what he was seeing and where he was at the time. It was like watching a videogame while someone else played."

Grimacing, I got frustrated and said, "And, of course, we couldn't find out who that player was."

The feeling of the group shifted, Dulaf slipping back from me just enough for it to be noticeable, a genuinely hurt expression crossing her face. "You know we're trying," she said sorrowfully. "We're all trying to get this under control."

I felt like an ass. The heat in my face and the blush coming on were impossible to ignore as I tried to look anywhere but directly at her. But when I looked away from her I inevitably ended up on similarly wounded expressions on her team.

"I'm sorry guys," I apologized, absently rubbing at my shoulder and rolling it a bit. "I'm not angry at you for not being able to crack this thing. I'm angry at the cloak and dagger bullshit going on behind the scenes on this."

Xander cracked a very slight smile and nudged me with a bump, "We get it, we're all feeling a little shitty about this case. Phillip over here's been feeling especially bad."

I peered at Phillip past Xander and thought about how bad he looked after Alice. He still had those dark circles under his eyes as he gave an understanding nod.

Glancing back into the room, I asked, "Come to think of it, were any civilians hurt this time?"

Dulaf scratched behind her ear for a moment in thought. "Actually," she said, "I think there were a few hurt but none of them were critical."

Phillip nodded earnestly and said, "They left here with everything intact, that's for sure."

Eyebrow raised, I prodded curiously, "So were any of them a match for the profiles?"

Xander replied, "There was one woman among the three that were sent to the hospital, but I'm not sure if she was an Alter or not. I only caught sight of her on the way in."

To which Phillip quickly chimed in, "She was a Nymph!"

The others stopped to look at the suddenly energetic Phillip as he nervously shrugged and added, "I had to see for myself."

Finally, a survivor: someone who could answer questions for us after so many victims. I rushed past them, slapping Phillip on the shoulder and turning to face him as I continued down the hall backwards. "The names are on the system already?"

Dulaf called out to me, "Of course they are, we're the professionals here."

Stopping at the door, I quipped before ducking outside, "Since when have you been a professional?"

Out the door and down the stairs, I made my way out to the bike Lucian had taken to the coast. After losing my car I found that it was actually unclaimed, left lying and waiting to be assigned to some unlucky sap like me that'd lost his car. It wasn't as secure as the cars and not nearly ready to take a punch from something like Patch. At the time I was siding with speed over defense. Patch had already had his way with one car, after all.

Though the majority of the people taken from the building were carted off to the Headquarters' medical wing, the civilians went to the nearest Emergency Room. I found myself at the doorsteps not long after, searching through the information on the system in the hopes of finding something I could use without having to actually talk to them. None of them were particularly injured when I arrived, though. Even if the SOL team failed to capture the creature when they took their shot at it, they could at least have some consolation in that.

The woman among them was Erica Fields, still actually sitting in the ER's waiting room when I arrived. She looked young, possibly around Alice's age, and showed very little signs she might have been an Alter. Her sandy blonde hair was a bit disheveled, hanging a bit loosely over her face and partially covering the scrape across her cheek. Her clothes were covered in dirt, dust and a couple spots of blood that didn't appear to be hers.

All the same, she was cradling her arm in a fashion that haunted me just a bit and made every step in her direction a little more urgent. Seeing an ACTF agent march up to her with a purpose probably wasn't the best thing for her mental health, suddenly sitting upright with wide eyes like a poor little animal struck in the path of a car.

Shaken, she stammered, "Can I help you, officer?"

"You were there when that thing hit your office?" I asked. "Did it hurt you?"

Calming, likely getting the impression of why I was in such a rush, she lifted her elbow towards me with a wince. "That thing, whatever it was, shoved me out of the way and I ended up smashing my elbow into a desk."

Inspecting her elbow, still trying to reassure myself that the arm was still there, I asked, "Did it try to grab at you any, maybe try to claw at anything?"

Erica looked me over and inquired softly, "Why would it try to do that?"

I wavered for a moment but finally answered, "It's been going after women like you for a while and we're not entirely sure why."

She scoped out the rest of the room before leaning in towards me and whispering, "You mean women that look like me or..."

"Alters," I interjected, trying to be as soft about it as her. "It's been targeting Alter women for weeks and we can't figure out why." Pausing, I looked into her eyes and said with a surprising relief, "Actually, I think you're the first one to get away from it."

She didn't seem nearly as relieved as I did when she asked, "Has it done something like this in broad daylight before?"

Something about it did feel off to me too, it really hadn't done it in broad daylight, definitely not in front of groups. For weeks they'd been able to convince people that a giant bat had been doing it. So why was it suddenly there, in the open, attacking a woman in front of a room full of people? Maybe it wasn't the woman. Maybe it was the room.

Curiously, I asked, "What exactly does your company do?"

She seemed confused at first, but shrugged it off and answered, "We're a security firm. We set up cameras and alarm systems for local businesses, keep track of the backups in case something happens on site. You know, watching out for people."

She didn't need to elaborate much. As soon as the word "security" left her lips I'd known exactly what had happened. She hadn't escaped maiming like the others – she wasn't even the target. There was something in that company's backups that was a threat to the one at the wheel. And, if that were true, I suddenly had a lead that we couldn't have had before.

Seeing Patch on a security feed wouldn't have taught us anything new. The only reason to destroy recordings was because something on those feeds showed who was controlling him. Maybe they were on the scene of one of the murders. Maybe one of those feeds had a motive. So when she said "local businesses", only one thought came to mind: there was a damn good chance there was something on The Moirae's tapes.

Chapter 26
Recorded Nightmares

I stayed with Erica for about an hour, waiting to make sure that her and her coworkers really did come out of it mostly unscathed. The SOL team had taken the brunt of it but I knew that if I were one of them I'd want to know that what I'd done had meant something. When the last of them had been checked and cleared by the doctors I left with that message in mind and flew across town to get back to the headquarters.

I couldn't be sure, right away, that my hunch on the tapes was right. But Dulaf already told me that she'd been able to see through that thing's eyes, even if it wasn't all that helpful. If my hunch was right, if it was what I'd thought it'd been, then it would be clear the thing was aiming for their equipment and not their people.

The headquarters was tense again, everyone on pins and needles as they moved through the shared office space. From the ceiling I could see an entire monitor had been dedicated strictly to the status reports for the SOL team. Every single one of their names glowed red above us and showed critical by them. It should have made me feel worse to see them listed like that but I was too relieved that none of them were dead.

The labs were as busy as I'd ever seen them while the crews did their best to catalogue everything. Standing at the door, I waved to try to get Dulaf's attention without having to get in anyone's way. After a couple attempts she finally caught sight of me and handed off a clipboard to Xander before practically jogging over.

She asked a touch impatiently, "Well? Did you find anything?"

"I'm going to need to see the recording of what we got off of that thing," I said. "Will I be able to access it from one of the desks or will the line eat it before it gets there?"

Resting a hand on her head and chewing on her lip, she considered for a moment before saying, "I guess I can send it over without any problems. I don't think the line's intercepting any of the office networks." An eyebrow raised and her ears coming to attention, she asked slyly, "And what exactly will you be looking for in there?"

"A break in the case," I said. "I think he wasn't there to go after the people. I think he was there for the equipment."

She stood a little straighter and tilted her head slightly while she exclaimed, "No way, you think they were trying to remove evidence?"

Holding back the snort, I tried not to laugh when I said, "That really seems to be everything they've done in the last few weeks."

Still chewing on that lip, she shrugged tossed up her hands. "You know, I should have realized that was kind of stupid before I said it," she mused. "I'll try to put the video on the network for you."

It was the fastest I'd ever gone to a desk in my life. In the years I'd been part of the Force, the desk was the site of the unpleasant things like paperwork. For the first time I would have something waiting for me that felt truly important. Well, I hoped it would be waiting for me. I couldn't be entirely sure as I sat down.

Watching the network for signs of it to arrive left me time to do a few things anyway. Starting up a search, I looked for information on Oliver Smith: Rufus' inside man with the Sindri researchers. The system returned nearly a thousand hits across the country. With a whistle I punched in a few commands to filter and let it work away at weeding out the false positives. Minimizing the window, I saw the network again and realized there was another video that could be waiting for me there. Checking the system for the tapes, I found the files lying there.

Marionette had followed through and sent the security tapes to me. With luck, maybe those girls really did run across a senator in the depths of that club. When I went to open the files, a tone rang out and a new icon appeared from the dark recesses of the network. The name was easily identified, Dulaf's typical smartass attitude shining through as I saw a file marked "Nate's Date" appear on my screen. Reaching over, I opened that file instead and sat back bracing for what horrors could come.

He moved so fluidly, like a cat through a jungle. Even through his own eyes I had trouble following his movements across the Seattle skyline. The Nosferatu's wings and the way it moved made it easy for people to spot it crossing overhead as it cut a shadow across the sky. But Patch here moved too fast, too purposefully. He leapt from one building to another with the same sort of grace that Lucian had when he scaled the side of the Sindri headquarters on the sea. The split second to travel from one point to another leaving no chance anyone could have seen something even his size moving by.

Along the edges of his view there were colorful lights and streams of data. Was it part of how he saw the world or just an overlay from the Oracle? I wouldn't have known and I certainly couldn't read the code. I could only watch as it waved and danced along what would have been his peripheral vision. I kept glancing at it every few seconds, like I expected something to jump out of it at me.

Surprisingly, something did.

With a sudden flash and a burst of new data I saw that field of junk cluttering his peripheral vision jump out and expand with a giant block of information that hadn't been there before. Pausing the video, I tried my best to decipher that block only to see a great deal of coding that I couldn't have understood in the least. But when I hit play again I noticed that Patch had stopped moving at the same time. That block, whatever it was, caught his attention the same way it caught mine.

Turning, Patch changed his course for no apparent reason except for that sudden burst of information. It became pretty obvious what I'd just witnessed and before too long I could see the building ahead of him where the incident took place. He landed on the roof and rushed for the access door. He took the time to stop and grab at the knob before finding it locked and frustratingly ripping it clear like he'd done on my roof. And then he was down into the building and sweeping through it with a purpose.

That stream of data had changed now. It wasn't in a way I could understand, but the nature of it, the quality of it was different. Something about how fast it was streaming by and the amount of it moving at once felt more aggressive than it had been before. And, as it moved more aggressively, so did he.

Reaching the office, Patch pushed through the door like a sheet of paper and sent shards of wood flying everywhere. The people inside screamed and flew out of his path, some running and others literally being slapped aside with an extraordinary ease. I could see a few in his path and recognized the faces of the three I sat with in the ER. Erica stood from her seat and practically froze in the face of this humanoid rhinoceros that had graced their door.

Patch hunched low, ready to pounce, and leapt at her with all of his might, colliding with her and sending her tumbling against furniture. He followed her movements as she fell to the ground and loomed over her, ready to strike. Then, as he was preparing to maul her, another block of information surged into view. In a flash he swung his whole body around and lashed out at the nearest computer. It vaporized into sparkling lights and splinters of glass, plastic and bits of metal. Not hesitating for a moment to appreciate his work, Patch vaulted over the desk and went for the next computer. Before long he was tearing through every electronic in sight like a whirling dervish. And that's all I needed to see: he was definitely ordered to hit the computers.

The search I ran for the name returned results as I watched Patch chew through the office equipment. I paused the video and opened the other window, taking a good hard look at Oliver's profile. There wasn't a touch of silver anywhere on his files: all of it was just black as the dead of a moonless night. The reports for his death were mostly redacted in the good old fashioned black marker that came to me as a refreshing change of pace. But what I could gather out of it was that it was being labeled an "industrial accident".

Clearly it was a sign that his accident had to do with something top secret. I imagined that one of the other creatures got out of its bottle and got its hands around his throat. But when

I looked at his actual job title I found that hard to believe. In fact, his title practically knocked the wind out of me.

Oliver Smith was the head of the transplant committee.

An executive with no business being anywhere near those test-tube soldiers.

Hairs rose on my arm as I reached for the video out of the Moirae and hit play. I knew what to expect from it: someone was going to talk to the girls that were killed, someone I would recognize. In fact, I had a good hunch I knew who it was going to be now. And there, in the surprisingly high definition feed, wandering through the neon lights and weaving through the packed crowd, a man approached the first of these girls and talked to her as she danced atop her little stage. Grabbing at the video and twisting my hand across my desk's surface, I turned the POV to another camera in the room, angling towards his face.

I watched on as this girl danced her last dance and the meek little man stared up at her. The neon lights weren't kind to him, making him gaunt and reflecting off his scalp through the wispy hair atop his head. His glasses caught every stray light in the room, turning his eyes into two large beacons that made him stand out against the crowd. Sitting there, a ghoulish figure at her feet, Archie watched her last dance too.

Chapter 27
Uncovering Evil

Hours later we were standing on the threshold of Archie's house. Twilight was setting in and the sky turned a burnt crimson as we approached that unnatural façade. We brought two SOL teams, a set of investigators and every agent Port Angeles could muster. Piling out of the vans as quickly and cleanly as we could, we crossed the fence and approached the door. It was a little surreal, like an army coming to wage war with his rose bushes and those creepy little lawn gnomes hiding in the shadows.

SOL took the lead and surrounded that house; a wall of faceless black figures encircled the cozy looking home and manning every door and window possible. One squad gathered around the door, a man attaching a preset Wisp and backing away as the others readied their rifles. Visors and earplugs were up all around, ready to block out the blinding white flash of the Wisp as it made a powerful bang and wrenched that door from the frame. And then the dark figures flooded the house, their polished helmets turning blood red under the light of the setting sun.

Months, if not years, of dust flew through the air as the men trampled the frozen shrine to a lost love. Plowing through the house, everything was overturned as they scoured that building for a sign of him. Glass broke, furniture was overturned indiscriminately and doors were kicked open. Following them inside, I nearly choked on the air, struggling to watch them as they rampaged through this house. In the back of my mind I knew that they were out of control but I couldn't fault them for it. I understood why they were destroying this place.

When the dust started to settle, we found no sign of Archie and the way he controlled Patch. Walking through the debris, feeling glass crack under my boot, I wondered if maybe they'd smashed his control to splinters without knowing it. But nothing on the floor looked like scraps of electronics. Nothing in that place seemed advanced enough to do what he had done.

At my back, coming in last, the investigative team started to sweep through the wrecked house and look for signs of what he might have done. They started in the living room and the other spaces towards the front of the house. Clearly they weren't going to find anything there; he never would have gone into those rooms and disturbed his personal shrines. I cut through the house and went to the back instead. Peering through the doorways, I kept going until I found a bedroom and entered that cautiously.

Thick curtains cloaked the room in shadows, the smell of dust once again on the air. When I turned on the lights it became clear that one half of the room had dust and cobwebs in it like the living room had. A queen size bed was left unmade with a missing pillow. An impression of a human form was left in the far end, faint cobwebs forming in the path between that side of the bed and the nearest wall. On the floor was a sleeping bag, left open with a pillow lying at the head.

Snapping shots of the room, I resisted the urge to curse at myself for missing all of this. I walked through and saw how troubled the man had been and still walked back out once I was sure he hadn't poisoned me. I almost let my personal feelings get in the way and this time it was going to be guys like Richards who'd paid for my mistake.

"Felt bad for him, didn't you?" Dulaf asked quietly from the door.

Regretfully I replied, "Might have had a little sympathy for him, yeah."

"Wouldn't be the first time you overlooked something staring you right in the face," she said sharply. "But you usually get back around to it."

Kneeling over the sleeping bag, snapping shots of it, I knew she registered why Archie's story dropped my guard. I lingered on the parallels for a moment before asking, "I did it again, didn't I?"

"I don't know," She said solemnly, quickly following with sarcasm, "Did you want to sleep with Archie?"

"Actually…" I trailed off, trying to avoid eye contact. "I didn't sleep with Janice."

The jaw dropping out of the corner of my eye made me cringe. Throwing her hands into the air and rolling her eyes, Dulaf snapped, "Then why the hell have you been hung up on that case for the last year?!"

Swept up in the emotion, I shot back, "Because I fucked up! She was stalking me for months and I never even registered it. I even thought *I* was the one being creepy! And I was so caught up in a little flirtation that I didn't even notice she never even had a pet!"

A jarring silence hit us, Dulaf taken aback and her face lighting up with shock and confusion. Her ears rose, then sank again very slowly as she leaned in closer and asked very quietly, "Why would it matter if she had a pet?"

Grimacing, I muttered, "I ran into her in the grooming section of Chester's during the Wolfendown situation."

"So, you were staking it out," she replied, "and she was staking *you* out?"

Solemnly, I nodded.

Reaching over to me, putting a hand on my shoulder, Dulaf said with an earnest nod, "You *really* fucked that up."

It was a typical Dulaf reaction and I couldn't quite figure out how to respond. I suddenly wasn't contemplating my own mistakes. Really I just started picturing the various ways I could make her pay for it, muttering, "Do you ever let up?"

Leaning in, whispering in my ear, she asked, "Angry?"

Studying her face, I tried to picture what was going on in that screw-ball head of hers, admitting, "A little."

"Good," she said quietly, pinching my cheek. "Because everyone's watching."

Wincing, I heard the sound of the team outside and realized how bad it was going to look if I broke down on a raid. Though her method sucked, she was right: I needed to keep my mind off of it. Searching the room for anything that I could use or at least focus on was pretty much all I could do to keep from being embarrassed or upset about my failures. Though, I honestly didn't expect to see something that could actually help the case in that room verging on a living memorial.

It was almost invisible in the shadows, only partially there and in colors that nearly blended with the dark. But there it was, staring me in the face, the remains of a footprint for a pair of shoes sitting in the corner by a dresser. They had a heavy tread, more than the smooth sole of any shoes he would be wearing to work, more suited for rough terrain. The dirt left behind in the carpet was caked in like mud, dried out and crusting over the top of the fibers, leaving behind only half an impression. Better than that, there were some signs of relatively fresh mud not far away like he'd just used them not too long ago.

"Dulaf," I called over, waving excitedly. "He has hiking shoes!"

She wiped at her face and walked over, saying, "I don't exactly see what that has to do with anything."

Mockingly, I waved around the room and remarked, "Well Miss Investigator, do you see them around the room anywhere?"

She stood straighter, ear-tips bouncing up as her head shot around and she explored the room with a frantic energy. Opening a closet door and shining a flashlight around, she cried back to me, "You don't think he's wearing them, do you?"

Standing, I left the room, feeling her hot on my heels as I pushed through the teams clogging the hallway and went to his little shrine in the kitchen. With everything else overturned and smashed, it was eerie to see that one table and the one photo on the wall still pristine. It hung there untouched, a smiling face reaching across the room to me and calling my attention. And as I peered into her smiling face, I took a look at the bigger picture and saw exactly what I needed to see.

I remembered that woman with the golden hair, the photo of Archie's wife as she smiled against the majestic backdrop. And when I saw those footprints my mind leapt to this one place. Clearly, they had hiked in the past. And with us catching onto him, it seemed to me that if he was going to run off somewhere it wasn't that long a drive to get into the park.

"Dulaf," I called out, "You've beat down a lot of rookies in that park, right?"

She scoffed, "Thousands!"

Pointing to the photo, I glanced back at her and asked, "So do you recognize the location?"

Her eyebrows quirked while she eyed the photo. "You know," she said, "I think I actually do."

Several hours passed after kicking in Archie's door while Dulaf and I tried to argue that a mountain search was necessary. There weren't that many ways in or out of Port Angeles and the local office was covering the city itself. With a roadblock at each end, the only place left to go was the park. Despite this, the idea of devoting resources to wandering a national park over a couple of photos seemed a little too silly even for our outfit. In the end, only half a dozen guys joined the search in the mountains as the rest scoured the neighborhood for the man. Dulaf identified the place as Obstruction Point, a mountain about half an hour drive and a decent hike south of where we were. So with that half dozen we trekked into the woods, across old mountain roads and to what looked to be fairly popular hiking trails in the dead of the night.

A near endless array of footprints was lit by nothing more than the moon.

"Needle in a haystack," one of the agents groaned.

Dulaf shook her head and held out her hand-link to show the map. Packing in shoulder to shoulder, the group did their best to get a view as she explained, "The photos from the house all indicate that he'd be most familiar with this region here on the east side of Obstruction Point. We're going to hike up to a point and then spread out to begin searching for any tracks that might have strayed off of the trail. If not, we backtrack and then move further up the trail and try again."

"It's too bad we don't have dogs," I commented, looking uphill and taking in the path ahead of us. "It's going to be a pain in the ass trying to find this guy in the dead of night."

Dulaf nodded and turned on her flashlight, smirking a little as she remarked, "Or at least Werewolves. But the Alters United group let us know that either one of them was probably some sort of rights infringement."

"Even dogs?" I asked, fishing out my light.

She started walking ahead of us, leading the pack up the trail the best she could, her light waving around like a beacon against the inky shadows. "Well some of the activists in Argyre are former animal rights activists," she said whimsically. "And in the end they kind of figured that animal and metamorph rights dovetailed."

Putting the strap on my visor before following her up the path, I secured it on and watched the forest light up under the enhanced ambient light. The brush around the trail was thick with activity, nocturnal animals wandering the shadows, watching us from their shrouded spaces. Small glowing eyes shined from every little corner and shelter as they watched us cautiously from a distance.

"What if it's out here?" an agent asked behind me.

Dulaf and I peeked over our shoulders as she replied, "What? The creature?"

The agent meekly nodded, waving his light into the bushes around us. "Out in this, if it happens to pin us down we're pretty much fucked, aren't we?"

Dulaf looked around thoughtfully, ears folding back, and shrugged her shoulders. "The last time we saw any sign of it on the system was back in Seattle. It's a couple hours' drive from there and we took the roads. I couldn't imagine it could have gotten here before us while crossing mountains."

Bemused, I questioned her confidence. "Yeah, well, let's just assume it is out here somewhere. Will our emergency beacons work if the thing happens to pin us down?"

Answering with a little irritation, she shot me a look and said, "Of course, the radios and all of that are satellite based, we're going to be in communications still. Now would you guys suck it up already?"

Not fond of shutting up, I figured the morale could only be helped by a little more needling. "We have satellites?"

Snorting, she threw up her hand and snapped, "Well who do you think sent the first one into space?"

"The Russians?" I snottily remarked.

"Oh come on," she said playfully, "Explosives stuffed in a tube to shoot a metal sphere into space from a country that figured out how to turn potatoes into liquor?"

Stopping to consider the wonders of vodka, I suddenly realized the deep, dark secret of the Soviet space program. Lightly slapping my forehead, I declared, "Dwarves!"

She stopped on the trail and gestured into the woods with her light. "This is where we split up," she said, "everyone stay in radio contact and stay within sight of the trail as much as possible."

We confirmed with each other which directions we planned to go and scattered into the brush, heading away from the path and into the dark unknown. Weeding through the brush and wandering semi-aimlessly, we each gave up after a distance and retreated back to the path, met up again, moved further up the trail and spread out once more.

Finally, one of us had to say it: "I don't think we're going to find him out here."

No one looked comfortable with it but it was probably true. With no dogs and only a handful of guys there was very little potential behind our wild goose chase. The gloomiest expression was the one on Dulaf's face. Her ears hung as low as they possibly could, her eyes glistening with the subtlest hint of frustrated tears. Looking into the brush again, starting to consider just where I would go if I wanted to disappear.

"One last go," I said quietly at first, beginning to raise my voice, "Just pick a direction, take a shot, if no one finds anything we start heading back and figure out another way. I'm not letting this guy get away without exhausting every possibility. Too many girls have died for us to just quit because it's gotten hard."

The others looked at me weary and frustrated. Growing determined once again, they nodded and started to search off in the distance for the direction they'd take. I wasn't expecting any miracles but I couldn't stand the feeling that he could go deeper into the woods and never be seen again. I just looked at the peaks cutting through the air and looked for something, anything that may be recognizable. And, getting a vague sense of the terrain, I chose the worst possible direction in the hopes that he did the same.

My direction was rather overgrown; the ground was a bit soggy from the last few days of rain and an apparent constant shade keeping it all from drying out. The rustling in the bushes was only mildly disturbing to me as I did my best to scour the ground for any footprints that could still be there. The good thing about the muddy ground, I figured, was the fact any footprints that might have been there were probably going to be there to stay. And, thinking about it a little further, I realized the muddy tracks in the house probably meant he'd been hiking sometime fairly recent.

Lost in these thoughts, I nearly overlooked something ahead of me: broken branches hanging from the sides of otherwise healthy looking shrubs, leaves still looking fresh as they hung from the snapped twigs. Examining the space around me produced a discovery almost immediately. There they were, frozen in the mud, a set of tracks of an all too familiar pair of soles.

Tapping my beacon, I tried to call them in and found that the usual indicators did nothing. Looking down at the badge, I tapped a couple more times just to be sure and found that nothing at all seemed to work. No lights, no sounds, just the dull shine of ambient light against the polished surface. Confused, I took out the hand-link and tried to call with that. Static buzzed from the link, no signal found at all and even the GPS functions failing to run.

My ass might have clenched a little at the time.

There weren't a whole lot of options about what to do just then. They clearly weren't going to get a signal out of me, but did that mean that all signals were bad in this area? Dulaf was able to run a map on her link earlier, but how far did the field go? The choices between pressing ahead without radio contact or going back and potentially losing the guy's trail somewhere weren't exactly pleasant either way.

Looking at the area around me, I realized how hard it would be to find this exact spot again in the dead of night like this. Nearly everything was covered, and, worse, it all looked almost exactly the same under this light. A thought crossed my mind and a memory came back of a girl with pointy ears teaching me something once in these same mountains. Pulling my gun, I fired a round into the nearby tree, scorching the surface and leaving a mark for the others to follow.

Everything lit up under the flash of my blue bolt and creatures all around scattered from the alien light and sound I just produced. I'd always known it was surprisingly bright, being a light-based weapon, but in that environment it was practically a flare gun. Studying the gun, an eyebrow raised and humming to myself, I lifted it into the air and fired off another one into the sky. The blue glow and distinctive hiss carried across the rolling terrain, treetops lit all around me.

Watching it for a moment, seeing it fade into the sky like a dying star, I hoped someone would see it. Either way, I had to turn and follow the tracks in the mud, following them through the woods. I made a point to keep shooting into trees as I passed, leaving the breadcrumbs for someone to follow if they spotted my flare. Even so, in the end I knew that it was a good chance that it was just going to be me and Archie out there. At the very least, I was comforted in the idea that I didn't see any extra-large, semi-human tracks by his side.

When I continued forward, the visor started to lose resolution too. Colors began to fade and distort, the light enhancement starting to weaken. For the first time in a very long time I'd had to take off my sunglasses because they were too dark. I was actually relying completely on the flashlight as I followed the winding trail up the mountain side.

And because I was relying on that flashlight, I almost completely missed the partially obscured wood shack to my side. Shrouded in brush and hanging tree limbs, it was almost camouflaged and far enough off the trail that no one likely saw it on a regular basis. Looking downhill, I struggled to remember where exactly the trail was and hoped once again that someone else could at least follow the breadcrumbs I'd left behind. Aiming into the sky again, I fired another shot and waited as it faded from view.

273

After a moment to steel myself, I turned to the door of the old shack and felt the resistance of a strangely durable lock and a door heavier than it should have been. Despite the run down wood paneling forming the surface, it was clear there'd been something much heftier below. Struggling for a few moments led to me giving into frustration and taking a few quick shots into the lock with the gun. Hissing and cracking, the lock blew out and released, showing me an electronic mechanism hidden behind that door, attached to the steel door those planks camouflaged from view.

Marveling at the thing, I pushed it open further to see that the rest of the shack was just clever disguise for a concrete bunker that shouldn't have existed so deep into the woods. The stairwell ahead of me dug deep through the ground, dim lights buzzing from the ceiling, a single bulb flickering as it did. The scent of formaldehyde drifted out, overwhelming the fresh pine tree scent coming from every other direction, and made me feel nauseous. It smelled like an old biology lab fresh after a class of dissections and sent me back to my high school days and memories of an unfortunate frog pinned to the table.

Turning away, I took one last cleansing breath of the fresh pine tree air outside before going down into the darkness. And then, trying to breathe through my mouth, steadying my gun, I marched down into the depths… hoping I wouldn't find anything worse than a frog.

Chapter 28
Fiendish Intent

Each steel step groaned lightly under my feet and the bolts rattled against the concrete walls. It was far too complicated for a single guy to have put in place, and yet, the deeper down I went, the thicker that disgusting smell became, the more I realized this had to belong to Archie. The walls of the stairwell were solid concrete surrounding a shaft that went a couple dozen feet into the ground. The implications were unsettling and the first thing I saw at the bottom of the stairs didn't help all that much. Hanging at the far end of the room, lit by the faint glow of chemical vats and terminal screens, was the emblem of a griffon ready to strike.

The room was full of capsules like the ones in the labs of Sindri and the relay room on the docks. Chemical cocktails produced sickly green and violet glows as lights shone through them, blocked by the vague outlines of grotesque, incomplete, inhuman forms. Their outlines cast across the walls, stretching and climbing towards the ceiling as they loomed over me with fearsome shapes. A stray claw, elongated limb or contorted spine cast onto the wall and projected a far larger shape, a funhouse mirror of what was already an unfortunate design.

Approaching cautiously, I leaned close and peered into the chemicals, hoping to see some sign of detail past the backlit shadows and cloudy concoction. Through the colored fluid, warped by the light bending through the thick gunk around it, an eye stared back at me from a desiccated socket.

"What the hell have you been doing?" I muttered breathlessly.

Cutting through the gurgling noises and electrical hum of the room, Archie's voice echoed off the walls, "I've been putting things right!"

Whirling around, I swept the gun through the air and scanned every dark crevasse of the room I could find. The shadows didn't much help, even if one of them might have been his, with each of them looking like the same sort of gaunt, gangly shape. Tightening my grip on the pistol, I slowly moved the gun towards a vat and considered destroying all of them. Studying the room, the fumes of a nearby vat reminded me of the hideous smell in that room - a smell I'd strangely started to get used to. Clearly, the gunk flowing through these tubes was the source of that horrid scent.

"If this is putting things right," I murmured, beginning to circle through the room, "I'd hate to see what you'd think of as wrong."

With a touch of disappointment he replied, "You told me you understood."

His voice was coming from everywhere, everything, like a hissing whisper from the nether-realms. I kept exploring the room, looking for something that might actually be him in this little haunted house. With the visor down, I couldn't rely on that either at a time like this and clearly he could still see me. I needed to keep him talking.

Defiantly, I replied, "I meant I understood someone dying when I felt like it could be prevented. I had no idea you were going to go berserk on dozens of other women."

Quietly, starting to become a bit more tangible and echoing less, he said, "I did what I had to do, to make things right. Don't you understand trying to make things right?"

"How did you go about finding these women, Archie?" I asked angrily, "What the hell did any of them do to you? Did they get transplants?"

Turning a corner around a counter and making my way to a wall, I pressed my back to it and started to ease through the room. Sliding towards my best guess at where his voice came from, I kept an eye on the shadows again, watching for one that might move. Sadly, my eyes landed on something a lot more disturbing than the things he kept in the rest of the jars.

"No," he said darkly, "I found the girls who had what I was looking for."

Suspended in the fluids was the piecemeal body of a woman hastily stitched together from what were clearly dozens of other bodies. The sick truth about what happened to Alice's forearm hit me like a hammer as I stared at this twisted creation. But the thing that terrified me more was the resemblance: Archie had recreated his wife's form out of the bits and pieces of dozens of others.

He'd put her back together like a jigsaw puzzle.

"I needed to see how it all fit," he said as I stared on at his creation. "So that when I used their genetics I would know that it was correct."

Closing in on this tube, I was half afraid the thing would wake up as I watched it bob slowly in the fluid, moved by jets of air bubbling from the bottom of the tank. As he mentioned genes a second figure caught the corner of my eye. Hesitantly, I turned my head just enough to see a second form not far from the first. And there, mirroring the movements of the patchwork doll he'd sewn from the flesh of his victims, one of the incomplete forms floated while his wife's face was slowly growing from the fleshy mass.

The thing that crept into my mind, looking across all of the jars, is that each of those was probably a prototype. Twisting, pulsating masses around me, some beginning to writhe and twitch as I watched, were suddenly more disturbing than the "apples" in their bloody vats.

"Do you really think she would have wanted this?" I asked uneasily. "You really think she wanted you to kill random women and start trying to stitch together a duplicate of her?"

With conviction in his voice, he replied sternly, "They were far from random; they each had genetic qualities I could use for her."

Clenching my jaw, I waved my gun out at the shadows and yelled, "If you were going to do something illegal the least you could have done was just clone her instead of leaving this trail of blood!"

"Her genes killed her," he hissed, "I won't see her die again."

Adjusting my grip on the gun, I started to scour the room for him again, heading in the direction I was sure the voice had come from. The fact I'd let someone this deranged go was running through my mind over and over again. I'd had a chance to stop this guy and I failed to see someone this warped sitting right in front of me. And, more than that, I'd realized that I wasn't the only one who'd enabled this man. Because as I walked through the rest of this strangely complex structure, I realized I could recognize a lot of the equipment around me.

The monitoring terminals lighting the room had the same displays I'd seen only recently. The tubes were clearly designed to store things like these, since he'd so easily used them for his little project. The old cobwebs in the corners of the room and the moss growing over some of the wet concrete walls made me think that it wasn't anything recent though. The only thing I knew for sure is that I had a very unnerved feeling about just how and why my badge would be cut from the network. When I entered the room at the back, a control panel at the far end with the same security interface of the buffering station, my fears were justified.

He sat there enveloped in the warm colored lights of the terminal as a shadow. His form was cast across the walls and the ceiling as phantasms dancing around the room while the lights shifted like candlelight. When I approached, keeping the gun leveled at his head, a new pair of shadowy figures in the corners of the room caught my eye. A shiver ran through me when I realized what I thought I was seeing next to me.

There are things in this world that you figure you'll never get used to. Of these, most obviously for me, was the sight of a brain in a jar. But seeing two of them? That was a new level of freaky. Especially as the one to my right was clearly human and still attached to the vestiges of a spinal column long degraded.

I did my best to fight back the gasp. "That can't be what I think it is."

"Oh, but it is," he replied coldly, turning the seat away from the terminal. "I preserved her, the part of her that I knew I couldn't replace."

Quickly I examined him, seeing he was unarmed, and hesitantly edged towards him. A white hot flash of rage came over me, my hand tightening around the grip. I wanted to put two shots through his face for one moment, wanting to use those lenses on his face as shining bullseyes.

"How could you do that to your wife?!" I yelled. "This is a crime against nature! This is a crime against human decency!"

He was so unmoved, so still. The faint running lights of the Helios reflected off of his glasses and the mouth of the gun appeared to be centered on both eyes. Yet it didn't faze him at all. The meek, quivering little man was gone right now. Either it'd all been an act or I'd found him now in a place where he'd let go of everything.

"Are you going to shoot me?" he asked quietly with a growing smile. "Are you going to kill me and kill her again?"

"She's gone," I corrected, "and you're going to rot in prison for the rest of what I hope to be a very long life."

He pushed back his glasses up the bridge of his nose and sat back in his chair. Stammering again, he replied, "Oh, oh you're very wrong there on both counts. You see, first, she's not gone, she's right over there. And second, I am not going to prison."

"This is just a brain in a jar," I said angrily. "It hasn't been alive in a long time now. What were you planning to do? Stitch together a new soul? Hope she hasn't suffered brain damage and will be the same as she always was?"

Turning around, I leveled the gun at the jar. "Do you think she'd want to wake up and find out what you'd done?"

The light from the next room was suddenly blocked out, a looming figure filling the door frame, shining eyes glaring through me.

"I wouldn't fire that if I were you," he said mockingly. "I sent the command to him a while ago to defend me and everything in this installation."

Freezing in place and doing my best not to make direct eye contact with it, I realized Patch in a confined space was going to easily tear me apart. My mind raced for places to go and things to do to try to fix this problem. But all I could remember was the shattered windshield and the bits of ballistic glass scattered across the blacktop.

"I had a feeling that you were going to find me eventually," Archibald said behind me, rising from his seat. "So I called him back to this place and figured that he'd be the best security I could possibly have."

Shifting my footing slightly, I tried to gauge how likely it was that I could slip between Patch's legs or disorient him long enough to make a difference. But in that space, with those conditions, I knew it was a matter of who could pull the trigger first: me or Archie. And unfortunately, with the laser guided missile in the shape of a hulking man at that door, Archibald had pulled the trigger long before I even knew we were in a fight.

Common sense has never been one of my strongest points. I've always been someone who feels their way through a situation and does what feels right at that exact moment, even if a small part of me kept screaming that it was wrong. And at that exact moment I was having one of those internal debates between the rational side and the part of me that made me do stupid shit.

So I shot Patch in the face again.

Chapter 29
Utter Terror

Everything after pulling that trigger was a blur. There was a flurry of motion, sound and jolts of pain as I flew through that lab at the end of a powerful arm. Shattering glass scattered everywhere and the smell of noxious fumes began to overwhelm as the two of us plowed through half of that lab. The whole way, despite the feeling of glass cutting across my face and the nauseating fumes filling my lungs, I held onto that gun. And, despite his enraged, wild screams, I kept shooting him in the face.

The blinding light in his eyes and the charged particles across his skin was slowing him down, each new bolt being met with a confused scream as he continued to charge through the room with me. And with all of his weight behind it he threw me into a hard concrete wall with that one powerful arm and knocked the wind out of me with a crack. My head bounced and I felt myself slip away, everything going dark for one quick moment. But as it did I felt the gun beginning to slip from my hand and knew one thing.

You can't let it go, I thought to myself. *If you let it go, he's going to kill you.*

My whole body flexed as I forced myself to stay awake and grip that gun again, like the jolt you'd have when falling asleep and feeling yourself suddenly falling. And with that jolt I squeezed the trigger again without even meaning to, sending a searing round across his ear.

His head snapped back as he roared, a faint light of burning particles shining from inside that ear. Whipping his head back towards me, screaming at me, he bared his fangs like an animal at a zoo. I was literally trapped in his cage. With his mouth open at me, the stench of dried blood on his breath from who knows how many people he'd torn into, I had only one thought cross my mind.

So I shot him in the mouth.

Shimmering lights pushed through every orifice in his head while he choked on that roar. His eyes grew wide and his grip went loose. I collapsed to the floor at his feet when he released his grip, too winded and too wounded to notice him letting go. I lay there in the festering smell of those rancid juices, seeing scraps of malformed flesh all across the floor. Trying to remember to breathe through my mouth, I looked away, glancing up at his face and watching as his eyes glazed over.

His shoulders slumped and his knees started to buckle while he fell back from me. His eyes were rolling back, his jaw fell slack and blood ran down from his ears. But something kept him upright as that dense figure of his swayed but wouldn't topple. While I knew I'd mortally wounded him, I needed to see him fall.

Kicking up at his groin area, I pushed him back with my foot as hard as I could. He fell back with the motion, a wheeze of air escaping him. But then, with little warning, he planted a foot again and kept himself upright. I jolted again and scrambled back up against the wall, pushing my shoulders up it while bringing myself up to my feet and leveling the gun at his face again. Surely he couldn't have survived that: I'd just put a round through his brain. All of that stopped mattering when he started to breathe again.

It was like watching a computer reboot. First his face started to twitch and contort as he struggled for a moment to close his jaw and his eyes. Then the muscles along his arms began to tremble. He was coming back to life, coming back online like a piece of hardware that'd taken a sudden power surge. I'd mortally wounded him and yet it wasn't enough. All I could do was run.

I staggered up the stairs and out into the fresh air with what strength I could muster. Looking over my shoulder to see if it was following was out of the question; even thinking about it was too taxing at that moment. A shooting, searing pain running up my side told me that there was a damn good chance those ribs I cracked earlier in the week were now officially broken. It was hard to breathe, the stinging stitch running up my side every time I inhaled through my nose. And as I gasped hard up in the pine-scented air, I realized the smell and taste of my own blood was in my nose and mouth, overwhelmed by the sweet yet foul scents below.

I spit some blood out of my mouth and took a knee, holding my side and hoping that my ribs weren't just bobbing around freely inside my torso. I needed to get away from this place and escape the field, something that wasn't about to happen if I couldn't breathe. The pain started to subside as I caught my breath, becoming a dull throbbing ache along my side and back. I looked to the scorched trees I left and realized if I chased that path I could find my way back out of the jamming signal. Maybe then I could send a call for help.

"Don't just stand there you idiot!" Archibald shrieked in the bunker, "Get him before that damned beacon of his can give them our location!"

A surge of adrenaline pushed up through me and washed away the aches and pains I'd felt. It was going to come for me and regardless of how I felt I knew that staying right there wasn't a good idea. Like the last time I'd been in these woods, I ran for all I was worth, hoping a stray branch wouldn't do Patch's job for him and kill me in the dead of the night.

The rumbling at my back as steel steps strained against concrete walls sounded like thunder echoing from a cave. It was the only thing I could hear in that place outside of the panicked, strained breathing sounds and twigs snapping under my feet. When it stopped and new rustling started, I knew without looking that Patch had not only reached the surface but was following me. Only one thing could smell like an embalmed mummy in that area, even I could have tracked that scent.

It was strange, the moment I heard him starting to come after me. I instantly knew that I wasn't going to escape, that I wasn't going to get away from this thing. The fear of death was never one of my biggest hang-ups, the idea that I could pass on was pretty obvious from the day I put on the uniform. I'd always felt that, if I was going down, I was going to do it fighting. But now, in this situation, a different feeling came over me and I found myself pushing harder.

My sides felt like they were ready to tear open, the air being squeezed out of me every time I twisted just wrong. My arms and legs were starting to feel about the same. I had to keep going, though. I knew I would never outrun this thing, even after giving it brain damage. But this wasn't a run to escape anymore. Somewhere, in the middle of that mad dash through the woods, it became a race to warn the others.

All I had to do was outrun Patch long enough to get outside of the jamming field. If I could do that, if I could just push that long, then I knew that at least then the others would be warned. They wouldn't go into it blindly following my flare; they would know that there was danger here.

I started to choke on the air, unable to catch my breath as I did my all to ignore the fire burning across my sides. The smell of the chemicals started to become overwhelmed by the smell of my own blood and the taste began to form at the back of my throat. With everything about ready to collapse on me, I had a moment of complete and utter relief when the light of my beacon flashed from the badge and I heard the tell-tale ring of its alarm. I knew they'd get the signal now, I knew they were warned. And not a moment too soon because I quickly found the giant hand at my back and felt the ground fly out from beneath me.

Lightning rushed through me when I hit the dirt, a surge that set everything on fire and made my vision black out for a moment. When I stopped tumbling and ended up flat on my back in that dirt, my eyes started to work again and I took in the sights of the stars sparkling through the branches as a few stray clouds floated across the now indigo sky. And for that one moment, I was at peace, even as the towering figure darted in and loomed over me.

It was okay right then, I was ready to let go and had already started to fade. Everything hurt so much and my vision was beginning to blur, distorting every time my heart beat. My eyes started to drift close and I think, for a moment, I sighed. And then a brilliant flash of light broke me from my stupor and a much smaller shadow flew into Patch's side while silver plates sparkled and chestnut hair flew through the wind. It was like watching lightning strike him in the ribs, thunder clapping as his side actually gave way to her fist for even the slightest moment.

Elves are close relatives to the Vampires, so I shouldn't have been surprised to see that small form bringing that kind of force to bear on Patch. But as I turned my head and started to drift away, the last thought on my mind was how shocked I was to see Dulaf send that monster reeling. It was like an angel had come down to save me, and not the kind that would have run for office. And as everything started to go dark, I could still see the small flashes of light off of her gear and hear the cracks of her vicious strikes.

Unfortunately, the last thing I saw before passing out entirely was her being on the receiving end of a powerful backhand, thrown from her feet the way I had been. And despite every fiber in me wanting to move right then, I couldn't do a thing. The darkness enveloped me and everything went incredibly still.

***

A roar shook me awake. Blood had dried across the side of my face, sticking twigs and mud across my cheek. Leaves in my hair crackled as I turned my head. And everything, absolutely everything, ached while my arm and my ribs in particular shot pain through me with every pulse of my heart. The sky was turning from indigo to an eggshell blue over us, birds scattering among the treetops to avoid the fierce creature that woke me. I forced myself to sit up, hoping the sound was from far away, since at that moment everything was feeling equally distant.

But he was standing there, cutting a figure across the horizon, roaring towards the sunrise in the distance, lost in some sort of blind rage. I studied the terrain, trying to understand how I was still alive and contemplating my chances of escaping if I tried to run again. The ribs were on fire and my legs felt like lead, but there was still a chance so long as he was looking away.

I might have even escaped if she wasn't still there.

Dulaf was face down in the dirt and the twigs no more than ten feet from me, a bloody ear turning crimson in the faint morning light. I couldn't tell how hurt she was from where I sat. Part of me was afraid to know. Thankfully, as I watched, I could see her sides gently move and heard a pained whimper. She was alive and I was in no condition to get her out of there with me.

Pushing to my feet, my mind raced for ideas on how to respond, how to fix this. I'd wounded it before, maybe I could do it again and shoot it in the same space. Maybe I could feed him a Manticore and hope the needles would shred whatever auxiliary nerve clusters had kept him alive once the brain shut down. I just knew I had to try... something.

"Hey ugly," I coughed out, feeling my dry lips crack from the effort, "I've had my nap, ready for round two?"

He turned towards me, eyes shining against the dark wall that was his body. If she'd landed any decent shots on him, I couldn't tell from there. There was bloodlust and confusion in his eyes, of the sort I couldn't define as either from the pain or from the surprise that I wasn't dead. Whatever it was, he sent another powerful roar through the area, shaking me down to my bones and feeling like a much larger animal on that hill. And with that sound he charged down the slope, carving a path through the mountain itself to get to me.

It was as he charged me that something else caught my eye, a Will O Wisp lying between us, clearly spent. Grasping at my belt, I realized mine was still there. And, while it didn't seem to stop him completely, for that moment I had faith that Dulaf knew better.

Pulling it from my belt, I closed my eyes and threw my weight behind the throw, flinging it towards his face as hard as I could while my shoulders cracked from the motion. An electric shock of pain ran through my whole torso as I did, the feeling of either tearing something inside or pinching a badly positioned cluster of nerves. My knees buckled and I crashed back down to the ground, bracing myself with my remaining arm and hoping it was going to hold. But as the wind was knocked out of me from my own throw, I saw the flash of the Wisp and heard the sound of the air being pushed out of him too.

She'd figured it out, somewhere in the middle of fighting for my life, and hit him with the first part. Slow to the uptake, I didn't have it figured out until I'd already acted on it. All the data streaming by on the videos we saw were telling us something about his very nature, something we already knew even though I hadn't put it together. Though he was organic he was clearly controlled by a machine. And in the course of fighting us right now, we'd exposed him to two electromagnetic pulses. They surged through him and hit the electronics at work behind whatever was left of his brain.

The leash was off and it was time to meet the real beast.

Looking up, he was closer to me than I'd have thought and halted dead in his tracks no further than Dulaf was in the other direction. Wild eyes had gone wide and dilated, darting around rapidly as he started to breathe just as fast. His jaw slacked and he stepped back from us, looking aghast over something as he lifted his meaty claws in front of his face and studied those massive palms. I'd almost say he looked... afraid.

Every fiber of his being shook and trembled. His features twisted and his nostrils flared while panicked hyperventilating started to bellow out of him. In that moment, it was like the first time he'd ever seen his own hands. If he was sentient, if he was capable of thought, it was also probably the first time he was allowed to realize what he'd done. For all the fear I saw in his face, I think it was the first time I was really seeing Patch's true personality, his soul. I hesitated to guess what kind of person he really was behind all of that and braced for the possibility that we just cut a rabid dog from its leash.

After a moment of near-silence he turned on a heel and bolted for the woods again, running from us like a frightened animal and leaping into the brush with a terrifying grace. The dust settled and the birds began to chirp nearby again, life returning to the forest as the alpha predator was away. The subtle crack of the twigs nearby almost didn't even catch my attention as Archie crept up on us.

"In the end," he said quietly, "it's just an animal without the transceiver."

I glanced over my shoulder, struggling to keep my eyes focused while I looked at him. "Animals don't look horrified by what they do."

"Yes, well," he said a bit more confidently, pulling an old pistol from under his coat, "Sometimes they lack conviction."

It was a relatively low caliber, nothing to worry about if hit in the coat. But even Archie, shaking hands and all, could have hit us in the head from that distance. It was still a definite step down in terms of threat. So I started to fight my way to my feet again, doing my best to look him in the eye.

"Yeah, conviction," I muttered, "like the ability to do the job with your own hand instead of through a computer screen?"

It was a hunch but it seemed to be one that stuck. He was sweating and shaking, nervous about our confrontation as he held the gun on me. It must have been a lot easier to kill randomly from a distance. It must have been so easy to forget those profiles were people when he pressed the buttons. Now, as I watched his hand, I saw it twitch as he adjusted his grip and I knew he couldn't pull it.

So imagine my surprise when a gunshot cracked the air and echoed across the mountain range. I almost flinched as the sound broke through the peace of the forest. A crimson streak ran down the side of Archie's face as I watched on. Crumpling over, he fell into the dirt, his gun sliding down the hill away from us. Searching downhill, I laid eyes on the shooter standing at the foot, gun still leveled in the air. Carlson, with Lynch at least twenty yards behind him, stared at me looking completely unfazed.

"I trust that was the right thing to do," he said smugly. "Assuming you didn't want him to fire."

I wanted to run down the hill and punch that smug look off his face. Granted, that would have meant being able to run again. He just looked so pleased with himself for finally doing the right thing after all this time. Furious, voice cracking from a dry throat, I cried, "You don't get to be smug about this! It only got this far because you people covered for him with your bullshit!"

Carlson's subtle smirk faded and he straightened his tie, still wearing that damn suit out in the woods. Walking up the hillside, he stopped by Archie's body and rolled him onto his back, commenting idly, "It wasn't my job to stop him."

Looking into my eyes he said coldly, "It was my job to stop others from finding out what he was doing."

Disgusted, I chided him, "Well everyone's going to find out really damn soon now that his monster's out there."

He adjusted his tie carefully and looked over his shoulder at the rising sun, taking out his sunglasses. "First impressions are a funny thing," he said confidently, "You see Alters every day and yet I'm the one standing here fairly certain that I just shot the *real* monster."

If I could have leapt at him and punched him across the face, I would have. I couldn't have, of course. Even if I could have lashed out at him I would have been forced to admit that he was right. One way or another, the real monster was lying dead at our feet. I hated that he got to be right after all he'd tried to do.

Donning the sunglasses and beginning to walk away, he waved over his shoulder and commented, "I'm sure we'll have that thing under control soon. Even if we don't find him I'm sure he won't be eager to continue his rampage."

Carlson and Lynch left us behind, their dark suits contrasting against the vibrant green colors of the forest around them. I watched them as they continued down the hill, disappearing down by the mountain trail. With a heavy sigh I gave in again and lay in the dirt next to Dulaf, watching the sky and waiting for the others to track my beacon. Listening intently to the rustling of the woods, I also kept an ear out for any distant cries or screams from the park's newest predator.

Chapter 30
Survivors' Tales

After all of that it was understandable that I would be laid up in the medical wing of the headquarters for a good long while. Omega was running through me and doing its very best to mend my broken bones. Freaky as it always was to me, I couldn't protest it this time. Besides, I was far too busy contemplating just how bad the situation might have really been. My only consolation was the fact I was far from the only one down there for once.

The SOL team was there for most of that time, some of them longer than others and a few even able to talk to me and share the stories of how exactly Patch put them there. Everyone got a good laugh about it when I informed them I'd shot him in the brain and kicked him in the crotch. It wasn't all fun and games though; some of the conversations got a little dark as we described the thoughts going through our heads before blacking out. But even that was a welcome change from the mindless chatter of Anatole talking my ear off in the next bed over.

I'd never been so happy to see a prisoner released.

Eventually, I had no choice but to get up and find out for myself, even if the SOL team tried to convince me to stay down. My arm was in a sling, my ribs were wrapped and my legs were stiff. I was too high on painkillers to care. Walls danced as I wandered down the corridors, swinging and swaying around me rhythmically. From time to time, I reached out with my good hand and tried my best to seize them and stop the motion, somehow not realizing right away that the thing swinging was me. Keeping my hand on the wall did the trick either way as I continued into the shared office and set eyes on Lucian.

He stood under the monitors stoically as the rest of the room buzzed with activity. Everything had calmed and life had returned to normal. The news broadcast on the monitors above had nothing to do with our little nightmare and seemed preoccupied with a Siren's attempts to start a singing career. Surely Lucian wasn't a fan, but I imagined he was keeping vigil for any reports of people missing in the woods. After all, that's what I looked for as I gazed up.

We stood together while I tried my best to remain upright and watched the news scroll by. There was an uneasy silence between us, thick with tension and questions left to be answered.

Cutting through that tension, I asked the inevitable, "Now what do we do?"

He smiled a big, fanged smile and replied sarcastically, "Now we go home."

"That's not what I meant," I chided. "There could be hundreds of them out there and we barely dealt with one. If that one even counts seeing as he's still out there."

His grin faded and he nodded solemnly. "First, we try to make sure the one out there doesn't do any serious harm. We have teams searching, but so far it's been remarkably quiet out there. Eventually we'll either find it or determine it's gone. Either way, we fight this politically," he said. "We get our people to pressure their people to stop."

I looked down into the black tar that the headquarters considered coffee and watched the bit of cream I put in it swirl and try to spread. "And what do we do if they don't stop?"

Confidently he proclaimed, "Then we deal with them by force."

I wasn't quite so confident, probing anxiously, "And what if we can't 'deal with them'?"

That uneasy quiet returned and I could feel his eyes turning to me. He fidgeted out of the corner of my eye like he was struggling to find the words. And after contemplating for what felt like an eternity he finally asked, "Do you know why there's a lion on the badge?"

"Not a clue," I answered with a shitty grin. "I just assumed it was for me."

A surprisingly thoughtful look crossed his face before he chuckled and waved it off. "It's based on an old Argyrean folktale," he said.

Surprised, I asked, "You guys have folktales?"

He laughed. "Everyone has folklore of some sort."

I nodded along and took a sip of the nasty sludge in my cup. Shuddering as the concentrated power rushed through me; I cleared my throat and said, "Hit me with it."

"Once," he said, "in the land of the beasts there was a griffon, the king of the griffons. He had ruled over the land of beast for some time but he eyed the land of man and could never quite take it from them. So he explored his land for a way to defeat man and found an answer among the rodents. The rodents had a curse that they claimed could turn man into beast. So the Griffon King gathered the rodents and the men and placed them into cages, saying none of them would be released until the men came out as beasts."

"Charming," I quipped, "Plague-Rats: The Home Game."

He chuckled along and continued, "So one day a lion crossed by. He stood up to the Griffon King and told him 'you can't do this, these men aren't meant to live like us'. And the Griffon King was furious that this lion would defy the lord of the land, king of the beasts. He lunged at the lion and the two of them fought ferociously. When the dust cleared, the griffon flew away and the lion was left wounded. With the last of his strength the lion killed the rats and set the men free. And as the men left one stopped to look at the lion, whom lay dying by the cages, and asked 'What do I do if I have the curse? What do I do if I become a beast?'"

Nodding, he rested a hand on my shoulder and squeezed lightly. "And the lion looked up and said, 'If you must become a beast, you will become the lion and fight the griffon in my place'."

I stared at him while he smiled earnestly and let the story sink in some. After a moment of thought I said, "That's really not making me feel any better."

Slapping me on the back, he remarked, "It's a good story, though."

Exasperated, I replied, "The moral of the story seems to be if you fight a monster you should die fighting."

With a shrug and a nod he replied, "Yes."

Examining his expression for any sign I was being toyed with and finding nothing, I eventually exclaimed, "That's a *horrible* story! It means we're all supposed to die!"

Turning and walking away, he threw his hands into the air and shrugged again. "I didn't say it was a happy one!"

Yet again I was left wishing I could run over and punch someone only to realize I couldn't run. It was probably for the best that I couldn't make a move since I'd already watched him and Dulaf both deck much larger creatures that'd thrown me around like a toy. Even if I landed the punch I'd probably have only broken my fist on the sleek stone carving he considered a jaw.

But how was Dulaf doing?

I couldn't quite fathom why that thought crossed my mind. At random I'd frozen on the image of her hitting Patch in the ribs while meandering through my imagined fight with Lucian's face. Starting to walk back towards the medical wing, those images halted me and made me look to my right, towards the corridor down into the sanctuary. Despite the fact the doctor was going to chew me out for it, I waddled down to that sanctuary, hoping to find her there.

The sky projected across the ceiling was as clear as I'd seen it in a long time, stars shining all around and the moon peeking through branches with rays of silver light. A cool artificial breeze brushed past my face and gave me a breath of the freshest air I'd had in days despite being a couple dozen yards below ground. The children ran across the fields, the smell of freshly cut grass filling the air as they laughed and kicked piles of clippings. Even Amelia was all smiles and cheers while she danced around completely covered in little green blades. And Dulaf sat with the parents, watching it with a serene look, a dark bruise still healing on her forehead.

"Got you a good one, didn't he?" I asked softly, gesturing to the mark.

She looked up and smiled softly for a moment, the gentle grin turning mischievous as she sniped, "Could have been worse if he wasn't worn out from pounding you."

Sitting by her carefully, I joked, "Well, curling up and playing dead seemed like a silly way to go."

We sat quietly and watched the kids play, Amelia in particular as she seemed so lively despite where we found her.

"Does she know?" I asked, nodding at the bubbly little girl.

Dulaf nodded and rested back on her hands. "I told her a couple days ago," she said, "a little after Lucas released me."

"Seems to have bounced back pretty well," I mused.

A thoughtful look crossed Dulaf's face and she said, "It's still rough, but I told her I was going to take care of her. I even put in the paperwork already."

Taken aback, I turned a little too hard and felt my side seize for a moment, exclaiming through a pained whimper, "You're taking her?!"

She glanced down at my side and rolled her eyes, getting up and shaking her head, walking out of sight as she retorted, "I *have* raised children before, you know."

Cradling my side, wanting to follow but knowing I couldn't move, I called out to her, "And how did that turn out?"

To my surprise, she walked back to me, sat down and gently pulled my arm away. She pressed a pack to my side, a warming sensation relaxing the muscles around my tender ribs. Lightly, she answered, "Some of them turned out a little hard headed, but I think most of them turned out all right."

Letting the pack do its work, trying to relax myself so it wouldn't seize up again, I thought about that story of the lion and what Dulaf and Rufus had implied so many times before. "It's funny you know," I said, mulling it over, "I think along the way in this case I started to worry about whether or not I was letting you and Lucian down. When we found that lab I felt like maybe my people had done something horrible to yours."

Sweetly smiling at me, she said, "You are our people, dumbass."

Ignoring the word, appreciating her tone, I continued, "We're the lions, aren't we?"

"Family," she corrected warmly.

Feeling a blush starting to rise in my face, I looked away and tried to cover it from view. Needing to keep the conversation

294

going so she wouldn't pounce on it, I tried to change the subject and remarked, "I saw you hit the thing, I'm surprised it was able to keep standing after that."

Leaning over and gazing at my face, she grinned and wrapped an arm around me, giving me a painfully strong hug. Cheerfully she replied, "Well I wasn't entirely ready to fight him at the time. I saw what was happening and reflex took over."

"So you were worried about me?" I asked smugly.

Kissing the side of my head, she answered the only way I could have expected of her, "Not until I saw you fall over like some woman in a slasher flick with a broken heel. It was kind of pathetic."

As much as that should have gotten under my skin, it almost felt comfortable to hear her jab at me again. No matter how close we got, no matter how bad things could get, I always knew two things for sure: Dulaf always had my back and she would always be a pain in my ass.

About the author

A longtime fan of science fiction and fantasy, **Jeremy Varner** has been writing speculative fiction for most of his life in one form or another. First introduced to the genre through his father, a huge fan of sci-fi and fantasy from the days when that wasn't very cool, some of his earliest memories formed around watching aliens, creatures of legend, and robots of all shapes and sizes. It wasn't long before Jeremy wanted to create his own worlds and tell his own stories. From fan-fiction to original works that he dare not ever show the public, Jeremy's childhood notebooks were littered with fantastic worlds inspired by the works of greats.

It was during a particularly rough time that Jeremy realized that he didn't want to just dream anymore. After years of treating it as his secret, geeky hobby, Jeremy eventually decided to take his work professional and bring his own quirky brand of world building to the real world he was often escaping. Following his debut novel, **Shards of Glass**, Jeremy released **A Patchwork Soul** with encouragement from friends in 2013. With the rerelease of the first two books of the **Agent of Argyre** series in 2019, Jeremy introduced new audiences to the world of the Alters in preparation for future installments.

These books are dedicated to lost loved ones, dear friends, and the people that introduced him to these wonderful worlds.

You can find more about Jeremy through his website, blog and twitter account at:

Website: JeremyVarner.com
Twitter: @JDVarner

Acknowledgements

Christi Sawyer	Andrew Schiffbauer
Dawn Prato	Sean O'Dell
Gerald Varner	Kai
Karen Varner	Thor